"VIVIANNE, YOU'RE WITH ME."

Jordan stalked from the bridge, without waiting to see if she followed. Ever since he and Vivianne had gone back to the engine room, he'd been riled.

His skin prickled. No matter how much he tried to repress the need, he was close to losing control again.

"You think us being together's a . . . good . . . idea?" Vivianne's tone was soft and raw. She might as well have caressed his flesh.

He gritted his teeth. "It's . . . happening . . . again."

"No. It is not." Vivianne spoke as if she was in agony.

It took every ounce of his control not to rip off her clothing and take her right there in the hallway. He swallowed hard. "I'll be in the captain's quarters."

Not in his entire life had lust ever pounded him like this. They were in danger. But it didn't matter. They might die tomorrow. It didn't matter. The crew would know exactly what they were up to. It didn't matter.

He had to have her. Now.

"Fast-paced and sexy otherworld adventure."
    —LINNEA SINCLAIR, RITA award–winning
          author of *Hope's Folly*

*Please turn this page for more
praise for Susan Kearney . . .*

JORDAN

THE PENDRAGON LEGACY

SUSAN KEARNEY

FOREVER

NEW YORK   BOSTON

Copyright © 2010 by H.E. Inc.
Excerpt from *Lucan* copyright © 2009 by H.E. Inc.
Excerpt from *Rion* copyright © 2009 by H.E. Inc.
All rights reserved. Except as permitted under the U.S. Copyright Act of 1976, no part of this publication may be reproduced, distributed, or transmitted in any form or by any means, or stored in a database or retrieval system, without the prior written permission of the publisher.

Forever
Hachette Book Group
237 Park Avenue
New York, NY 10017
Visit our website at www.HachetteBookGroup.com.

Forever is an imprint of Grand Central Publishing. The Forever name and logo is a trademark of Hachette Book Group, Inc.

Printed in the United States of America

First Printing: March 2010

10 9 8 7 6 5 4 3 2 1

To all the booksellers out there who read, love, and sell romance books. Without you, writers would have a hard time connecting with readers. Thank you.

ACKNOWLEDGMENTS

First, I need to thank my editor Amy Pierpont for all her hard work on the book. She's very much appreciated. And to Alex Logan for keeping track of all the little details. To Melanie Moss and Anna Balasi, your work behind the scenes makes promotion painless. I'd also like to thank Claire Brown and Christine Foltzer for my best cover ever!!!!! And thanks to Anna Maria Piluso in book production for taking care of JORDAN at the last minute. And of course, Bob Levine and his team in the sales department, the book wouldn't be out there without you.

And as always I'd like to thank Julie Leto, Charlotte Douglas, and Jeanie Legendre for all their wonderful suggestions, but mostly thanks for being my friend.

JORDAN

As we lay in the sweet grasses under the constellation of Orion, I knew that what we had done was not so much lovemaking as a release of an inexplicable act of passion.

—HIGH PRIESTESS OF AVALON

1

Damn it, Jordan. You lied to me." Vivianne Blackstone, CEO of the Vesta Corporation, tapped the incriminating report against her leg and restrained her urge to fling it at Jordan McArthur, her chief engineer. The world was in a total meltdown after learning an ancient enemy had infiltrated Earth's governments and major industries, and Vivianne was determined to keep her Draco Project safe.

Head throbbing, she stared at the spaceship's complex wiring. The *Draco* was the only ship of its kind, the most advanced spaceship Earth had ever built, and she had to fly as planned. It had to work out. So much was riding on this venture to find the lost and legendary Holy Grail. Vesta's future. Earth's future. Her future. Everything she'd ever wanted, everyone she'd ever loved, might be lost if this project didn't succeed.

When Jordan didn't respond, she nudged his foot with her shoe. "I'm talking to you."

Lying on the deck with his head halfway through a hatch, Jordan shifted until she could just see his intense blue eyes.

"I heard. How did I lie to you?"

She dropped the papers, but she'd already lost his attention to the ship. He'd wriggled back inside the compartment, pulling another wire to hook into the circuits, no doubt following an electrical schematic that existed only inside his head.

He threaded a wire into a panel box of delicately networked circuits. "Pass me a screwdriver."

Scowling at his back, she slapped the tool into his hand.

"Tell me these findings are wrong," Vivianne demanded.

"What findings?" He didn't so much as spare a glance at the folder she'd dropped. His profile, rugged and somber, remained utterly still, except for a tiny tick in his jaw that told her he was unhappy she'd interrupted his work.

"You've never attended Harvard. Never got your PhD at MIT. Never taught at Cambridge."

"The Phillips head." He held out his hand again, impatience lacing his voice. "It's the screwdriver with an X on the tip."

Like she didn't know a Phillips head when she saw one? While her specialty was communications technology, she'd designed and built her first hydrogen rocket by age twelve.

However, when it came to spaceship design, Jordan was the go-to guy. Despite his doctored résumé, the man knew his aeronautical engineering. From hull design to antigrav wiring, no detail on the *Draco* was too small for Jordan to reengineer and make more efficient.

One of Jordan's engineers spoke over the ship's intercom. "These voltage-converter equations can't be right."

"They are," Jordan answered evenly.

"They're frying the circuits." The man's frustration was evident in his tone.

"Sean, you'll find a way to keep them humming. You always do."

"I'm stumped."

"I'll give you a hand as soon as I can."

"Thanks, boss."

"But I'm sure you'll figure it out before then."

Sean chuckled. "I'll do my best."

While this was a side of Jordan she hadn't seen, his easy relationship with his team didn't surprise her. But it wasn't his leadership skills that she questioned. Vivianne's gut churned. "Jordan, we really need to talk."

"So talk."

Vivianne paused and considered precisely what to say. She'd already made one mistake by hiring Jordan before he'd been properly vetted. She couldn't afford to make another—like accusing him outright of being a spy for the planet's worst enemy.

"The *Draco* is Earth's first and only spaceship that can carry a full crew to the stars."

"So?"

"This ship has caught the imagination and attention of the masses. Everything we do is under intense scrutiny and makes headline news, and when the press finds out that my chief engineer falsified his employment application—"

"Damn it, Vivianne, I know what I'm doing."

"To the public, a liar is a liar. And if you lied to get a

job, they'll wonder what else you've lied about. In these dangerous times, we can't have our loyalty questioned."

"So we don't tell anyone. Problem solved."

Vivianne pinched the bridge of her nose to ease her headache. "But if your lies come to light, you don't just lose your job, you ruin my credibility. My company's reputation. It could crash Vesta's stock."

Jordan threaded one of myriad wires into a nexus of circuitry. "As long as this ship doesn't crash, your stock will be fine."

She could handle the business end. What she couldn't handle was a traitor. Who was he? The PIs she'd hired had found nothing on him back further than six months ago, when he'd applied for a job with Vesta. His fingerprints and eye print weren't on file. He had no military record. No record of birth. With the entire planet on the alert for alien moles, Jordan's nonexistent background and his lies had her suspicious as hell . . . and yet, she was good at reading people.

Maybe his brilliant blue eyes and intellect had fooled her. Hell, if she put his picture on the news, the female half of the planet would fall in love at first sight and forgive him anything. Mr. Dark, Tough, and Brilliant's gorgeous face might just sway the general population and perhaps her stockholders, as well. And she needed his expertise badly enough to give him the chance to convince her he had a damn good reason for his deception, before she called in the authorities.

"What other lies have you told me?" she asked.

"Whatever would get me this job."

"Real inspiring. Why didn't you respond to the memo I sent last week?"

"If I spent all my time reading your memos, how would I get anything done?"

Vivianne tried coming at him with another tactic. Last week's change orders had been over the top—even for Jordan. "You've installed miles of wiring that aren't in the specs."

"We're ahead of schedule, so why are you concerned?"

She frowned. Before she'd known about his lies, she'd shrugged off his clever modifications. But now she wondered if his alterations had been necessary. Or simply a sneaky way to delay and undermine the entire project.

She'd tried to hire theoreticians to double-check his work. But the specialists couldn't keep up, remaining bogged down in theory while Jordan had gone on to build working prototypes. Now even his brilliance seemed suspicious. How did he know what he knew? Where did he come from?

In a desperate attempt to suppress her frustration, Vivianne reminded herself how far she'd come. Peering at the *Draco*'s shiny metal, she had difficulty believing they'd built this ship in just over three months. Almost every system was a new design, and while the number of things that could go wrong was infinite, she had high hopes for success.

"If the story of your doctored credentials leaks, our client may get cold feet," she explained.

"Chen won't back out." Jordan sounded completely certain.

She didn't bother to keep the exasperation from her voice. "Billionaires willing to buy a spaceship in order to search the galaxy for the Holy Grail aren't a dime a dozen."

Jordan grunted.

"If Chen does back out, I'll have to refund his investment. And with the way you've been spending, not even I have that much credit."

"Down to your last few billion, are you?" Jordan teased without glancing in her direction.

She clenched her fists in irritation. "That's not the point." She wished he'd trust her with the truth. Maybe he would if she reassured him. Because in truth, the government had gone a bit overboard looking for alien moles. As far as she knew, they hadn't found even one. "Maybe we can break the news, spin it in our favor." She pictured an advantageous story. Something like "Genius engineer discovered." "The article could praise you and some little-known college. I'll have my PR department put together a package."

"Not a good idea."

His blue eyes glittered dangerously, and his response made her uneasy. Something wasn't right. He should be grateful that she was willing to fix the publicity nightmare he'd created. Instead he was acting like a man with something else to hide. But what? Was he here to damage her ship? But if so, why would he work day and night to build it? Why give them all his marvelous inventions?

She needed more information. She'd hire new PIs. Dig deeper and watch him more closely.

"Do you always make contingencies for contingencies?" he asked.

She snorted. Orphaned at age ten, Vivianne had become a ward of the state. Control became her lifeline. She'd used her obsession to earn herself a first-class education and to build a successful small business into a worldwide conglomerate.

The downside of running a huge company, however,

was that she had to rely on others. Brilliant engineers like Jordan didn't give a damn about her minute-to-minute expectations. He got the job done—but he certainly didn't do things her way.

But was his allegiance to Vesta, the *Draco*, and Earth? Why wasn't he trying to reassure her?

"In your case, I haven't planned enough."

Jordan rubbed his ear and stood, reminding her just how tall and broad he was. But if he was attempting to use his size to intimidate her, he'd learn she didn't back down.

"What do you want me to do?" he asked. "You have someone else who can build the *Draco* on budget and under deadline?" He didn't wait for her reply. Why would he? They both knew the answer was no.

"Where *did* you go to school?"

Jordan shrugged. "Here and there."

Her blood pressure shot up ten digits, but she did her best to keep her temper under control. "Could you be a little more specific?"

He shot her a nonapologetic smile that was way too charming. "I'm pretty much self-taught."

Hell. She needed more than a damn charming smile to convince her he hadn't been educated on another planet. That he wasn't a spy.

"You don't have a PhD?"

He didn't answer.

Vivianne reminded herself that she'd dealt with many difficult situations in the last few years. She'd funded archeologist Lucan Roarke's risky mission to a moon named Pendragon to find the Holy Grail. While he hadn't brought back the Grail, he had found a cure for Earth's infertility problem.

Vivianne stared at the scales on the inside of her wrists. Like one-tenth of the population, she now had two hearts and could shapeshift into a dragon and fly.

Too bad her new genes hadn't increased her intelligence. How could Jordan have fooled her so easily? More important, what was he hiding? "What about job experience?"

"Nothing verifiable."

"I suppose you fudged the glowing recommendations, too?" Her pulse pounded, and she massaged her aching temple. Was Jordan her ally or her enemy? "Who are you?"

"You might want to take an aspirin—"

"Thank you, *doctor*." Her sarcasm escaped unchecked. "Oh, excuse me, you aren't a doctor of anything, are you?"

"I don't need a medical degree to see that your head hurts and you're taking it out on me." His tone was calm, low, and husky, and that she found it sexy irked her even more.

"So now you're a shrink."

He'd barely glanced at her before turning to work on his beloved circuits, but it was so like him to notice details, even her wincing in pain.

Vivianne willed Jordan to turn around. "How did you do it? It's as if you appeared in Barcelona six months ago. Until then, you had no credit. You attended no schools. Even your birth records are fake. I can't find anyone who knew you before you walked into my office to apply for a job."

"And you've never regretted it."

"Until now." Damn him.

"You don't mean that." Jordan shrugged again. "You don't regret letting me design this ship."

Vivianne hadn't built up her company by allowing handsome men to sweet-talk her into trusting them or by ignoring urgent government warnings that alien agents may have infiltrated her company. Both Vivianne and the Tribes were after the Grail, but her goal was to save Earth, theirs was to enslave it. And according to legend, whoever possessed the Grail held the upper hand. So it was very possible that the reason her chief engineer had faked his past was because he was a spy—for the Tribes.

She couldn't put Earth's future into Jordan's hands until she knew more. Feeling sick to her stomach, Vivianne's tone snapped with authority. "Jordan, put down your tools. You can't work on the *Draco* until security clears you."

In typical Jordan fashion, he kept right on working. "Don't you want to see if the new engine's going to work?"

"We'll straighten that out later." Her temper flared because Jordan knew just how to pique her interest. From the get-go, the engines had been a major issue. It almost broke her hearts to know that the *Draco* might never fly now that she was pulling him off the project.

"I'm about ready to test a new power source."

His words teased her curiosity as much as they raised her suspicions anew. "What are you talking about? What new power source?"

"The Ancient Staff." Jordan reached to a sheath he wore on his belt and drew out an object that resembled a tree branch with symbols carved into the bark. When he flicked his wrist, the rod telescoped and expanded with a metallic click.

Oh, God. Had he just unsheathed an alien weapon?

The air around the Staff glittered like heat reflecting off hot pavement. It was if the Staff folded and compressed the space around it, the eerie effect and haze continuously rippling outward.

She peered at Jordan. The cords in his neck were tight, his broad shoulders tense as if he were bracing for her reaction.

She tried to tamp down a pinch of panic. "Don't move."

He turned to place the staff into position. "The Ancient Staff will supply far more power to the *Draco*'s engines than a cosmic converter."

That Staff wasn't in the plans. She'd never even heard of the mysterious artifact. For all she knew, that power source was alien technology and once he attached it to the *Draco*, they'd all blow up.

Hiring Jordan had been a gigantic mistake. One that might cost Earth . . . everything. Unnerved, she reached for her handheld communicator to call security, but there was no time. It would take only a second for him to snap the Ancient Staff into the housing.

She'd have to stop him herself. "Turn it off."

"The Staff doesn't have an off switch."

Stiffening, she forced authority into her tone. "Don't attach that thing to my ship."

"It's meant to—"

"I said no." Mouth dry with apprehension, she clamped her hand on his shoulder.

Before she could yank him back, Jordan snapped the rod into place. The anxiety she'd been holding back knotted in her stomach. Sweat broke out on her brow, and her nerves stretched taut.

But controlling her fear was the least of her worries as the air around the rod shimmered, then spread up his arm.

Voice trembling, she asked, "What type of energy is this?"

"The powerful kind."

"The engines can deal with that kind of power?"

"I hope so."

Energy crawled all the way up his arm and stretched toward her hand. Terrified, she tried to jerk back, but her body refused to obey her mind. Her feet wouldn't move. Her fingers might as well have been frozen.

Panicked, she watched the glow of energy flow over his shoulder to her hand. Every hair on the back of her neck standing on end, she braced for pain. But when the glowing energy engulfed her fingers and washed up her arm, then sluiced over her body, the tingling sensation somehow banished her headache and expelled her fear.

The effect was instantaneous and undeniable. Her breasts tingled. Her skin flamed as if they'd spent the past fifteen minutes engaging in foreplay rather than arguing over his nonexistent past. She'd always found Jordan attractive, but now it was as if the Staff had turned on a switch inside her.

She swallowed thickly. If he was feeling the same effects, he wasn't showing it.

Every centimeter of her skin was demanding to be stroked. Unwarranted sensations exploded all over her erogenous zones. Her nipples tightened, exquisitely sensitized. The scales on the insides of her arms and legs fluttered. Sweet juice seeped between her thighs.

Drenched in pure lust, she shook her head, trying to clear it. "What the hell is going on?"

"Don't know." Jordan practically growled, as if it took superhuman effort just to speak.

So he felt as totally, inexplicably aroused as she did. Obviously, he wasn't handling it well, either, but that didn't stop desire from rushing through all her senses.

She craved him like a starving dragon needs platinum, yet this could not be. Not without an emotional connection. She didn't do chemistry. She didn't do one-nighters. She didn't crave a man she barely knew, a man who was very likely a traitor.

But there was no fighting or denying the potent passion that blazed within her. Sexual need burned into her flesh, smoldered through her blood, the sensations fiery hot.

If she didn't have sex in the next few seconds, she was certain she would spontaneously combust.

Beneath her hand, Jordan's shoulder tensed. Mouth tight and grim, he turned and faced her head-on, those blue eyes seemingly searching into her soul. Tingling and breathless, she suddenly found it very hard to breathe. Heaven help her, she wanted him. It was a terrible thing to lose control over her own desire, to crave sex with a man she didn't trust, but she could no more stop what was going to happen than she could prevent a hurricane.

Jordan was clearly caught in the same sexual firestorm. Eyes flashing with a primal blue-ringed flame, he focused on her with a fevered intensity, right before he crashed his hard mouth down on hers, his kiss so demanding he bruised her lips and her heart jolted.

Wrapping her arms around him, she arched her back and thrust her breasts against his chest. She ground her hips into his straining sex.

Lips locking, they ripped off their clothes. His flesh was smooth, muscled, male. She couldn't breathe enough

JORDAN 13

of his scent into her lungs. She couldn't touch enough of his warm bronzed flesh to satisfy her cravings.

All coiled tension, he backed her against a bulkhead and she could see desire flash in his eyes, hear the sexual rasp in his breathing.

Wrapping her arms over his powerful shoulders and around his corded neck, she clamped her legs around his sturdy hips. And she attacked him like a savage, with lips and nails and teeth, while his strong hands clenched her bottom and he lifted her onto his straining sex.

She took him inside her, greeting his fullness with molten heat. She was burning, going up in flames. Nothing mattered—not her suspicions, not this raging spark of need that neither of them had kindled—nothing mattered, except having him.

When she squeezed her thighs, he groaned and pumped into her hard, deep, and fast. With cold steel at her back, his warm male flesh sliding over her and his sex thrusting in and out, she couldn't get enough friction, couldn't draw in enough air, couldn't think past the mind-jarring explosion.

Powerful sensations, inexplicable pleasure swept her into a vortex of energy that took him over the edge with her. The pleasure was too extreme. No way could she hang on to consciousness.

Never will those who wage war tire of deception.
                        —The Art of War

2

J ordan opened his eyes to find himself floating in the engine compartment. Weightless.

Earlier, when Vivianne had accused him of lying about his past, he'd read the heightened suspicions in her eyes. He didn't blame her. How could he when he didn't have the credentials? Nor could he deny that the Staff was an alien object. He understood she thought he was an enemy mole. But he couldn't risk her shutting down the project.

Nor could he risk his mission. So when he'd attached the Staff to the ship's engines, he'd set a timer to launch the ship.

And the *Draco* was now in space.

Before Jordan could check the engines' power, a memory slammed him. Not a recent memory. Not *his* memory.

> *"Vivianne, honey, come on down, and don't forget your party hat."*
> *"I'm coming, Daddy."*
> *Vivianne placed the silver hat on her head and tugged the rubber band under her chin. With a gig-*

gle, she picked up her mom's present and hurried to the kitchen, her mouth watering at the aroma of chocolate cake.

Dad was dancing Mom around the kitchen, singing "Happy Birthday."

Mom was laughing, her hair all messy, her eyes happy. She twirled over to Vivianne and took her hand, and the three of them kept dancing around the kitchen until the oven timer went off.

Mom took the cake from the oven while Vivianne watched with impatience. As she held her mother's present behind her back, she'd never felt so grown-up. She was seven years old and couldn't wait to share the secret surprise.

Finally, Mom turned from the counter. Vivianne took her hand from behind her back and held up her present. "Happy birthday, Mom."

"Oh, sweetie. You made me a present?"

"All by myself." Vivianne had carefully made the card. Then she'd colored a picture and used it for wrapping paper.

Her parents looked at each other over her head. Her mother had questions in her eyes. Her father shook his head. "I know nothing."

"Come on. Open it, Mom." Vivianne couldn't wait to see her expression.

"All right. This is going to be the best birthday ever." First, Mom opened the card. And as she read, "Happy birthday, I love you very, very, very much. Love Vivianne," tears filled her eyes. Mom's fingers shook as she took care not to tear Vivianne's wrapping, a picture of red roses.

Vivianne picked up the box and placed it back into her mother's hands. "Open it, already."

Her father chuckled. Her mom lifted the lid and gasped at the sight of two shiny silver chains, each with its own puzzle piece. "Oh, my goodness. Bless your heart. These are sterling."

"One is for you, and the other for Daddy," Vivianne told them, so excited she'd pulled off the surprise.

Her mother put the two silver pieces together, and her father read the words carved into the puzzle, "You are the missing piece to my puzzle."

Vivianne jumped up and down. "Were you surprised? Do you like them?"

"I love them, and you totally surprised me." Mom put one necklace around her neck and the other around Daddy's. Then she picked up Vivianne, kissed her cheek, and hugged her tight. "Where did you find such pretty necklaces?"

"And how did you pay for them?" Daddy asked.

"My friend Allison's mother makes jewelry, and I saved up my allowance for a whole year."

Dad smoothed back Vivianne's hair, his face proud. "That's my little planner."

The brush of Vivianne's hair against Jordan's cheek brought him out of the memory. What the hell had just happened?

Jordan had been through a lot of strange things during his very long lifetime, but the last few seconds of having someone else's memory downloaded into his head was a first. Why and how had that birthday party ended up in his head?

Was Vivianne a telepath who could send and receive? He hadn't ever heard even a rumor to that effect, but suppose she was getting his memories while he saw hers? He turned to look at her. If she was broadcasting or receiving, she didn't seem aware of it. Her eyes remained closed, her breathing steady as she floated weightless.

Asleep but restless. Her eyelids fluttered, her fingers twitched, as if she were dreaming. The tiny motions only drew attention to her beauty, her high cheekbones, her slim fingers. Fingers that had clutched him with a desperate passion that teased his lips into a grin.

Even as he fought to grab hold of the hull so he could propel himself to the ship's bridge, his own memories crept into his mind. Vivianne's suspicions, her widened eyes at the sight of the Staff, her passion. Her blacking out as he'd launched the *Draco*.

He could only imagine her fury when she awakened and learned what he'd done. He supposed she'd see it as yet another reason to call him *enemy*.

And without a doubt, he knew she'd be furious if she learned that he'd had an inadvertent glimpse into her childhood. He'd deal with what had happened between them later. He'd deal with her later, too. Right now he had to focus on keeping the ship that he'd launched into space flying.

The steady purr of the engines told him that his spur-of-the-moment plan had worked. As he pulled himself toward the bridge, his clothing reassembled around his body, the nanotechnology repairing the rips.

Clothing was the least of his concerns. Those alarms

could be due to leaking air, loss of pressure, or overheating engines. The ship was a few systems shy of ready. They hadn't tested navigation or propulsion, not to mention that his untrained crew of civilian engineers had no experience in space.

They'd adjust. Adapt.

Yet Jordan knew only too well what it was like to be ripped from home. He remembered the crippling pain of the loss of his home world, Dominus. The terror of knowing he would forevermore be alone. The rage that he had survived when everyone else had died.

It was his destiny, his fate, and he'd lived through the centuries with a heavy heart and one purpose—to make sure his enemies never destroyed another world. The brutal loss of Dominus had cost him family, friends, teachers, everyone he'd ever known. Like Vivianne, he had come from a loving home. Although recalling his parents' faces after so many centuries had become difficult, Jordan never, ever, forgot his vow—to make certain the Tribes fell.

But in all his years of living, he'd never experienced anything as simultaneously confusing and overpowering as his lust for Vivianne. When they came together, it was like two pieces of her missing puzzle. What the hell had happened when he'd connected the Staff to the power grid? He'd been on fire and out of control. And he'd never felt that way before. He'd had no choice but to drive into her, just as she hadn't seemed to have a choice but to take him with equal ferocity.

He was sorry the sex happened that way, and baffled by how her childhood memory had ended up in his mind. But there was no time for regrets.

If that meant her feelings were hurt or that he had to take a bunch of raw recruits into space, then he'd do it. He didn't like acting with ruthless disregard for the wishes of others, but he'd lived too long to go soft now. If it meant retrofitting the *Draco* along the way, he'd manage. Nothing was more important than stopping the Tribes. Nothing.

Of all those aboard the ship, Vivianne would be hit the hardest by her new circumstances. The *Draco* was his means to an end—finding the Holy Grail and stopping the Tribes before they reached Earth. Vivianne didn't belong on this mission. But he couldn't take her back to Earth without the risk of being arrested. Unfortunately for her, out here there were no schedules to keep—just life-and-death decisions.

Jordan surged through the corridor and onto the *Draco*'s bridge, which was filled with engineers. "Lay off the controls."

"Whatever you say." Tennison threw his hands into the air.

Once upon a time, Tennison had been in charge of this team. But at sixty-five years of age, paunchy and bald as an eagle, he'd been happy to step back and let Jordan take the lead. Jerking away from the data stream on the monitor, Tennison bumped into Sean, who was studying the readings over his shoulder.

Sean was Jordan's fix-it guy. He might be short on theory, but he had the knack for puttering. Over the last decade he'd worked on anything that moved—ships, airplanes, and heavy machinery.

"What's going on?" Gray, the thirty-year-old chemical, mechanical, and industrial engineer had strapped himself into the communications system.

"Give Jordan a moment to assess." Darren clung to a porthole and looked down at Earth. Quiet, thoughtful, and short in stature, the man thought first and spoke rarely. He was the best chess player among them, and although he could calculate differential equations in his head, he wasn't worth a damn at poker.

"Someone help me." Lyle, the most recent addition to the team, floated helplessly in midair. Ever since human resources had assigned him to Jordan's team, the man had complained about the working conditions, the hours, the pay. Jordan had heard the gossip. A cheating wife, a nasty divorce. Alimony payments he couldn't afford. But he performed his job well, even if he whined a lot. "I expect hazard pay added to my check, and I'm going to—"

"Silence." Jordan had no time to coddle the man.

Of course, they weren't prepared, and all hell had broken loose. Alarms screamed. Warning lights flickered.

"Damage reports?" Jordan asked.

"Communications are down," Gray summarized, "and life support's on the backup generator."

Jordan grabbed hold of the command console, seized Lyle's foot, and plucked him from the ceiling. A blinking light on the monitor drew his gaze back to the engineering readouts. Dozens of systems were in the red zone.

"Turn on artificial gravity," Jordan ordered Sean. "Do it slowly."

"Gravity's not responding." Sean yanked a panel off a console, pulled a soldering iron from his tool belt, and went to work.

"What the hell just happened?" Lyle rubbed a giant bruise on his forehead.

Tennison grinned. "We're flying through space. That's

what happened." He cracked his knuckles. "And my arthritis . . . is almost gone."

Darren and Tennison high fived.

Lyle's face turned ashen. Jordan handed him an airsickness bag. They might not have gravity, navigation, or stabilizers, but they had barf bags.

"Lyle, I need an immediate inventory of our supplies," Jordan snapped. "Tennison, Vivianne Blackstone's in the engine compartment. Check on her, and see who else is aboard. Then do what you can to solidify life support. I'd rather not rely on backup power."

Darren and Tennison launched themselves toward the stern.

Lyle didn't throw up, but his eyes bulged. "How did this happen? Can we get back in one piece? What's powering the *Draco*? The cosmic converter hasn't even been delivered. Do we have landing—"

"Lyle." Jordan snapped his fingers in front of the man's panicked eyes. "Go down to the cargo bay. If you need Darren to help with the inventory, take him with you."

"You just want to be rid of me, and—"

"Now." Jordan hardened his tone. The crew needed to understand their lives now depended on following orders.

Lyle took one last frightened glance through the circular viewscreen where Earth was receding behind them, then nodded. Sean moved away from his console and fiddled with a dial. "Artificial gravity might work now. I tied into the new power grid."

Jordan settled into his chair. "Good work. We're at eighty percent?"

Sean signaled a thumbs-up. "Eighty-one point five."

"Captain." Gray pulled off a headset, his eyes apprehensive. "You need to hear this message."

"Put it through the speaker."

Vivianne stepped onto the bridge and took in the view of Earth. Wearing her cream blouse, gray slacks, and olive jacket, she looked every inch the corporate executive and nothing like the Vivianne who short minutes ago had had wild, savage sex with Jordan. Not until he looked into her eyes. Turbulent with tension, her eyes green and vibrant, she looked like a volcano on the edge of erupting.

A strange urge to reach out and touch her jarred him. But she wouldn't appreciate an intimate geture. Nor was it appropriate. Although they were now something more than boss and employee, they had to forget the sexual encounter. Put it out of their minds. Sweeping back a mass of red-gold hair, Vivianne spied Jordan at the controls and speared him a barbed glare.

Before she spoke, the message from Earth filtered through the speaker. "To the unidentified spaceship that just launched from the east coast of Florida. By emergency order of the North American States, return to Earth at once, or we will shoot you down. I repeat, return at once—"

"Turn it off." Jordan had heard enough. Since learning that intelligent life existed on other worlds, Earth's leaders had totally panicked. Politicians feared war. But isolationism would not stop the Tribes.

These people needed to suck it up and embrace the fact that the universe didn't revolve around Earth. There were allies like Pendragon and Honor out in space, and if Earth could summon the courage to reach out despite their differences, they might actually improve their lot.

Instead, the idiots were ready to shoot down their own people to try and control contact between the worlds. Vivianne's company had built this ship, but Earth had never given permission for them to fly.

"Tell them we'll return immediately," Vivianne said with self-possessed authority.

Jordan swiveled to face her. "We're not going back."

Tennison and Gray exchanged a long look but remained silent.

Vivianne squared her shoulders, straightened her back, and locked gazes with Jordan. "You aren't in charge. The *Draco* isn't yours."

"Actually, she is."

Her voice, though quiet, held an ominous accusation. "Because you're stealing her?"

"Because I paid for her." He took a perverse pleasure in challenging her, especially as he recalled the fire in her as she'd ripped off his clothes. She was one gutsy, passionate, intelligent woman. The kind he was always attracted to—the kind he avoided at all costs.

Vivianne's tone remained cool, tight. "I don't pay you well enough for you to afford that command console, never mind this entire ship."

Enjoying her annoyance, he allowed a tiny smile to reach one side of his mouth. "I'm Chen. And I've paid for half this ship."

She narrowed her eyes. "I don't believe you." Her lips tightened, and she folded her arms across her chest, a very delicate, perfectly proportioned chest.

"If I wasn't Chen, I wouldn't know that you've sold only part ownership, would I?"

Vivianne gasped.

Jordan knew her PIs had never been able to find the source of Chen's income. So revealing his dual identity might only have increased her suspicions that he was funded by the Tribes. Baiting her was one thing, but Jordan didn't enjoy watching Vivianne lose all the color in her pink cheeks. She deserved to know the score.

The voice from Earth blared through the speaker. "Two minutes until we launch missiles."

"Tell them we'll be returning as soon as possible," Vivianne ordered Gray.

When Gray looked from her to Jordan, Jordan nodded.

But Vivianne didn't wait for Gray to obey. Just as impatient as the seven-year-old Vivianne had been for her mother to open her present, the adult Vivianne strode over, snatched the headset, and placed it on her head. "This is Vivianne Blackstone, CEO of the Vesta Corporation. We launched accidentally and will return immediately."

Jordan shifted back to the controls and motioned for Gray to join him. He kept his tone low. "She'll buy us time. Can you engage the hyperspace transporter?"

The HT was Jordan's adaptation of ancient machinery. Theoretically, the new HT design allowed the *Draco* to transport itself to any coordinates.

Gray whispered tensely in his ear, "But sir, we haven't tested—"

"Is the system working?" Jordan asked.

"It's operational, but we require more time to charge it up." Gray chewed on a fingernail. "But these numbers can't be correct."

"What do you mean?"

"The power source feeding the batteries is phenomenal."

"I just installed a new power source." Jordan grinned. "Glad to hear it's working."

"If these energy figures are right, we'll be up to speed in minutes."

"That's the idea."

So the Ancient Staff was powering the *Draco*. It was good to know that after all these centuries, Jordan hadn't lost his touch. Back on Dominus, he'd planned to make a career out of spaceship design, but then the Tribes had decimated his world. The people, their history, art, and culture, were gone. The oceans and mountains were gone. Not even dust remained.

Vivianne removed her headset. "I've explained we have system failures. The North American States has given us five additional minutes before firing missiles."

"Excellent work," Jordan told her and then peered at his gauges.

Vivianne glanced at the receding planet. "Why haven't you swung us into orbit?"

"I told you, we aren't going back."

She lifted her chin and spoke softly, but anger flickered in her eyes. "We don't have a choice. They're going to shoot us down."

His crew exchanged uneasy looks, and Jordan spoke loudly enough for all to hear. "I'm not into suicide."

She arched a brow. "Excuse me?"

"Thanks to you, we've time to power up the HT."

She peered at the spiking energy readings on the monitor, but she still shook her head, a lock of fiery hair framing her high cheekbones. "All we have time to do is get blown up. With the world government spooked of alien spies, they need to make certain that everyone on this ship is loyal to Earth before they'll give permission to leave the solar system."

"Let's hope you bought us enough time to outrun the missiles," Jordan replied.

"Are you insane?" she asked, her tone low and urgent. "Even if they don't shoot us down, we can't go anywhere. The *Draco*'s not ready. We haven't tested most of the new systems."

As if to emphasize her words, a monitor shot sparks at the ceiling. Smoke curled in the air. Gray put out the fire with an extinguisher.

Vivianne's eyes watered. She coughed and raised her wrist to breathe through her sleeve. But she didn't panic. Instead she transferred the data to Jordan's screen.

The ship's hull hadn't buckled. They still had life support. "There's no time like the present to test the *Draco*'s systems."

She frowned at the smoking monitor. "And if they don't work?"

"We'll fix them."

"It's more likely we'll blow ourselves up. We don't even have spare parts aboard to make repairs."

"We'll make do."

She gestured to the crew. "These men didn't volunteer to leave their families."

Jordan shrugged. "It can't be helped. Once they understand the choices—"

"You gave them no choice." Vivianne placed her hands on her hips, her entire body vibrating with anger. But she kept her temper under tight control, her voice locked down so low he had to lean forward to hear her. "You're giving *me* no choice."

"Two minutes until HT reaches full power," Gray reported.

The voice from the North American States started a countdown. "One minute until missile launch."

"Damn you, Jordan." Vivianne's eyes blazed. "Turn this ship around and land."

Jordan's fingers danced over the monitor. "I'm laying in the course."

The fury of the wise never shows.

—HIGH PRIESTESS OF AVALON

3

Vivianne watched Jordan lay in the course, but . . . not . . . for Earth.

The lying son of a bitch!

No way could this man be the same boy she'd dreamed about when she'd blacked out.

The Jordan in her dream had been leaner, lankier, and sweeter.

Adrenaline pumping, Jordan dived into the pool. He'd trained hard all season for this race. The winner attended an elite summer camp and received expert coaching and offers to prestigious schools. And Jordan, in the best shape of his career, was determined to win.

K'dark, a good friend in the lane beside him, popped up half a body length behind.

Jordan breathed evenly, kicking strongly, letting his warmed up muscles carry him through the water. His stroke seemed effortless, the long hours in the pool giving him an edge in stamina.

K'dark had trained hard, too. The two friends pushing one another.

Jordan turned his head to breathe and saw K'dark's father on the pool deck cheering for his son. It was a first. The first time he'd ever seen him swim. His father worked long hours, double shifts, to support the family.

Jordan checked to his right, his left, flipped at the wall and headed back. He and K'dark were leading the race.

It would come down to the two of them.

He breathed again, glimpsed K'dark's father jumping up and down. Winning meant a lot to Jordan, but winning this race might be K'dark's future. Without a scholarship, his family couldn't afford to send him to the university.

Jordan already had an academic scholarship. He eased up. Slowed his pace.

K'dark pulled ahead.

Vivianne's mind had played tricks on her. The real adult Jordan couldn't have been that selfless kid. Because the adult Jordan was deceptive. Dangerous.

Vivianne had to stop herself from lunging toward the controls. Instead she kept her face expressionless and strolled casually toward him. She knew the *Draco*'s specs as well as the layout of her beach penthouse. That meant she could disengage the nav system and turn the ship into orbit as easily as she could change the channel on her TV—if only she could get close enough to the controls.

Pulse racing, she made herself sound breezy. "Shouldn't we be turning by now?"

"Missile launch in thirty seconds," the North American States warned.

Vivianne's pulse sped up. Jordan stood at the control center, a study of calm.

Gray leaned over his monitor. "One minute until hypertransporter is fully powered."

"Missile launch in twenty seconds."

Still too far away to reach the controls, Vivianne stared at the monitor and ran equations in her head. "They're not bluffing. They'll fire unless you comply."

"I know." Jordan's tone was cool. "But after they launch those weapons, it'll take fifty-three seconds for the missiles to reach us. By then, we'll be gone."

"Ten seconds."

He was risking their lives for no good reason that she could discern. "Stand down, Jordan. We aren't provisioned. We don't have enough food, water, oxygen, or—"

"Five seconds."

Expression determined, he hovered over the transporter control.

"Two seconds."

Praying he wouldn't suspect she was up to anything, Vivianne edged closer, her nerves raw. Another step. Then one more. Taking all her resentment and fear, converting it into raw force, she lunged and slammed into Jordan, knocking him sideways.

She was fast, but Jordan was faster.

Even as she crashed into his rock-hard body, his fingers began the transporter sequence. And the *Draco* jumped from sub–light speed and normal space . . . into hyperspace and faster-than-light travel.

Earth vanished from view. Stars streaked by the viewport.

Damn him to hell.

He'd just shot them into a place where space folded in on itself, a wormhole. Over the years Vivianne had heard many explanations of wormhole theory. But her high school physics teacher had described them best. She'd told them to think of the universe as a towel. Wring the towel and certain parts touched where they wouldn't normally do so. Those new connections were the spatial equivalent of three-dimensional wormholes. Hyperspace.

Without a map, the *Draco* could end up anywhere.

Starlight streaked across the viewscreen, and the *Draco*'s hull groaned in protest. Deck vibrations radiated through her shoes and into her bones. Someone shut off the ringing alarm.

Gray frowned over his console's readings. "The forward bulkhead's starting to collapse."

Vivianne held her breath.

"I'm rerouting power to the shields." Jordan reconfigured the systems, his hands a blur over the touch screen.

Gray glared at his monitor. "That worked, but we just overloaded the power grid." Sirens blared once again. A panel popped open and sparks hissed, a bulkhead light exploded, and the plastic shattered.

"Engines are running hot," Sean said.

"We have bigger problems," Jordan muttered.

Bigger problems than being without a working engine? Bigger problems than a collapsing hull?

"What's wrong?" Vivianne was certain they were going to die.

"We're on a collision course." Jordan peered straight at the viewscreen.

"With what?" Vivianne asked.

Up ahead, a cluster of objects headed straight at them. At hyperspeed, even if the objects were dust particles, they'd slice through their hull like a knife through butter. And these were way bigger than dust particles. To the naked eye, they looked about half the size of the *Draco*.

"Get us out of hyperspace," Vivianne ordered.

"We'll wipe out our power reserve," Sean warned.

"Do it," Jordan agreed.

Gray made the adjustments. Jordan coordinated the controls. And they popped out of hyperspace. The stars stopped streaking. Space looked normal. Too bad they'd lost power and gravity again—which left the *Draco* tumbling.

Vivianne clutched at the console but missed. She ended up floating halfway between the two decks. Gray reached to tug her down.

Jordan shook his head. "Leave her. She can't cause trouble up there."

Vivianne struggled but failed to reach a bulkhead. "I'm not the one who launched this ship and almost got us blown up. Or who shot us into hyperspace."

"No, you just sent us into the wrong damn wormhole," he drawled.

"You're accusing me?" Outrage almost choked her. "I haven't so much as touched one control."

"True," he admitted. "But when you knocked into my hand, we vectored off course. We're now thousands of light-years away from Earth."

A few thousand . . . light-years? She twisted in midair to peer out the viewscreen, but nothing looked familiar. Earth was gone. So was the sun. Mouth dry, she forced out the words. "Where are we?"

"Damned if I know." Jordan brought up several familiar star systems seen from Earth and tried to place them over the ones shining through the viewscreen, but clearly nothing matched. "I set our coordinates for Pentar."

"Pentar?" Where had she heard that name? It was hard to think when she was spinning in midair. But suddenly it came to her. "Earth's intel from Honor had said Pentar's the last reported position of the Holy Grail."

"If we were anywhere near Pentar, the Staff would lead us straight to the Grail. But we're nowhere near it," Jordan mumbled.

Ice stabbed her spine and chilled her bones, even as sweat trickled under her arms. Pentar was in Tribe territory. Did Jordan intend to steal the *Draco* and hand it over to the enemy?

In all fairness, she supposed he still could be adhering to the *Draco*'s original mission—heading to Pentar to steal the Holy Grail back from the Tribes. But she couldn't ignore the fact that the *Draco* was being powered by an alien artifact, heading into enemy territory, and captained by a man with a suspicious background.

So far, Jordan had offered no explanations. And she had no clue to his intentions.

Vivianne clenched her hands into fists. Her head ached and her stomach was churning. Between the lack of gravity and her body's slow spin, she was growing dizzy. "If I promise not to touch anything, will you please pull me down?"

"Why should I believe you?" Jordan muttered, but he reached up, grabbed her arm, and thrust her behind a console.

"Before we ran out of power, the engines redlined,"

Tennison reminded them over the speaker system. "There may be damage. Self-diagnosis isn't working, either. I could use Sean's help down here."

"Let them cool off, and I'll reboot the system," Sean told him.

"Before anyone eyeballs the engines, we should shut down the power," Tennison countered.

"We have no stored power," Jordan explained. "We used all the reserves."

Was he trying to get them killed? Vivianne rounded on Jordan. "If Sean and Tennison are going to crawl between the engines, I'd feel a helluva lot better if we knew the power wasn't going to come back on and fry them," she said. "And there might be residual energy. Or they could encounter loose wires, electronic feedback—"

"Fine," Jordan agreed, "but shutting down the power's not necessary."

Sean scrambled out from behind his station. "I'll go see what—"

"No. Vi and I will take care of it from engineering." Jordan swiveled away from the console.

She'd hoped Jordan would leave and give her a few minutes alone with Gray. That Jordan had neatly ruined her plan before she'd made a move to stop him frustrated her, but what had her nerves skittering was the notion of returning to the engine compartment. With Jordan.

"Let's go." Jordan shoved away from the console, launched himself into the air, and grabbed her hand. Warmth flooded back into her and she recalled his hands all over her breasts, her belly, her butt. God. What the hell was wrong with her?

She had to get herself together.

She supposed now was not the time to tell him she didn't like him calling her Vi. A nickname implied intimacy. But intimacy was not what they had shared. They'd had sex. But what really stopped her from saying anything was the erotic tingle going up her undulating scales.

What was wrong with her? Jordan was a liar, a thief, a hijacker, who'd put all their lives at risk. The wild sex they'd had earlier was totally inexplicable. Why had her dream about Jordan as a teenager seemed so real? What had made her hormones go crazy? She'd been no more able to resist him than she could counter the lack of gravity.

Something was very, very wrong. Because she didn't have sex with employees, clients, or strangers. If there was one thing that defined her, it was self-control. Vivianne always did her research. She always had options. Always had a plan. And a backup plan. To turn the *Draco* around, she'd have to do some hard thinking.

She jerked her hand from his. The motion changed her trajectory.

"Careful." Jordan grabbed her ankle and saved her from banging her head on the bulkhead. "You may not have weight, but you still have mass."

"Thanks."

Soaring through the corridor, he latched on to the engine-room door to slow his flight, made certain she stopped safely, then neatly slid toward the glowing Staff.

She recalled him touching the Staff, that otherworldly shimmer engulfing him. And she'd been touching his shoulder. So the shimmer had crawled over her, too.

The rest was history.

Lust that came out of nowhere. There had been no lead-up. No coy flirting. No kissing. No touching. No foreplay.

Hell, since she'd discovered he'd lied about his identity, she didn't even know if she liked him. She most assuredly didn't trust him.

Reluctant to go anywhere near that Staff, but needing answers, Vivianne followed. Deep in thought, she didn't pay attention to her progress and almost soared into another bulkhead before wrenching to an awkward halt.

No longer glowing brightly, the Staff now appeared like a real bough with carved symbols in the bark. Runes. But it was way more than a branch with ancient carvings.

Jordan slid his hand over the Staff with a familiarity that suggested he knew every rune, every centimeter of it by heart. His pointer finger stopped over a marking that reminded her of a key. A straight piece of metal connected a crystal at one end and a triangular stone on the other. He pushed on the crystal, and the staff slowly lost its very dim glow.

"It's like no power source I've ever seen," she murmured, edging back to avoid touching him. But that wasn't really protection. The self-confidence that always radiated from him was sexually potent, and now he seemed more certain of himself than ever. She ignored the ruffling of her scales, the racing of her pulse. "What fuels the Staff?"

As if he suspected she was fighting desire, his stare was bold and assessed her frankly. "The Staff eats pure energy."

She didn't have a clue what he was talking about. "It eats? You're speaking as if it's alive."

He stood, his broad back to the Staff, and eyed her with a critical squint. "I don't have time to teach you basic six-dimensional quantum physics."

She'd never heard of six-dimensional quantum physics, and he'd just called it basic.

In the confined space, she boldly met his glittering blue gaze. "Who are you?"

He raised a dark eyebrow, his voice sounding husky and weary. "If I told you, you'd accuse me of lying again."

"Try me." She folded her arms across her chest, determined to ignore his smoldering look.

"I've gone by many names. Chen. Jordan. The one you'll recognize is . . . Merlin."

Merlin. "As in King Arthur? Camelot? That Merlin?"

He nodded.

"Okay, so your mother had a romantic bent, but—"

"My mother didn't name me after Merlin. My real name's unpronounceable to most of your people, so I took one that was close. Jordan."

"Sorry, I'm not following you."

"When I came to Earth to join King Arthur Pendragon in the fight against the Tribes, I lived in Camelot and I took the name Merlin."

Holy shit. He was right about one thing. She didn't believe him. In the last few years, she'd come to accept that the legendary King Arthur Pendragon was not from Earth but had come from a moon called Pendragon, that he'd traveled to Earth in an ancient transporter that was currently known as Stonehenge, and that he'd come to Earth with a contingent of aliens, Knights of the Round Table, to help Earth fight the Tribes.

Arthur had been only partially successful. Before his death, he'd hidden the Holy Grail safely away in Avalon, an ancient edifice on the Pendragon moon. And now the

Tribes had the Grail once again. But for Jordan to claim he knew King Arthur . . . he'd have to have lived for more than fifteen centuries.

Half in anticipation, half in dread, she asked, "You're saying you're over fifteen hundred years old?"

Again, he nodded.

"Funny, you don't look a day over thirty."

His eyes glinted with humor. "I don't age."

"You don't age?"

He looked her straight in the eyes and nodded.

Okay. He seemed to lie without a conscience. She'd remember that. But she played along for the moment. "Wasn't Merlin an old man with a beard in Arthurian legend?"

"Just one of my many disguises."

"You're immortal?"

He eyed her with a calculating expression. "Let's just say I have the potential to live a very, very long time."

He was as serious as engine failure. Clearly he believed what he was saying. Or he was the best liar she'd ever met.

Vivianne hadn't reached her position in life without being able to think outside the box, too. Time to reassess.

Wrapping her skepticism around her, she eyed him warily. "Are we going to play twenty questions, or are you going to explain—"

"Captain." Darren poked his head through the hatch. "Look what I've found."

He held a black-and-white Boston terrier, with mournful brown eyes and one floppy ear. Vivianne petted the dog's head and it leaped into her arms.

His warm little body snuggled against her. "Hey, fella. Where did you come from?"

"He doesn't belong to any of the engineers," Darren said. "I've already asked."

She scratched behind his ears. "He's a stowaway?"

"If we run out of food," Jordan muttered, "I suppose we can eat him."

"Over my dead body." She clutched the dog to her chest and he licked her neck. "Don't worry, fella. I won't let the mean old man eat you."

Darren started to chuckle, caught sight of Jordan's scowl, and uttered a choking cough instead. The dog settled happily in Vivianne's arms, his nose tucked under her chin.

Darren cleared his throat. "I also found . . ."

"Yes?" Jordan prodded him.

"My girlfriend, Knox."

Darren's expression looked sheepish, and Vivianne focused her attention on him. "How'd she get onboard?"

"My fault." Darren rubbed his temple. "I just wanted to show Knox the *Draco*. I thought she'd left, but she fell asleep in the bunk."

The bunk? Vivianne didn't want to think about that too hard. "Does Knox have a security clearance?"

"Yes, ma'am. She works in payroll."

"That's useful," Jordan said, and Vivianne suppressed a smile. She was beginning to learn that Jordan looked tough and talked rough, but at times, he was more growl than bite. "Sorry, how's the inventory coming?"

"Lyle and I are working on the list. There's a lot of supplies in the cargo hold. Knox's helping, too."

"Can your girlfriend cook?" Jordan asked.

At just the mention of food, Vivianne's stomach twisted. Eating without gravity was something she'd prefer not to try.

"I'll rustle us up some grub." Darren hurried away.

The dog didn't seem to mind when Darren left. He closed his eyes and relaxed. Apparently he had no trouble with space sickness. Or men who told the most outrageous stories.

"You believe me?" Jordan asked her, with those strange glittering eyes piercing her. And she recalled another part of him piercing her, pleasuring her. The memory taunted her as details came back. His five-o'clock shadow rubbing against her neck. His hands gripping her hips. "Do you?" he prodded, drawing her from her daydream.

"Huh?"

"You called me an old man. So you believe me?"

She'd reserve judgment until she had more facts. "So what planet are you from?"

"Dominus was my home world. It hasn't existed for over fifteen hundred years." He rested his hands on his hips.

So Jordan was older than even King Arthur? So old that his world no longer existed? Alien technology might explain how he knew how to design systems that no one else understood. It might also explain how he knew how to enflame her lust against her better judgment. She reminded herself he might be old, but he was still a man with desires like any other. And he'd just told her his world was gone.

"What happened?" she whispered, sensing tragedy from the harsh twist of his lips and the haunting pain in his eyes.

"While I was exploring a nearby moon, the Tribes shot a planet buster at Dominus."

That sounded terrible. "A planet buster?"

"Missiles that fire in sync into the nickel-iron core and change the world's pressure. The planet collapses in on itself, then explodes, the pressure so great that nothing larger than cosmic dust particles survive."

Earth also had a nickel-iron core, and Vivianne's gut tightened. "I thought the Tribes want to enslave people and steal other planets' natural resources."

"They do."

"But they can't benefit from such planetwide destruction. So what's the point?"

"The Tribes couldn't conquer Dominus, so they destroyed it. They believe that any independence or freedom is a threat to their authority."

"So if a world isn't an ally of the Tribes, they're an enemy?"

Eyes grim, he nodded. "In one instant, they killed billions."

He must have lost family, friends, and coworkers. No wonder he was bitter.

Resisting his magnetism when she was angry was difficult; resisting when she felt sympathy was almost impossible. "Oh, Jordan. I'm so sorry."

She wanted to reach out and hold him. Just hold him. Even though they'd been physical in the most intimate sense, this wasn't a relationship. Couldn't be.

She couldn't forget he'd lied to get the job as chief engineer, lied about being Chen. He was good at spinning tales.

As if sensing her doubts, Jordan actually volunteered information. "I joined Arthur to stop the Tribes. We almost succeeded."

"Almost?"

"There's an ancient galactic legend that says that when the Ancient Staff and the Holy Grail are united, only then will the Tribes fall. By the time Arthur found the Holy Grail on Earth, the Ancient Staff had been stolen from me."

"That Staff?" She pointed at the *Draco*'s power source.

He nodded. "I recovered it on a world the Tribes had enslaved."

"Where did the Staff come from originally?"

"Dominus."

"And you needed the *Draco* to unite the Staff with the Grail?"

He nodded.

"How did you pay for your half of this ship?"

"The city of Barcelona runs on solar power. But remember a few months ago when atypical rain caused rolling brownouts?"

"What of it?"

"I sold them power." He jerked his thumb at the Staff.

That would explain his having the funds, but she still had doubts. "Don't you think it's a tad dangerous to bring that Staff into Tribe territory? They already have the Grail. According to your legend, if they steal the Staff again, they win."

"Uniting the Staff and the Grail is the only way to defeat them."

She shook her head. "There's always another way."

"Captain," Tennison interrupted as he floated around the threshold. "The engines look okay. Sean thinks they just overheated but aren't damaged. Gray said if you restore the power, we can recharge and turn the gravity back on."

"Good work."

Kneeling, Jordan pressed the crystal at the top of the Ancient Staff and the artifact began to hum and glow. He'd told her it didn't have an off button, but clearly he could adjust the flow of energy. But it was hard to think. Her scales undulated. Her breasts ached.

God, no. Not again. She couldn't afford to have her mind clouded by lust. Dealing with Jordan was difficult enough without the added complications of sex. But her blood stirred. Her pulse kicked up a notch.

She stared at the Grail. "What's going on? What is that thing doing to us?" she asked.

"I'm not sure." He shot her a piercing look. "You aren't telepathic, are you?"

"If I could have read your mind, I would have stopped you from launching the *Draco*." And she would have avoided ending up in that engine room with him. Avoided this desperate wanting.

"Turn down the power," she whispered, trying not to sound as if she was begging.

"I can't." A shadow crossed his face. "We need everything we've got to power the *Draco*."

*All that we are is the summation of our experiences
and thoughts.*

—KING ARTHUR PENDRAGON

4

L et's get the hell away from here." Jordan stalked from
the engine room. After over fifteen hundred years of
mostly solitary endeavors, he now had to become accustomed to working with others. But being around Vi was
a major problem.

For one thing, she was independent and accustomed
to doing things her own way. For another, every time he
came near her, he recalled her vivid memories from her
mother's birthday. Her excitement. Her childish joy.

Just reliving her happy memory had made him want to
know the adult Vivianne much better. He groaned. Like
the recollection of how soft her skin had felt under his
fingertips wasn't tempting enough?

Their lust had caused a savage meltdown. One taste of
her had only whetted his appetite for more. Being with
her had been one of the most memorable moments in his
long life. Vivianne Blackstone was too smart, too bossy,
and much too damn sexy for him not to like her, but he
couldn't afford the distraction.

He'd made a solemn vow to stop the Tribes from doing to any other world what they had done to Dominus. While he hadn't expected that losing the Staff would delay him fifteen centuries, his resolve to stop the Tribes had never faltered. He wouldn't allow himself to get sidetracked.

Not even by Vi.

Although he'd love to know more about her, what made her laugh, what made her happy, what drove her to be such a successful businesswoman, he could not afford to indulge his curiosity.

Floating through the corridor, he headed toward the galley. Holding the dog under her arm, Vi had no difficulty keeping up. Yet her voice was breathless, no doubt because of the Staff's effects.

"So that Staff is responsible for what happened between us?" she asked.

"The Staff's more than an energy source."

"And?" she prodded as if she sensed his reluctance.

"It can nourish all kinds of energy. Electric. Magnetic. Cosmic."

"Sexual?" Her green eyes darkened with intensity, yet her voice remained calm and contained. Still, she couldn't totally suppress a hint of yearning that was the Staff filling her with desire.

"Sexual energy? Yes. But it can be *any* kind of energy. For example, when I live in a dragon's shape it takes tremendous energy. Living as a human takes less. When I don't have enough to maintain human form, I can morph into a creature that needs even less energy to survive."

"You can shapeshift because of the Staff." A delighted grin lit up her face. "Are you saying you're a dragonshaper, even though you don't have scales in human form? And you also can change to . . . ?"

"An owl." He damn well wasn't going to tell her he couldn't morph without the Staff nearby. But if she thought she could cleverly pull a secret from him, she might go along with his plans more easily.

"Prove it," she said.

"There's not enough room to dragonshape here." He halted in the middle of the corridor and gave her time to catch up.

"Show me the owl," she requested.

Gray's voice filtered through the speakers. "Warning. Gravity coming back on."

"Good work, people." Jordan believed in complimenting his team. It cost nothing and boosted morale.

Vi shoved her feet toward the deck. Jordan did the same, and then he morphed into an owl. His cells compressed. His limbs shrank and his arms became wings and his skin grew feathers. His pupils changed from blue to golden, and his eyesight sharpened. He lost some of his intellect. His clothing shrank with his body, the nanobots leaving him with only a collar. He flew around her head, then humanshaped back into a man. And the nanobots quickly clothed him again.

"When King Arthur suffered a mortal wound, he feared the Grail would fall into the hands of the Tribes. So before he died, we brought the Grail to the Pendragon Moon and placed the healing cup inside Avalon." Jordan had spent his time on that moon, trapped in owl form, unable to fight the Tribes. While he'd often accompanied each High Priestess, his abilities were severely limited without his Staff. "When Lucan Roarke, your archeologist, made his journey home, I accompanied him and his wife Cael from her Pendragon moon."

"Lucan filled me in, but he never mentioned you were a dragonshaper."

"He didn't know. Neither did his wife, Cael. At the time, they thought I was only an owl."

Her eyes lit with suspicion. "Why did you tell *me?*"

"Because you and I have to work together to recover the Grail from the Tribes."

"You want *my* help?"

"It seems preferable to locking you up in a cabin for the duration of the voyage," he muttered.

She cocked her head and petted the dog, not looking the least bit scared. But she should be. Ignoring his threat to her freedom, she circled back to the subject. "So exactly why did we have sex when we don't much like each other?"

He bit back a snort. She could speak for herself. He liked her plenty. He just didn't *want* to like her. He had no time for a woman in his life. He'd had a few flings, but never had he allowed himself more than physical gratification. There'd be no emotional entanglements. He needed to focus all his energy on stopping the Tribes.

"The Ancient Staff has powers that I don't fully understand." The Tribes had blown up Dominus before he'd been fully trained in the Staff's powers. "You saw me switch up the power by pushing the crystal?" he asked, certain she'd carefully watched his every move. "There are two other crystals that serve as keys. We must find them to make the Staff fully functional."

Her eyes widened. "You're saying the Staff's working on minimum power and may not be at full capacity?"

"Yes."

"And if you find the missing keys, the Staff might be stronger?"

"Perhaps."

She shook her head. "Suppose it increases our lust even more?"

He shrugged. "You're free to get off at the next stop."

"That's a birdbrained idea."

He choked back a chuckle.

"I don't like that thing randomly messing with my libido." Her lower lip trembled, and she bit it to control the quiver.

"I'm sorry. But we need to—"

"Don't tell me what I need to do." She raised her head and glared. "You only paid for half this ship. That means I still own half." He'd known this was coming. If she wanted to believe she was in charge half the time, he'd do his best to support her theory—as long as she didn't get in the way of his mission. "And we may be cocaptains, but I'm keeping my distance from that Ancient Staff. And you, too."

"If you must." Keeping her distance wouldn't help, but he didn't have time to argue or explain. She wasn't fooling him with that cocaptains offer. Vi was too much of a control freak to share command. They'd be going head-to-head.

And perversely, he looked forward to it. He liked that she had a backbone. Enjoyed the way her mind worked. And he loved her sexy ass.

It was a good thing she couldn't read his thoughts, or she would have decked him. Hell, for his own sake, he shouldn't be thinking about how great she smelled or tasted or felt with those long legs wrapped around his hips. It was better for the mission if he kept his distance.

He started to turn toward the galley. "You want to run systems checks while I figure out what those things were coming at us in hyperspace?"

"All right. But do you have any idea where those missing keys are?"

He'd been trying to figure that out for fifteen hundred years. "During my first trip to Earth, I gave one key to King Arthur for safekeeping, but it was stolen. Later, Trendonis, the Tribes' leader, stole my Staff with the other two keys still embedded in the bark. When I finally got the Staff back, all the keys were gone. I found the triangular one on Tor, but the others could be anywhere."

"The staff was stolen in King Arthur's time on Earth?"

"Yes."

"And you found it again on the same world where Marisa, Lucan's sister, visited and found evidence that the Tribes are about to invade Earth?"

"Yes."

Her forehead wrinkled. "But how could that have happened?"

"One of King Arthur's knights was a man named Gareth. Long ago, he betrayed me and all dragonshapers to Trendonis. Gareth helped steal the Staff for the Tribes."

"Why would he do such a thing?"

"The Tribes were very powerful in those days, and Arthur couldn't defend every world. He had to make hard choices, like which planets to defend and which to sacrifice. One of the worlds Arthur sacrificed was Tor, and Gareth blamed Arthur."

"So Gareth made a deal with the enemy leader Trendonis?"

"In exchange for Gareth's help to murder King Arthur and steal my Staff, Trendonis promised Gareth that Tor would remain free of the Tribes." Jordan sighed. "When I was last on Tor I found the Key of Space, in Gareth's ancient home."

"Key of Space?"

"The key changed a rusting ship into a shiny new one so it could fly through space. The other keys are Wind and Soil. When all the keys are attached to the Staff, they create a fire strong enough to unite with the Grail."

"But if Trendonis wanted to prevent the Staff and the Grail from ever uniting, why didn't he destroy them when he had the chance?"

"According to legend, the Staff and the keys are indestructible."

She frowned skeptically. "So Trendonis scattered the keys across the galaxy?"

He nodded. "Without the keys, the Staff isn't at full power and can't unite with the Grail and utterly destroy the Tribes."

"So why didn't he drop the keys into a black hole?"

"Maybe he did. He's kept me from finding them. And he's used that time to rebuild the Tribes. Now that he has the Grail in his possession, he believes he's strong enough to take on Earth."

"What happens if you unite the Staff and the Grail without all the keys?"

She sure had a way of driving right to the point. But just because he'd lived a long time didn't mean he had all the answers.

"I guess we'll have to wait and see."

"That's not good enough."

He raised his eyebrow. "Would you prefer I lied?"

"I'd prefer you had a plan to take us home, but that's not going to happen is it?"

"Not just yet."

She sighed. "So we might as well go find the keys and our Grail."

"That's my girl."

Her eyes blazed with heat. "One very short, very meaningless sexual encounter does not make me yours."

"For something so *meaningless,* you're certainly talking about it a lot." He took pleasure in annoying her. He could grow to love her scowl, he really could.

The greatest dangers have their allurements.
—PHILIP DORMER STANHOPE,
4TH EARL OF CHESTERFIELD

5

Vivianne headed for the bridge with the dog tucked under her arm. But at the delicious aroma of frying burgers, the animal squirmed for his freedom. She set him down and he raced off. She followed more slowly and poked her head into the tiny galley to see the canine had already begged a hamburger patty from a slender, blue-eyed woman with her black hair pulled back into a ponytail.

"Hi." The woman smiled in greeting. "I'm Knox. Darren's fiancée."

"Vivianne. And those burgers smell delicious." She prayed the gravity would stay on long enough for her stomach to remain settled and for those burgers to cook.

"They're almost done." After wiping her hands on an apron, Knox kneeled to pet the Boston terrier, who'd inhaled his burger in one bite. "And who's this?"

"Another stowaway like you." Vivianne grinned. "I'm sorry you got caught up in this mess, but I do appreciate your cooking."

"Perhaps the dog will end up being good company for all of us."

"He's so curious I think we should call him George."

George wagged his stumpy tail, then sat. Looking up with expectant eyes, he stared at the stove.

Knox washed her hands, then flipped the burgers. "Looks like he wants some more."

"I don't suppose you've found any dog food?" Vivianne asked.

Knox shook her head. "There's frozen steaks and hamburger in the freezer. Rice and beans in the pantry. No vegetables. No fruit. No spices. I found a few soft drinks, a moldy sandwich, and leftover lasagna in the fridge."

Vivianne noted the countertops were immaculate but the ceiling was spattered with assorted crumbs, no doubt due to the sudden lack of gravity earlier. She opened a control panel. "I'm going to program a floater to clean up the ceiling."

"A floater?"

"It's technology we bought from another planet called Honor. The floaters help clean the air and incinerate the garbage before it clogs the filters."

"Cool." Knox filled a bowl with water and pushed it over to the dog.

George lapped it up. And Vivianne realized what went in was going to come out. "I'll program another floater to clean up after George."

Knox returned to her cooking. "This is way more exciting than payroll. But my family is going to worry about me." She bit her lower lip. "You think we might be heading back soon?"

Vivianne doubted it. Especially since the engines

might have sustained damage after they'd overheated. "I have no idea."

"It's just that I promised my little sister I'd be there for her graduation."

"I'm sorry. I'm afraid all our lives have been disrupted." Vivianne wondered how many of the crew were married. Had children. Except for Jordan and her, everyone else likely had some kind of family worrying about them.

"I wish we could send a message home. So at least my family knows I'm alive."

Vivianne clapped her hand to her forehead. Even after Sean fixed the communications system, their normal channels wouldn't work in hyperspace. However, they might have another communicator onboard—one that only Vivianne knew about.

Knox peered at her. "What is it?"

Vivianne didn't want to raise false hopes about her untested system. "Maybe we can fix our communications." Vivianne peered hungrily at a burger. Torn between food and her need to check on the prototype unit she'd had installed in the captain's quarters, she decided her stomach would have to suffer. But did she have time for a test before Jordan wondered why she wasn't running the *Draco*'s diagnostics as he'd asked?

"Another few minutes and these burgers will be done. You can take some with you. Maybe take some to Jordan—"

"Sorry, I can't." Arriving on the bridge with cold food wouldn't be appreciated. "Jordan's asked me to run diagnostics on the gyro circuits—"

"No problem. I'll bring them to the bridge." Knox's tone remained friendly, but she teased, "I can see why you'd want to keep your distance."

"Excuse me?"

Knox grinned. "I have six married brothers. And all of them look at their wives—just like Jordan looks at you."

"Jordan works for me. Other than that . . ." They'd shared lusty sex.

Knox winked at her. "That man only lets you think he works for you."

"You're mistaken." Vivianne hurried aft. Knox had come to the wrong conclusion. True, Jordan's eyes held a challenging gleam when they met Vivianne's. But that was merely due to the fact he enjoyed baiting her, not out of genuine interest.

And she wasn't wasting another moment thinking about him when this might be her best opportunity to test the prototype. If it worked, if she could contact Maggie, her former college roommate and an astronomer, Vivianne could stay in touch with Earth and learn what was happening back home, even notify the crew's families that their loved ones were all right.

She headed straight for the master cabin. None of the private quarters were luxurious. Space was at too much of a premium. However, the captain's quarters had a desk, its own tiny bathroom, and, best of all, its own porthole.

The view outside, glinting pinpoints of light scattered across a black velvet universe, was as spectacular as it was daunting. Yet there was also the most magnificent promise just outside the porthole. A promise of adventure. Of the unknown. Of a tomorrow that might be better than today.

Vivianne shut the door and keyed the lock. Anticipation thrumming through her, she headed straight to the monitor that tied into all *Draco*'s systems—it was bolted to the desk. She flipped open the side panel, toggled a switch.

A tiny green light signaled that the prototype she'd designed was drawing power and good to go. Vivianne was first and foremost a communications expert. This baby was her own invention, but there'd been no way to test it on Earth.

Vivianne heard a whine, and she jumped, then realized George was scratching on the door. She couldn't work with him distracting her and hurried to let him inside. He leapt onto the bed, circled, and settled, resting his head on his paws.

Vivianne turned back to the prototype. What should she say? That they were on a ship with an unproven hyperspace transport device and an untrained crew? And no navigation charts? And an alien power source that filled her with lusty energy? Oh, and let's not forget the captain, claiming he used to be Merlin and was at least fifteen hundred years old and fully intending to take the *Draco* into enemy territory, if they could find it.

Maggie would think she'd lost it.

Maybe she had lost it. She no longer knew what the truth was. How could she? While Jordan had answered some of her questions, his explanation hadn't proved or disproved his allegiance to Earth.

Even if she shared her doubts and Maggie agreed that Jordan might be a traitor, what could they do? The *Draco* was one of a kind. Earth didn't have another ship to send after them. They were on their own.

A hard knock had her pulse racing. "Vi?"

It was Jordan. "Just a minute."

Combing her fingers through her hair, she opened the

cabin door, ignoring her elevated pulse and refusing to let his implacable expression unnerve her.

Jordan held up a plate with a two hamburgers and two glasses of water. "Thought you might be hungry." His tone was casual, but she didn't miss his sharp gaze roaming over the cabin or how he immediately made himself at home by settling into a chair.

At the scent of food, George jumped from the bed with a bark. Before he could stand on his hind legs and beg, she jerked him back. "Down."

George paid no attention.

"Sit," Jordan ordered and, to her shock, the dog obeyed.

"Wow. Thanks." She accepted the food and placed it next to the desk.

Jordan's gaze settled on her prototype. "What are you working on? Is that a communicator?"

"It's a prototype and has never been tested. I've calibrated it to bounce zeta waves along magnetic wormhole lines."

"Zeta rays work like dropping a penny into a pond, the waves rippling outward," Jordan said. "Only the ripples travel through wormholes and three-dimensional space."

"Exactly." There were only about three people back home who could understand the theory behind her work. Again, he'd impressed her. "It could take hundreds of thousands of years for a message to arrive . . . if it arrives at all. Or if it works as planned, it might be instantaneous."

"Fascinating." He lifted his gaze from the prototype to her. "Your design, will it work in hyperspace?"

Pride zinged through her that he recognized the machine as her design. "That's the idea, but even if our end does what it's supposed to, we left before I set up Earth's end of the system."

"But you have a backup plan, don't you?" he guessed, laughter in his eyes.

She grinned and dialed down her excitement, told herself her reaction was normal. After all, she'd waited a year to test this machine. "I have a former college roommate, Maggie. She's an astronomer at Sunnyside Tech Observatory. Perhaps one of Maggie's instruments will pick up our message."

"Won't she just slough it off as a wormhole echo bouncing off Earth's atmosphere?"

"Other astronomers might. But Maggie won't. Not if she thinks it's from *me*."

He eyed her with curiosity. "And why would she think that?"

"Because in college we had a special code for when we went out. If I texted *qxq,* she'd call and make up an emergency excuse for me to return immediately to the dorm."

Amusement lit his eyes. "Did you use that tactic often?"

"Often enough that she'll remember."

He picked up a burger and bit into it. George got off the bed and sat at his feet, the animal watching him chew. "So what message will you send?"

Vivianne typed and pretended not to notice him feeding bites of his burger to George. "I'll tell her we're testing the *Draco*. Give her the names of everyone onboard and ask her to notify their families about the journey. And I'll ask her to retrieve the second zeta communicator from Vesta's headquarters in Florida so we can have a two-way conversation."

"Sounds like a plan."

Vivianne finished, left the communicator on to record a reply if one came in, but shut the panel. Jordan lifted the plate and once again offered her a burger. She bit into her burger and savored the delicious meat.

"Captain," Tennison's voice came through Jordan's handheld communicator.

Jordan lifted his wrist and spoke into the speaker. "Yes?"

"We picked up an unidentifiable energy surge . . . a burst we've never seen before. It appears to have come from inside the *Draco.* Do you think it's the Staff?"

"It's possible. Continue to monitor the situation."

From the moment she'd picked up the burger, George's attention had shifted from Jordan back to her. Such a little beggar. Vivianne fed George a bite. "Why would the Staff spike now?"

"Why does it change our body chemistry?" Jordan asked her back.

"It's almost as if it has a mind of its own," she said between bites.

A few crumbs of the hamburger roll stuck to the corner of her mouth. She wiped it with her finger and looked up to find Jordan watching her mouth.

He pulled a clean white handkerchief from his pocket and dabbed at the corner of her lips. "You missed a spot."

"Thanks." Was it her imagination, or was his voice lower? Huskier? She took the handkerchief from him and stood, a little uneasy at the intensity of his gaze. Knox's comment about how Jordan looked at Vivianne crossed her mind. Was he interested in her? She filed the thought away to examine later. "Any idea what those objects in the wormhole were?"

"No." He seemed to be staring into space.

"Is something wrong?" she asked as she gave the last bite to George.

"Those objects seemed . . . familiar. I'm just trying to remember . . ." Jordan opened the cabin door for her. "We should head back to the bridge."

She supposed centuries of memories might be difficult to process. The idea of living so long boggled her mind. Jordan claimed he'd been around since before the time of King Arthur. Yet he seemed so vital, alert and sharp.

Not to mention passionate. The man knew how to please a woman. Knew how to please *her*.

Sex with Jordan had been the most savage of her life. The most exciting. And ever since Jordan had come to the cabin to find her, she'd been much too aware of him. Could the Staff be affecting her from a distance? Or was it simply human nature to be aware of the man with whom she'd had such magnificent sex?

As they strode onto the bridge, she tried to tell herself that it was natural to dwell on what had happened between them. That it was natural for them to share private conversations over a meal, considering they were cocaptains. If she'd been male, he might have brought food, stayed for a conversation.

But he wouldn't have dabbed her mouth with a handkerchief.

Again, she shoved the thought away.

Lyle showed Jordan the completed inventory list on his handheld. "Do you realize we'll be out of food in a week? Knox didn't even have the sense to ration. And you"—he glanced from Vivianne to George, who was licking the last crumbs from his whiskers—"are feeding a dog?"

Jordan looked up from the inventory and frowned. Years of business had taught Vivianne to play with the big boys. She could handle the likes of Lyle.

She picked up George and tucked him under her arm. "Did *you* eat a whole burger?"

"Everyone did."

"Well, the dog had some of mine. So back off." She didn't mention the bites Jordan had fed George, or the one Knox had fed him, either. Breezing past Lyle, she slid behind the captain's console, set George to one side of the monitor, and began a systemwide diagnostic check.

Gray came over and scratched George behind the ears. "The engines seem to be all right, but let me know if the readings fluctuate more than one percent."

"Will do."

"Are communications back online?" Vivianne asked Tennison, since he stood behind the com station.

Jordan put a hand on Lyle's shoulder. "Your organizational skills are excellent. So why don't you work out a food schedule? And then perhaps you can help with assigning quarters to everyone."

Vivianne shot Jordan a thankful nod, went back to work, and tried not to think about how he kept surprising her. Whether in his arms or in his presence, there were levels to the man she'd never imagined.

Lyle slid behind the weapons console and booted up a screen. At least he couldn't do any harm. No weapons had been loaded onboard.

Tennison scratched his bald head. "As far as I can tell, the navigation system is up and running, but . . ."

"But?" she prodded.

Tennison's voice was tight. "I can't find Earth." His

head wrinkled from his forehead back to the crown. "I'm not even sure we're still in the Milky Way Galaxy."

Oh . . . God. That wasn't possible, was it? Her mind couldn't even calculate how many light-years away from home they might be. Her hands shook, and she clenched her fingers on the console so no one would notice. They might never see Earth again.

Gray must have overheard the conversation. "Tennison, see if the computer can backtrack our path."

"I already tried that. The attempt crashed the system. Sean's trying to reboot it."

Jordan's tone was calm. "There are too many possibilities for the computer to handle."

"Why can't we just turn around and go back?" Lyle asked, his tone high-pitched and nervous.

"Because when the ship opens a wormhole," Vivianne answered, "we have no way to tell where that wormhole will take us. And once we're through the wormhole, it closes behind us."

Lyle's face turned ashen. "Are you saying we're lost?"

A disaster is an opportunity to sail with a dangerous wind at one's back.

—CHINESE PROVERB

6

"Find us a planet." Jordan strode to the viewscreen and paced.

"A planet?" Lyle asked. "Like, just any planet will do?"

"We need food. It doesn't grow in space. Ergo, we need to find a planet to restock our supplies." Jordan pressed the intercom. "Everyone please come to the bridge."

A few minutes later the crew had arrived, and Jordan addressed them. "You've all heard that Earth may be attacked by the Tribes."

"Aren't those just rumors?" Knox asked.

"Intel from Pendragon and Honor say otherwise." Jordan's gaze went to Vivianne. "You've seen reports that the Tribes have the Holy Grail?"

"Yes."

"The *Draco* was built to recover the Grail. If we don't succeed, Earth will fall." Jordan's gaze went from one person to the next. "I know you people didn't volunteer. But now that you're here, I hope you'll agree that despite the danger, we must all do what we can to save Earth."

"We aren't trained," Lyle protested.

"No one's trained for this," Tennison argued. "Count me in."

Gray didn't even look up from his monitor. "Whatever it takes to save Earth."

One by one, everyone agreed. Even Lyle.

"Thank you for your support," Jordan said, ending the meeting.

"What exactly do you want us to do?" Darren asked.

Jordan stared at the stars on the screen. "For starters, work together to find us a planet with food."

Several crew, including Knox, left the bridge, their expressions determined and hopeful.

Gray hovered over his console. "What parameters should I plug into the search engine?"

"A planet with atmosphere and gravity similar to Earth would be best," Vivianne suggested, placing George under a console, where the dog curled up and promptly went to sleep. "One with water."

"A planet that's close enough for the *Draco* to reach within three days without reentering hyperspace," Jordan added.

Vivianne scanned the diagnostics she was running. "Why a planet only three days out?"

"In case the first world turns out to be a dud, we'll still have time for a second try," Jordan said.

Lyle threw his hands in the air. "I vote we search for Earth, not hunt for food on some strange world where the natives may decide to eat *us*."

Jordan eyed the man coldly. "The *Draco*'s not a democracy. If you don't hunt, you don't eat. And if you don't obey orders, I'll shove you out the nearest airlock."

A few of the crew chuckled.

Lyle opened his mouth. Jordan raised an eyebrow.

"Understood, sir." Lyle's face reddened. He ducked his head and walked off the bridge.

Jordan wondered where Lyle had gone to sulk. He also wondered exactly what Vivianne had been doing in the captain's quarters before he'd arrived. Vivianne had told him she'd tried to send a message to Maggie, but had she also tried to contact anyone else? Perhaps someone on Pendragon or Honor? Had she told him the truth? Although she'd settled down, he knew better than to think she trusted him.

With Lyle's departure, for a long minute or two an awkward silence fell over the crew. Then Sean strode onto the bridge, Darren behind him. Darren held out a scanner. "I've got that cargo inventory you asked for. Want me to download it?"

"Yes, please," Vivianne answered. "You find anything useful?"

"That depends how you define useful." Sean vibrated with excitement.

"Star charts?" Vivianne asked.

"None."

"Food?" Darren guessed.

"Nothing edible."

"What did you find?" Jordan asked.

"A first-aid kit." He held it up. "Vitamins and spare clothing, which I left in the hold. And"—Sean broke into a wide smile—"three spacesuits."

"What?" Vivianne exchanged a long, surprised look with Jordan. "Those weren't due for delivery for another two weeks. Good work, Sean."

"Lyle found them." Sean still looked pleased at the compliment, and his grin widened. "I've already checked them out. They hold pressure and air. Would you like me to go outside to see if we've sustained any damage?"

Before Jordan could answer, Gray's monitor beeped. "I've got three possible planets. Want me to post them on the overhead?"

"Yes, please," Vivianne answered.

"This one is closest." Gray pointed at a world with four continents and a polar ice cap. "The planet's similar in gravity to Earth. Ditto for distance to the sun. We can probably breathe the atmosphere, but the oxygen's thin."

"Maximum magnification," Jordan requested. All four continents on that world were black, the sea brown.

Gray switched the visual. "These two planets are in the opposite direction and share a solar system. The smaller one's only land mass is one icy and mountainous island in a planet of blue seas. The air's breathable, but the weather seems extreme. I'm currently counting five class-ten hurricanes and another building off the southern hemisphere. The last world in this system is larger, colder, with lots of ice, but still within our parameters."

Vivianne looked at Jordan. "What do you think?"

Gray's jaw dropped as he listened through his headset. "There's also a planet four days out. They're sending a message. I wish I had a universal translator."

"I have one," Lyle said as he returned to the bridge.

Jordan also had a translator, as did Vivianne, who used it for frequent talks with Pendragon and Honor, though she hadn't mentioned it. The tiny machine under the skin in his forearm was new technology that had recently made it to Earth from Pendragon. The subcutaneous device translated language. All the regular crew would have had them, but unfortunately Vesta's engineering team didn't usually have much use for anything beyond math and science.

Lyle started to don a headset, but Jordan signaled for Gray to put the sound through the speaker system.

The alien language came through intelligible and shrill. "Turn back. Any craft attempting to enter our atmosphere will be shot down. Turn back. Any species—"

"Turn it off," Jordan ordered and thrummed his fingers on the console.

"Do they know we're here?" Vivianne asked.

Gray shook his head. "I think it's nondirectional. Like a buoy at sea. Anyone within ten light-years would hear it."

While Lyle translated the message for the crew, Vivianne sighed. "They really don't sound friendly."

Jordan made up his mind. "Head to planet number one."

"The one with the black dirt and brown seas?" Tennison asked in surprise.

Gray's fingers moved over the console. "Course laid in."

Jordan double checked the readings and gave him a thumbs-up.

"Engines engaged," Gray said.

Jordan knew the crew would be happier with an explanation. "We need food. Since we're alone out here and the *Draco*'s not armed, I'd prefer not to knowingly fly into hostile territory. So we heed the warning and stay away. That leaves us three choices: "Tempest," the bad-weather planet; "Frigid," the cold one; or "Shadow," the dark one. On Tempest those hurricanes could rip us apart. And Frigid's temperatures are less likely to produce food. That leaves Shadow, the dark world. Any questions?"

"If we can't breathe the air on Shadow . . ." Lyle's voice trailed off.

Jordan folded his arms over his chest and kept his tone neutral but firm. "It's borderline breathable. And we have spacesuits."

Tennison shot Lyle a thoughtful frown. "We're going to have to make hard choices, and we need to stick together."

"Of course." Lyle laughed, his look sly. "Jordan's real good at sticking to her. Or should I say sticking her?"

Vivianne went white. But she compressed her lips and lifted her chin.

In the year he'd worked for her he hadn't heard or read so much as a whisper of gossip about her private life. Not even in the scandal sheets.

"Lyle's losing it." Gray gestured for Darren to open the first-aid kit. "Are there any tranqs in there?"

"Believe what you want," Lyle sneered. "I saw Jordan and Vivianne going at it in the engine compartment."

Jordan punched Lyle in the jaw, wishing he could have done it sooner to shut the man up. Lyle's eyes rolled back in his head and he sagged, then collapsed to the deck. At eighty percent gravity, he didn't fall as hard as he would have on Earth. But one punch and Lyle was out cold. Hell. Jordan would have enjoyed hitting him again. And again.

He didn't care that Lyle's wife had cheated on him and that he believed any other couple who were enjoying themselves deserved his rage.

Vivianne came around her console, her fists on her hips. "Damn it. Have you killed him?"

"Who cares?" Jordan scowled, then forced his face to go stoic. But it pained him that she would worry over a man who'd just insulted her. Because he knew what the accusations had cost Vivianne.

Another woman might have fled or burst into tears. Or ignored the situation. Chin high, eyes dark with suppressed hurt, voice calm, Vivianne addressed the bridge crew. "What I do in my own time is my business." She shoved Lyle with her foot and he groaned. Kneeling, she spoke quietly, her tone threaded with steel. "Lyle, you aren't welcome on this bridge until I receive a public apology."

"Get him out of here," Jordan ordered.

Tennison dragged Lyle to his feet. Lyle wobbled and leaned against Tennison, and although his tone was strong, the fight was gone from his voice. "I'm sorry. I was out of line." He raised his head, rubbed his brow. "And . . . I overreacted. I'm an engineer, not an explorer. I didn't sign up for this kind of stress."

"Apology accepted." Voice tight, Vivianne jerked her thumb. "But do me a favor and stay out of my way for a while."

Her demeanor was strong, feminine, sexy as hell. And like a switch had been turned on, Jordan's blood was suddenly simmering with lust. He gaze caught Vivianne's, and he could see twin pinpoints of light in her irises.

She wanted him. At least, he prayed the answering gleam he'd seen there was real. Because he had to get them off the bridge fast. Like a vibration from loud music, tremors rocked him. Starting in his bones, echoing through his tendons, radiating outward through his muscles, the thrum of sensuality was a drumbeat he couldn't ignore.

Jordan approached the viewscreen. "How long until we orbit the dark world?"

"About ten hours," Gray said.

"You and Sean have the first watch. Don't hesitate to call me if anything unusual happens. Vivianne, you're with me."

Jordan stalked from the bridge, not even waiting to see if she followed. He was in serious need of . . .

Jordan halted in midthought. Ever since he and Vivianne had gone back to the engine room, he'd been riled. If Lyle hadn't set him off, something else would have.

His skin prickled. He had a hard-on the size of Jupiter, and no matter had much he tried to repress the need, he was close to losing control again.

"You think us being together's a . . . good . . . idea?" Vivianne came up next to him. Her tone was soft and raw. She might as well have caressed his flesh.

He gritted his teeth. "It's . . . happening . . . again."

"No. It is not." Vivianne spoke as if she was in agony.

It took every ounce of his control not to rip off her clothing and take her there right in the hallway. He swallowed hard, unable to keep the gruff need from his tone. "I'll be in the captain's quarters."

And if she didn't follow, he was going to die. Not in his entire life had lust ever pounded him like this. It was as if some universal joker was playing cruel tricks. They were in danger. But it didn't matter. They might die tomorrow. It didn't matter. The crew would know exactly what they were up to. It didn't matter.

He had to have her now.

He heard her first hurried steps behind him. And he began to run.

Her matching sprint should have made him feel joyous. But he was in too much need for joy.

Breath coming harsh in his throat, he opened the cabin door and spun around, snaked out an arm to grab her, and dragged her to him. She kicked the door shut behind her. He couldn't wait one more second to kiss her. Thank the Universe, she lifted her head, grabbed his hair, and yanked his head down.

Then he was tasting her. Holding her, crushing her against him.

He had to force himself to ease back so she could breathe. "I hope to hell you want me," he growled.

"Like I have a choice." She bit his neck.

"I'll take that for a yes." He scooped her up and was in the process of carrying her to the bed when the *Draco*'s artificial gravity failed.

They floated into midair. "Captain," Gray said through the intercom. "We have a short. Sean says it's going to take about an hour to fix the gravity."

He leaned over and hit the toggle. "Understood. Make certain the damn dog doesn't break its neck." He killed the intercom and eyed Vivianne.

"Thanks for looking out for George." She was already removing her jacket, blouse, and slacks, a task eased by the lack of gravity. Spinning slowly, she was like a tempting piece of eye candy, all pink satiny skin and feminine curves.

Jordan knew how to make a woman feel good. He knew how to make a woman want him. He knew how to caress and stroke a woman's body. But last time, in his hurry to have her, he'd not taken the time to worship her as he should.

He'd taken her with a savage need. Luckily, her desire had matched his own. And once again, he was simply too charged up to take this slow. Besides, she was fierce, pushing off a bulkhead to get to him, then ripping off his shirt, attacking his pants. Eyes wild, breath panting, reddish-blond hair framing her face, she was like a hungry predator, wild and independent and so fierce that he knew she was right there with him. Feeling what he felt. Wanting what he wanted.

"Hurry," she demanded as she placed his hands over her breasts.

God, she was soft. He caressed her flesh. "Better?"

Her nipples tightened. "Much better."

They floated in the cabin. He tried to fight the compulsion to hurry, but she wasn't having anything to do with slow.

She yanked him to her, until they were face-to-face. "Fill me."

He tried to stroke her with gentle caresses, but she writhed with impatience.

"Now. Damn you." Parting her long legs, lifting her slender hips, she took him inside her.

Thrusting into her, then pulling back, had the blood rushing through his head and roaring through his ears. The ship could have caught fire and he couldn't have stopped. Pressure was building, growing in intensity, blinding him with need.

He pumped, his hips grinding. She matched him stroke for stroke.

He could feel the orgasm tensing in his balls, and from the top of his head to his toes, he craved release.

Vivianne slapped his ass. "Faster."

"Yes, ma'am."

"Harder."

He grunted, his body slamming into hers as she pumped her hips to meet his. "I'm burning."

"Yes." He could feel the heat. Sweat broke out on his flesh, but he never stopped moving. He couldn't stop moving. The need was too primal.

She raked her fingernails across his back and drew him in tighter.

Too tight.

They were floating in midair. Gravity no longer dictated their moves.

"Unhook your legs," he demanded.

"No."

He stopped moving, gazed straight into her eyes. "Do it."

"But—"

"Do it," he urged. And this time she yielded. They floated prone, touching only where he was inside her. He spread his legs wide until each foot braced against a corner alcove. Then he placed his hands on her shoulders for a moment and set her into a spin.

"Oh . . . my. Ah."

He'd never been so hard in his life. And she was spinning on him. Every time her face passed his, her breasts skimmed against his chest. A riot of sensations swelled as he viewed her from a variety of angles. Her passion-filled face, her lovely breasts, her toned legs, her tight ass.

And those sweet sounds that came out of her mouth were like music.

"Ah. Oh. Oh, oh, oh." She squeezed her eyes closed. "Faster. Spin me . . ."

He slapped her ass and she moaned.

"More."

He slapped her again and she spun so quickly he felt as if the top of his head was going to explode.

And when she tensed and clutched him, stopping the spin, he poured into her, the orgasm so strong that he could have sworn he saw starbursts of purple and sizzling gold.

When he opened his eyes, Vivianne floated above him, the fringe of her lashes casting shadows on her high cheekbones. She was studying him, her face flushed, her lips bee-stung from his kisses, but her eyes were like a caged wild animal's in full panic.

When a single tear escaped from one of her eyes, he didn't know what to say.

Life is a space wreck, but we must not forget to sing in the life pods.

—DOMINUS ADMIRAL

7

"Vi," Jordan drawled. "Vi, come here." She'd been through so much. All because of him. He wanted to take away her pain but he wasn't sure how. So he did what felt right. Reaching out, he gathered her against his chest. "It's going to be all right."

One moment he was holding her, the next, another of Vi's memories hammered Jordan, dropping into his brain as if out of regenerated air.

"Are we there yet?" Vivianne asked her parents. Belted into the back seat of their Prius, she sat behind her father. A cardboard carton of cranberry juice with a straw sat on a tray next to a plate with sliced apples and carrots, and peanut butter for dipping.

Headlights from the oncoming cars on the four-lane highway kept lighting up her dad's face. "Do you need a bathroom, honey?"

"No. I just want to smell the leaves again."

Her parents were taking her north to see the leaves change color. So far, the leaves had been orange and red, gold and brown. And they smelled ripe, like Mom's garden after a hard rain.

"Look out!" her mother screamed.

Her father slammed on the brakes. Tires squealed.

Vivianne's drink flew off the tray. Her carrots and apples spilled. Then she was turning upside down, then back up. The seat belt cut into her waist and shoulder. Metal crunched. Glass broke.

Mom screamed and screamed.

The screaming scared Vivianne. She would have screamed, too, but her throat froze.

Vivianne's head hurt. Her chest ached. And she couldn't seem to breathe. The car kept flipping. Over and over. The horn blared. The air bags popped, and Vivianne choked on the powder.

Mom had stopped screaming, and that scared her even more.

Vivianne didn't open her eyes until the car stopped skidding. "Mom? Dad?"

"Sweetie," Mom said in a sob. She was crying. "Are you okay?"

"What happened?" Vivianne tried to unlock her seat belt, but her fingers didn't seem to work right.

A car pulled up, and headlights shined through the broken windshield. Their car was tipped sideways in a ditch. "Mom, your head. You're bleeding."

"I'm sorry. I'm sorry." Her mother kept saying that over and over.

Vivianne finally freed her seat belt. She put her hand on her father's shoulder. "Dad. Mom's hurt. She needs you."

"Don't look at Daddy, baby. Look at me."

Vivianne didn't understand. Dad always helped her mom. Why wasn't he doing something?

"Mom?"

Her mother reached up to the necklace Vivianne had given her for her birthday three years ago. She jerked it, snapping the chain. She loved that necklace. Wore it every day. Why would she break it?

"I'm sorry." Mom pressed the necklace into Vivianne's hand. "Keep this, and remember how much we loved each other."

Her mother's head slumped. Her eyes closed. With a horrible gurgle, a bubble of blood oozed from her mouth and her hand fell away from Vivianne.

Vivianne clutched the necklace. She didn't understand. She heard sirens. Saw blinking red lights. Strangers talking.

"We'll have to cut the little girl out of the back seat."

"The parents?"

"Dead."

No. No. No. They couldn't be dead.

Hands reached for Vivianne. She tried to fight, reached for her parents. "Mom. Dad. Don't leave me. Don't leave me all alone."

Jordan had to inhale a deep breath, tell himself that Vivianne had lost her parents a long time ago. But her pain . . . he didn't want to feel her pain. He didn't want to feel sorry for her. And he most certainly couldn't afford to give her his sympathy. He couldn't afford to form emotional attachments that clouded his judgment. He'd made that mistake once, befriending Trendonis, a stranger whose betrayal had cost Jordan his world.

But how could he not feel more for her after living her pain?

At least he'd been an adult when his parents had died. She'd been only a child.

He had no idea how she'd grown into such a strong woman. But he wanted to know. Had relatives raised her? Had she gone to a loving home?

And that's when he realized there was a price to be paid for the lovemaking. Both times the Staff forced them together physically, Jordan had received another of Vivianne's memories.

Damn it. He couldn't stay detached when he knew so much about her. He didn't want to admire what she had made of her life. He didn't want to be involved. Apparently, the Staff was determined to show him all the little details that made Vivianne so special.

But he couldn't let it matter.

NOTHING WAS GOING to be all right again. Ever. As much as she told herself what they'd done was just sex, it didn't feel like just sex. Not when he invaded her thoughts at all the wrong times. Not when she found her gaze roaming the bridge to gauge his reactions. Not when she took solace in his arms. Not with Jordan's memories flooding Vivianne's mind.

A bloodied sword swung at Jordan's head. React-ing on instinct, Jordan raised his shield to block the blow. At the same time he advanced, and, with his sword arm, counterattacked. His weapon glanced off his attacker's chain mail but still came away bloody as part of the blade caught unprotected flesh.

The man moaned in agony and fell to his knees. Before Jordan could finish him, two more men at-tacked, one from either side. Jordan shifted, par-ried, and sliced with lightning speed, dispatching both men, then another.

In a matter of seconds Vivianne saw him slay half a dozen men, his arm tireless. And then he slipped. While he rolled in the mud, Vivianne caught sight of other men battling for their lives. One man in particular drew her attention, a knight, his face masked behind armor. But for a moment Vivianne could clearly see his stunning silver-colored breast plate embossed with three golden horses.

The memory ended as suddenly as it had come to Vivianne.

Either Jordan had told her the truth about his age, and his memories had somehow entered her mind, or some-one or something was implanting false memories. And she had no idea which scenario was more likely. Both seemed impossible.

Vivianne could deal with being lost in space. She could deal with the danger. She could even deal with the sex.

But this total loss of control of her mind . . . was like losing her strength, the part of herself that she relied on most.

How could she make good decisions when her enemy might be the one offering solace? With both of them floating, it was almost cozy and peaceful, like the quiet after a storm.

But she shouldn't rely on him or trust him. She had to stay on guard. That Staff was Jordan's. For all she knew he'd programmed it to place memories in her head, to have this effect on her. No way would she admit to him that the Staff was getting into her mind.

Jordan might control the Staff, but he didn't control her. And she still planned to find a way to stop him from driving her ship into enemy territory.

And while the memory of him fighting seemed so very real, she had no proof that it had happened. But how could she not look at Jordan differently on the bridge after she'd watched him fight for his life? She'd been rooting for him. And that feeling of their being on the same side remained. Could she remain impartial? Wouldn't their intimacy and his memories influence her judgment?

And if she couldn't trust herself . . . then what?

Just then, Jordan reached out and caressed her shoulder and back with soothing strokes. "We'll figure this out."

"How?"

"I don't know," he admitted, his tone husky. "But we'll be all right."

The last thing she'd expected from Jordan was . . . tenderness. Or sympathy. Damn him for being so kind. When he was rough and tough, she kept herself together, fighting instinctively.

But his tenderness undid her.

Tears choking her, Vivianne swallowed down her rising panic. She forced herself to think. "The Ancient Staff is changing our hormones, right?"

He nodded. "But I can't turn down the power, or the *Draco* won't fly."

"But why isn't the Staff affecting anyone else?"

"It's my Staff, so it always affects me."

She lifted her head to peer into his glittery blue eyes. "I don't understand."

"We share energy."

"Are you saying it's always made you feel—"

"No. This insatiable lust . . . has never happened before."

She sensed there was much more he wasn't sharing, and once again frustration made her uneasy. He was answering her questions, but she suspected she wasn't asking the right ones.

"The Staff came from Dominus? And you had it with you when your world was destroyed?"

"On Dominus, everyone had a Staff. When I was conceived, my parents' Staffs united and began to grow. On my world, after a child is born, the Staff separates into three pieces, one for each parent and one for the child. We keep our Staffs by our side at all times."

She frowned. "But you told me that you lost it before King Arthur found the Holy Grail."

His tone was flat. "I was tricked. A woman named Nimue pretended she was drowning. To save her life and swim her to shore, I had to let go of the Staff. When I swam back for it, her cohort, Gareth, had stolen it. Then he took it to Trendonis."

He spoke without bitterness, and yet she sensed a wound so deep that it pained him to his very core.

"You went after Trendonis?" she prodded.

"It took me fifteen hundred years. I finally found Trendonis on Honor. He and the Tribes were using my staff to power their torture machine."

Fifteen hundred years. Vivianne was a master of setting long-term goals, but even she couldn't imagine pursuing anything for so long.

"And Trendonis, what happened to him?"

Frustration filled his tone. "I almost caught him on Honor, but he fled. But I have sworn before the Goddess to stop the man who destroyed my world."

Trendonis had lived at least as long as Jordan. "Are the Tribes immortal?"

"No. They can be killed in battle—or they could be before they possessed the Grail."

"But if the Tribes already have the Grail," she asked, "how can we win?"

"We steal it back. Once we possess the Grail and drink from it, then no matter how severe our wounds, we will not die in battle."

"Being immortal might be the most powerful defense of all time."

"Exactly." Jordan turned onto his side, his face serious and glum, but he kept his hand in hers. "When a soldier of Earth risks his life of only a hundred years and dies, the loss isn't as great as a soldier of the Tribes who might otherwise live for thousands of years."

"I could easily argue that when a life is short, each day is more precious," she countered, wondering why she couldn't find the strength to pull away from the small circles his thumb was making on her wrist.

"Perhaps." When he caught her watching him stroke

her wrist, he jerked. Almost as if he'd been unconsciously caressing her, then had realized what he'd been doing, he pulled away. "But despite their warlike and dominating natures, the Tribes have difficulty recruiting soldiers. That's why when a planet doesn't fall easily to their domination, they destroy it."

"If Trendonis now possesses the Holy Grail, he can promise his soldiers that they won't die of battle wounds."

Jordan added, "And their ranks will swell with recruits."

"How well do you know Trendonis?" she asked.

"He's fearless. And evil."

"Did he ever wear armor with a coat of arms bearing three horses?"

Jordan's eyes pierced hers. "That was King Arthur Pendragon's coat of arms. Why did you ask?"

"While reading about medieval history, I've read references to the three horses."

"Three horses was definitely Arthur's coat of arms."

If Jordan knew King Arthur's coat of arms, then he could have lived in that time as he'd claimed. But he also could have read up on King Arthur.

Still, he could turn himself into an owl, and possessed a Staff that powered the *Draco,* so if his knowledge was accurate, it was another clue that lent credence to his story. Vivianne would check the computer the first chance she had to see if she could verify his statement. "So Trendonis is still alive?"

"I'll destroy him." Jordan spoke in the same flat tone, and yet his eyes darkened to a turbulent deep blue.

His private war of revenge had lasted over a thousand

years, and yet she could see that he hadn't lost one iota of determination. With all his people gone, she supposed she couldn't blame him.

And yet living only for revenge seemed an empty existence.

"In all those years, you've had no home? No family? No friends?"

He hesitated, then spoke softly, "There was no time. I was searching for the Staff."

"The Staff must be very precious to you."

It was just her luck that the object that was causing all her difficulties was the key to keeping Earth's enemies at bay. She wasn't certain how she would reconcile herself to the way the Staff affected her, but she was beginning to believe Jordan was over fifteen hundred years old. That he had known King Arthur.

But was he on the side of Earth?

While she wasn't totally certain she could trust him, she was leaning more in that direction. She just prayed the shared memories and the physical intimacy weren't altering her perception.

Gray's voice came over the speaker. "Prepare for gravity."

Jordan shoved off the ceiling, rotating their feet down toward the deck. Five seconds later, as the gravity kicked in, they dropped.

Jordan steadied her, then sat on the bed. He scooted over and left enough room for her to join him. But with the restoration of gravity, the return of responsibilities weighed on her.

She reached for her clothing.

He locked his hands behind his head. "You need sleep."

"Here?" she asked.

"Why not?" He raised an eyebrow. "It's not like the entire crew doesn't already know what we've been doing."

"True." She slipped into his shirt. "Just let me check the communicator to see if Maggie's answered."

He shot her the most charming grin. "You look good in my shirt."

For a moment, she lost her breath. She yearned to get right back into bed and let him take the shirt off of her. But she really needed to check out his story.

From the bed, he couldn't see her screen. She tapped into the main search engine, but everything she found about King Arthur was legend. Then she recalled that they'd downloaded all of Pendragon's history into another module.

When she pulled it up, she found King Arthur's coat of arms. At the sight of three horses that matched the one she'd seen on the breastplate, she bit back a gasp.

She tried to tamp down her excitement. She supposed Jordan could have come across Arthur's coat of arms while he'd been on Pendragon. But it was the kind of esoteric information that wasn't found on Earth, that only a historian or someone who'd lived during that time would know. Jordan could have looked it up in Pendragon's history on the computer, just like she had. But what were the chances? While she still didn't have real proof that his fantastic story was possible, she was beginning to think he might actually have told her the truth about his past.

"Find anything?" Jordan asked.

"Maggie hasn't answered yet." She turned off the monitor but left the system running. Vivianne slid out of his shirt and climbed into bed.

She'd sleep better snuggled next to Jordan's warm body, knowing that he probably was exactly who he'd claimed to be. Jordan, Chen, Merlin. Still, she'd give up her entire fortune to know with one hundred percent *certainty* that he was now telling her the truth.

Exhausted, she felt as if she'd just closed her eyes when she awoke to the sound of alarms blaring. Before she could force her eyes open, Jordan had leaped out of bed and dressed. He toggled a switch to open communications with the bridge. "What's wrong?"

"Those things that came at us in hyperspace," Tennison's voice piped into their cabin, "they're back."

"I'll be right there." Jordan was out the door in less than ten seconds. But before he left, he pointed to the closet. "There's a change of clothes for you in there."

"Thanks." With a sigh, Vivianne swept aside the covers, shocked to discover she'd actually slept for eight full hours. Gazing out the porthole, she viewed the objects in question. And ice slid down her spine.

The objects looked like barbells, but instead of round ends there were cubes of polished rock. While the material might be confused with a naturally formed object, their precise shapes suggested these things were manufactured.

They could be spaceships. Weapons. Hurrying to dress in the clean clothes Jordan had had placed in the cabin for her, her thoughts flew. Jordan could be surprisingly thoughtful, his face when unguarded expressive. And his eyes had darkened with concern at the news of those cubes.

Jordan had left the toggle on the bridge open, and she could hear a multitude of busy conversations.

Gray's voice was firm. "Everyone quiet down so I can listen to the headset."

"You picking up anything?" Jordan asked, and she pictured him striding onto the bridge, taking immediate control.

"Nothing."

Tennison raised his voice. "Energy readings indicate they are powering up. Preparing to fire?"

Vivianne didn't wait to hear more. She hurried down the hallway.

And everything went dark.

You cannot build moral fiber and devotion by taking away people's initiative and liberty.
— KING ARTHUR PENDRAGON

8

Totally blind and weightless, Vivianne pulled herself toward the bridge.

Where were the emergency systems? Why hadn't the backup lights and generator kicked in? Had they suffered a total power failure? Had the Ancient Staff stopped working?

She might not be able to see, but she could hear shouting coming from the direction of the bridge. And George was barking. He must be terrified.

Damn it. He wasn't the only one. Had those objects sucked out all of the *Draco*'s power?

Mind whirring with fear, Vivianne reached the bridge. Gray had turned on a tiny portable penlight and held it between his teeth as he helped Tennison remove a panel. Sean had snagged George, but the moment she entered he thrust the dog at her and went to help with the generator.

Vivianne caught George and soothed him. Although she was full of questions, she didn't want to add to the confusion.

Jordan wore the headset and spoke quietly. At first Jordan was calm, but then his eyes narrowed, his mouth tightened, and she suspected he'd begun to issue threats.

Jordan tore off the headset, his eyes dark and furious. "No one's answering. After we shot at them, I suppose they have their reasons."

She gasped in surprise. "How could we shoot at them? We have no weapons."

"Sean rigged up a laser during his shift. When the objects appeared, Lyle panicked and fired."

"I was trying to protect us," Lyle said.

She bit back a curse. This was why they shouldn't have left with an untrained crew. With no self-discipline or rules to serve as guidelines and no plan to deal with a first contact with an alien species, Lyle may have doomed them all.

And they had no contingency measures to deal with hostility, either.

Jordan spoke as he leaned over his monitor. "Lyle destroyed one cube, and then the others put us in some kind of stasis field."

"Stasis field?"

"An energy dampener," Gray explained. "We have power, but somehow they're suppressing it."

"What about life support?" she asked, and set George on the floor.

"It's on the fritz," Sean said, "like every other system onboard."

Jordan remained calm, but she heard an underlying thread of fury in his tone. "Shut down everything that's still emitting even one amp. I want to go totally dead."

His orders shocked her almost as much as his anger. He seemed to be taking the blackout personally.

"You're going to kill what little life support we have left?" she asked.

He nodded.

"Even our air scrubbers?" Tennison asked.

"If they think we're dead, maybe they'll lose interest." Jordan's tone was hard as a cut diamond.

He edged very close to her and whispered into her ear, his tone so low no one else could possibly hear. "If killing all our power doesn't work, you're in charge."

"What?" She spun around to face him, but Jordan had disappeared. Vanished. Had she imagined he'd told her to take charge? Not that she needed any urging, but it was so unlike him to just depart during a crisis that her gut churned.

She floated before the viewscreen. "Without the ship's scrubbers, how long can we keep breathing?"

Gray came up beside her. "All our instruments are down, but I'd estimate about a half hour."

Sean joined them. "Air isn't our problem. The cold's going to get us first. Without the ship's heaters, we'll freeze long before we run out of air."

George whined, and she grabbed him from midair. The poor little dog was not adjusting to the lack of gravity. He pushed his cold nose into her hand. Already the bridge temperature had dropped ten degrees, and she held the dog against her stomach, sharing heat.

"Sean, Tennison, grab Darren in the galley and you three go down to the cargo bay and don the spacesuits," she ordered.

"What about you?" Sean asked her.

"Go," she snapped, and the three men hurried off the bridge while Lyle hung his head.

· "Let me help," Lyle demanded. "I caused this mess. I want to fix it."

"I appreciate that. And you may get an opportunity to help." George licked her hand and she cuddled him tight, his body lending comfort and heat. "If the ploy to cut all power doesn't work, I need everyone to help implement plan B."

"Plan B?" Gray asked.

"We wait as long as we can to convince them we're dead. If that doesn't work, we turn what power we have back on—"

"And shoot them?" Lyle asked.

She shook her head. "We don't have enough power for that. But I want to talk to them."

"Talk?" Lyle shook his head. "If Jordan's threats didn't work, you think they'll be afraid of you?"

"Maybe they're afraid of women—you never know." She tried to joke, but her mind was working furiously. She needed to reason with them.

"Where's Jordan?" Gray asked.

"He went to check on our power," she lied, and her teeth began to chatter. "Lyle, please go find us some jackets and blankets and hurry back."

After Lyle tugged himself off the bridge, Gray said quietly, "I can turn on the power by myself."

"I know." She sighed and forced her jaw to open wider to prevent her teeth from chattering. "But Lyle needs to feel useful."

"Captain?" Tennison's voice came over the speaker system.

"Yes?" Vivianne answered.

"Darren's giving his spacesuit to Knox."

He was disobeying her orders to save his girlfriend. Vivianne didn't like it. "Darren?"

"Yes, ma'am."

"Next time you want to disobey an order, you ask for permission to do so. Is that clear?"

"Yes, ma'am."

"Then zip Knox into that suit and make sure she knows how to use it."

"I will. And th-thanks."

She peered back out the viewscreen. "Th-they aren't leaving, are th-they?" No longer able to stop her teeth from chattering, she stared at the strange cubes. Had Lyle's hostility caused this crisis? Would those machines be dampening their power if they hadn't fired first?

Very likely they were going to die. Freeze to death.

She'd heard that it wasn't a bad way to go. But as her core temperature dropped, she began to feel light-headed.

To her surprise, Lyle returned with blankets, and he and Gray wrapped one around her and George. "Th-thanks." In truth it didn't help much. Her fingertips had gone numb. Ditto for her toes.

As Lyle and Gray wrapped more blankets around themselves, she knew they had only a few more minutes left before they froze. "Huddle close," she ordered. "We n-need to share body heat."

The three of them floated shoulder to shoulder, but without gravity they kept moving apart.

"This isn't working," Gray said.

"All right." Vivianne had to do something. "T-turn th-the power back on."

Gray and Lyle soared over to the panel. Gray's fingers were so clumsy with the cold, it took both men to kick in the power—such as it was.

"D-done." Gray moved slowly. "You want power to go to heat or communications?"

She picked up the headset. "First we talk."

Blessed heat would have been wonderful. But Vivianne knew it would take hours to get their core temperatures back up, and she had a job to do first. "Tennison, Sean, report to the bridge." She placed the icy headset over her freezing ears. "Gray, route all power to my station."

"R-routed."

Lyle floated unconscious. Vivianne prayed she hadn't waited too long. Her eyelids were heavy. But going to sleep meant never waking up. "You are k-killing us. We have no heat, which we need to s-sustain life. If you continue to t-take away our power, we'll die. When you surrounded us, one of my crew panicked and fired at you. We hope you did not suffer a loss of life, but if you did, I'm willing to give you my life in return. There's no reason to k-kill others aboard who are innocent. I repeat, you are killing everyone on this ship. If you do not restore power immediately, we'll all die. We're at your mercy."

Gray crumbled against a wall. Vivianne swayed on her feet. Her plea was their last chance. Had anyone heard? And if they'd heard, would anything she'd said make any difference? As the cold seeped deep into her bones, her mind drifted.

To Jordan.

Where the hell had he gone?

Some of us are looking to the stars.

9

W ake up." Jordan had piled blankets on top of Vivianne, but as the *Draco*'s heaters kicked in, her flesh had remained cold. So he'd crawled under the covers to warm her with his own body heat. While he'd broken into a sweat, her face remained pale, lifeless.

At least she was breathing. But her pulse was weak.

So weak, Vi's sudden thoughts barreled into Jordan's mind, and he was suddenly back in another of her memories.

A teenage Vi hadn't eaten a good meal in so long her hands shook.

But the little kids were suffering more. This foster home was the worst she'd ever been in. With a chain around the refrigerator and a locked pantry barring the children from food, they were all pale, skinny, and hollow-eyed.

"Haven, you're the lookout," Vivianne said to the second-oldest girl. "Let me know if anyone comes home."

Haven shoved a bookcase over to the garage window, then climbed up. "All clear."

"James," Vivianne told a little boy, "stop crying." Vivianne plucked a penknife from her pocket. "We're all going to eat soon."

She inserted the penknife into the lock. And twisted. But the lock held.

Vi's real parents wouldn't have called this stealing. The state paid for their food. Only, the greedy people who were supposed to care for them never gave them enough.

Vivianne had become accustomed to the gnawing hunger pangs, but she couldn't get her hands to stop shaking.

The penknife slipped out of the hole. Vivianne wiped her sweaty fingers on her jeans, then tried again.

The lock clicked. Yes!

"All right." Haven let out a whoop.

Vivianne opened the cabinet where the foster parents stored their hurricane supplies. She had to choose something that wouldn't be noticed. After spying several blue boxes, she snagged one and held it up. "How about mac and cheese?"

The kids cheered. Vi helped Haven replace the bookcase, then lifted the little boy onto her hip. "All right. Now, who wants to help me cook?"

Jordan knew children went hungry. But to feel the gnawing pain in Vivianne's empty stomach had him angry and frustrated, and puzzled at this new connection between them. They hadn't made love. So what was going on? Had he been wrong about the Staff causing them to share memories?

Whatever was happening, it was too late for him to stop caring about her.

He placed his fingers on her pulse. Still weak.

"Come on, Vi. You're a fighter. *Fight*." He smoothed back a reddish lock from her forehead, massaged her arms and fingers with his hands, rubbed her calves with his toes. He'd give the *Draco*'s plumbing another five minutes to warm up, then he'd take her under a hot shower.

"Vi?" He breathed warm air onto her face. She remained still. Deathly still. He cupped her jaw and stroked her cheek. "We need you with us. Wake up."

Her eyelids fluttered and stilled.

"Vi? Please. Open those pretty eyes for me."

Her lids fluttered again.

"Come back to me, Vi," he murmured. "You can do this. Open those clever green eyes. Look at me. Just open your eyes and look at me."

Ever so slowly, she woke up.

Finally.

But although her eyes were open, at first she didn't seem to see him.

"You're safe." He gathered her against his chest, inhaled her scent.

But then she pulled back, focused. Frowned. "Where the hell did you go?"

He was so happy to see that she was all right, he threw back his head and laughed. Then he reached for her again.

She pummeled his shoulder with her fist. "It's not funny."

Jordan couldn't have been more pleased when his shoulder hurt. It meant she had strength. It meant she would live to fight with him some more.

"How do you feel?" he asked, sitting up and tucking the blanket back around her.

She craned her neck to look out the cabin's portal.

"Thanks to you, the cubes are gone," he said, rubbing her forearms through the blanket. "Your plan worked. They left, and the energy came back on."

"Everyone's okay?" she asked.

"Yes." He pointed to her feet where he'd wrapped the dog in part of her blanket. "Even George. He wouldn't leave, so I figured you might as well get the benefit of his body heat."

"Here, boy." She wriggled her fingers and the dog crawled up the blankets to lick her hand, then plopped onto her chest and peered right into her face. "I'm okay. But George is heavy." She slid him to one side but kept him cuddled against her hip.

Her eyes fluttered closed again and she slept. Relieved, Jordan eased back beside her and slept with her. When she wakened a second time a few hours later, their legs were twined, one of his arms resting intimately on her hip.

He got up and fed her some hot broth. Again they slept, and this time when she woke up, her strength had returned.

But tension arced between them. It didn't take telepathic powers to know she was still furious with him for abandoning her and the bridge.

He took the chair next to the bed. "I left to protect the Staff. If it had gotten too cold, the power might not have come back on."

She locked gazes with him. "So how did you keep it warm?"

"I removed it from the *Draco*'s housing, retracted it, and placed it inside my shirt."

"So you could have returned to the bridge?" she challenged him.

"Yes. But I feared the cold would slow me down. So I stayed in the engine compartment, waiting for the moment when you'd need me to place the Staff back into the housing." And he'd prayed that the Staff's power wouldn't drop so low that he'd be forced back into owl form, unable to help her when she needed him.

She stared at him, her eyes swirling green pools of skepticism. He had no idea if she believed him. But he suspected any ground he'd gained by telling her his history had just been lost. He realized he'd made another mistake. "I'm sorry. I should have explained before I left you on the bridge."

"You should have."

"I'll do better next time," he promised.

But he wasn't going to tell her that when the Staff lost power, or when it was out of his possession, he didn't have the energy to maintain his human form, couldn't protect her, couldn't fight the Tribes.

Until he'd been tricked out of his Staff, he'd never once let it out of his sight. That error had cost him centuries. Centuries the Tribes had used to increase their domination over the galaxy. He had to remain human. Had to stop them. Had to make her understand they were on the same side.

But he didn't have a clue how to do that. Sensing she didn't want his touch, he fell back on normal conversation. "We should be orbiting the dark world within the hour. If you're up to it, I'd like your opinion on where we should set down."

"I gave Lyle busywork to keep him out of my hair." She cocked her head and pursed her lips. "Is that what you're now doing with me?"

"Hey." He took her hand, pleased when she didn't withdraw. "You saved the *Draco*. We all owe our lives to your quick thinking."

"You mean my plea for mercy?"

He grinned. "I would never have thought of that tactic, and it worked. You were brilliant."

He recalled her picking the lock to feed the hungry kids. She'd always been resourceful.

"And you were brave to offer your own life to save everyone."

Although he was sincere, she wasn't buying it.

"We were dying anyway. I had nothing to lose."

Standing, he strode to the door. "I'm glad you're better."

He shut the door behind him, shocked to find his hand shaking. Apparently all that warming her up had made him cold.

He clenched his hands into fists a few times and the tremble receded before he reached the bridge. As always, he would do what must be done, but sometimes he wished he didn't have to put the mission first.

Sean and Tennison looked relieved to see Jordan walk onto the bridge. Sean was at command, Tennison at the science station. Neither man had suffered from hyperthermia, thanks to the protection of the spacesuits. And while Jordan had nursed Vivianne, they'd pitched in, repairing frozen transistors.

"Status report," Jordan requested.

"Gravity and life support are stable," Tennison reported. "Darren and Knox are preparing lunch."

"Good." Jordan swung around to Sean. "What's up with the dark planet?"

Taking up a third of the viewscreen, the Shadow planet didn't look promising. The land was blackened as if singed by fire, and the brown sea looked mudlike.

"The good news is that Shadow appears to be uninhabited," Tennison said. "And the bad news is that the planet appears to be uninhabited. No sign of plant or animal life."

"Do we even want to land?" Sean asked.

"How's the air down there?" Jordan stared at the polar cap of white ice.

"Breathable. No poisonous trace elements."

"Then we land." Jordan hated to waste fuel, time, and energy. But they might find algae in the mud, protein in the ice. And they'd come too far not to go down and see if they could find food.

Vivianne, with George on her heels, stepped onto the bridge. "Have we scanned to see what else is nearby?"

Jordan nodded. "We either find food down there or we jump blindly into hyperspace and pray we come out near an Earthlike planet."

She peered at the data stream on the science monitor. "Have we figured out where we are?"

"Darren's been working on it," Tennison said.

"How?" Vivianne asked.

"He's assuming we're in the Milky Way Galaxy, and

by calculating the rate the stars are moving, their speed should give us our approximate distance from the Milky Way's center."

Jordan exchanged a long look with Vivianne. Both of them knew that such a rough estimate wouldn't do them much good. But it was a start.

"What kind of topography is down there?" Vivianne asked.

"Funny you should ask that." Sean scratched his head. "These readings are peculiar. In fact, I'm wondering if the cold damaged the sensors."

"Why?" Jordan asked, peering over his shoulder.

Sean pointed. "Can a world be this flat and uniform? Every reading's the same. Shadow's seas register the exact same depth. The land is exactly three feet above sea level everywhere. There's no variety. It's almost as if the world is artificial."

Jordan clapped him on the shoulder. "You're a genius."

"I am?" Sean's eyes rounded with puzzlement.

"If Shadow's artificial, then someone created it. That ups the likelihood of finding food down there." Jordan smiled.

Tennison shook his head. "The entire planet seems to be shielded."

"A shield might mean that whoever's down there doesn't want to be found." Vivianne peered at the planet as if willing it to give up its mysteries.

Jordan wondered what kind of people could create such technology. "Between the warning we already received to stay away from one world and those cubes that chased us out of hyperspace, this part of the galaxy isn't exactly friendly."

Vivianne followed his reasoning. "Maybe it's not so surprising they've made Shadow look unappealing."

Knox entered the bridge with a plate of burgers and a tray of drinks. "Anyone hungry?"

They helped themselves. Although they were rationing food, Jordan spied Vivianne feeding George part of her burger. Sean and Tennison did the same. And when George came over begging, Jordan tossed him a bite, too. When Jordan looked up, he caught Vivianne watching him, a smile softening her expression, then hardening.

Did she think he'd fed the dog to get on her good side? Come to think of it, that wasn't a bad idea.

Except Jordan shouldn't be thinking about Vivianne at all, never mind the dog. He couldn't afford distractions.

He picked a spot where the land met the sea at random. "Let's set down here."

To be wronged is nothing unless you do continue to remember it.

—CONFUCIUS

10

❧

The *Draco* dropped from a high orbit around Shadow into a landing pattern. Vivianne blinked, then blinked again, still unable to believe her eyes. The brown seas they'd seen at the higher altitudes were gone. In their place was a gorgeous turquoise ocean. And the flat, barren view of the continents had been replaced by lush forests and verdant valleys with quaint villages dotting the landscape.

"You might want to rethink the landing site," Vivianne said.

"Set us down in that open field," Jordan directed, his voice tight.

"I'd love to see the specs on Shadow's shield technology," Sean muttered.

Jordan's eyes narrowed. The cords in his neck and shoulders tightened.

Vivianne would have thought he'd be happy to see a healthy planet with abundant flora and fauna. She moved close to him and kept her voice low. "What's wrong?"

Jordan stared at the peaceful village, the rolling farm-land, the clean skies and blue waters. Did Shadow remind him of home?

"I'm not a big fan of making first contact," he said.

"Why not?"

"It's too easy to have misunderstandings. People always fear what's different. They might attack us the instant we open the hatch because they think we're hostile, or because we smell bad. Or they fear people with two arms and two legs. We should have experts in first contact here with us—not a bunch of nerd-brained engineers."

"Speak for yourself, boss," Tennison chipped in.

Vivianne gave Jordan a sharp look. "We would have had those experts with us if you hadn't taken off ahead of schedule."

"True. But this crew"—Jordan folded his arms across his chest—"has enough trouble socializing on Earth."

"We're not here to socialize." Vivianne redirected the conversation. "What do we have to barter for food?"

Jordan toggled the intercom. "Lyle, pull up that inventory list."

"Yes, sir."

A few minutes later, Vivianne perused the inventory on the tiny computer monitor strapped to her wrist. While she recognized the parts, she wasn't certain which were essential and which they could spare. "What do we have aboard that isn't necessary?"

"The mutt," Jordan teased.

Vivianne dug her elbow into his rib. "Be serious."

He quirked an eyebrow. "Don't you think George would be happier running through the fresh air and grass than being terrified every time our gravity goes down?"

Maybe. But she liked having George aboard. She'd never had a dog before. Just petting him calmed her, and to deal with Jordan she needed all the calm she could get. She held out her wrist so he could read the screen. "What else here is expendable?"

"Lyle."

"Not funny." She kept her gaze on the screen, determined not to let him get under her skin. The crew might be on the nerdy side and Jordan authoritative, but Vivianne was good at negotiating and bartering. This didn't have to be a tense, warlike meeting. Once she explained that they'd come in peace, they . . .

Her stomach swooped. What was she thinking? If aliens had dropped out of the sky and landed on Earth, they'd have been lucky not to have been shot down.

"Maybe landing in the open field isn't such a good idea," she said.

Sean looked up from the controls. "Tell me now."

When Jordan didn't say anything, Vivianne answered. "Can you set us down someplace where we can hide the *Draco*? Somewhere we can sneak into town without the authorities—"

"These people have a shield that hides their entire planet. You don't think they have radar?" Jordan smirked.

"So you just want to fly into a public area and—"

"We'll figure it out from there."

"That's it?" Vivianne restrained a sigh.

Jordan toggled the intercom. "Darren."

"Yes, sir."

"Keep an eye on Lyle for me. Make certain he knows that if he sets foot on Shadow, I'm leaving him behind.

And he's not to be allowed near a communicator or anything resembling a weapon."

"Yes, sir."

Lyle sighed sheepishly. "I may not be astronaut of the year, but I don't make the same mistakes twice."

"Good." Jordan snapped off the toggle and motioned Sean to take them down.

Vivianne held her breath as the *Draco* flew through the clouds and over a small city. Muscles tense, she braced, expecting at any moment that the natives would scramble military aircraft, and they'd be shot out of the sky. At the very least, she expected Shadow's equivalent of police cruisers to come screaming in, sirens wailing.

But no one attacked.

Sean set the ship down in the middle of a field of what she assumed was waist-high grass. But then she saw bean pods growing on the stalks.

She sighed. "We may have made our first error. We've just squashed part of a farmer's crop."

Departing the bridge, she headed down the corridor toward the exit. George stayed at her heels.

Jordan fell in beside her and handed her a leash. "You might want this."

He'd taken a rope, separated the threads, then re-braided them so that not only would the leash slip over George's head, she even had a loop for her hand. She bent and slipped the makeshift collar over George's head. "Thanks."

"If you're going to keep him, it'll be better if he doesn't try to eat anyone."

"From what I've seen," she teased, "George is pretty much like you, all bark, no bite."

Jordan's eyes smoldered. "So those aren't my teeth marks on your shoulder?"

Thanks to her dragonblood, she'd already healed from their turbulent sex games. But if he kept looking at her with that kind of heat in his eyes, she soon might be ready for a repeat performance.

"Are you coming outside with me, or are you going to pull another disappearing act?" she asked, careful to keep her voice breezy.

His eyes crinkled at the corners. "That depends."

"Depends on what?"

"On what we find."

"Damn it, Jordan. Now isn't the time to be vague."

All traces of amusement gone, Jordan jerked her to a stop. "Then let me be very, very clear."

She raised her chin. "Please do." It was about time he leveled with her.

"Don't count on me for anything." His eyes burned with blue fire. "Is that plain enough for you?"

"Yes, you're very clear." She wouldn't have expected his declaration to hurt. After losing her parents, Vivianne had learned that not even the people who loved her most could always be there to offer their support. But her parents had died.

They'd had no choice. Jordan did.

To be fair, pretty much ever since they'd left Earth she'd known Jordan was on a mission to stop the Tribes, and he wasn't about to let anyone, or anything, get in the way.

His kind of determination didn't rattle her. Or frighten her. In fact, she admired Jordan's drive and sacrifice.

Still, disappointment flooded her. She couldn't forget his abandoning her on the bridge. Or his lame excuse. He was hiding things. She needed to watch her own back. Because Jordan would only do so . . . up to the point where she remained useful to his mission. And if she impeded his end goal, she might be not just irrelevant, but expendable.

Eying Jordan, she spoke calmly. "I'd like for either Sean or Gray to join us."

At her request, Jordan's expression didn't change. Neither did his voice. "Fine." He spoke into the handheld communicator. "Gray, please meet us at the main hatch with the Staff."

Gray joined them by the hatch, anticipation glowing in his eyes. He handed Jordan the Staff. "We're going out?"

Jordan nodded, retracted the Staff, tucked it into a sheath at his belt, and pulled the airlock handle.

Without the Staff and power, the *Draco* couldn't fly. As long as Jordan had the Staff, the ship couldn't leave without them. She didn't like taking the Staff from the *Draco,* but knowing how precious the Staff was to Jordan, she didn't argue.

The airlock opened.

George took one sniff of Shadow's fresh but thin air, let out a soft woof, and tugged on the leash.

Jordan gestured for Vivianne to step outside. "After you."

"Wow." Vivianne allowed George to tug her out of the *Draco*'s airlock. She'd often dreamed of flying through space in one of her ships and of stepping onto other worlds, but she'd never thought she'd be one of Earth's first explorers on an alien world.

Shadow's smells hit her first. Lush grasses, rich soil, and something tangy and sweet. The temperature was downright balmy, the gravity slightly lighter than on Earth.

Beyond the landing site, huge trees with spindly trunks stood like sentries around the *Draco*. At first the flat grassy area seemed empty, but then she spied a pair of latte-hued eyes in a caramel-colored face staring at her through the high stalks. Then another set of eyes. And another.

They were surrounded.

A man has no more character than he can grasp in a time of crisis.

—LADY GUINEVERE

11

After Vivianne's eyes adjusted to the bright sunlight, she glimpsed human faces. Their bodies were clothed in dark layers of nanocloth, their heads bald except for double arches of hair over their very human ears.

Jordan stepped beside her. "Keep your voice low, and don't make any quick movements."

"We wouldn't want to scare *them*," she murmured, her quick head count suggesting she, Jordan, and Gray were outnumbered at least a hundred to one.

"Exactly," Jordan muttered.

Even with the sun shining so brilliantly, she still couldn't see these people very well. Either they were crouching low in the grass or they were about as tall as George when he stood on his hind legs. But as men, women, and children stared back at them in total eerie silence, goose bumps rose on her flesh.

"Hello," Vivianne said, careful to modulate her tone to what she hoped sounded friendly.

George lifted his leg and christened one of the plants. Vivianne hoped these people wouldn't take offense.

"Now what?" Gray asked.

"We wait," Jordan murmured, and she had the feeling he'd done this a time or two before.

"Wait for what?" Vivianne asked.

"For them to lose their fear of us." Jordan seemed certain of the protocol, and it made sense.

But Vivianne wondered what would happen if these people never lost their fear. Would they attack?

Nose to the ground, George sniffed and wagged his stub of a tail. Quickly, he found the limit of his leash, then yanked.

"Easy, fella." Vivianne pulled him back. "Sit."

George paid no attention to her command. She suspected she had to make her voice more firm, but she didn't want to frighten the natives. So instead, she pushed down on his lower haunches. "Sit."

George sat. She straightened, and then he promptly stood up and tugged toward the natives again. Frustrated, she bent and pushed on his hindquarters, again. "Sit," she repeated.

George sat, then again bounced to his feet and tugged the leash.

One of the natives chuckled.

Vivianne smiled, sat down cross-legged, and lifted George into her lap. "We might be less intimidating if we're more their size."

Gray kneeled, and Jordan squatted next to her, but, if the natives attacked, his legs looked ready to lunge. She heard whispers and soft hoots from the natives, but her translator couldn't pick up their words.

George grew tired of sitting and yanked, straining to the limit of his leash to explore. This time when she tugged him back, there was much laughter and the tension eased from her shoulders.

"I'm glad we're so entertaining," she said. "How much longer—"

"George is winning them over." Jordan petted George behind the ears. "Good boy."

"Someone's coming," Gray murmured.

Although her cheeks began to hurt from smiling, Vivianne didn't change expression as one of the natives slowly shuffled out of the grasses. She'd assumed these people were small, but the man slowly straightened to a willowy six feet.

He was quite human in appearance, with the usual number of limbs, but he was extremely slender, almost delicate, his knees and ankles seemingly double-jointed as he approached with a graceful gait.

"Don't make any sudden moves," Jordan warned.

George didn't listen. He stood, tugged on the leash, and wagged his tail, eager to greet the stranger.

Vivianne was about to jerk him back when the native reached out to the dog, pushed his hindquarters down, and said, "Sit."

George sat.

Everyone in the audience clapped their hands in applause. Many stood to see better, their fears seemingly forgotten.

"Hello." Vivianne pointed to herself. "Vivianne."

"Viv?" the man repeated.

"Vivianne." Jordan pointed at her, then at Gray, saying,

"Gray," and then at himself, "Jordan." Then he gestured to the man.

"Pez." The native puffed out his thin chest.

Once again, Jordan pointed to all of them and said their names. This time, Pez repeated them, too. And then, eyebrow lifting, he patted George.

"George," Vivianne told him.

Pez motioned for Jordan, Gray, and Vivianne to follow him.

"He doesn't seem hostile," Vivianne said.

"Don't make assumptions," Jordan murmured. "For all we know, he may have decided we're the perfect food for his pet lion."

"Somehow these people don't seem the type to domesticate lions," Vivianne said. "But why aren't our translators doing their job?"

"Sometimes it takes a while for them to work," Jordan said. "The syntax or grammar here must be very unusual. If we can get them to name other things, it might speed the process."

Jordan touched his nose. "Nose."

Then he gestured for Pez to give him the alien word. But Pez said, "Nose."

And no matter what Jordan said, Pez didn't seem to understand their wish to learn the native language. Eventually he gave up. "I'm no linguist."

"Mind if I try?" Vivianne asked.

"Go ahead."

She strode up to Pez with George. She patted George's head. Then she patted her own head and said, "Head." Then slowly she reached out to Pez's head.

"Tskky."

Vivianne clapped her hands. Then she touched her nose and said the word. Then touched his.

"Brrighgt."

Again she clapped. Then she touched the ground, pointed at the sky, held up one finger, then two, then three. Each time the man gave her a word. But then he seemed to tire of the game and she didn't press.

"That was perfect," Jordan told her, and his compliment made her feel good.

"The translator still isn't working," she said, because she could hear these people talking among themselves and she couldn't understand them.

"Patience," Jordan said.

"I'm working on it." She supposed that after living so many years, patience was something he'd acquired.

Pez led them through the farmer's field and onto a winding two-lane dirt road lined with homes that reminded her of English cottages with thatched roofs. On top of the roofs were what she at first assumed were weather vanes. But instead of a pointed arrow at one end, there was a circle and on the opposite end was a square. The shape seemed familiar, but she didn't know why.

She glanced at Jordan. His blue eyes were focused on the roofs, too.

And then she remembered. "Those things on the roofs, they are the same shape as one of the indentations on your Ancient Staff."

"The proportions look identical to one of the missing keys." Jordan rubbed his forehead, his expression thoughtful.

"What does that mean?" Gray asked.

"It means we aren't on Shadow by coincidence." Jordan's tone was threaded with excitement.

"I don't understand," Gray said.

"We jumped out of hyperspace to avoid colliding with those metal cubes," Jordan reminded them. "Those cubes may have wanted us to find this world."

"Why?" Vivianne asked. "Do you think your missing keys are here?"

"I don't know." Jordan's pace remained steady. "But from the beginning, Shadow has not been what it seemed."

All the natives who watched from their yards and houses joined in the procession, falling in behind the group from the field. At least four hundred men, women, and children followed in that odd gait, reminding her that although these aliens looked human, they had probably never seen anyone who looked like Earth people. Children held one another's hands and chattered under the watchful eyes of their parents. Most of them wore tan shirts and slacks, but one little girl had a pink ribbon braided into her hair. Another wore a simple bead bracelet. Contributing to the carnival-like atmosphere, several boys played catch, running back and forth, never getting too close to the strangers.

She glanced back at their retinue. "I'm beginning to feel like the Pied Piper."

"Where do you think Pez is taking us?" Gray asked.

"To their leader." Jordan seemed certain, but he'd told them not to make assumptions.

Vivianne frowned as they headed straight through the tiny village and into a dense forest. "Wouldn't their leader live among them?"

Jordan shook his head. "Leaders in many cultures live

apart. The king in his castle. The medicine man in a hut just outside the village."

"The minotaur that demanded a blood sacrifice every spring," she said with a tiny shudder. Maybe it was the shade, or the odd shape of the trees, but she didn't like leaving the town or traveling so far from the *Draco*.

"Surely they have food in their village." She glanced uneasily over her shoulder. "Why don't we try and trade for the food we need and get out of here?" Get out while they still could.

"Easy." Jordan moved beside her and whispered into her ear. "I need to find out why those key-like objects are over the roof of every home. There's no need for anxiety. These people aren't armed. They aren't carrying so much as a paring knife."

"That doesn't mean we should go along with their plans for us. They might want to sell us off to their neighbors in the next village," she warned him.

"Let's give them another half hour," Jordan suggested. "That way we can still make it back to the *Draco* before the sun sets."

His suggestion sounded reasonable. But the hairs on the back of her neck prickled. Sensing danger in the dark forest, she kept peeking over her shoulder, staring into the bushes, searching for something menacing. But she saw nothing beyond a couple of feral cats that George tried to chase.

Shadow's weather changed quickly. The wind keened through the trees. And the air chilled and darkened as dark clouds blocked out the sun.

"Sorry, fella." She petted the dog, and he whined, then tried to bolt. If she hadn't been holding the leash tightly, he would have escaped. He kept pulling hard and started barking.

Pez stopped and almost backed into them, fear shadowing his eyes to a dark chocolate. Trembling, he dropped to his knees.

Jordan picked up the dog and held him under his arm. "Next time we leave him on the ship."

"George broke the ice with the natives," she reminded him.

"George also either saw or smelled something over there." Jordan pointed with his chin.

Thunder boomed. The natives grabbed onto one another, their thin bodies swaying in the gusts.

Gray muttered, "Probably just another cat."

The treetops rustled, the branches shaking. Vivianne tugged on Jordan's shirt. "Over there. There's something big hidden in those trees."

George kept barking. Jordan tensed and placed his hand on his Staff, almost as if it was a weapon.

The natives chattered. The children kept playing. Surely if there was a danger, these people would recognize it and protect their children?

Yet something had shaken those tree trunks.

It was big.

And moving straight toward them.

A true friend is one who walks in when the rest of the world runs out.

—HIGH PRIESTESS OF AVALON

12

Jordan tensed and peered into the forest. While he didn't believe the villagers had brought them out here to murder them, he also knew better than to accept that Shadow was what it seemed. There were no footprints on the dirt path, as if no one had passed this way before, but this close to the village, how likely was that? There was no buzz of insects in the forest, no humming mosquitoes, no fluttering butterflies, no crawling ants. And the natives themselves were a bit generic.

Artificial world. Artificial people? If so, had someone created this world as a trap?

Ever since he'd spotted the blatant key shapes atop the thatched roofs, his imagination had soared with outrageous possibilities.

When a golden dragon flew down from the treetops, Jordan automatically reached for the Ancient Staff. It wouldn't be the first time he'd used the energy contained in the Staff as a weapon.

The dragon possessed huge spikes and dark purple

eyes, and with his golden coloring, he had the exact opposite of Jordan's purple dragon form. But this golden dragon sported the same clawed forearms, thunderous hind legs, and long, spiked tail as other dragons he'd known.

"A golden dragon?" Vi turned to him, eyes wide with wonder.

"Rumors about such creatures have drifted around the galaxy for eons," Jordan told her. "I thought they were legends."

"What kinds of legends?"

"Supposedly, the golden dragons are guardians of the four kingdoms, Soil, Space, Wind, and Fire." He tightened his hand on the Ancient Staff.

"He's done nothing hostile." Vivianne placed her hand on his arm.

"Not yet." Jordan stepped forward and placed himself between the dragon and Vi, Gray, and the villagers. "Dragon, we have come for the key."

The dragon roared fire, but the flames shot over their heads. Oddly, the treetops didn't catch fire, but the natives retreated and disappeared into the forest.

"Now what?" Gray asked.

"We wait?" Vivianne raised an eyebrow.

"It won't be long." Jordan sensed the dragon's impatience.

George didn't even bark. He curled up at Vivianne's feet, rested his head on his paws, and closed his eyes. Either the dog was very accustomed to dragons, or the animals were communicating on another level.

"Should we dragonshape and try for a telepathic connection?" Vivianne asked.

"I'd rather not show our hand," Jordan said. Besides,

changing shape took energy, energy that he'd have to tap from the Ancient Staff.

As thunder rolled and lightning clapped and the first drops of rain began to fall, the golden dragon morphed into a man. Blond-haired and black-eyed, his bronzed skin tight over bulging muscles, he stood naked for only a moment before his nanoclothing produced a loincloth to cover him low on his hips to his powerful thighs. He wore no weapons, and from the set of his shoulders, he feared nothing.

With dark eyes he perused them, his nostrils flaring, his high cheekbones softened by full lips. "I'm the last scion of the House of Tarpon. You may call me Devid."

"You may call me Jordan."

Vivianne stepped into the testosterone-charged air. "I'm Vivianne, and this is Gray. We're visitors to this world."

"It took you long enough to arrive." Devid gestured them to follow him, turned, and walked deeper into the forest. "Let's get out of the rain."

Vivianne didn't hesitate. While Jordan released the hilt of his Staff, he followed more slowly. For now he'd let Vivianne negotiate . . . while he watched for treachery.

Devid strode through the forest, and as the storm rolled in, the rain became a downpour. The canopy of trees prevented them from being soaked to the skin, and soon they reached a cave. Set into a hillside of rock, the opening shielded them from windblown rain, yet there was no welcoming fire, no food, no utensils of any kind. In fact, there was no indication that man or animal had ever used this site before.

"Please sit." Devid turned and frowned as if noticing the cave's lack of creature comforts.

Chairs and a glowing fire suddenly materialized in the space of a heartbeat. Logs crackled, and Jordan could feel real heat from three feet away.

Gray gasped. Vivianne kept her expression serene and took a seat. But her fingers clenched the arm of the chair as if to make certain it was real. "I've heard of machines that materialize matter, but I've never seen one in action. Are they available for purchase or trade?"

"I'm afraid not." Devid folded his arms across his chest, but he didn't sit.

Jordan also remained standing.

"So you've been expecting us . . ." Vivianne let her voice trail off.

"Yes."

"What do you want?" she asked simply.

Jordan noted how she had yet to mention their need for food. Clearly she was testing Devid, without displaying their weakness.

"I don't want anything from you."

Devid's answer might have surprised Vivianne, but she didn't let it show. Instead, she lifted her hands to the fire. "It's good to be out of the rain."

She allowed a silence to descend while the wood crackled and popped, and Jordan suspected Devid was waiting for them to say or do something.

Jordan figured it was time to make a move. "During our walk through the village, we noticed wind vanes on the thatched roofs. Each vane had a square at one end and a circle on the other. I have been searching for an object like—"

"Finally." Devid smiled. "You seek the second key to the Ancient Staff?"

"Yes."

Vivianne's gaze sought Jordan's, and the questions in her eyes weren't hard to read. How did Devid know what they sought? How did he know about the Ancient Staff?

Devid spat out words as if in a great hurry. "When Trendonis stole your Ancient Staff, he learned it was indestructible. So he removed the keys and hid them throughout the Galaxy. On Tor you found the Key of Space."

"Is another key here?" Jordan asked. "Is that why Shadow has the Wind Key weather vanes?"

"The weather vanes are merely indicators that you are on the right path." Devid glanced at the Ancient Staff in the sheath Jordan had made. "The Key of Wind that you seek can be found on the hurricane planet in the next star system."

"You have coordinates?" Gray asked.

"They'll be in your nav system by the time you return to your ship." Devid snapped his fingers. "Oh, yes. I've seen to ample food supplies, as well."

"Thank you." Vivianne spoke graciously. "What can we do for you in return?"

"Just find the damn key."

"Why is our success important to you?" Jordan asked.

"Your mission's important to every dragonshaper in the Galaxy." Devid's arrogance vanished. "Trendonis of the Tribes has a master plan. Once he and his ilk got hold of the Grail, they set the rest of their evil plans in motion. They seek to destroy the light in the Milky Way Galaxy, and they intend to expand into the Four Kingdoms."

Vivianne shot him a puzzled look. "What are the Four Kingdoms?"

"Other galaxies. The Tribes want them, too, and must be stopped."

"How do you know so much about us and our enemies?" Jordan asked.

"I'm not permitted to answer that question."

"Why not?" Vivianne asked, her eyes flashing with banked exasperation.

"You have yet to prove yourselves worthy."

"Of you?" Jordan frowned.

Devid snorted. "I'm only the messenger."

"This world," Jordan asked, "is not yours?"

Devid ignored his question. "The Tribes are amassing for a strike on Earth. Trendonis is on the move. You haven't much time." Devid's expression grew stormy. "You must leave Shadow and go to Tempest, the hurricane world. Retrieve the second key."

"And the third key?" Jordan asked.

The irises of Devid's eyes grew black until no whites showed. For a moment he seemed to burn with inner fire, and Jordan thought he would dragonshape. But he beat back the blackness in his eyes, until once again he appeared quite human.

Muscles taut as if fighting some internal battle, Devid intoned, "Change will come to those who fight for the light."

"I don't understand," Vivianne said softly. "Are you quoting ancient myths, proverbs, or . . ." Her eyes widened.

In a flash of light, Devid disappeared.

If you keep looking back, you'll miss the present and the future.

—LADY OF THE LAKE

13

W hat just happened?" Vivianne asked in astonishment.
At the man's disappearance, Gray sucked in a noisy breath.

George didn't react. Asleep, he lay on his side next to the fire, his feet twitching.

Jordan rubbed his forehead, but he didn't look surprised at all. "Devid may not have been any more real than this fire or the chair you're sitting on."

"There are machines that can materialize people, heat, and dragons?" Gray asked.

"He could have used a transporter." Vivianne was thinking out loud. And what a wonderful device that would be—instantaneous travel—no on-site machinery required.

Jordan leaned against a wall of the cave and stared into the fire. "Devid said he was a messenger. He might have been a four-dimensional hologram."

Vivianne shivered despite the heat from the fire. "How

did Devid know so much about us? Or about the Ancient Staff and the keys? He seemed so certain that Trendonis and the Tribes would strike Earth soon. But who is he, and is his information accurate?"

Gray's eyes darkened with speculation. "If Devid really has the power to move instantaneously through space, that would certainly help account for his knowledge of us, of Earth, of the Tribes."

Jordan peered out of the cave. "The rains stopped. Let's head back to the ship."

"Someone's gone to a lot of trouble to point us toward Tempest." Vivianne's mind was spinning.

She would have appreciated more of Jordan's insight, but she'd learned that Jordan neither spoke about the Ancient Staff unless necessary, nor jumped to conclusions about their circumstances.

Perhaps in private he'd share his thoughts. In the meantime, decisions needed to be made. Vivianne recalled the planet Tempest, with its one icy island and hurricane-force winds. Landing the *Draco* there wouldn't just be dangerous, it might be impossible. "You think the hurricane world's a trap?"

Jordan raised an eyebrow. "It's crossed my mind."

His suspicions matched her own and left her uneasy. They retraced their steps, but when they reached the place where they'd entered the forest, the road and grass were gone. The thatched huts had vanished, too. Instead, the *Draco* perched on a dirt plain that swept like a black river to the horizon.

Vivianne spun to look back at the forest, but it, too, had vanished. She rubbed the heels of her hands into her eye sockets. But when she dared to look again, she was still standing on black earth, the terrain now matching the sight they'd first seen from space.

George growled, yanked, and tore the leash from her hand, then bolted for the *Draco*. With a frown she turned to Gray and Jordan. "Did we just have the mother of all hallucinations?"

Jordan rolled his shoulders as if to clear the tension. "If so, the dog had one, too."

George made a beeline for the ship, covering the distance on his short legs quickly, and scratched the hatch to enter. When no one immediately opened the airlock, he stood on his hind legs and barked for admittance.

Gray raised his handheld. "Tennison?"

"You aren't going to believe this." Tennison's voice thrummed with excitement. "We didn't open the hatch, but the hold's stocked with food. Enough to feed us for a year."

A year? Her knees weakened. Was that how long Devid expected them to be gone?

When a loud boom reverberated through the thin air, Vivianne automatically ducked and looked up. Three slender silver spaceships had just broken the sound barrier. As they descended and braked, their shields hit the atmosphere and flames flared.

While she stared, Jordan grabbed her arm. "Run. We're a sitting target on the ground."

So was their ship. Vivianne lunged into a full-out sprint.

Tennison's voice came over their handhelds. "We've got company. Hostile."

"You're certain?" she asked.

"They're locking weapons on the *Draco*. Get back here. Now."

Gasping for air in Shadow's thin atmosphere, Vivianne sprinted for the *Draco,* running toward the one place those ships would surely attack. But they had no choice—staying here would likely get them just as dead.

Legs pumping, lungs burning, she ran alongside Jordan and Gray. Without trees or roads for perspective, judging the distance was difficult. It was farther than she'd thought.

Suddenly the ships disappeared from the sky. But Jordan and Gray weren't slowing, so she kept running.

"Hurry," Jordan urged. "They're orbiting. We have to launch the *Draco* while they're on the back side of the planet."

"I'm trying," she panted.

Jordan spoke into the handheld. "Open the airlock."

From their angle she couldn't see it open, but George stopped barking and disappeared inside.

Another few steps. Sweat beaded her forehead and dripped into her eyes. She could see the ships returning on the horizon. Her legs felt like lead, and Jordan and Gray were pulling her now, but she couldn't keep up with their longer strides.

"I'm slowing . . . you down," she gasped. "Just go without me."

Jordan yelled, "We aren't leaving you. So if you die, we all die."

Talk about motivation. The sting of his words gave her an extra spurt of adrenaline. She told herself she didn't need air. If her lungs couldn't grab enough oxygen, she'd just run without it.

Still, she staggered the last few yards. Jordan picked her up and carried her, running full tilt into the *Draco*. After setting her on her feet, he sprinted for the engine room.

Gasping for air, she made her way to the bridge. Jordan had to reinstall the Ancient Staff to power the ship. Meantime, maybe she could keep the ships from attacking. "Open communications."

Through the viewscreen, she watched the ships as they flew in ever closer.

"You're good to talk," Tennison told her. "But they have us in a weapons lock."

Anger forged her voice in steel. "Back off, or we'll blow you out of the sky."

Tennison leaned over his monitor. "I think . . . yes. They're slowing."

Surely her threat hadn't worked?

"Come on, Jordan." Vivianne paced. "We need power."

"Message coming in," Tennison reported.

"Put it on speaker," Vivianne said.

A cold and arrogant voice crackled through the speaker. "Prepare to die."

Despite herself, she shivered.

Jordan spoke over the intercom to the enemy commander. "Go to hell, Trendonis."

Cold laughter mocked them. "Earth is about to fall. And this time, you won't be able to stop us."

Jordan swore.

She signaled Tennison to cut communications. Somehow she didn't think the two men cursing each other would do them much good. But something else beyond

Trendonis's threat against Earth niggled at the back of her mind. The exchange had seemed oddly intimate. The hatred . . . personal.

Sean frowned at the viewscreen. "Each ship has launched four missiles."

There was no place to run. Nowhere to hide.

"Power's ramping up," Tennison reported. "But the engines won't be hot before those missiles . . ."

"How long have we got?" Vivianne asked, her pulse pounding.

"Three minutes."

"Can we trigger those missiles to detonate early?" she asked Gray, who'd swiveled into the science station.

"Hell, we're talking alien technology. I don't know what makes them tick."

"Throw some energy at them," Vivianne ordered. "Radio, Electromagnetic. Laser. Maybe we'll luck out."

"Two minutes."

Gray's hands blurred over the console. "Nothing's working."

"How much power have we got?" Jordan asked as he strode onto the bridge. The sight of his strong face, his lack of fear, and the determination in his jutting chin gave her hope.

"Not enough power to take off," Tennison said, his voice steady.

Vivianne's stomach churned. If the *Draco* was destroyed, Earth's best hopes of defeating the Tribes would disintegrate with them.

"Missile strike in one minute."

Life is not measured by the number of breaths we take but by the number of moments that take our breath away.

—GEORGE CARLIN

14

So what do we do now?" Vivianne asked.

"Working on an idea," Jordan murmured, his expression as hard as industrial diamonds.

"Thirty seconds until impact."

A shiver shimmied down her back. "You don't have a plan, do you?"

"It's a work in progress." Jordan made an adjustment at the command center and pulled up the hyperdrive screen.

What was he doing with hyperdrive controls when they were still on the ground? From their current position, the *Draco* couldn't safely initiate hyperspace maneuvers. On planets, the transporters were tied deep into the bedrock, which allowed them to launch in a predetermined direction. Here, with the ship merely parked on the surface, engaging the hyperdrives could blast them straight up, or straight down, where they'd end up encased in the planet's core.

Jordan had started a two-second burn. He was blasting

off—without setting a course. They could end up in a fold in space or inside the heart of a star or a black hole.

"Ten seconds until missiles impact."

Lyle ran onto the bridge, eyes full of panic. "We're going to die."

"Not yet." Jordan slammed the hyperdrive into gear.

She sucked in a breath. Held it while the streaks of hyperspace flickered and replaced normal space.

As they popped back into sub–light space, she finally breathed out a sigh. The *Draco* was intact.

"Any sign of Trendonis and his ships?" Jordan placed a steadying hand on her shoulder. No doubt he could feel her trembling.

"He's the least of our worries," Gray said.

Jordan kneaded her shoulder. "Don't be so certain. Trendonis can track a comet by its dust."

She should move away before anyone noticed. But his fingers felt too damn good as he kneaded her knotted muscles.

Lyle's voice trembled. "You know Trendonis?"

"Yes," Jordan spat.

"Are this ship and Earth under attack because that man hates you?" Lyle asked, this time his tone thoughtful.

"I'm not that important." Jordan stepped away from Vivianne, turned to the command console and busied himself with the nav system. "Lay in a course for Tempest," he ordered. "Use Devid's coordinates."

"We aren't lost?" she whispered.

Jordan grinned. "Courtesy of Devid, we're the proud owners of a galactic set of star charts. The best I've ever seen."

She walked closer to the viewscreen and stared into

space. While there was nothing particularly fascinating outside, she needed a little distance from Jordan. "How far is Tempest?"

"We need to be heading to Earth to warn them, not onto another alien world and into a damn hurricane," Lyle said.

"Earth's already been warned," Jordan reminded him.

Both Lucan and Marisa had brought back reports of the Tribes' intentions to attack Earth. The planet had already prepared as well as possible.

When no one said anything more, Lyle stalked off the bridge.

Gray peered at his screen, a green glow from the monitor highlighting his worry as well as the silver in his hair. "You want the good news or the bad news?"

"Just tell us," Jordan ground out, his fingers tightening on the console.

"The hyperspace trick shot us halfway to Tempest. At sub-light speed we should arrive in eight hours."

Vivianne remained tense. "And the bad news?"

"The entire weather system has splintered. Where there were ten hurricanes before, now there are fifteen."

She didn't understand his concern. If the hurricanes were breaking up into smaller storms, that would make landing on the world easier. "What's bothering you?"

"The intensity of the storms isn't diminishing." Gray punched up the viewscreen and displayed the planet. Sean gasped beside her. Each storm had its own distinct swirl and its own eye, but the major storm systems blanketed the oceans, blocking the entire island from view.

Sean whistled. "I'm clocking wind speeds of over four hundred miles an hour."

Vivianne stared at the swirling eye. "This hull isn't designed to fly in that kind of weather."

"We'll have to wait out the storm," Jordan agreed, folding his arms across his chest, but she recognized the stubborn tension running through him. He wasn't giving up, and he wouldn't turn back.

As if sensing her worries, George trotted onto the bridge and headed straight to her. She lifted him up, and he tried to lick her ear.

His breath smelled like hamburger, and despite all her concerns, her stomach growled. "I'm heading to the galley for food, then to the cabin for some rest."

She hoped Jordan would join her. She had so many questions to ask him in private. But ever since Devid had mentioned Trendonis's name and then Trendonis had attacked, he'd been tense, brooding, and even less communicative than usual.

She entered the galley and accepted a salad from Knox.

The other woman grinned. "Enjoy. I never knew fresh vegetables could taste so good." She handed her a small carafe. "Raspberry dressing with nuts and mandarin oranges."

Vivianne slid into a chair, drizzled the dressing over the salad, and stabbed a carrot. "When you're hungry, almost anything is good. But you've outdone yourself. This is fantastic."

Vivianne closed her eyes and let the taste slide over her tongue. The years of hunger during her childhood had made her appreciate good food.

"So how are you and Jordan getting along?" Knox asked.

"I don't know." Vivianne opened her eyes, scooped up lettuce, baby peas, and fried noodles, and took her time chewing. "He told me not to count on him, but back there on the planet he refused to leave me behind. That could have cost us our lives."

"Of course he wouldn't leave you behind." Knox sat across the table from her. "Did I mention I have six brothers?"

"You did."

"Well, one thing I've learned about men is that they often say one thing and do something else."

"And which do you listen to?"

"I go with my heart."

Vivianne laughed. "I take it you and Darren—"

"Are going strong." Knox sighed. "He hasn't told me he loves me, but he does."

"How can you be so sure?" Vivianne asked.

"When the ship went cold, he gave up his spacesuit for me."

Maybe he would have done that for any woman. Some men were chivalrous that way. But Vivianne kept the thought to herself. She saw no reason to ruin the dreamy look in Knox's eyes.

When Darren entered the galley, Vivianne informed him that his shift on the bridge began soon, then she retired to the cabin and slept. She awakened in the morning to an empty bed. But Jordan had invaded her dreams. Moisture seeped between her thighs, and her breasts tingled.

She tossed aside a pillow, determined to ignore her needs. If Jordan had come by, he'd left no evidence of his presence.

Either something new was wrong or he was avoiding her. Maybe both.

As she stretched she expected the tingles to fade, but instead the sheet seemed to caress her skin and the scales on the insides of her limbs undulated. Heat flushed her neck and . . . Damn it. Not now.

Gritting her teeth, she dressed and forced herself to think about their current situation.

Jordan had told her the Tribe leader Trendonis had destroyed his world. He'd said he knew Trendonis by reputation. But was that the entire story? And could the animosity between them be affecting Jordan's judgment? Would returning to Earth and using this ship to fight the Tribes do any good?

Anyone who possessed the Grail had the ultimate defense weapon, an army of immortals, and held the upper hand in the coming battle between the Tribes and Earth. Stealing back the Grail from the Tribes was imperative. As far as she was concerned, the Wind Key was of lesser importance, since Jordan wasn't even certain if he required all the keys to unite the Staff with the Grail.

She glanced out the porthole. The hurricanes remained at full force. Perhaps if the hurricanes didn't abate, she could convince Jordan to return for the Wind Key on Tempest later.

She toggled the intercom. "Jordan, where are you?"

"Engineering."

That did it. He'd gone to the one place in the *Draco* she wanted to avoid. Damn him.

But she was done hiding her sensual side. Done pretending she didn't have a flirtatious cell in her body. She had a plan, and Jordan wasn't going to stop her.

No man deserves punishment for his thoughts.
                                          —KING ARTHUR PENDRAGON

15

❦

W hy are you avoiding me?" Vivianne asked as she walked into engineering. In the tight quarters, the scent of her soap wafted to Jordan. Turning over on the hard deck, he looked at her. And his hormones went ballistic. Ponytail bouncing, her shirt collar open at the V of her neck, she looked more like a college student than a corporate CEO—until he saw her turbulent green eyes.

He'd removed his shirt and wadded it up under his head. Clearly, she hadn't expected him to be shirtless. The pulse in her neck kicked up a notch before she forced her eyes to his face.

He didn't bother to deny her accusation. Not when he'd spent the night tossing on the hard floor while he tried not to think about her asleep in their cabin, her chestnut hair fanning the pillow, her skin smooth and silky.

But he'd been determined not to go to her. He'd spent too many centuries on his quest to unite the Grail and the Staff. Now that he was closing in, the last thing he needed were carnal distractions. Or worse, emotional ones that affected his judgment.

He told himself that if it had been Knox, not Vivianne, slowing them down during that run back to the *Draco,* he would have waited for her, too. But would he have been as frantic?

It was hard to think straight with all his blood going south. Jordan turned onto his side and faced her. "The Staff's up to mischief again. Or haven't you noticed?"

"I noticed."

"I wish we knew what triggered it."

She flushed. "I have an idea."

"Really?" He rolled onto his back, again, lacing his fingers behind his head.

"Instead of that Staff ruling us, it's time we take control of the situation."

Leave it to Vivianne to see lust as a control issue. He supposed yielding to desire was scary for her—especially with her background. She'd lost her parents young and grown up in a system that left many people unable to cope. She'd replaced the family she'd lost with an empire that spanned the globe. However, now she was once again alone. In a world she didn't understand. And Vivianne would abhor being at the mercy of anyone . . . or anything.

The Ancient Staff's power over her had to be undermining her independent spirit. He wasn't thrilled, either. Sure, the sex was great, but so was the guilt. Guilt that he'd enjoyed what she hadn't freely offered. Guilt that he knew things about her that she hadn't shared. Guilt that the Staff would throw them together again and again when he had nothing of himself to give Vivianne, not even hope.

His eyes found and held hers. "And how do we take control?"

"We have sex."

They locked gazes, and the heat that sparked between them could have fused metal. Still, he shook his head. "I don't get it. You want to have sex so that we don't have sex?"

"I want to have sex—so we can choose the time and place. I want to take away the Staff's hold over us."

So if she couldn't have total independence, she was angling for a measure of control. While he appreciated her suggestion—and how could he not when it was to his benefit?—he knew there would be consequences if he followed through on her idea.

At first her memories had come to him only after their sexual encounters. But the last one had come out of the blue. He feared that the physical intimacies between them were somehow triggering some kind of mental bond to develop.

All their touching had just made it more difficult to put her out of his mind. Being with her was like playing with fire. And he couldn't afford to get burned.

Jordan chose his words with care. "There's no guarantee that anything we do will alter the Staff's effect on us. I could make love to you right now for hours and it still might kick in five minutes after we're done."

Hands fisted on her hips, she lifted her chin. "I'm willing to test my theory. Perhaps if we satisfy ourselves, that Staff won't be antagonizing us during a crisis."

The idea of actually taking his time to kiss her, to explore her tenderly and caress her skin, to stroke her where she was soft—it held undeniable appeal.

A dangerous appeal.

He could stay detached. After all, he'd had centuries to practice cutting off his emotions, but he suspected she would be more vulnerable. And he had too much respect for her to play her.

He made his voice flat, hard, cold. "I can't bond emotionally with you."

"Can't? Or won't?" Vivianne sat on the floor beside him and crossed her legs, curiosity in her eyes.

"As long as the Grail's out there, I'll search for it. That doesn't leave me extra time for . . . you."

"And?" she prodded.

He owed her the truth. "I've already told you that when the Holy Grail and the Ancient Staff unite, the Tribes will fall. According to the ancient myths, each is half of a whole. When they join, they will form something new."

"But?" she prodded him again.

"When I connect the Staff and the Grail, the Staff and I lose connection. I will die."

Horror and fear shadowed her eyes. "But that's just a legend."

"It's my destiny."

Her eyes softened. "Let me see if I have this right. You don't have time for me while you complete your mission. And after you finish, you'll be dead?"

He nodded. "So if you're looking for someone to get you through the night, I'm your man. But . . . I won't be there for you in the end."

Her eyes were filled with shadows. "Thank you for being honest."

"Yeah, well, you have my permission to be impressed."

Sadness filled her eyes. "How do you deal with such a hopeless destiny?"

"Alcohol, drugs, and wild women." He didn't want her pity.

"Yeah, you're such a party animal." She gazed at him, speculation in her eyes. "All right, I consider myself warned. And you needn't worry, I'm not going to fall in love with you." She held out her hand. "So are you coming back to the cabin with me or not?"

He grinned and took her hand. "That was an invitation."

"It was."

He placed his free hand over his heart. "I think I'm developing a sudden coronary."

She winked. "I hear those pass very quickly."

He escorted her down the corridor, and for once fate was on his side. They didn't bump into anyone. No one called him from the bridge. Nothing was attacking the *Draco,* and nothing was breaking down.

Yet he was set on a course that could only end badly. In his death. He'd warned her. She was an adult. His conscience was clear.

"What are you thinking?" she asked as they passed the galley.

"About which article of your clothing I'm going to remove first."

"Oh."

"I'm going to take my time."

"But—"

They reached the cabin, and the moment they were inside, he kicked the door shut behind them. She turned around and faced him, her eyes seductive.

He twisted the lock because he wanted her to hear the finality of its click. "For the next few hours, you're mine."

"*Hours?*" she purred.

He stood close enough to breathe in her scent, without touching one luscious inch of her skin. "We want to be thorough."

She grinned. "Yes. We do." She placed her hands onto his shoulders, pulled him close, tilting up her face. "Kiss me."

Ever so slowly, he lowered his head, until their lips were a mere inch apart. She raised onto her tiptoes, combed her fingers into his hair, and tugged his head until their lips met.

Her lips softened, and her mouth parted with a whisper soft promise of a cascading heat. Heat that put him on a slow burn.

While he yearned to make the sex good for her, to make up for the pain of what was coming, he reined in his own feelings, locked them down tight.

She began to remove her shirt. He closed his hand over hers. "Allow me the pleasure." His tone was low and husky. "We've already done fast and furious."

"Twice."

He traced the tip of his finger from her temple down her cheekbone to the excited pulse at her neck. "So this time, I was thinking slow and easy was the way to go."

Vivianne lifted her eyebrow. "I'm not the patient type."

"I can be," he teased, hoping she could read the promise in his tone as he swept the hair off her neck, slowly leaned in to nip her earlobe, her neck, her collarbone.

"You smell like nectar of the gods." He nuzzled her shirt aside. "You're an amazing woman."

"You're not just saying that to win brownie points with your boss?" she teased.

"You deserve to be cherished."

"Fine. But you might want to start cherishing a little more of me before I expire from anticipation." She cocked her hip at a saucy angle. "Surely you aren't waiting for inspiration?"

"Inspiration's for neophytes." He'd spent most of last night dreaming of unbuttoning her creamy blouse. But not even his unconscious could have dreamed up this new side of her. A flirty attitude he hadn't seen before.

First, he slid the jacket from her shoulders and noted the elegant lines of her neck, her dancer's posture, and the green fire in her stunning eyes. "By the Goddess, you are one gorgeous woman."

She groaned. Leaning into him, she licked his neck and traced a sensuous path to his ear that made the blood roar through his veins. "You're moving slower than a glacier, and compliments would work better if we could lose the clothes."

"Fine." He tossed her jacket unto a chair. Staring into her eyes, he unbuttoned the top button of her blouse and let his fingertips feather her flesh at the V of her neck. When the soft material parted, he kissed the exposed morsel before finally moving on to the next button. Then the next. Each time he took the opportunity to tease, to taunt, until she trembled with anticipation.

And when he finally finished with all the buttons, he didn't part the blouse. Instead he merely ran a fingertip from her throat to her bra, over her ribs and taut stomach.

She quivered under his touch, and her eyes blazed. "Are you going to spend all those hours you promised me just taking off my clothes?"

"Not even I can wait that long," he teased. Then he slid his hands under her blouse and placed his palms on her bare hips. "But I like making you wait for the pleasure I will give you."

She sucked in a breath. Her nipples went hard. She tossed her head. "I didn't know you were into games."

"I'm into what turns you on."

"Really?"

"Really. And you most definitely like my game plan." Even if she didn't want to admit it.

"You have a plan? That's a first."

He slid his hand up her rib cage to cup her breasts. "My plan's very detailed. I had all of last night to think it up." Watching her eyes, he flicked his fingers over the lace at her nipples.

Her irises dilated.

"You liked that."

"I'd like even more."

He flicked her breasts again, then smoothed his hands up to her blouse and peeled the silk over her shoulders. Then, ever so slowly, he slid the material down her arms.

He relegated the blouse to the chair. "Hmm. What next?"

"You're giving *me* the choice?"

"I can live dangerously."

She shot him a wicked smile. "Then by all means, re-move my bra."

"If you insist." He hadn't enjoyed himself like this in a very long time. Her banter alone could turn him on. And while he was playing it cool, inside he was heating. He was so ready to have her right now, but he was willing to undergo a little discomfort to achieve maximum pleasure. And tough CEO lady was enjoying the role reversal of having nothing to do . . . but to think of when and where and how he would touch her next.

He would not disappoint.

Unsnapping her bra, he bared her breasts to his hungry gaze. The pink buds were pointy and hard. Even her areolas had goose bumps. But when he leaned down and kissed first one breast and then the other and she sucked in her breath, he redoubled his determination to hold out for as long as he could stand his raging hard-on. Because opportunities and women like Vi came only once in a thousand years.

If you love someone, you'd give up everything for them. But if they love you, they won't ask you to.
                                        —LADY GUINEVERE

16

"Take your time," she challenged, thinking if he could hold out, she'd somehow hang on, too. But it might be the hardest thing she'd ever done. She'd had no idea that standing before him half naked could be so sexy. Or erotic. Her flesh tingled, her blood simmered, and with all his intensity focused on pleasing her, she'd never felt so powerful. So feminine.

She could make love without falling in love. She'd already proved that by having been with him twice. And now that he'd so clearly told her there was no future for them, there would be no broken heart, either. Vivianne was a realist. She would deal with the future on her own terms.

After he'd slipped off her bra, her mouth had gone dry with anticipation. The gleam in his eyes, the angle of his jaw, and the sudden tightening of his mouth told her that she might be trembling in expectation but he was right there with her.

Lightly, he pinched her nipples, shooting a zing of

pleasure straight to her core. A soft moan tore from her lips. With his gaze locked with hers, he'd made just the act of touching incredibly intimate. She forced her knees to lock. "Right about now . . . would be a good time for the . . . ah . . . gravity to go out."

"Perhaps that can be arranged," he murmured, his voice mysterious and silky. "But not just yet."

Again he cupped her breasts and lifted one to his mouth, and the sensations of warm heat on her bare skin had her rocking forward on her toes for more. His lips closed on her breast, his hot tongue laving the nipple. Moisture seeped between her thighs, and she plunged her hands into his hair to steady herself.

"You have no idea how good . . . that feels," she murmured, in a voice that was already breathless.

Tingling heat seemed to pour from his mouth into her. Her breath grew ragged, her legs trembled, and her thoughts spun. Light-headed, scales fluttering, she gasped for air but couldn't seem to draw enough into her lungs.

When she didn't think she could take one second more, he raised his head and began anew on her other breast.

She squirmed and his teeth delicately tightened, holding her in place. Keeping her exactly where she wanted to be.

All her muscles were tensing, and she wondered if it was possible to orgasm from this delicious pleasure alone. She might have found release, except once again he stopped, leaving her floating.

"Are you ready?" he asked, his tone as smooth as syrup.

"For you?" she asked, slightly confused. How could she think when she was light-headed, wanting, wanton?

"Ready for me to remove your pants?"

"Yes."

She was flushed. Hot. The *Draco*'s temperature controls had to be on the fritz, because she felt bathed in tropical heat. It was all Jordan's doing, his hands that caressed and stroked, his mouth that teased and taunted.

He removed her slacks without delay. But her wish for the lacy panties to go the same way didn't look like it would happen. For one thing, he'd placed his hands on her hips and turned her around, and then, as he nibbled on her neck, his hands slid around to her breasts, cupping them, cherishing them, repeatedly stroking her nipples.

When she tried to lean back into him, he pinched the tips lightly. "Stay still for me."

"Why?" She thrashed her head, unable to hold still.

"Because it will please me."

God. He was assuming she wanted to please him. In truth, she wasn't so sure.

She didn't answer. She couldn't. Not when his hands fluttered down her rib cage to her panties.

She wriggled her hips and demanded, "Take them off."

"I will." But instead of pulling down her panties like she wanted, he caressed the curves of her buttocks, lifting the panties higher until he'd created a thong.

"Hey." Moist with her scent, the lacy material tucked into her folds and created delicious constraints.

"I will take them off . . . eventually." He slipped his fingers around her waist and dipped into the tiny triangle. "Part your legs for me."

"Finally." She breathed out a sigh and did as he asked. She'd assumed he'd dip his fingers lower into her curls. But instead he played with her panties, tugging and teasing, the friction making her crave him all the more until she grew so tight with need, she thought she would surely burst.

It took all her self-control to remain still. A glance into the mirror revealed her standing there nearly naked, aroused, breathless. And damned if he wasn't still fully dressed and enjoying every second of her squirming. His eyes practically glowed, and a five-o'clock shadow made him look rough, bold, and dangerously sexy.

"You can do better," she taunted.

"Much better," he agreed as he flipped a switch on the console. "Gravity's going off."

"Everywhere?"

"Last night from the engineering bay, I rigged this cabin with its own gravity controls."

"Oh." What was he up to? Had he known she would come to him? Ask him to make love? Was she that easy to predict?

Or did he have other reasons for messing with the gravity?

He snapped the elastic at her hips and drew her attention back to his hands. She was floating in midair, which meant she was at his mercy. She could move. But she had no leverage.

Finally, he slid her panties down her legs.

"What about your clothing?" she asked.

"Not yet." His eyes gleamed with blue heat. "I have plans . . ."

She swallowed hard. He floated her facedown and over to a straight-backed padded chair that was bolted to the deck.

"Grab the seat."

She did as he asked, and he folded her over the chair so that her bottom rose into the air, her feet unable to reach the deck.

"Now part your legs."

She gulped and did as he demanded. She couldn't see him. But he could see her. All of her.

"Don't move."

Heat flared through her. She started to turn her head, and he swatted her bottom.

"No looking."

The playful sting of his hand only added to the heat. She was on fire for him, and he had yet to touch her core. But she liked the heat of his hand, so again she turned her head to look at him. He'd removed his shirt and had just unhooked the top fastening of his slacks when he caught her ogling his washboard abs.

With a grin, he swatted her rear again.

And the heat escalated. All the blood in her body had to be stampeding to her core. She was so damn sensitive, she could barely hold still.

When his hot mouth came down on her core without warning, she would have bucked, but his hands kept her hips elevated. Already so sensitive, she moaned. As he lapped and licked and stoked, tension inside her ramped up until she quivered with need.

From the top of her head to the tips of her curling toes, she drew tight, tighter, the sizzling sensations ripping through her. And then he drew back.

"Don't come." And he slapped her bottom several times.

Shocked at the fiery sting that escalated the tension to another level, she released the chair.

"Hold on." With one finger he caressed her, floating her back into position.

"But—"

"Hang on."

Her nipples ached. She couldn't seem to draw in enough air. But most of all, if she didn't find release soon, she was going to scream.

And that's when he replaced his finger with his sex. Finally. His fullness, sleek and hard, was exactly what she needed right now. His hips slid against her hot bottom, and he reached around to her clit.

And then as he ever so slowly thrust in and out of her, his fingers kindled a red-hot fire.

"Ah . . . oh . . . oh." A delightful explosion ripped through her, and she spasmed inside, clutching him. But he didn't increase his pace. He stayed with slow and easy friction, and his fingers kept playing with her, never stopping their magical rhythm, extending the explosion until her body fired again and then again.

She clawed the chair, pumping her hips as moans of pleasure escaped from the back of her throat. The orgasms went on and on and on, crashing over one another until they melded into one giant explosion of pleasure.

And still he didn't stop.

Her pulse skyrocketed. It was suddenly hard to breathe. And she lost it.

Like some feral thing, she embodied the pleasure. She became pure wildfire. Locking her legs around his calves, she raised and lowered her hips, demanding he take her faster, harder, deeper.

When he thrust into her and finally spasmed, her name on his lips, she exploded once again and saw stars.

Several minutes passed before her pulse settled and she opened her eyes to find herself floating, her head on Jordan's chest, his arms wrapped around her, their legs entwined.

Total satiation had left her every muscle relaxed. "Thank you."

"It was my pleasure."

He was a surprisingly sensitive lover. He'd known when to push, when to surprise, when to hold back, and when to give her exactly what she needed.

She could come to care for such a sensitive man. But she couldn't nurture those feelings. She reminded herself how they'd come to make love—to avoid the Staff from forcing them into it.

So what if he'd been kind, attentive, and tender, as well as ferocious and demanding and exciting? So what if he was the best lover she'd ever had?

Jordan's memory dropped into her head like a nightmare. Only Vivianne was awake. And she could only watch in horror.

"Trendonis, what have you done?" A younger version of Jordan ignored the blaster pointed at him, fought down the panic honed to a razor sharpness welling inside his chest.

With a triumphant gleam in his eyes, Trendonis gestured with his blaster for Jordan to move toward the space ship's portal. "I've lowered our altitude so you have a perfect view."

Jordan peered out the spaceship's triangular porthole to see his home world, Dominus. At the sight of hundreds of deadly missiles racing toward his home, Jordan's blood went cold.

"No." Jordan's hands fisted. Those missiles would strike farms, cities, schools, and hospitals. So many would die.

Jordan spun and advanced on Trendonis, who lifted one smirking eyebrow. "The Tribes don't accept defiance."

Jordan's voice cracked. "Don't do this."

"Watch." Trendonis shoved the blaster into Jordan's side.

He stumbled back to the portal. The missiles had yet to reach the atmosphere. "Call them back."

"It's too late."

"Detonate them while they're still in space, please," Jordan pleaded, knowing it was a waste of breath.

Trendonis laughed, his eyes sparkling with amusement. "Once planetbusters are released—"

"Planetbusters?" Jordan sagged, barely able to take in the reality. The man had purposely ordered the destruction of his entire world. "Have you lost your mind?"

"See what happens to people who resist the Tribes." Trendonis snapped his fingers. "They vanish."

Jordan cringed. Below, the full force of the missiles struck, the warheads primed to sink to critical depths. The seas came to an instant boil. An entire continent jumped, dropped, and buckled. The poles erupted into tidal waves of lava and ash.

The air itself turned to liquid fire. And he could do nothing to stop the incineration of Dominus.

The end of everyone and everything he knew. His home. His parents. His friends. The planetary core boiled, reached ignition temperatures, exploded. Billions of people gone in an instant. Their history, their culture, their art. Gone.

"You killed them all." Tears running down his cheeks, Jordan turned to face the man he'd thought of as friend. "Kill me, too."

The memory ended as suddenly as it had begun. The destruction of his world might have happened centuries ago, but with Jordan's memory branded into her mind, his pain saturated Vivianne. She could now taste his bitterness. Comprehend his rage. He'd told her the story, but this time she'd suffered with him. Had felt the fury that clawed at him, the determination to stop Trendonis and the Tribes.

Jordan was on Earth's side. The last of her doubts fell away.

And yet she still couldn't let down her guard.

While Jordan's warning that he would not be there for her in the future seemed far away, Vivianne was a pragmatist. She would work with him, she would make love with him, but she would not care about him just because he'd insatiably caressed every inch of her. She would not fall for a man set on saving her world—not when his success meant his death. She wouldn't do that to herself. And she wouldn't do that to him.

The time to dream is now.

—LADY OF THE LAKE

17

After three days of waiting for the weather to break, Vivianne sat behind the helm, her patience near its end.

"Any change?" Jordan asked Darren.

"None." Darren checked the storm readings on the planet below. The hurricanes on Tempest never seemed to run out of energy. Warm water from the seas kept feeding them, and they showed no sign of diminishing.

During the downtime, the crew had tried to keep busy. Tennison was calibrating one of the navigation sensors. Sean tweaked the engines. Knox kept trying new recipes, and when she wasn't in the galley, she and Darren disappeared for hours into their cabin. Gray and Sean played endless games of chess when they were off duty. Lyle was reading and keeping to himself.

Jordan had spent his time studying the star charts. He'd finally pinpointed the *Draco*'s galactic location, and Vivianne tried not to think about how many light-years they were from Earth. Hyperspace could take them home—if they could figure out how to navigate through it. But first they needed the storms to ease on Tempest, and then after they found the key, they'd fly to Pentar for the Grail.

Vivianne had tried to keep busy, too. But mostly she'd felt useless, and she paced, George often at her heels.

"How long are we going to wait for the storms to clear?" she asked Jordan.

"Not much longer."

She eyed Jordan cautiously. "So you've figured out a route to Pentar?"

"Actually, I'm working out a way to fly down there." He gestured to Tempest.

She should have known he would never give up. "The *Draco* can't maneuver in those winds."

"I know." Face hard, he tossed aside a calculator and leaned forward. "There's another way to get down there."

"How?" Her stomach knotted.

"Dragonshape and fly down."

Sean stopped tinkering and gasped. Gray turned white and shook his head. Vivianne felt as if he'd just thrust her under a cascade of icy water. "Those winds will rip off our wings. It's suicide."

"Not if I fly through the eye."

Oh, God. It just might be doable. The eyes were huge and moving at about twenty miles an hour. "But even if we can make it down, we can't search the entire planet for the key—not under those conditions."

The winds were ripping through at hundreds of miles an hour. Although the surface was dirt, the fierce sand-storms would flay off tough dragon hide within minutes.

Jordan let out a long, low breath. "I know where the key is."

"You do?" How could he know that? Vivianne's gaze

locked with his, and he shook his head slightly. He didn't
want to say—not in front of the others. She pursed her
lips but didn't ask again.

"Where's the key?" Gray asked.

"Here." Jordan tapped a spot on the island in the southern hemisphere. "I'll shoot the coordinates over to your
screen. We need a hurricane's eye to pass over that spot.
We fly down, grab the key, and then fly back. The *Draco*
will only need to go into a low orbit in the upper atmosphere to drop me off."

"We jump out the airlock?" Vivianne asked.

"Just me."

She narrowed her eyes. "And after you jump, you'll
dragonshape. But how will you get back?"

"That will be trickier."

No kidding. A dragon couldn't fly into the airlock—it
wasn't big enough. "You'll have to change shape in the
air, time the shift to match the *Draco*'s velocity. Have you
ever done that before?"

"It's possible."

"Gray," she ordered, "notify us if a suitable storm crops
up." She didn't want to argue in front of the crew and motioned to Jordan to follow her.

He hesitated, looking reluctant to discuss the issue, but
then he escorted her from the bridge. They stopped in the
empty galley. She fixed coffee, then took a stool by the
counter.

Jordan sipped, then shuddered and set the coffee aside.
"Can I be honest with you about this coffee?"

"Of course not." She sipped and grinned. "You're my
employee, and then I'd have to fire you immediately." She
shoved his cup back at him. "It's an acquired taste."

He ignored the coffee. "The Staff has homed in on the key."

"Homed in?"

"The Staff's pulsing with light. The nearer I go, the more it pulses. I'll have to take it with me to pinpoint—"

She almost choked on her coffee. "If you take the Staff, you'd leave the *Draco* with only limited backup generator power."

"There's enough to descend, for me to drop out an airlock, and then while I dragonshape and retrieve the key, the *Draco* can maintain a low orbit."

"Not for long it can't. The orbit wouldn't be stable."

"I've run the numbers. The ship would have an hour until power runs out."

She sighed in frustration. "And how would you return?"

"Reverse the process."

She did rough calculations in her head, then did them again on her handheld. "You're cutting it too close."

"On the upside, maybe retrieving the key won't take an hour."

"Damn it. This is too dangerous."

"Some things are worth dying for. We need the key."

"So you say. But *you* won't die down there, will you?" she asked. "Not as long as you have the Staff."

At her accusation, pain flickered in his eyes, and then his face turned hard, bleak. "There are some things worse than dying."

"I'm sorry." She felt badly for accusing him of risking their lives after she'd felt his pain, seen exactly how his entire world had died.

"I'm going with you."

"No. It's too dangerous."

This was her ship, too. She had just as much say-so as he did. "I'm not staying here and just waiting for you to return."

"You're not strong enough. You'll slow me down. You'll hurt my chance of success."

She didn't take offense. "Two people have a better chance than one. Besides, the shape-shifting back into the airlock is going to be tricky. We can help each other."

"No." He shook his head to emphasize his words. "I've had centuries of flying experience. My timing will be better than yours."

The last thing Vivianne wanted to do was go down to Tempest. Just the idea of jumping out of a perfectly good spaceship into a hurricane was enough to make her hands tremble.

"It could take more than just one person to retrieve the key," she insisted, her every instinct telling her she needed to go with him.

"I'll call on the handheld if I need—"

"By the time you know the situation, it might be too late for me to come down. And if something goes wrong down there, you shouldn't be alone. That's why scuba divers have a buddy system. That's why astronauts spacewalk in teams."

"I'll be fine."

"But if you fail, we should have a backup person to retrieve the Staff. And that has to be me. I'm the only other dragonshaper on board."

"You're not going. You'll get yourself killed."

She shrugged. "I have to die sometime."

He reached over the counter and placed his hand on

her shoulder. Warmth flowed into her, and she realized he was worried about her. "Are you always so—"

"Stubborn?" She allowed a smile to tease her lips.

"I was going to say brave."

Her smiled widened. "It's not every woman who'll get to tell her grandchildren that she flew into the eye of a hurricane."

"Grandchildren?" He scowled at her. "Aren't you getting a little ahead of yourself?"

She tossed her hair over her shoulder. "Having children's on my to-do list. Right up there with—"

"Jordan," Gray interrupted on the intercom. "We've got a gale-force storm brewing over Tempest's equator that appears headed for your island coordinates."

"Is there a defined eye?"

"Not yet. But if the winds keep building, there will be."

"I'll be right there." Jordan stood, and his fingers slid from her shoulder to her hand. He kept hold of her, even after they stepped onto the bridge.

Vivianne peered at Tempest and her stomach churned. From here the spinning cloud rotations looked harmless as pinwheels. But she knew better.

Even if they timed their descent with perfect precision, could they survive? While she'd flown in winds of twenty, maybe even thirty, miles per hour, she'd never dared to fly into hurricane-force winds.

"What's the ground temperature at our landing site?" Vivianne asked.

"You're going?" Gray asked.

"She isn't," Jordan said.

She didn't argue. "The temperature?"

"Thirty below."

"What?" she frowned. "Hurricanes need warm water to feed them."

"Arctic storms are shallow, short-lived pressure systems that create fierce blizzards. When this kind of storm passes over water, it can ice over the seas," Jordan said.

"How long until we know if an eye will form?" she asked.

Gray peered at his data. "I'd estimate anywhere from fifteen minutes to an hour."

"I need to be ready to go." Jordan linked his handheld into the computer's weather data stream. "Sean, plot a course to intercept with the eye. Keep in mind that this kind of transient arctic storm typically doesn't last as long as a warm-water hurricane and will produce severe weather and heavy precipitation."

Sean didn't look happy. "Sir, the cloud vortex at the center's walls are where the strongest winds are located."

"True, but like their tropical hurricane counterparts, winds farther inside the eye wall are calmer."

"Won't the storm system decay when it passes over land?" Vivianne asked.

"Normally you'd be correct," Jordan said. "But on Tempest, the one island is only large enough to stall the storm, not break it up."

Vivianne left the bridge while the men continued to talk. She was done arguing. Jordan was not in charge of her. And if he thought he was, he would soon learn differently.

The greatest lesson is to love and be loved in return.
—KING ARTHUR PENDRAGON

18

❦

Jordan filled the emergency batteries, then removed the Staff from the housing in engineering. The *Draco,* already in low orbit, shifted to backup power with smooth efficiency. Jordan contracted the Staff, placed it into his sheath, and headed for the airlock. The leather nanobot sheath would expand when he dragonshaped, and the Staff would remain strapped to his body as he flew down to the island.

"What's the progression of the storm's eye?" Jordan asked Gray through the handheld strapped to his wrist.

"Looking good."

While he couldn't speak in dragon form, the handheld's nanotech bracelet would also expand to dragon size and shrink when he transformed back to human shape and allow him to communicate with the *Draco.* In addition, he carried a harness with winter clothing and a knife. He didn't expect to need anything else, and more weight could adversely affect his flying.

He'd wanted to say goodbye to Vivianne, but she had disappeared. It wasn't like her to be off pouting. But perhaps she needed space to cool down. Jordan pulled the slot-like handle that opened the airlock and shut the door behind him. The seals hissed. He toggled his handheld. "How's the eye now?"

"Stable and going to pass right over the island in four minutes," Gray reported.

Jordan had to allow time for freefall, then time to fly with the eye as it moved over the island. He pressed a timer on his wrist. "Starting countdown."

"Fifty-eight seconds and looking good," Tennison monitored.

"You can abort any time up to the last five seconds," Gray reminded him. "Then the outside hatch will begin to cycle open."

"Fifty seconds."

Jordan didn't remind the man he'd designed the system. Instead he rechecked his gear. Knife, Staff, harness, and winter clothing all packed and ready to fly.

"Forty seconds."

"The eye's spinning. Wind speed at the wall is over two-fifty," Gray said.

"Still on target?" Jordan asked.

"Yes, sir."

"Thirty seconds."

The *Draco* shuddered.

"Status report." Jordan demanded.

"We caught an air pocket and slipped a little. I've corrected," Gray responded.

"Twenty seconds."

Jordan turned to the outer hatch and peered through the airlock's tiny window. Dark skies and a few pale stars winked through the thin upper atmosphere. Again the ship shuddered.

"What's our exterior temperature?"

"Fifty below. You need to drop down fast."

"Ten seconds."

"Tell Vivianne that I'll be back soon."

"Roger that," Gray said. "Five seconds."

Jordan clasped the ball on the airlock's handle and tugged. The outside lock began to cycle.

Jordan heard a thud. He glanced over his shoulder to see Vivianne beside him. Fuck. All this time she'd been above his head, plastered against the ceiling, waiting until the very last moment to reveal her presence.

He swore. "What in the seven hells of Hades are you doing here?"

Battle-hardened soldiers had cowered at his fury. She didn't so much as wince. Her eyes flashed fire.

"Like it or not, I'm going with you."

It was too late to send her back.

"Hell's ass, you're one stubborn woman." Furious and worried about her safety, he glared at her. "Don't blame me if you get yourself killed."

Just as the door opened, he threw both arms around her and held her tightly. Then together they tumbled out of the airlock. Into freefall.

Freezing cold slammed into him, and subzero winds plucked at his clothing. He pulled Vi's face against his chest, shielding her from the worst of the wind. "Don't dragonshape yet, or the wind will tear off your wings."

"I know the plan."

"Don't talk. Don't breathe." The air could freeze their lungs.

At least she wasn't panicking in the icy freefall. However, once they got down, if they got down, he would . . . he would . . . what? Damn her. She'd left him no options. He could only do so much to ensure that she stayed alive. She'd had no business coming along. He didn't even know if *he* could fly through this storm, and she hadn't his experience, his muscles, or his mass.

Even as his fury hammered him, he kept count of the time. After sixty seconds they could dragonshape. He just hoped his limbs weren't frozen solid by then.

"Ready?" he shouted to be heard against the snapping wind.

Vivianne quipped through half-frozen lips, "I was born ready."

VIVIANNE COULDN'T LET Jordan come down to Tempest alone. She just prayed she'd be useful, because fury radiated from him in fierce waves. She'd prove herself able.

Just a few more seconds and she could dragonshape. Until then, she ignored the swooping in her stomach that she told herself was from the freefall and not Jordan's anger.

"Now." Jordan released her, and for a second the wind bit into her from every angle.

Then she morphed into her dragon shape. Her clothes shredded. Her dragon skin thickened and protected her against the cold. Her eyesight sharpened, and her bones changed to a honeycombed structure that allowed her to spread her wings. She also lost much of her superior human intellect, but she gained strength. She didn't try to fly. Instead she ducked her head, tucked her wings against her sides, and streamlined her massive body to dive toward the eye, easily discernable in the swirling storm below.

Aim for the center. Jordan sent the order telepathically.

Of course. Dragons didn't have vocal cords but could convey simple conversations through mental telepathy. Even if this world had been full of dragons, she would have recognized his tough, dominant, and angry mental signature as easily as his voice.

Jordan, with his heavier mass and stronger muscles, could have withstood a steeper descent, but he spread his wings to slow his dive. She supposed later he would blame her for slowing him down. But she hadn't asked him to wait.

When they reached the swirling white cloud system of the upper eye, the pressure systems changed and the wind gusted in blasts that battered her. She opened her wings a bit, testing, trying to stabilize, but mostly trying to ride the air gusts.

Careful. He nudged her away from the eye wall.

I'm fine.

Just stay that way.

The wind blasted sideways, and she spread her wings wider to fly level. A giant downdraft almost flipped her upside down. She corrected to the right, overcorrected to the left, almost somersaulted, then flattened out.

She peered down through the eye at the steep, icy cliffs rising from the island. At lower elevations the blizzard was blowing so much snow there were swirling white-out conditions.

Hurry. Jordan's worry came through with his thoughts.

She didn't understand his sudden concern until she looked directly below. The eye wall where the winds were most severe was calving the mountain cliffs like a glacier. House-sized chunks of snow and ice broke off from the sheer face. If any of that frozen debris hit them, it would hurt. A lot.

Tucking her wings closer to her body, she squinted against the snow and plummeted. The last few thousand feet, Jordan took the lead.

Flying in formation directly behind Jordan, she spied a hunk of debris shooting toward them. *To your right,* she warned.

He banked and she followed as rocks the size of her Lexus—and black icicles so huge that any one of them could cause a deathblow—whizzed by.

Talk about flying blind. She couldn't see the ground through the thick snow. She couldn't see her own wings.

In that moment she decided that Hell wasn't rife with red hot fire, Hell was deadly white and miserably cold.

She kept her nose right on Jordan's tail to avoid losing him in the whiteout. Sensing the ground coming up before she actually saw it, she extended her legs and claws to touch down. Just as she landed, the wind blasted. She stumbled and rolled, her dragon's body tumbling over ice and snow. A chunk of ice dug into her leg, and another slammed her wing. But finally she stopped somersaulting and skidded to a stop. Rising to a crouch in the high wind, she spat snow and pebbles from her mouth, the taste bitter.

Jordan?

You okay? He lumbered up behind her.

She prayed he hadn't witnessed her clumsy landing. She was lucky she hadn't broken her neck. Or leg. A lot of damn help she'd be if she'd gotten seriously hurt.

He humanshaped and changed into the heavy clothes he'd packed. She stayed in dragon form. Unless he needed her, she saw no reason to freeze alongside him.

Jordan removed the Staff from the harness, and it pulsed with light. He held it in front of him and slowly turned in a full circle. But when he faced into the wind, the Staff's flashes were closer together.

"This way," he shouted. He took two steps and fell in snow up to his waist.

Swearing all the while, he struggled to dig himself out. Finally he was free, until five steps later he fell into another drift up to his neck.

This time, she flattened the snow next to him with her wing and he easily walked out. "Thanks. I'd ask for a ride, but I don't think we have far to go."

Four steps later, the Staff's light stopped blinking and remained bright. He stopped and turned. No matter which way he stepped, the light weakened. He resheathed the Staff. "The key must be under me."

She gestured with her wing for him to move back so she could dig with her powerful rear legs to clear about ten feet of snow. Then she hit something hard.

"Let me see." He jumped into the hole. "There's nothing down here but solid ice. Lift me out."

She ducked her head into the snow hole, and he grabbed her harness and she easily hauled him out. Now what?

He pointed. "Melt the ice for me."

For a guy who hadn't wanted her to come along, he sure didn't hesitate to order her to do his bidding. Of course, he could do all this himself, dragonshaping, then humanshaping. But at least she was saving him time. And energy. When he stepped aside, she roared out a long, hot flame and focused the blaze on the ice.

When he grabbed her harness, she carefully lowered him into the hole. The bottom of the crater was now filled with water, but the surface was quickly refreezing.

"I don't see—wait—over there." He pointed to the water. "It's right down there. But I can't swim in this gear. Lift me out."

She complied and watched him remove his gear and begin to shiver. "H-heat the water for me. Not t-too much," he instructed. "I don't want to b-boil."

She breathed fire into the water. Then watched him jump in. He swam underwater for what seemed like a long time. Then his head burst to the surface, his blue eyes gleaming with triumph. "Got it!"

Quickly, she ducked her head down to lift him out and watched as the water froze on his skin.

After setting him down on the snow, she roared more fire near him, careful not to singe him. Quickly, he snapped the key into the Staff and dragonshaped.

That was close. His thoughts came at her with a blast of cold. He'd almost frozen down there.

More fire?

No time. Let's fly.

He lifted off. She began to follow. Out of the corner of her eyes, she saw a boulder heading right for Jordan.

To your left.

He banked right. But since he was only about a meter off the ground, he couldn't maneuver well. There was no time, no room, for him to duck or swerve. He wasn't going to make it.

Lunging with her powerful dragon legs, she jumped

onto the boulder, hoping to crush it into the snow with her great mass. The snow crunched under her weight, and she slowed the boulder's progress just enough for Jordan to fly away uninjured.

But the boulder didn't stop dead. It skidded and kept rolling.

Next thing she knew, she was plowing snow with her face. Snow in her eyes, snow in her ears, snow under her talons. Her world went white.

Keep your face to the stars and you can't see the dirt.

—LUCAN ROARKE

19

*W*ake up. In dragon form Jordan nudged Vi's body, his fear battling with his anger. What had she been thinking to throw herself on top of the boulder like that? He'd seen the danger and had been about to veer safely away when she'd jumped onto it. She might as well have been trying to stop a charging bull by leaping onto its back. And if she couldn't fly . . . Goddess, she had to be all right.

Wake up. Wake up.

She didn't respond. But he could see her dragon's chest rising and falling.

He swore and nudged her again. With his wing, he gently swept the snow from her face.

She groaned and opened her eyes. Thank the Goddess.

But then she closed her eyes again and she didn't move. Panic and fear twisted inside him. He'd lost so many people. He couldn't lose Vi, too.

Are you hurt?

She didn't respond. Was she conscious? He saw

no twisted limbs or blood, but she could have internal injuries.

Damn it. She had to fly out of here with him. The *Draco* couldn't set down in these storms. And he had to return with the Staff.

But leaving her . . . was not a choice he could make. Just the thought made his double hearts ache with sorrow and frustration. He was not going to lose her.

Damn it, answer me. Am I going to have to fly you out of here?

She moaned. Her eyelids fluttered.

Come on. Wake up, Vi.

She shuddered. And then finally, she opened her eyes, and this time they remained open. She raised her head. Blinked.

I'm here. Are you hurt? he asked again.

She shook her head and snow went flying all over him, then she lumbered to her feet. *Just got the wind knocked out of me.*

He wanted to give a mental shout at her that she shouldn't have followed him. That it was insane for her to have risked her life to stop that boulder. That she could have died and he would have had to go on alone.

He trembled as the aftershocks whipped through him. But he sent none of those furious thoughts. He was too damn relieved to see her climbing to her feet.

How long was I out? she asked.

A few minutes. It had seemed like hours. He shifted position to block the worst of the wind from her. Glancing at the sky, he tried to spot the advancing eye wall, but the whiteout hid the encroaching danger.

She tested her wings. *We need to get back to the ship.*

You can fly?

She launched into the air. He would have preferred she'd used more speed and that she wasn't favoring one wing, but they had no choice.

The winds were already increasing, signaling the eye wall was closing in. They'd delayed too long. The deadly eye wall was like a tornado, spinning madly. In human form he wouldn't have been able to stand. And not even his dragon strength could fly through this biting, blinding snow.

While Vivianne didn't even suggest turning back, to continue was . . . death.

They would fail. And be stranded here.

But then lightning seemed to illuminate the entire sky. Vivianne's dark dragon silhouette was outlined in startling white.

What's happening? she asked.

It took him a moment to comprehend; the light wasn't a natural phenomenon.

Light radiated from the Ancient Staff and shined right through the sheath.

The Wind Key's containing the storm.

Vivianne didn't question him. She caught a thermal updraft and soared toward the *Draco* in a long spiral. He followed, watching her carefully. At the first sign of trouble, he'd demand she humanshape and he'd scoop her out of the air, carry her on his back. But she kept flying.

Even with the wind knocked back, his wings iced, snow clung and weighed him down. And she must be having trouble, too. *We need to deice.*

How?

He slowed to gain a little distance, then roared fire in

her direction, using just enough heat to melt the snow without singeing her wings.

Your turn, she offered, her mental tone weary.

They switched places, but when she tried to return the favor, she couldn't shoot fire. *I'm low on platinum,* she admitted.

Not good. Dragons ate platinum and hydrogen to fuel their bodies. But they'd expended huge reserves to retrieve the key. Every time she'd roared fire, she'd burned massive amounts of energy. Just keeping warm used more reserves, never mind flying against these gale-force winds. While he could draw energy from the Staff, if her platinum level fell too much, she might not make it back to the *Draco.*

He put extra muscle power into his heavy wings, but his concerns for her safety escalated. With the snow and ice weighing him down, there was no way he could carry her, too.

Timing would be critical. They had to match the *Draco*'s speed, but they didn't have instruments to guide them. They had only their keen eyesight, their tired wings, and the tiny airlock for a target. And a ship that likely didn't have enough fuel for a second attempt.

When they finally cleared the planetary storms, they flew higher into the thin atmosphere. The wind diminished, but the temperature plummeted. He tapped one ankle against the other that held the communicator, his signal to the ship.

I don't see the Draco. Exhaustion came through her thoughts on a layer of pain.

They'll be here soon. You go first, he ordered, and when she didn't even argue, his concern deepened. *Don't try to match the* Draco's *velocity. Fly a little forward, a little high. I'll signal when to morph. Then grab the airlock and pull yourself inside.*

The ship, a tiny dot on the horizon, approached with startling speed. *There they are. Fly closer. Closer.*

Wings dipping unsteadily, she was clearly at the end of her strength.

He tried to encourage her. *You look good. Now wait for it. Wait. Wait.* The lock opened. *Now.*

She morphed into human form. Reaching out with her arms and hands, she grabbed the airlock's deck. And dangled. She kicked. But the wind tore at her, and she didn't have the upper-body strength to pull herself inside.

No one could cling to the airlock for more than a few seconds. Jordan humanshaped. With one hand, he latched on to the airlock. With the other, he shoved her inside.

But then the wind was tearing at him, and he couldn't pull himself up with only one hand, couldn't reach a handhold with the other.

Vi scrambled around to face him, braced her feet on either side of the airlock. She held out her hands to him. "I've got you."

He had to release his handhold on the airlock. Had to trust her to reel him in. Her exhaustion flashed through his mind. But seeing the determination on her face, he let go of the ship.

For a split second, he slid backward. Then she grabbed his hands, heaved, and pulled him inside so hard that he landed on top of her. Reaching up, he jerked down the handle to shut the outside hatch.

"That was fun," she panted.

"You almost got us both killed," he muttered, scowling into her beautiful eyes.

"I just saved your life—"

"Which was only in danger because I had to delay my entrance to push you inside."

"You wouldn't have had to push me, if I hadn't strained my arm saving you from that boulder."

"I would have shifted out of the way. I didn't need you to—"

"Right." She shoved him off her. "You can do everything alone. Fly through hurricanes. Find the key and the Grail. And you know what? You can damn well sleep alone, too."

"Hey—that was your idea."

"A bad one." She ground her teeth together.

The airlock recycled and she stepped out, refusing to look at him.

Gray glanced from one angry face to the other. "Did you get the key?"

"Yes," Jordan said.

"Then install the Staff. Our orbit's deteriorating. You two can kill each other later."

Never live for someone else's dream.
                                        —LADY OF THE LAKE

20

After checking the bridge and learning Tennison was at the helm and ready to take them out of danger the moment the power kicked in, Vivianne headed to her cabin. She was certain after Jordan installed the Staff he would go to the bridge, and she wanted to check the communicator in the cabin and be gone before he arrived.

She opened the cabin door and George raced to her, stood on his hind legs, and demanded petting. It was nice to be appreciated, and she petted him, then tried to step inside the cabin. "Down, boy."

When he didn't listen, she bent, scooped him into her arms, then slid behind the desk. As she settled George in her lap, the *Draco*'s power kicked in.

After opening the monitor's side panel, she adjusted the circuitry. Had Maggie received the first message? Had she secured Vivianne's spare unit?

Vivianne let the unit warm up, then fiddled with the controls. "Maggie, are you listening? Talk to me."

Vivianne hit the toggle and scratched George behind the ears, welcoming his warmth. "It's okay, fella. We have to be patient. Maybe she's sleeping." Maybe the system wasn't working. Or maybe there weren't any hyperspace wormholes within range of the *Draco* for the messages to pass through. Space wasn't stable. Or predictable.

Vivianne tried the unit again, and again received no reply. She was about to give up when she heard Maggie's excited voice. "Vivianne, is that really you?"

Hot damn. Her machine was working. And there wasn't any delay—even with light-years of distance. Amazing. "Yes, it's really me."

"Have you found the Holy Grail?" Maggie asked.

Vivianne frowned. "Not yet."

"The whole world knows your mission now. When you blasted off, the government announced how the *Draco* is going to save us all."

"Oh." She recalled their departure and the North American States threatening to shoot them down. Now they probably wanted to take credit if the *Draco* succeeded.

"Are you close to finding it?" Maggie pressed.

"We're working on it. Tell me what's going on."

"We're under martial law."

"Why?" Vivianne's stomach lurched. Had the Tribes already attacked? Were they too late?

"The politicians are telling us the lockdown is for our own protection." Maggie sighed. "Maybe it is."

"I don't understand."

"Rumor has it that the Tribes are about to strike Earth. Scratch that. It's no longer rumor but headline news. And it's crazy here. People are looting and hoarding food, fuel, cigarettes, and alcohol. A loaf of bread costs a week's pay. Yesterday there was a mass suicide—hundreds killed themselves preferring death to alien domination. People think they're going to die, so they do whatever they please. It's too dangerous to go out. The police can't keep up. The world is close to anarchy."

Vivianne's pulse raced. "Have there been any real attacks?"

"By the Tribes? No. But Iran's invaded Iraq. India's invaded Pakistan. North Korea took over the south, and Alaska is trying to secede. The major powers are doing nothing to stop the rampant violence. People are accusing their neighbors of being part of the Tribes. Everyone's suspect."

Vivianne tried to get a handle on the scope of the problem. "Are you talking about isolated incidents or—"

"I saw a man on the news lynched last night—in Beverly Hills."

Vivianne swallowed hard. If they made it back to Earth, they'd return to a different world. "Are you all right?"

"Yes, but getting your little machine home was tricky. I was lucky no one stopped me or accused me of conspiring with the enemy. Or of *being* the enemy."

"Maggie, I'm sorry. I didn't realize you'd be in danger. Call my office. Have them send over twenty-four-hour protection. Or better yet, take your husband and kids to my headquarters. It's vital that you monitor that machine twenty-four/seven."

Vivianne's top people knew Maggie was her friend. They'd do as Maggie asked.

"All right. And thanks." Maggie lowered her voice as if she feared being overheard. "Vivianne, people are saying it's the end of the world."

"They're panicking."

"Their panic is scaring me more than the Tribes. I didn't know civilization could fall apart so fast. Kids aren't going to school or to piano lessons or baseball practice. It's not safe to go to work. We've actually boarded up the sliding-glass doors to prevent anyone from seeing us eat. They might kill us for our food."

"Where are our government leaders?"

"Watching after their own asses. Probably holed up in some cushy underground bunker with twenty years of food and the military to protect them against the masses. Yesterday, we had a major brownout. If the power goes down, we'll lose what little food we have in the freezer."

Vivianne's stomach danced up her throat. "We have food and a generator at Vesta's Headquarters. Get over there now."

The sounds of gunshots traveled through the communicator. Maggie lowered her voice. "It's not safe to go at night. But tomorrow, we'll do as you say."

"Good. And once you're there, have my people build more communicators ASAP. I want two units in every Vesta headquarters, so that once we have a plan we can coordinate our efforts. Make sure Lucan gets one, and tell him to use Stonehenge to transport units to Rion on Honor and Cael's people on Pendragon. We need all the allies we can get."

"I'll try. But I don't know if the transporter's operational—"

Vivianne heard the sounds of breaking glass, a child crying, then more gunshots. She bit her lip, waited, prayed her friend was all right. "Maggie, are you still there?"

Maggie whispered, "I've got to go."

The communicator went dead. Again Vivianne waited,

hoping Maggie would come back to assure her she was all right. But she never did.

George let out a low growl just before someone tried to open the cabin door. Vivianne scooted George to the floor, flipped back the panel, and turned off her communicator. She yanked open the door, expecting Jordan to be standing there with a scowl and demanding why she'd locked him out.

But it was Knox. She held out a sandwich and a cup of coffee. "Thought you might be hungry."

"Thanks." Vivianne sipped her coffee, welcoming the heat and comfort.

"Are you okay?" Knox asked.

"Why do you ask?"

"Because Jordan is in a mood. Edgy. Dark. And he wants you on the bridge," Knox added.

"What's wrong?"

Knox wrinkled her nose. "He said something about picking up some strange energy signal."

"I'll go to the bridge as soon as I eat."

Knox lowered her voice. "I've seen Jordan handle much worse emergencies without . . . well . . . Look, I heard you two had a fight."

"Yeah, we did."

"If you want to talk—"

Alarms blared.

Now what? She shoved her coffee into Knox's hand. Eating on the run took on a new meaning as Vivianne dashed from the cabin.

"Vi, I need you here." Jordan's voice came through her handheld and urged her into a full-fledged run.

She skidded onto the bridge, sandwich still in her hand. The moment she arrived, Jordan spun around, his hands on his hips, his face hard, his eyes suspicious. "Do you know anything about these peculiar frequency spikes?"

Clearly, he was still angry with her over what had happened back on Tempest, but they had to put it aside. They needed to work together.

She glanced at the streaming data. "Why are you asking me about the spikes?"

"Because you're the communications expert, and the last time we read that kind of energy, a wormhole opened up off the bow."

"And those cubes found us," she whispered, her stomach sinking.

His tone was harsh. "Your prototype, did you just use it again?"

"Yes." Vivianne squared her shoulders. "Maggie answered me. It works."

Jordan raked his fingers through his hair. "So your experiment probably caused the energy spikes."

"I couldn't have known . . . The prototype's not designed to open a wormhole, just find existing ones."

"But the cubes may have homed in on your signal, tracked us, then opened their own wormhole."

"It's possible," she admitted, sliding into the communications seat and studying the readings.

"Captain." Gray interrupted Jordan's stare. "Something's coming through the wormhole."

"Raise shields," Jordan ordered.

"Get us the hell out of here," Vivianne added.

There is music in space, but to hear it you must be still.

—ANONYMOUS

21

F ull reverse," Jordan ordered.

Tennison was one step ahead of him, kicking the power into overdrive. As Jordan waited to see what would emerge from hyperspace, his glance fell on Vivianne.

Vi was clearly upset, still furious with him over what had happened between them in the airlock. Maybe that was for the best.

Vivianne wasn't looking at him. Hadn't shared her conversation with her friend, and her reticence bothered him on several levels. First, their chances of finding the last key and the Grail were slim enough if they worked together and shared information. Second, whatever she was keeping from him might prove to be important. And third, she was too smart to have her working against him.

"Sensor readings indicate three objects approaching fast," Gray reported.

Lyle walked onto the bridge, took one look at the viewscreen, and turned pale. "Those machines are coming back after us. I should have shot them all down the first time."

"Maybe Trendonis tracked us through hyperspace," Sean suggested.

Vivianne's eyes narrowed. "No one is to fire any weapons without a direct order."

"Wormhole's ejecting," Tennison said. Three cubes flew out.

Vivianne gasped, then her gaze flew to meet Jordan's. "Are those the exact same machines that surrounded us last time?"

Trendonis was out there hunting them, but Jordan didn't know if the advancing spacecraft were under his control. He turned to his crew. "How's the power?"

"Steady, but—" Tennison squinted at his data as if he couldn't believe his readings.

"We aren't going anywhere," Gray said.

"What?" Lyle's face went from pale to white.

Darren's voice came over the speakers, "Engines are starting to overheat."

Gray explained. "Power and engines are working perfectly, but we are at a full stop."

"How is that possible?" Vivianne asked.

"Power down," Jordan ordered. Obviously retreat wasn't an option, and he'd prefer not to drain the Staff. "If we can't escape, there's no reason to risk blowing the engines."

"I'll open a channel." Vi placed the headset over her ears. "Maybe we can find out what they want."

"Put them on the speakers," Jordan ordered.

She flipped the toggle switch without hesitation. "Hello. Can anyone hear me?"

Jordan shot her a thumbs-up. She nodded, but there was a distance in her eyes, a barrier she'd put up.

"You will follow us." The alien voice sounded mechanical.

Vivianne paused for a moment. "Follow you where?"

Jordan held his breath, waiting for a response. But they didn't reply.

Instead, the machines surrounded the *Draco*.

"Here we go again," Gray muttered.

"Power status?" Jordan asked

"It's ramping back up." Gray's hands moved over the screen. "I can't stop it. My controls are dead."

"Helm's dead, too." Tennison said.

"We're moving again," Vivianne said.

"Those machines are kidnapping us." Lyle's voice was close to panic. "They're taking us into the wormhole. We should shoot them down before—"

"No shooting," Jordan ordered.

"But—"

"Last time they cut our power and nearly froze us to death," Vi reminded him, and Lyle settled down.

Jordan hit the toggle. "Prepare for hyperspace."

Over the communicator, Knox swore. "The floaters are going to have to scrape dinner off the ceiling again. A little warning would have been—"

Vivianne grabbed George with one hand, the console with the other. She'd barely braced herself before the alien machines whisked them right into the wormhole.

"Can we plot our course?" Vivianne asked. "Or are we going to be lost again?"

"No and no." Jordan looked at his streaming data. "I have no idea where we're going, but once we return to normal space, our new star charts should pinpoint our location."

He should have known better than to make a statement

like that. It was almost as if his words jinxed them. The stars streaked by and the hull shook. They must have remained in the wormhole for about twenty minutes. And then they popped out, the machines still escorting them.

"Where are we?" Vivianne whispered.

"Nav charts are picking up only one star," Gray said. "It's behind us, and there's also a planet nearby. I'm running an analysis to see if I can match the light and magnetic spectrum to anything in our charts."

Jordan had a bad feeling. There were only a few places in the universe where the stars were so far away they couldn't be picked up at all. They were between galaxies or in another dimension. Either possibility was mind-blowing.

"Report," Jordan said, keeping his suspicions to himself.

"All systems are operational," Gray said, "but we still don't have control back."

The cube machines turned the *Draco,* and a yellow planet came into view. It was approximately half land, half ocean, with both poles covered with ice. From above, the land masses appeared to be mostly sandy deserts, with no jungles, rain forests, or greenery.

"What's the atmosphere like down there?" Vivianne asked.

"Barely breathable, and without plants, yet, I don't understand how that can be," Gray said.

"We should fire on them," Lyle repeated. "Before they come aboard—"

"They've gone to a lot of trouble to bring us here," Vivianne said. "Let's see what they want."

"They almost killed us last time," Lyle sputtered.

"Only because you fired on them," Jordan reminded him. "I agree with Vi, let's see what they want."

*Start by doing what's necessary, then what's possible,
and suddenly you are doing the impossible.*
                                    —ST. FRANCIS OF ASSISI

22

Vivianne knew Jordan was trying to get back on her good side. While she wasn't immune to his backing her up, or his thumbs-up over how she'd handled the communications, she also wouldn't put it past him to try to manipulate her.

The man was complex. Brilliant. He'd lived so long that he was adept at hiding his real feelings—if he had them. She had no idea where she stood with him, and it bothered her that she cared.

She reminded herself that just because they'd been lovers didn't mean she required a deeper connection. Vivianne already knew she could count on Jordan to save her life, even at the risk of his own.

But she must guard herself against forming deeper attachments. She shouldn't even be this angry or hurt about his refusal to acknowledge her contributions down on Tempest. His opinion shouldn't matter. She didn't need him to recognize her help. All that counted was that she'd done what she'd had to do. They'd succeeded in retrieving the Key of Wind.

When he came alongside her and placed his hand on her shoulder, she wanted to shrug out from beneath it. Irritated with herself over how much she enjoyed his casual touch, she forced herself to step away, to move closer to the viewscreen. "What is this world?"

His tone was quiet, thoughtful. "On Dominus, we had a legend about Arcturus, a world far out of the Milky Way's rim."

"You think this world is Arcturus?"

"It's possible. Look at the equator. That desert isn't sand, but stone." He pointed. "What do you see carved into the rock?"

She peered hard, then gasped. "Those carvings look like three horses running." They had to be enormous to be seen from this distance.

"Three fast steeds was King Arthur's coat of arms," he reminded her.

"But I thought Arthur was from Pendragon."

"Many worlds claimed him as their own."

"What else do you know about these Arcturians?" she asked.

"It was said that on Arcturus lived a race of ancient ones who possessed Goddess-like powers."

"But?" she prodded, sensing more.

"Supposedly, these Arcturians had lost their humanity. They weren't cruel, just cold, methodical, careful, and indifferent to the concerns of the rest of the galaxy."

She didn't like the sound of this legend at all. "If the Arcturians are so indifferent, what do they want with us?"

"I don't even know if this world is the same one from

the legend. But I doubt anyone would go to all the trouble to bring us here if they meant us harm."

She disagreed. Perhaps she was simply too suspicious, but she couldn't make such an assumption. Those machines hadn't invited them to come. They'd herded them here.

"How do you know this isn't a Tribe world?"

Jordan shrugged. "If the Tribes have the kind of technology that can take control of the *Draco's* engines, then we've already lost."

She locked gazes with him. "We can't give up."

"We won't." Blue fire blazed in his eyes. A muscle in his cheek vibrated. His shoulders squared with determination.

"Conditions on Earth are growing more dire by the day," she said. "We need to find the last key, go after the Grail, and return home before there's nothing left to return to."

"I'm doing my best," Jordan said in a soft voice so the others couldn't hear. Then he turned to the crew and requested, "Status report."

"We can't breathe the air without spacesuits," Gray said. "Gravity's within our normal limits. But there may be hyperspace frequencies our sensors can't identify."

"Can you be more specific?" Vivianne asked.

"Remember the energy from your prototype?" Gray reminded her, as if she could have forgotten. "Well, those kind of energies are all over this planet."

Vivianne scratched her head. The *Draco's* sensors might not have the sophistication to track her prototype's hyperspace frequency, but suppose other races out here could? Had her communications through hyperspace drawn attention? Was this delay her fault? Or was it merely coincidence that these people used the same kind of energy as her hypercommunicator?

"The atmosphere just changed," Gray reported. "It's now within very suitable parameters for human life."

"Were our former readings wrong?" Vivianne asked.

Gray shook his head. "I know it sounds impossible, but . . . someone changed the atmosphere."

"Who does that? Who changes the air of an entire world to make us more comfortable?" Vivianne's voice rose in astonishment.

Jordan's attention focused on his data pad. "We just passed through high-altitude orbital space. They're taking the *Draco* down to the surface."

Clouds covered most of the planet. But from this height above Earth she would have seen signs of civilization. The Great Wall of China. Lights from the big cities, London, New York, Hong Kong, Tokyo. Ancient petroglyphs in China, Pakistan, and Kazakhstan.

But these Arcturians didn't seem to build great cities, or bridges or roads. She caught sight of sweeping farmlands that dotted the countryside, and little else. They landed gently on a grassy hillside that overlooked a large, perfectly circular lake.

"The two dragonshapers will exit," the alien voice ordered them over the *Draco*'s speaker system.

"I'll get the Ancient Staff," Jordan murmured. "You might want to pack a few things."

"I'm on it." Her voice might have remained calm, but aliens had just ordered them to leave the relative safety of their ship. They'd issued orders she and Jordan couldn't refuse. And a shiver of fear shimmied down her back.

"Don't forget food and water," he reminded her.

And platinum and hydrogen. She had yet to replenish her platinum supply since she'd used up her energy reserves on Tempest. His reminder set her in motion.

Fifteen minutes later, she met Jordan at the hatch. "How do they know we're dragonshapers?" she asked.

"If their scanners are as sophisticated as those cubes that retrieved us, they've already downloaded our entire database."

She gasped. "That would mean they know all about Earth, Pendragon, and Honor, our capabilities and science, our history, our language."

"Only if they've read everything. And that would take some time." Jordan took her hand. "Let's assume they mean us no harm until they prove otherwise."

Vivianne patted the laser weapon strapped into her belt. She hoped Jordan's assessment was correct, but she would draw her own conclusions. At least Jordan wasn't arguing for her to stay behind—although she suspected he would have if given the choice. The hatch hissed open and she strode out beside Jordan. A field of golden grasses stretched as far as the eye could see, and the placid lake was so large, they couldn't determine what was on the other side. Along the sandbanks, the greenish water lapped quietly in the gentle breeze.

Only one metal cube remained beside their ship, and its mechanical voice sounded exactly as it had through the *Draco*'s speakers. "The Key of Soil will be yours if your hearts are true."

The Key of Soil? How could this machine know about the third key? That information wasn't in the computer databanks. And how would anyone determine what was in their hearts? A shiver of ice wound down her spine. This was just weird.

"What now?" Vivianne asked, her pulse racing. These beings knew entirely too much about them and their mission.

"Dragonshape and you shall learn."

Home is where you make it.

—LADY OF THE LAKE

23

So we dragonshape?" Vivianne asked.

Jordan nodded, then removed the Ancient Staff from the sheath. They morphed.

Where to? Vivianne asked.

Jordan now clutched the Ancient Staff in his talon. It was her first good look at the Ancient Staff since he'd embedded the Wind Key into the bough. It pulsed with more energy than she'd ever seen before.

Jordan turned in a continuous circle, using the Staff like a dowser trying to find water. When the Staff brightened, he clutched it in both front talons, then launched into flight. *This way.*

With a flap of her wings she lifted off, caught an updraft, and soared after him. Flying in the sunny, cloudless sky was pleasant, even if the landscape below was monotonous. She saw no animals, no people, no movement. Just ripe grains swaying under a blue sky.

How far? she asked.

This is very strange.

What?

To the right. That edifice looks like an exact replica of Camelot.

She turned her head and stared in surprise. *King Arthur Pendragon's castle?*

"Strange" might be the understatement of the century. With anyone else she would have questioned the facts, but Jordan had lived in Camelot. He'd been King Arthur Pendragon's adviser.

Jordan humanshaped, and she did the same.

The castle rose naturally from a cliff, its stone walls spiraling into the sky like a city out of some medieval history book. Surrounded by high, thick walls and a moat filled with striking blue water, Camelot was a fortress, a haven, large enough that they should have spied it from space. Massive round towers rose above narrow cobblestone streets crowded with horses pulling carts laden with cloth, foodstuffs, and animals. People wore cloaks trimmed with animal pelts.

"This city can't be real," she murmured.

"It's manufactured." Jordan sounded very certain. "Just like the air was manufactured for us."

"But why?" she asked.

"I don't know," Jordan said, his frustration evident. He lifted the Staff, and when he pointed it toward the city, the Staff didn't appear to change. Nevertheless, he offered her his arm in a gallant gesture. "Would you like to see Camelot, milady?"

She glanced down at her nanotech pants and blouse. "In these clothes, we're going to draw attention."

Jordan grinned, his gaze falling to her chest. "No one's going to mistake you for a man."

She didn't rise to his teasing. "I'd rather blend, at least until we figure out—"

Trumpets blew. A gate opened, and the moat lowered. Men atop war horses rode out of the castle, the Pendragon banner waving in the gentle breeze. Everything looked medieval to Vivianne, the knights and their armor, the saddles, the gear. Shields gleamed in the sunlight. Huge black horses with plaited manes and polished hooves pranced down the road.

"What's going on?" she asked.

A smile teased Jordan's lips. "If I'm not mistaken, you're about to meet King Arthur."

She swallowed hard. "King Arthur Pendragon?"

"Yes."

"But he died almost fifteen hundred years ago."

"Apparently not." Blue eyes glittering, Jordan folded his arms over his chest and waited.

She would have given one of her companies to read his thoughts. Did Jordan think this was real? Or had this alien civilization created this city out of their archives for some reason of their own?

"Is this some three-dimensional hologram made up for us?"

Jordan's expression didn't change. "We'll find out soon enough."

"How?" Her pulse raced.

"I knew the man. A hologram won't fool me. Not even a clone."

Right. Jordan and Arthur would have had private conversations that no one else knew about. But Jordan seemed so pleased to see his old friend that she was certain he believed King Arthur still lived.

Who would have thought it possible?

King Arthur rode as if he were part of the horse. Blond-haired, blue-eyed, he didn't look a day over fifty. With strong muscles and bronze skin, he held his head with a regal elegance.

"Merlin, my man." Arthur dismounted, his cape flaring out behind him dramatically. Striding over to Jordan, Arthur enfolded him in a bear hug. "Good of you to visit."

"I'm going by Jordan now." When the back pounding was over, Jordan stepped away with an ease that belied her own tension.

Arthur's focus shifted from Jordan to Vivianne. "Introduce me to your beautiful lady."

"King Arthur Pendragon, this is Vi Blackstone, CEO of the Vesta Corporation and half owner of the *Draco*."

"Vivianne," she corrected Jordan and offered her hand to Arthur.

Arthur began to lift her hand to his lips. Jordan bristled slightly and Arthur seemed to change his mind, and instead, he shook her hand. "Welcome to Arcturus, milady." Arthur slipped his arm through hers. "Guinevere will be so happy to speak with you. She remembers the many kindnesses of your people."

So Guinevere was an alien, too? "I shall be glad to meet her, but sir, we have come a long way. And we have far to travel. Why did you bring us here?"

Arthur's eyes twinkled. "Your lady's full of fire, Merlin."

"She's stubborn as hell," Jordan said to Arthur.

"Thank you," Vivianne said and turned to Arthur. "And you, sir, avoided my question."

"So I did." He winked at her. "But the story is long and should be told over good food and savory wine."

"Can you possibly give us the short version?" Vivianne insisted.

Arthur frowned at Jordan over her head. "CEO of the Vesta Corporation, you said?"

Jordan nodded.

Arthur cocked his head to one side, his face deep in thought. "Ah, so she's a powerful, self-made woman of industry. Interesting."

Vivianne banked her frustration. For all she knew, Arthur wasn't real. However, his arm holding hers felt real. And she could smell the scent of leather, the horses, the grass.

With the news on Earth so terrible, her patience was in short supply. When another knight lifted a gauntleted hand in her direction, she almost jumped. "Would milady prefer to ride?"

"No, she wouldn't, Lancelot," Jordan growled.

Jordan almost sounded . . . jealous. Her gaze flashed to him, but he refused to meet her eyes. Still, she couldn't miss the muscle ticking in his neck or the tense set of his jaw.

Lancelot? She peered at the knight with curiosity. He was handsome, with dark hair and playful eyes.

Vivianne recalled that Lady Guinevere had fallen in love with Arthur's best friend, Lancelot. Yet the two men had an easy way about them that suggested no hard feelings. And Jordan was reacting as if he believed these men were real. Not holograms. Not messengers. And in truth, this place felt real.

She might as well have stepped back in time. And yet,

Arthur knew what a spaceship was. And he'd obviously sent those powerful cubes to fetch them.

She really wished he'd get to the point. Almost as if reading her mind, Arthur patted her arm. "Easy, milady. I brought you here because I thought I could be of some help."

"That would be much appreciated. What kind of help do you offer, sir?" she asked.

Arthur threw back his head and laughed, his gaze on Jordan. "You must have your hands full with this one."

"Actually," she countered. "I'm the one who has my hands full with him. Jordan is a man of many mysteries. And he's determined to find the Key of Soil. Might you help us with that little task?"

Arthur stopped and released her arm. "Have no fear. I have safeguarded the key for Merlin."

Vivianne saw the hope flash in Jordan's face. "So you can give it to him?"

Arthur shook his head. "Not even I can reach the key."

"A king can do what he wishes," Vivianne challenged.

"If I went after that key, Guinevere would have my head—if I didn't lose it first. And since I have no wish to end my existence, I shall leave the task to the one who is most suited for it. But right now, I have one of my oldest and dearest friends to entertain and a feast prepared. Come. Both of you. Welcome to my home. Welcome to Camelot."

One should never consent to walk when one feels the impulse to fly.

—LADY CAEL

24

As they walked inside, Vivianne saw that the castle was not exactly what she'd expected. While the high stone walls looked like they could have been built on Earth during medieval times, the floors were polished stone. Torches burned but emitted no odors or smoke. Castles on Earth were known to be drafty; this one had radiant heating in the floors. And while the clothing designs looked medieval, the fabrics were modern, self-cleaning nanotechnology.

Camelot had been Disneyfied. She imagined sparkling kitchens with gleaming technology hidden in an ancient cellar and bathrooms with hot and cold running water secreted away in some crenellated stone tower.

"Guinevere, my love." Arthur gestured to a short, pleasant-faced woman whose hair was worn in an elaborate coif riddled with pearl-seeded pins. Her gown was elaborate, golden-embroidered nanosilk. "Come meet our guests from Earth."

Guinevere held a toddler by one hand and carried a

baby on her hip. She smiled, her eyes lighting with pleasure as she joined them. "We so enjoy having guests. And
Merlin, 'tis good to see you again after so much time."

With a whoop, Lancelot lifted a curly-headed toddler
onto his broad shoulders. There could be no doubting the
little boy with dimples matching his own was Lancelot's
son. Yet Arthur wrapped a protective arm over Guinevere's shoulders and held her close to his side.

Clearly there was no jealousy between Arthur and
Lancelot. And Guinevere didn't appear the least bit uncomfortable under the adoring and loving gazes of both
men.

Arthur kissed her brow, then made introductions before
continuing to beam at the baby. "This infant is Bethany."
Arthur smiled at his daughter, and his grin remained just
as wide and proud as he held out his arms to the toddler on Lancelot's shoulders. "And this big guy is our son
Grant."

"I'm pleased to see you again, milady," Jordan said to
Guinevere, then smiled at the child. "And pleased to see
the years have been fruitful."

Guinevere actually giggled. "I now have too many children to count. In just this last century alone, I've borne
Lancelot six, Arthur five more, and three whose genetics
we have yet to determine."

"Congratulations. I've never heard you so happy," Jordan said.

And no wonder. Not only had Guinevere finally borne
the children she'd always wanted, apparently she was
married to two men. Arthur, Lancelot, and Guinevere
had worked out their love triangle to the satisfaction of
all. "I have the two best husbands," Guinevere confirmed.

"And it's a good thing, because I think I might yet again be with child."

"So soon?" Lancelot raised his eyebrows, but Vivianne could tell he was pleased and only pretending surprise.

Arthur smiled widely. "Another child is always a blessing. Come, my dearest, sit and feast with us."

The king led them to a great hall where a bard was entertaining a group of knights with a long and complicated tale about a dragon slayer, his mate, and a war. Elegant, bejeweled ladies in floor-sweeping gowns and elaborate updos gathered and chatted, while children romped and musicians played stringed instruments.

Vivianne accepted a goblet of sweet red wine and was filling her trencher from the vast assortment of turkey, pheasant, wild boar, and meat pies at the table when Arthur raised his goblet. "A toast."

His people raised their glasses. "A toast."

"To old friends." He tipped his goblet to Jordan, then to her. "And new ones. May they make all their dreams happen."

"Thank you, my friend." Jordan raised his wine and drank.

But Arthur was not done. "If not for Merlin, I would not have made it back to Arcturus alive."

His words indicated that Jordan had always known Arthur still lived. Her gaze went to him. Jordan didn't seem pleased by her look or Arthur's attention, but he took the words in good spirit. Still, Jordan had more secrets than Arthur had horses.

"No thanks are necessary." Jordan shook his head but sipped from his goblet. "Surely you haven't forgotten that you already thanked me for tripping up Trendonis so you could leave Pendragon?"

Arthur raised an eyebrow. "Of course I remember what happened with Trendonis. Hmm . . . is this a test? Perhaps you don't believe I am . . . me?"

Jordan held Arthur's gaze. "Perhaps I've forgotten what you look like."

Arthur nodded. "My friend, you didn't trip Trendonis, you pecked out his eye with your beak."

"I had to be certain, old friend." Jordan lifted his goblet and drank, obviously getting the confirmation he'd required.

"With his beak?" Vivianne's gaze focused on Jordan, but his face remained hard, unreadable.

Eyes twinkling, Arthur explained. "I'd already suffered a mortal wound, but I could not die, since I'd sipped from the Holy Grail and possessed it still. Yet with Trendonis dogging my heels, I couldn't keep the Grail with me and risk the Tribes following me home to Arcturus. So I left the Grail safe in Avalon. Still Trendonis came after me."

"And Jordan saved you?" Vivianne prodded.

"Let's not speak of the past," Jordan said in an attempt to change the subject.

But Vivianne was too curious to drop it, and Arthur obviously relished telling the tale. "Sir, finish your story, please," she asked.

"Jordan had taken the form of an owl and guarded me even then, although at the time, I did not recognize him in his new shape. When Trendonis sneaked up on me while I slept, Jordan flew down and pecked out his eye."

The knights raised their tankards in many toasts to Jordan's bravery. They drank so much, Vivianne wasn't sure if she'd ever get the answer to her question of why Arthur had brought them to Arcturus. But finally he turned serious.

Arthur clapped Jordan on the shoulder. "Brother, I owe you my kingdom and my life. While no native born Acturan may leave this world and return more than once, I have not been idle. I've spent these centuries preparing for your return. The Key of Soil is here. And I've safeguarded it so that only the great Merlin can retrieve it." Arthur's eyes turned sly and crafty. "If you trust enough, the Key of Soil shall be yours. And in addition, I will grant you a boon."

"I ask for no favors."

"Don't be so quick to turn down this one. I offer you Dominus's history."

"I don't understand." Jordan's eyes narrowed.

Guinevere explained, "On Arcturus, we're fanatical galactic record keepers. We have a memory chip about Dominus that includes your customs, your history, your science, religion, and art."

Arthur leaned forward, his ringed fingers clasped around his silver goblet. "Find the Key of Soil and all the worldly knowledge of Dominus shall also be yours."

"You *have* been busy." Jordan grinned, but the smile didn't reach his eyes.

Something was wrong. Vivianne didn't know what, but she could feel the tension in Jordan. She would have liked nothing better than a private conversation with him, but there was no opportunity.

And then it was too late.

One moment it was evening and they were dining at a sumptuous round table in Camelot surrounded by Sir

Lancelot, Lady Guinevere, King Arthur, and his knights, and the next, the castle simply vanished.

She and Jordan were standing alone, beneath the stars in a grassy field.

Vivianne shook her head in a futile attempt to clear it. "Did I just dream that we met King Arthur, Sir Lancelot, and Lady Guinevere?"

"If you did, I had the exact same vision," Jordan said.

At his admission, her gut knotted.

"But where did they go? Where did Camelot go?" she asked, trying to accept what seemed like magic. Although if Earth could transport people across the stars, she supposed a higher civilization could transport an entire city.

"They probably didn't go anywhere. It's you and me who have left Camelot." Jordan's voice was gentle, as if he understood she was having difficulty coping.

She took a step toward Jordan and almost tripped over something on the ground. "What's this?"

"I'll get a light." Their daylight was fading with the setting sun. Jordan unsheathed the Staff and shined it over the bag she'd run into.

Vivianne kneeled, opened the pack, and looked inside. "Why do we have climbing gear?" She glanced around with a frown. It might be dusk for only a few more minutes, but she could see enough to ascertain that the land was flat, filled with grass and a gentle breeze. "Where are the mountains to climb?"

Jordan sighed. "You're looking in the wrong direction. According to the Staff's pulsing, we have to go down."

"Underground?" The knots in her stomach drew tight.

Jordan shined the Staff's light into a dark spot, hidden by the grasses that she'd overlooked. "Do you see that tunnel in the ground?"

"How far does it go?" Vivianne asked, hoping her voice didn't sound as reluctant as she felt.

"I have no idea." Jordan didn't sound happy, either.

In truth, they should both be elated. After all, he'd just met his old friend, and they'd learned the Key of Soil was here on Arcturus. She should have been thrilled that they were about to find the key and move on.

Perhaps Jordan sensed something wrong, too. She could still feel the tension radiating off him.

"What's wrong?" she asked.

He dumped out the bag's contents and held up two sets of climbing gear. "I'm supposed to take you with me."

*The pessimist complains about the weather, the optimist
expects it to change, the realist brings an umbrella.*
—ANONYMOUS

25

❧

Jordan held the Staff higher and peered into the cave. He
hoped that Arthur hadn't hidden the Key of Soil so well
that even he couldn't find it. While the ground maintained
a gentle descent through a dirt tunnel braced with wooden
beams, some caves wound underground for miles. "You
ever been caving?"

"No, but right now it's easier for me than you," Vivianne said, her tone upbeat. "I can stand upright. You want
me to carry the pack?"

"Maybe later." He strode inside and inspected the dirt-
packed walls. "There are no spiderwebs, no insects, no
sounds of nocturnal creatures."

"You think this cave is as artificial as Camelot?" she
asked.

"Maybe," he mused. She caught on quick. But he still
would have preferred not to have had to bring her along.
Arthur wouldn't have sent a woman into danger unless he
believed her presence was necessary.

Yet this was not Arthur's decision, but his.

By now Jordan knew better than to try to talk Vi out of accompanying him, but if he found an opportunity to leave her safely close to the entrance, he would take it.

He glanced at her sideways, and when she showed no overt concerns, he walked deeper into the tunnel. "This cave was created by an intelligent being. But it's as clean as if it had been swept free of dust."

"Perhaps Arthur buried the Key centuries ago but only recently created this tunnel for us."

Walking hunched over, he had to crane his neck to see in front of him. Yet even this awkward position was preferable to the sudden ninety-degree right-hand turn followed by a seeming dead end. Then he looked down to see a shoulder-width black hole in the dirt.

He shined the light over the opening. The shaft appeared to be a straight vertical drop into the bedrock. "The fun starts now."

As he shrugged out of his pack, she peered into the hole, her brows furrowed. "How deep does it go?"

"Listen." He tossed a rock down the hole. In a short moment, he heard a distinctive thud that sounded fairly close to the surface.

She grinned. "That didn't sound so far."

"Unless the rock landed on a protruding ledge and didn't reach bottom."

"Maybe this won't be too hard."

Nothing on this mission had gone easy, but he kept the thought to himself. Jordan set out lines, picks, crampons, boots, carabiners, and harnesses. He handed her a hardhat and the smaller pair of boots and knee pads. "See if these fit."

She pulled on the knee pads, then the boots. "Exactly my size."

"Yeah, Arthur always was good with supply details." He adjusted the harness, clipped the carabiner into a bolt already driven into the rock, and tested the strength with a hard yank. "Feels solid."

After attaching the other end of the line to his harness, he planted his feet, backed over the hole, and leaned into the harness. Balancing his body in an L shape, he prepared to descend. "I'll take a quick look. Maybe the key's just over this lip."

"You don't believe that," she muttered. But she didn't protest. Instead she dropped to her stomach and watched him descend.

At first he had exactly the right amount of room to rest his back against one vertical wall and keep his feet planted against the other. But soon the opening narrowed, so much so that he was forced to squeeze his knees against his chest.

Another two feet and he couldn't drop any farther. He stopped and looked around with his headlamp. "There's a narrow passage off to one side that travels horizontally again."

"How far?" Her voice echoed down.

"I'll check it out and report back." He unclipped the harness.

"Fine."

As he began to crawl horizontally, Jordan realized Vi had taken Arthur's kidnapping of the *Draco* better than he would have expected. Vivianne didn't panic, and she kept an open mind—even when faced with seemingly impossible scenarios. Like coming face-to-face with King Arthur, Lancelot, and Guinevere. Like dealing with Jordan. His history and his fate. Like dealing with the inexplicable keys to the Ancient Staff. Another woman might have doubted her own sanity, but Vivianne was strong.

"Talk to me," she demanded.

"I'm crawling along. All I see is more tunnel."

"Is there plenty of air?" she asked.

"There's actually a breeze."

"How narrow's the passageway?"

"Too tight for hands and knees. I'm pulling myself forward on my elbows."

"Don't get stuck. You're too big for me to have to pull you out."

"You worried about me?" he teased.

"You get stuck down there with the Staff, and my ship won't have the power to leave Arcturus."

"I'm touched." She didn't want to admit she cared about him even a little. "From the way the Staff's pulsing, I'm getting closer."

"That's the best news I've heard all day. Well, besides the fact that Guinevere seems to be happily married to Arthur and Lancelot."

"You approve of the threesome?"

"Who am I to judge? If they are happy, and they seem to be, it's right for them."

The tunnel was narrowing again. He had to hunch his shoulders to crawl forward. "I'm glad she now has the children she always wanted."

"What about you?" she asked.

"Huh?"

"You have any children?"

At the question, he bumped his head. "You aren't trying to tell me anything, are you? Because now is really not a good time."

"I've taken precautions. We're not pregnant. And we won't be. But it's good of you to think of it *now*."

Apparently there wasn't enough time in the day for all the things he did wrong. As dirt fell onto his face, he sighed.

But suddenly up ahead the tunnel widened, and when he crawled past the tight spot, he could finally stand and wipe the dirt from his eyes. "I'm in a wide cavern. And the key's just sitting here on a granite slab under a car-sized glass dome."

"You found it!"

Approaching the glass, he touched the smooth, cool surface and tugged a handle near the top curve.

"What's happening?"

"Nothing. The handle seems stuck. Looks like I'll have to break the glass."

He picked up a rock and slammed it into the dome. Nothing broke. He kicked the glass with his crampon. Still nothing.

"What's wrong?" Vivianne asked.

"Some kind of impenetrable force field is protecting the glass." Jordan rested his hands on his hips. "Since Arthur packed equipment for both of us, I suspect that means getting past the force field to the key will require your presence down here, too."

"Happy to oblige."

Jordan recalled Vi's current position, the ten-foot drop, the long horizontal crawl. He wasn't able to help her except by talking her through it. But even after she made it down here, they still might not find a way to release the key. "Arthur also mentioned trust."

"And trust takes two people. But how did Arthur know

when he buried this key that when you came for it you wouldn't be alone?"

"I've had to accept that Arthur can do things that I can't explain." Jordan hesitated. "How much do you trust me?"

"Just tell me how to get down there." Vivianne sounded determined and focused.

Even experienced cave climbers might be uncomfortable with the tight squeeze, the falling dirt, the risk of being stuck. If asking her to come down here weren't his last option, he wouldn't have mentioned it.

"The first downward drop's easy," he told her. "Pull the harness back up, latch in, and then lower yourself. It's only about a ten-foot descent. Just take your time."

He heard her swearing. Although she muttered under her breath, sound bounced off the walls down here. "All right, I'm lowering myself."

"Easy."

"This is not easy. I'm sweating up a storm."

He forced himself to be patient, but after ten minutes he was biting his lower lip and pacing. Damn it. While he didn't want to distract her and ask about her progress, he wished she'd talk to him. Suppose she slipped? She could break her leg.

"Vi?"

"I'm down."

"Good job." He heard her breathing hard, and he shuddered. The next section was going to be so much worse.

"Take off the harness and leave it hanging so we can use it on the way back. Then find the entrance to the flat tunnel. All you need to do is crawl to me."

Clothing rustled. The harness clinked. It seemed to take forever. What was she doing?

"God. This is a wicked tight fit. Did you shapeshift to get through?"

She was breathing hard.

"I can't carry the Staff in bird shape. I crawled through, and if I fit, then so do you."

She remained silent. Too silent.

"Vi?" he asked softly.

"I can't . . . crawl through this tunnel."

"You can. Here's what you're going to do. Take off your helmet."

"But I need the light."

"You don't." He peered into his end of the tunnel, but he couldn't see her since it wasn't straight. "Now close your eyes."

"What?"

"There's no way to get lost. Just close your eyes and start belly crawling." He heard a soft groan. "Think about scooting along a sunny beach, the waves lapping offshore, the wind teasing your hair. Breathe in the sweet, clean salt air and keep moving your feet, your arms, just a few inches at a time." He kept crooning, praying she'd appear soon.

"Uh-oh."

His pulse raced. "What's wrong?"

"I banged my head. The tunnel's too small, too narrow."

"You're almost here, and then it gets wider."

"I'm going to back out. Rest, then try again."

"No!" He swore. Backing out was way too difficult. When she found out how hard it was to maneuver backward, she might really panic. "Damn it, Vi. Earth needs us to release this key. Earth needs you to keep moving forward. Crawl to me, sweetheart."

He heard her gasping for air. His hands closed into fists, and his muscles were so tense, his nerves felt ready to snap. He was long past telling himself his concern was all about the success of the mission. His fear was for her.

"I'm not your sweetheart," she muttered.

Maybe not, but the futility of fighting his own feelings for her swept over him. The woman crawling through that tunnel wasn't a specialist at caving. She was scared, and he burned with the fierce need to banish that fear.

Even anger at him was better than her fear—he didn't want her to panic and freeze in one place. He could work with anger. "Hell, you wanted to come with me, wanted to prove you're tough. Well, be tough. No more whining."

"I don't whine."

"Right." *Come on. Come on.* Where was she? "A snail could move faster," he teased over his pounding pulse. If she got stuck . . . if she panicked . . . he wouldn't be able to bear it.

When she didn't answer, he broke into a sweat. All the while he waited with thudding anxiety, praying he hadn't encouraged her for no reason.

"I need . . . a rest."

"All right, darling, you rest," he agreed. She sounded spent. While he yearned to let her do as she wished, to help her to get through, he needed to toughen up. Up to now, he'd been too kind.

He knew how to push her buttons, forced himself to manipulate her. "I've been thinking about what Arthur said and how retrieving this key would take trust."

"And?" she prodded.

At least she was listening, still curious, not panicking. "So far you've trusted me by coming down here." Jordan glanced at the written instructions branded onto the force field. "After you arrive, I'll have to trust you."

"Huh?"

"You ever hear the story of the sword and the stone?"

"Of course."

"Arthur was the only man who could free the sword, and that's how he became king. Well, I arranged for the sword to respond only to his DNA. Now he's made this challenge specific to me."

"How did he do that?"

Jordan swallowed hard. "He knows what I fear most."

"What would that be?"

He heard her clothing rustling as she pulled herself forward, and his heart lightened. When he could finally see her, praise the Goddess, he had to cling to the rock face to stop his own trembling. "You're almost here. Just a little more."

Despite telling himself that he wouldn't come to care for Vivianne Blackstone in any special way, he'd lost control. Fear for her had been slamming him for so long, he was weak with it.

Even worse, he could no longer ignore how much she meant to him. It wasn't just her passionate lovemaking. Or her bravery. Or her intelligence. It was Vivianne's spirit, one as strong as his own, that drew him and made him so eager to gather her into his arms and reassure her and himself that she was going to be all right.

She covered the last ten yards quickly, and then he was pulling her through. Hugging her tightly, he kissed her dirty, tear-streaked face, realizing anew that she'd been terrified but she'd still kept going.

He held her trembling shoulders and gazed tenderly into her eyes. "You made it. You did good."

She buried her head into his shoulder and shuddered. "I thought I was going to die in there."

"You were very brave."

"I was scared out of my mind. If you hadn't talked me through it . . ." She clutched him so hard she cut off his circulation. "We still have to crawl out."

"Don't think about that now." He smoothed her hair from her forehead, wishing he could soothe her nerves as easily. He took her hand and led her over to the key. "Here it is."

A smile brightened her face. Placing her hand on the force field, she touched the glass. "So close . . . and yet so far." She dragged in another breath, steadied herself, then looked to him. "How do we get to it?"

"Arthur said it would take trust," he reminded her. "It's time for me to give you mine."

"I don't understand."

Stomach tightening, he gestured to a flat slab of rock and they both sat. "You have to remember that when the Tribes destroyed my world, I was not yet a fully grown man, not still a boy, either, but in that awkward age between. I had great powers, but little experience and no one to guide me."

She swigged from the water bottle, then capped it. "What does that have to do with the key?"

"On Dominus we had a ritual when a man turned twenty-five. I was only twenty-one when the Tribes destroyed my world, so I wasn't yet considered an adult.

Which meant I was never told about the full ritual powers of the Ancient Staff."

"You learned on your own?" she guessed.

He nodded. "But I've learned the hard way." He sighed. "I always knew that the Staff supplied the power to dragonshape and to morph into an owl, but I didn't know what would happen when I lost the Staff. I thought I would die."

Curiosity filled her eyes. "You told me the Tribe leader, Trendonis, stole your Staff, and that's why you and Arthur failed to unite it with the Holy Grail." Her brows furrowed. "But you never said anything about what happened to you."

"Without the Staff to feed me energy to morph, I could live only as an owl." He stood and paced, his eyes fierce. "That's why when Arthur's cubes dampened our energy I had to leave you on the bridge to disengage the Staff. If I hadn't, I would have been forced back into owl form."

"Why would Arthur do that to you?"

"Those cubes were machines following their programming to bring us to Arcturus and Arthur. Machines don't know about consequences to their actions unless their programmers—"

"Point taken, but the cubes could have tried direct communication." She frowned at him, her agile mind skipping along. "You didn't want to tell me you need the Staff to stay human because I might take advantage of your weakness?"

He nodded. "The last time someone knew what the Staff meant to my survival, they arranged to steal it. I was in owl form for fifteen hundred years."

"You spent all those centuries as an owl . . . God. I'm

so sorry." Her hand went to her mouth. "I don't blame you for keeping that a secret."

"There's more. My people believe the Staff is a life form. Our evolution is symbiotic with our Staff. It gives me power. I'm uncertain what I give it. Some of our people believe it may feed off of human emotions. But there's a third factor. With the keys missing from the Staff for so long, the Staff might not be working at optimum. I don't really know."

"Are you saying we may have come all this way to retrieve the keys for nothing? That the absence of the keys for so long may have damaged the Staff so it might not unite with the Grail?"

He shrugged. "It seems fine. Supposedly those Keys are indestructible. Everything should work exactly as planned." He couldn't contain his frustration. "But there are things about the Staff I should know that I don't. Like why it makes us pulse with lust. Like how it controls the elements of Earth, Space, and Wind."

"All this information is fascinating, but"—she glanced toward the glass dome—"how are we going to get that key? And can you read the writing on the force field?"

"It's written in my birth language. It says, 'Blocked trust is the reason for blighted dreams.' "

"I'm not sure I understand."

"For us to succeed, we must trust each other. I've trusted you by revealing my weakness." He spun and faced her, locking gazes. "Now it's your turn. What have you been keeping from me?"

The universe opens the door. You enter by yourself.
                                    —LADY OF THE LAKE

26

Stomach churning, Vivianne stared back at him and licked her lower lip. "You don't even know if *trust* will bring down the force field."

"That's true. I'm just following Arthur's words. And interpreting the instructions there." He gestured to the force field with the alien inscription.

"If he wanted you to have the key, he should have just told you what to do."

"He did." Jordan sounded so sure, but nothing was that simple. Not with men who'd lived for hundreds and hundreds of years. Not with the forces at work trying to destroy Earth.

She yearned to trust him. But she had to think without letting her emotions come into play. Or did she? Vivianne often relied on her gut instincts in business. But Jordan was difficult to read.

She hesitated. "You must realize I've always suspected you were one of the moles the government warned us about?"

"I hate the Tribes as much as you do. They ruined Dominus, killed everyone I know."

Stolen the Staff and kept him trapped in an owl form for over a thousand years. It was a wonder he'd retained his sanity.

"Surely you don't still believe I'm a spy for the Tribes?"

She could see the pain in his eyes, hear it in his voice. His shoulders stiffened, as if her lack of trust hurt him. Yet even as he tightened up, his voice remained calm and level. "The Tribes cannot dragonshape."

"So *you* say." Frustration gnawed at her. "How do I know that you didn't create Arthur, the Keys, this entire scenario, just to foil any chance Earth has to go after the Grail?"

His voice turned harsh and cold. "Are you forgetting I designed almost every system on the *Draco* just to give us a chance to go after the Grail?"

"I haven't forgotten," she kept her tone as soft and as nonconfrontational as possible. "But what better way to derail Earth than to subsidize our only hope, then ensure our failure?"

He raised an eyebrow. "Since then I've had many opportunities to take the Staff and leave you stranded."

He also would have left himself stranded.

She hugged her legs to her chest. "Eventually, I would have found another way to power the *Draco*."

"Maybe, but by then Earth will fall to the Tribes." He sighed. "Nothing I can say will convince you. But think of this—don't you believe I could have arranged to sabotage the *Draco* and make certain that neither you nor my engineers ever saw Earth again, without blowing myself up along with you?"

With his abilities, he had the knowledge to compromise any one of a dozen systems. But had he compromised her judgment? Had he somehow inserted those memories into her mind to sway her perceptions?

Her lack of trust was hurting him. When it came down to it, words didn't mean as much as actions. Jordan had saved her life several times. He'd saved the ship, and she sensed that if she didn't give him her trust, she'd be burning her bridges with him.

She'd come to care about him, more than she should. She didn't want to trade barbs. She didn't want to question why she was falling for him when they had no possible future together. She shouldn't trust him. But deep down in her heart, she did. Possibly she always had—even after she'd learned how he'd lied to her on his employment application, she'd still trusted him on an instinctive level.

Raising her head, she looked him straight in the eyes. "I have memories of yours, ones you haven't shared with me." She swallowed hard. "For a long time, I thought you might be planting false memories in my mind to get me to believe in you."

"I wouldn't do that." His eyes gleamed with a light she'd never seen before. Luminous, brilliant, they glittered a warmth she could feel across the cave. "In fact, the same things happened to me. I have memories of you buying a necklace for a birthday present for your mother."

Vi gasped. He was telling the truth. She'd never told anyone the painful story of that necklace. And if he was getting some of her memories, she wasn't losing her mind—or her judgment. A weight lifted from her chest. "Why do we have some of each other's memories? Is the Staff responsible?"

"I thought the memories might be connected to love-making," he admitted. "But one time, the memory came when we hadn't done anything."

"I saw you as a boy. You wanted to win the prize of spending the summer at a special training camp. But you threw the race so a friend could win."

"I'd forgotten about that." Jordan smiled an easy smile. "His father had never seen him race. He'd always been too busy working to make a living."

"So you lost so he could win with his father watching?" She leaned into him and placed a kiss on his mouth. "That was kind."

He wrapped his arms around her. "I have the memory of your parents' deaths. I felt your pain. Your fear of being alone. By the Goddess, I don't want you ever to feel that alone again."

"What else do you know?" She clung to him, raised her head, and locked gazes with him. It felt good to tell him her secret. Because now she felt as if she had an ally. Because the warmth in his eyes told her that he, too, had feelings he didn't want to admit.

"I saw you picking a lock to feed little children."

"And I saw your world destroyed," she told him. "And I don't want the same thing to happen to Earth. We have to stop the Tribes."

With a sizzle, the force field suddenly zapped with bright, bluish-white stars. She stared as the entire dome turned into a three-dimensional star field.

Jordan stepped over to the glass.

"Don't touch it," she murmured.

He paid no attention, lifting the dome. The Staff also pulsed with the bluish stars, a spiraling aura, an alien energy field that suddenly surrounded Jordan. His expression turned inward as the field took hold of him, surrounding him in a brilliant blue vortex.

The hair on the back of her neck raised. Everything inside her was shrieking at her to run. To get away from those devastating blue lights. Vivianne was practically jumping out of her skin.

"Jordan!" she cried. "Where's the off switch?"

He didn't appear to hear.

A crackling sound caught her attention, the energy swirling faster as Jordan retrieved the Key of Soil. The shimmer shined so brightly she had to hold her hand up to block the light, and still she had to squint.

"Jordan, talk to me," she pleaded.

But he didn't say a word. Was the energy hostile and killing him? Or was he simply absorbing the energy?

Vivianne had no idea what to do. Those hellish bluish glows looked ethereal, otherworldly. She didn't have a clue how to make them go away.

Jordan wasn't moving. Not blinking.

Backing away, holding her hand to her mouth, she stood dazed and uncertain.

As quickly as the light had turned on, it faded.

The light released its hold over him, and Jordan slumped to the cave's floor, unconscious, the key and Staff dropping from his hands.

Oh, God. Was he dead?

She rushed over. His flesh was clammy, and when she opened one of his eyes, his pupil was dilated and didn't react at all. Placing a finger to his neck, she felt for a pulse. Nothing.

His hearts weren't beating. His chest didn't move up and down. He wasn't breathing.

Vivianne rolled him to his back, slammed her fist onto his hearts, and began to compress his chest. She pumped hard several times, tilted back his head, pinched his nose closed, and breathed into his mouth.

"Come on, breathe, damn you, breathe."

For five minutes she performed CPR, the entire time tears streaming down her cheeks. So help her, if Arthur had sent them into a trap to die, she'd crawl out of this tunnel, find the bastard, and kill him herself.

"Jordan, you can't leave me." She pumped his chest, her breath coming in gasps.

And still he didn't respond.

She kept up the CPR until her arms ached and she grew light-headed from lack of air. Finally, she rocked back on her heels, the sudden loss sinking in. He wasn't responding. There was nothing more to do.

Jordan was gone.

A sob broke from her chest. She'd always known she would eventually lose him, but she'd never thought it would be this soon. Or that her agony and outrage would leave her shaking and sickened.

The cave grew dim. Without the Staff's bright light, she would soon be left in total blackness.

If she didn't act, this cave might become her tomb.

The idea of squeezing through that tunnel in total pitch blackness should have made her numb with fear. But the sorrow in her heart overwhelmed her. She was so weary. Somehow she had to summon the strength to shove to her feet.

Jordan was dead, and if she didn't crawl out, she'd die

with him. But she couldn't push to her feet, so she crawled over to Jordan to say a final goodbye.

She brushed against the Staff and it rolled away. Instinctively, she grabbed it and placed it in Jordan's hand, knowing the Staff was part of him and they belonged together for eternity.

His face was so still. The stubble of his beard shadowed his jaw. With his eyes closed, he looked as if he slept.

She prayed he'd find the peace he'd never had in life.

Goodbye, my love, she thought, admitting the truth too late. She'd loved this man. She'd just been too stubborn to see it. After he'd told her they could have no future, she'd denied her feelings. But it had done no good. How many precious moments had she wasted fighting the obvious?

Too damn many.

She should have grabbed every opportunity they'd had. Now it was too late.

"I'm sorry," she whispered. Finally, forcing herself to stand, she staggered toward the tunnel and tripped over the Key of Soil. The key glowed with only the dimmest of light, and the Ancient Staff was pale, too; the objects were dying with Jordan.

Bending, she scooped up the Key of Soil. Turning back, the key clutched in her hand, she snapped it into place at the bottom of the Ancient Staff. Then, hearts aching, she kissed Jordan on the mouth one final time. "Sleep in peace."

Feeling hollow and weary and discouraged, she turned and headed toward the tunnel.

Don't leave me.

Was she hallucinating? Hearing things that couldn't possibly be true?

I'm still here.

He was dead.

Not anymore.

She spun around to stare at Jordan and thought his pinky might have twitched. But his chest wasn't moving. Without a heartbeat, without breath for the last ten minutes, he couldn't be communicating with her telepathically.

Hoping for a miracle, she returned to his side, leaned over his mouth, and listened for a breath. "Jordan?"

Nothing.

"Jordan." She shook him. "I can hear you in my mind, like when we're dragons and telepathic. What do you need me to do?"

Take the Staff and insert it into the dome. She heard the words clearly in her mind.

With a feeling of dawning wonder, she picked up the Staff. But she paused by the dome. Jordan's touching that glass had caused those blue lights to envelop him. If she reached inside, would those blue stars attack her?

I wouldn't ask you to do something that would hurt you.

She spun around to look at him. He hadn't moved. He still didn't appear to be breathing.

Jordan was dead. She should be leaving—not reaching into the machine that had killed him.

Vi. Please believe. It's me. Warmth and gentle encouragement flooded her, and she felt bathed in his aura. But now that there was more of a reason to panic, she felt oddly calm. Because no one called her Vi. No one but Jordan.

"How did you get into my head?" she asked.

It's a pretty complicated head, Vi. You have a beautiful mind. For once, it's going to be all right.

Nothing might ever be right again. Jordan had died, and she was losing her mind. The stress, the heartache were too much to bear. She should ignore the voice in her head and just get out of here.

That would be a mistake.

"A mistake?"

For Earth.

"Please," she whispered. "Just tell me what's going to happen if I place the Staff inside that dome."

I don't know.

"That thing killed you."

I'm not dead.

She stared at his body. "You aren't breathing. You don't have a pulse."

She could feel amusement wafting along with his mental communication. *Vi, you don't talk to dead people, do you?*

With a shrug, she leaned over the dome. Inside was a housing similar to the one Jordan had built on the *Draco*. Holding her breath, expecting to be zapped by blue lights, she snapped the Staff into the housing.

She stared hard at the domed glass. But although the Staff pulsed more brightly, those blue stars didn't reappear. Slowly, she released a breath.

At the rustle of a footstep behind her, the hair on her neck stood up. She was no longer alone.

If it weren't for the last minute, nothing would get done.

—HONORIAN WARLORD

27

Spinning around, Vivianne eyed Jordan. He was standing, walking toward her in jerky steps like some zoned-out, nonbreathing zombie. Horrified, she edged away until her backside smacked up against the cave wall. That thing coming toward her was not her Jordan, who moved with the smooth grace of a panther. What had happened to the man she loved? Was he still there inside somewhere and fighting to get out?

When she'd felt for his pulse, had it only been weak and she'd missed it? Had he gone into some kind of hibernation? Suspended animation? Because he was now very much alive.

And the blue light shimmering in his eyes was the same. He spoke in his familiar deep voice. "It's me."

"Jordan?"

"I just short-circuited. And I haven't regained complete use of my muscles after the shock to my system."

Afraid to hope, she folded her arms across her chest to stop her shaking. Torn between hope and fear and terror, she forced the words from her mouth. "Y-you still aren't breathing."

"Huh?" One side of Jordan's forehead wrinkled. "What are you talking about?"

"Your chest isn't moving." She pressed harder against the wall, wishing it would open up an escape route.

He looked down and placed his hand over his chest. Then his puzzled eyes jerked to her. "You're right. I'm not breathing." Reaching for his chin and missing the first time, he finally rubbed his jaw. "I no longer seem to require oxygen."

Astonished, overwhelmed, afraid to believe he'd survived, she stared at him. "How's that . . . possible?"

"I don't know."

He combed his fingers through his hair, but a stubborn lock fell on his forehead, in a gesture she recognized from whenever he was trying to solve a puzzle. His movements were more coordinated now, almost normal. But he wasn't normal. He wasn't breathing. But she'd never realized how the simple movement of breathing humanized a person. Without his chest rising and falling, Jordan looked stiff, forbidding. Alien. This couldn't be her Jordan. Could it?

Yet if by some miracle he'd come back to her, she could adjust. Adapt. Be grateful for the gift of life.

She was judging Jordan by normal human laws of nature. This man had turned into an owl.

Jordan held out his hand to her. "We need to leave."

She looked down . . . and placed her hand in his. "Will removing the Staff hurt you?"

"I'd rather not find out." He raised an eyebrow. "At least until I know you're safely back aboveground." He leaned over the glass dome, and then he climbed inside and settled next to the Staff, which pulsed a little more strongly.

"What are you doing?" Had the lack of oxygen damaged his brain cells? She tried to contain her worry.

He gestured for her to come over. "Join me."

She glanced at the tunnel. "We need to leave."

He leaned back at an angle, and the glass supported him. Then he patted a flat piece of glass between his thighs. "There's room for you to sit right here."

She folded her arms across her chest. "Why would I want to sit in there?"

"Besides keeping me company?" he teased. "We can ride out of here in luxury."

"There's no motor." She pointed out the obvious.

"Don't need one," he insisted. When she frowned, he gestured to the Key of Soil. "We have all the power we need."

She recalled his story of how the Key of Space had turned a rusted space relic into a shiny new ship. She'd also seen the Key of Wind tame a hurricane on Tempest. So she supposed it was silly to think that the glass done was no more than what it looked like—a big empty glass dome.

She climbed in, and Jordan helped her settle. She tried not to think about how good it felt to touch his warmth, or how solid and secure she felt perched between his muscular thighs.

Then Jordan closed the dome above their heads with a click. Without making another sound, the glass dome lifted off the cave's floor. She held her breath. Would it jump into hyperspace? Transport them directly to the surface? Was the damn thing going to make her stop breathing, too?

She was wrong on all three guesses. The dome simply lifted straight through the rock, cutting through layers of bedrock, limestone, and dirt as if taking them up an elevator shaft.

"How is this possible?" she asked, staring through the glass as the Staff lit up just enough for her to see them slowly rise foot by foot.

"I'll have a much better idea after Arthur gives us the Dominus history."

"Why?"

"We might find some information on the Ancient Staff and the Keys."

Hope and frustration filled his voice, making him seem more like the Jordan she knew before he'd been swallowed by blue lights, died, and come back to life.

After they reached the surface, Jordan opened the dome and she climbed out. It was nighttime, but the starlight shined brightly over the fields of grain. He removed the Ancient Staff and folded it back into his sheath. As the glass dome sank back into the Earth, she spied the *Draco*. "Home, sweet home."

Jordan took her hand and squeezed. "Thanks for saving me."

"You're welcome." She had not forgotten her sorrow when she'd believed he'd died. Or her realization of how much he meant to her. Yet her chest remained tight and her nerves on edge. "How do you feel?"

He faced her and caressed her cheek. "You sure you want to know?"

"Yes." A few minutes earlier, she hadn't wanted to hear one more strange or incomprehensible thing. But now that she was aboveground with her ship in sight, she rolled her shoulders to ease the tension and faced him.

"I'm different. There's a part of me that I now have access to, new abilities I never knew I had." His voice was soft, thoughtful, as if he understood her curiosity and her wariness.

"What kinds of abilities?" she asked, trying to keep her fear from showing in her voice.

"Could you explain to a blind man the difference between red and yellow?"

"Beyond mathematical equations? Probably not." She gazed at him, troubled, her pulse racing. "Are you saying you can't even tell me what about you has changed?"

"Such impatience. Give me a chance to get a handle on things. I'm not even sure if I understand what's happened to me. Then I have to find the right words. It's like suddenly finding a new set of muscles and learning what I can do with them." Anger threaded his tone.

"What's upsetting you?" She shot him a level look, hoping he couldn't read her anxiety.

"If the Tribes hadn't destroyed my home, if Trendonis hadn't stolen the Staff, I wouldn't have spent centuries without these abilities. My people would have taught me . . . how to live like this."

Like what, exactly? She wanted to press him, but he'd asked her to give him time to figure it out himself. So she would do that.

Although his tone remained whispery soft, she sensed both wonder and fury seething inside him. She couldn't blame him. The Tribes had destroyed his family, his world, his birthright, and part of Jordan's self. There was no end to their evil.

Now that Jordan was whole, not only could he fully see what had been done to him, he was different. This Jordan was not the same man she'd known before. The differences were subtle, but he seemed both older and younger. Older because he was more self-contained yet more willing to be open with her. Younger because he was practically vibrating with eagerness and anticipation.

She recalled how he hadn't just connected with her telepathically back in the cave. When she'd believed him dead, he'd responded to her thoughts. He'd read her mind. "Can you still read my mind?"

"Do you want me to?" he countered, his tone a soft caress.

The Jordan she'd known had avoided her questions by countering with questions of his own. But this Jordan sounded sincere. "Do my wishes matter?"

"Of course. I'll only read your mind . . . if you invite me in." Jordan sealed his promise with a kiss to her forehead.

"Down in the cave, I didn't invite you in," she murmured.

"I apologize." He bowed with a formality that she'd never seen before. "I didn't have full control of myself then. I was still integrating the old me with the new me."

Hearts aching, she narrowed her eyes. "How much of the old you is still there?"

He chuckled, his tone warm and sultry. "I've lost nothing." He murmured into her ear. "I still remember exactly what you like."

His lips tickled her ear, but his warm breath didn't fan her neck. She hadn't realized how much such a simple thing would rattle her. She stiffened, then forced herself to relax. This was Jordan. He was alive and charming and sexy as hell.

But he was different, too.

"Did Arthur change you?" She still didn't understand what had happened down there and needed to make sense of it.

"Arthur played a part by finding the Key of Soil. But you did more."

"Me?"

"When you placed the Staff in the housing, you completed a circuit. With all three Keys in place, the Ancient Staff could draw on cosmic energy to revive me."

"Those blue lights I saw inside you were cosmic energy?" Her jaw dropped, and she couldn't stop staring at him. He looked the same. He sounded the same. His touch felt the same.

But she wasn't responding to him like she had before. Once she'd believed Jordan was just a brilliant employee. When she'd seen him change into an owl, she'd accepted he had unusual powers. But now she suspected he had godlike powers.

He could read her mind, and while he'd said he would do so only if she invited him in, she didn't know if she believed him. She wasn't certain she wanted to know all his abilities.

Not yet. Maybe not ever.

She wasn't that evolved. She wasn't ready to have someone know her every thought. Sometimes she was selfish. Got angry for no reason. Had doubts she didn't want to share. She couldn't imagine anyone liking her if they could read all the things that went through her mind.

But Jordan had already done so, and he still accepted her. Still wanted her. She could tell from his gentle touch that he knew she had doubts. But if he could read all that she was and still want her, she could do no less.

They'd been given a second chance. This time she didn't intend to waste it.

She lifted her mouth to his. "You still like making love, don't you?"

Crushing her to him, he angled his mouth down for a kiss. He didn't bother with nibbling. He took what he wanted right off, without any hesitation.

There was something very powerful about a man who could sweep her off her feet, and as he kissed her, her doubts fell away. Ignoring the past, putting aside the future, this moment was for them. She was going to take this time with Jordan and enjoy it.

When she'd been in foster homes, she'd planned how to go to college. While attending college, she'd planned her career. Once she'd founded Vesta, she was always looking down the road. All her planning had brought her unimaginable success. Yet . . . she hadn't stopped often enough to enjoy the perfect moments like this one with Jordan.

His mouth on hers was deliciously tempting, utterly sensual. She loved the way he smelled, even when dusted with dirt. Jordan's scent was all male heat. His scent was life.

Wrapping her fingers around his neck, she leaned into him, appreciating the hard muscles of his chest. But most of all she enjoyed how protected and cherished he made her feel, as if she was the center of his universe.

Having his total attention focused on her wasn't only thrilling and exhilarating, it turned her on. His wanting her seemed so natural, so uncomplicated. So justifiable.

His lips on hers were both hard and soft. As they kissed, her blood thrummed through her veins with a bubbly effervescence that intoxicated her. She wanted to tell him how good he was making her feel. She ached to tell him she loved him. But she couldn't find the strength to pull her lips from his kiss.

But finally, she had to come up for air. "*I* still need to breathe," she reminded him.

His chest lifted and fell, and he sighed.

She grinned. "Are you breathing again?"

"I'm faking it," he admitted and nipped her neck.

"You would do that for me?"

"There's not much I wouldn't do for you."

How could she not love this man? Under the starlight, the night took on magical qualities. All outside influences—Earth, the Tribes, Arthur, and the crew—vanished.

Her world consisted only of one wish—making love to Jordan. With her heart full, she was going to show him exactly how she felt.

As they kissed, she unfastened his shirt, smoothed it over his shoulders, and ran her palms over his broad chest. Damn, he felt so good. Vibrant. Alive.

As she caressed his chest, his nipples tightened and she played lightly with the tips.

Breaking her lips from his, she nuzzled his neck, sipping in his musky scent, teasing his flesh until she dropped her head and took a nipple into her mouth. Laving with her tongue, she trailed her hands lower and undid his pants. In almost no time at all, he stood before her nude, his sex hard.

But she had more to give before she allowed herself the prize. She released his nipple only to take his other one between her teeth. Capturing him, she held him still.

When he thrust his hands into her hair, his fingers tensing on her scalp, she slipped her hands over his tight butt.

Using her palms to swirl circles on his cheeks, while her tongue mimicked the swirls on his chest, she could feel him tightening. Good. She wanted him on edge. Hungry to see what she would do next.

Content to keep their progress slow and steady, she spent a long time exploring his ass. She slid her hands over the top curves, enjoying his tight flesh, the way his hips began to grind. But she wasn't done with him . . . and slid her hands over his hips.

She cupped his balls, which were wickedly firm, tight. She caressed him where he was soft, enjoyed the quiver that overtook him, that told her how much he was enjoying her touch.

Feeling powerful, feminine, she released his nipple and nipped her way down his ribs. All the while, her hands stayed busy, stroking him into a seething need. When she finally dipped her head and took the tip of his sex into her mouth, he released a small groan.

"Enough." He grabbed her shoulders and lifted her to her feet. He kissed her lips once again. At the same time, he slowly removed her clothes, not in a wild rush, but methodically, taking his time, using the excuse of disrobing her to touch and tease and taunt.

When they both stood naked under the stars, she leaned into his heat. "Whatever happens, I will never forget you or our time together."

He nodded, his eyes burning into hers. "I wish I could give you more."

"Tonight we shall make enough memories for a lifetime," she promised him. Those memories would never be enough. No matter how special this night, no matter how good they'd be together, she'd always yearn for more. Which made tonight even more special.

Jordan scooped her into his arms and laid her down on the pile of clothes they'd tossed onto the grass. Then he joined her, kissing her ear, her neck, her collarbone.

"Do you want me?" he murmured.

She giggled. "Now I know you're *not* reading my mind." Because if he was, he'd know that she was damp, the moisture seeping between her thighs.

"Say the words. Tell me you want me," he demanded.

"I want you."

As if her statement gave him permission, he slid between her parted thighs, entering her, filling her.

Blue lights danced before her eyes. At first she thought the lights came from the heavens, but then she realized that the lights she'd seen inside Jordan back in the cave had returned.

She stiffened, and he slipped his arms around her. "It's all right. The lights are part of us now."

"Us?"

She should be terrified. But she wasn't. He was still Jordan, and his hands skimmed over her chest, then down her hip to twine into her curls and open her folds, and she moaned with a pleasure she didn't understand.

Because not only could she feel how good his fingers felt, she could also feel *her* warm, slick heat on *his* fingers. Her warmth surrounding his sex. It wasn't just double the pleasure, it was so much more than two halves of the whole.

She was feeling from both sides. His and hers. It was a glorious sensation. Mind-blowing pleasure.

And when she burned, so did he.

A man can succeed at almost anything for which he has unlimited enthusiasm.

—KING ARTHUR PENDRAGON

28

Jordan awakened to find Vi against his side. Her breath fanned his ear, and she entwined her legs with his. He wrapped his arm around her and nestled her closer, wishing he never had to let her go. He didn't know what the hell had hit him in that tunnel. But being inside Vivianne's mind for that brief instant troubled him. The last time in the cave was different than the single incidents he'd gotten from her before. He'd had free access . . . to everything.

The wind blew a tendril of her hair across his forehead. And he no longer needed to breathe to recognize her scent.

She opened her eyes and smiled at him. "You okay?"

"Yes." He kissed her cheek.

She held his gaze. "How're you doing with your new abilities?"

She understood that he was no longer the same man who'd entered that tunnel. Yet she'd made love with him.

But he'd also read her thoughts. Until she knew exactly what he was, she might love him—but she had doubts.

While on the one hand he wanted her to love him . . . on the other, it would only bring her heartache.

"I'm adapting," he said. "How about you?"

"I'm getting there."

With a sigh of frustration, he understood that if any human could accept his true self, it was Vivianne. She was so open-minded and adaptable, a truly exceptional woman. But as alluring as he found her, he had to find the strength to keep from creating any deeper bonds, because that would be a path to disaster.

Vi caressed his chest. She lifted her head to kiss his neck.

Desire spiraled. His abilities might have changed . . . but his fate remained the same. Once he united the Holy Grail and the Ancient Staff, he would cease to live. So the more distance he could keep between them, the less she would feel the loss.

With a groan, he rolled away.

She yanked him back. "What's your hurry? Don't you want me?"

Over a thousand years of pent-up frustration made him growl. "Don't do this. Don't do this to us."

As much as he yearned to deepen and broaden their connection, to merge their bodies and minds in the Dominus custom, he could not permit himself more indulgence.

Pain filled her eyes. "You told me there is no us."

"I'm sorry. I haven't changed my mind." He clenched and unclenched his fingers. "I wish I had a choice that included you in my future."

His words might have just caused him to lose his one opportunity to bond with a woman in the manner of his people, but better he should suffer than Vi. For if the bond was complete, her life would never be the same.

Vivianne's face paled but she took his hand and squeezed it. "No one knows the future. We'll have to make do with the present."

At the sound of horses' hooves, Jordan rolled them off their clothes. "Someone's coming. Get dressed."

He stepped into his pants, then helped Vi into her own clothes.

"Who's out there?" Eyes heavy-lidded from lack of sleep, lips raw from his kisses, she tucked her shirt into her pants, brushed off the dirt, and stuffed her panties into a pocket.

He peeked above the grass. "It's Arthur."

He was about to stand when she grabbed his belt and pulled him down beside her. "Arthur almost got you killed. We shouldn't let him know we're here."

"He already knows." Jordan questioned how he knew that. It was almost as if he had a new sense, a way of putting things together in his brain that he couldn't yet explain. "But thanks for worrying about me."

"Somebody has to," she murmured and stood. "You attract trouble like a dust magnet."

Arthur, wearing full armor, reined in his horse and dismounted. "Did your woman just call me trouble?"

Jordan grinned. "Sire, she was complaining about my shirt." He flapped it, and dirt flew everywhere.

Vivianne placed her fists on her hips, lifted her chin, and glared at Arthur. "Your little plan got him killed."

"*Killed?*" Arthur blinked, his confusion genuine. "Has she gone mad?"

Jordan shook his head and took a moment to appreciate how magnificent she looked. Eyes flaring with anger, her hair curled all sexily over her shoulders, she was defending him.

"I'm mad all right." Vivianne marched up to Arthur's horse. "You're lucky I don't have a—"

"Vi," Jordan interrupted. "Arthur found the key for me. He's kept it safeguarded for centuries."

"And thanks to him, you no longer have to breathe." Vivianne glared at Arthur.

Arthur raised an eyebrow and looked to Jordan for answers.

Jordan changed the subject. "Sire, why are you here?"

"As promised, here's the information on Dominus." Arthur plucked a data chip from the folds of his cloak and tossed it to Jordan.

Vivianne folded her arms across her chest. "Have you anything else for us?"

Arthur frowned. "Excuse me?"

"Surely there's more you can do to help us defeat the Tribes?" She squared her shoulders and challenged him.

Arthur refused to meet her gaze.

Interesting. Vivianne was on to something that Jordan hadn't considered. But what? "Arthur?"

"I'm not supposed to take sides." Arthur grimaced and gave them a lame shrug.

Jordan glared. "What the hell are you talking about? You gathered the Knights of the Round Table on Earth to fight the Tribes. I fought at your side. You sent those cubes and Devid to us so we'd find Tempest and the Key of Wind, and you protected the Key of Soil for me."

"I've already told you that every Arcturian is allowed to leave only once. During that time, we are free to do as we wish. But once we return, we can no longer interfere with the affairs outside this realm."

"You can't?" Vivianne pressed. "Or you won't?"

Arthur held out his arms to her. "I've done all that I can."

Jordan expected her to slap Arthur's hands away. But Vivianne surprised him by changing tactics.

She took Arthur's hands and held them. "Jordan saved your life."

"He did." Arthur cocked his head to one side. A smile played over his lips.

"You haven't forgotten?"

"We forget nothing. We're the galaxy record keepers."

Vivianne's eyes pleaded. "So tell us something useful. Like where's the Holy Grail? How can we defeat the Tribes? Are there other worlds out there who would ally themselves with us?"

Arthur spoke over her head to Jordan. "She speaks like a warrior."

"I'm trying to save my world," she countered softly, drawing Arthur's attention back to her. "Please."

Arthur's eyes sparkled, his lips quirking into a huge grin. "'Tis a good thing you make ready to depart." He winked at Jordan. "Or I might be inclined to stray from my Guinevere."

Jordan braced, ready to step in and stop Vivianne from slapping the man. But instead, she laughed. "And, sir, I might be tempted. I always knew King Arthur was a hero, but I didn't know he would be so charming."

Jordan didn't move a muscle. Vivianne was playing Arthur. But would the man fall for it?

Perhaps.

Arthur leaned forward and kissed her on the cheek. Then he whispered into her ear.

Vivianne's laughter stayed on her lips. But her eyes stopped smiling. It wasn't until after Arthur departed that Jordan asked her what had been said.

"Weakness will strengthen you," Vivianne repeated. "What does that mean?"

Jordan wished he knew.

A patriot must always be ready to defend his country.
—GEORGE BERNARD SHAW

29

Vivianne was looking forward to contacting Earth to find out the latest developments. Anything to take her mind off this new Jordan would be a huge relief. Because while she still loved him, she wasn't certain if she could live with him. Before his death and rebirth, he'd been difficult. But now he seemed so certain of himself, she didn't know if she could still feel independent.

She wasn't the kind of woman who turned to a man for answers. While she'd never hesitated to take his engineering advice, and she'd be stupid not to take advantage of his new powers to defeat the Tribes, she wanted to be autonomous.

When she heard the shouts up ahead, she automatically changed direction from her quarters to the bridge. She'd never heard this much shouting aboard the *Draco* before, and curiosity had her almost running. But once she could see the bridge, she skidded to a halt.

The sight was so normal, it rocked her back onto her heels and she grinned. During the captains' absence, the crew had moved a Ping-Pong table onto the bridge.

Ponytail swinging, Knox was playing at the opposite end of the table from Darren. But the shocker was seeing the Boston terrier jumping over the net from side to side chasing the Ping-Pong ball. The crew were all laughing, shouting for George to get the ball.

"Fetch," Knox encouraged the dog.

Leaping happily over the net, George twisted and turned, his mouth just missing the ball before Knox lobbed it back to Darren.

"Fetch." Darren hit the ball back across the table.

Vivianne couldn't stop her own laughter at George's comical antics.

At the sight of the captains, the game stopped. George finally caught the ball in his mouth, then leapt off the table into Vivianne's arms.

One glance at Jordan and Vivianne understood why the game had ended. Jordan was bristling beside her, his eyes fierce, his lips thinned.

Despite his reaction, she saw no harm in the game. The crew had needed time to regroup, and they'd be sharper if they were more relaxed.

She petted George. "I didn't know you were so talented."

"He just leapt onto the table," Knox told her, then glanced at Jordan's frown. "Should we get ready to leave?"

"Yes."

"Where are we heading?" Gray asked, already moving toward the bridge while the others folded up the table.

"Earth," Jordan announced, shocking Vivianne, but she didn't question him in front of the others.

However, she didn't like the hard look in his eyes. She knew that look, and her gut churned. What was he up to? Why the change in plans? They were supposed to be heading straight to Pentar and into Tribe territory for the Grail.

"I'm heading to our cabin to freshen up," she announced and then took George with her. Her words didn't fool Jordan. She could feel him staring at her back. If he wanted to hear Maggie's news report about Earth, he'd have to follow her, and then she'd make sure they had a private chat.

He might have some kind of new superpowers, but that didn't mean she'd follow his lead without any explanations. So she marched off to the cabin.

She'd barely opened the panel when she felt the *Draco* lifting off into space. Vivianne tried to settle George on her lap, but he wanted to play, releasing the Ping-Pong ball into her hand.

"Fetch." She grinned and tossed the ball where it rolled under the bed. George crawled under and brought the Ping-Pong ball back to her with a wiggle of his short tail. "Good boy."

Vivianne opened a channel on the hyperspace communicator and spoke into the mic. "Hey, Maggie, you there?"

"Vivianne Blackstone?" Lucan Roarke's voice came through the speaker, and Vivianne recognized him immediately. As he was the archeologist who'd figured out that King Arthur had come to Earth from the Pendragon moon, his perspective would be invaluable. And since he was married to Cael, the Pendragon spiritual leader, he would have news from two worlds.

"Lucan, I'm so glad you have a hypercom unit," Vivianne told him. "Is Maggie all right?"

"She's fine. It's just too bad we couldn't get a unit to Rion as you instructed." Lucan paused. "There have been some complications."

"The Tribes?" she guessed, her pulse escalating.

Jordan walked through the door, and she turned to him. "I'm talking to Lucan."

Lucan spoke quickly. "The Tribes have shut down our transporter. Earth's isolated."

Jordan leaned over Vivianne, his hand on her shoulder. "How did they shut it down?"

"We're working on it. But we suspect one of the soldiers guarding Stonehenge was compromised."

"You've questioned him?" Vivianne asked.

"Yes. He's not talking, but two men are dead. One's vanished. But that's the least of our worries. We're panicking down here. Everyone suspects everyone else of working for the Tribes. Soldiers are deserting their units, and the police can't contain the civilian problems. I'm back in Florida at the family homestead. In Europe, there's chaos. No news is coming out of Asia, and the last we heard from Pendragon were reports that the Tribes were gathering to make one final attack on Earth."

"So would you recommend that we come home?" Vivianne asked.

"Not until you have the Grail." Lucan's voice was grim.

Lucan had once held the Grail in his hands. But when the Tribes had captured the woman he'd loved, he'd sacrificed it to save Cael. Vivianne knew that choice still haunted him, and she wanted to give him good news. "We now have all three Keys to the Ancient Staff. Hopefully we'll find the Holy Grail soon."

Lucan sighed. "Although the government announced your mission, you may still have surprise on your side. No one will expect you to fly straight into the heart of Tribe territory."

"We'll do our best," she promised.

"Look, I hate to put any more pressure on you, but if you don't get back soon, there may not be much to come back to."

"Understood." Vivianne closed the panel and turned to Jordan. "We need to fly straight to Pentar."

He rested his fists on his hips. "I'm dropping you off on Earth first."

"We don't have time to spare." She frowned at him. "And it's still half my ship."

He shook his head. "When we arrive on Earth, I'll buy you out."

She didn't like him standing and hovering over her. "It's not about the money."

"No, it's not." He leaped onto the bed and laced his fingers behind his head. "You aren't prepared to fly into Tribe territory."

"So tell me what to expect." She must have tensed. George woke up and leapt from her lap. The ball went flying and he chased it again.

"I've never been to Pentar," he admitted.

"So I'm just as prepared to go as you are." She stood and strode over to him, not liking how he stared at the ceiling instead of back at her.

She sat beside him, her hip against his side. "What's really wrong?"

"You don't know what it's like to lose an entire world. It's like a big aching hole inside that you can never fill."

He finally looked at her. "Let me show you what it was like on Dominus."

"All right." She expected him to pop the data chip Arthur had given him into the computer. Instead, he put a vision in her mind of himself when he appeared about ten years younger.

Vivianne saw a modern kitchen, a tall woman who resembled Jordan setting a heavy platter in front of him. The scent of freshly baked bread and cream sauce over pasta, and a whiff of sparkling wine, made her mouth water. This woman must be his mother. The memory was over a thousand years old, yet every detail remained crisp and clear.

White curtains billowed in the breeze. A cat scampered over immaculate tile. Holograms of the entire family were in frames over the hearth.

Jordan was directly sharing a memory with her, totally in control of it. She didn't know how he was doing this, but there could be no mistaking his love for his mother or vice versa.

His mother ruffled his hair, smiled fondly at Jordan. Another door opened and his father strode in. Jordan had inherited his powerful shoulders and dark hair. The man swept his wife into his arms and kissed her. Then he clapped Jordan on the shoulder, set a gift beside his plate.

"Go ahead. Open it," his father urged.

There could be no doubting the love in the room as both parents smiled down at their son. His fin-

gers made short work of opening the box. Inside
was some kind of mechanical device.

    Jordan's eyes lit with excitement. "The computer
core. How did you ever find it?"

    His father chuckled. "I have my ways."

The memory dissolved. She peered at Jordan on the
bed, and he spoke softly. "The core was the last piece
of equipment I needed to explore the asteroids around
Dominus. The next day, I left." He swallowed hard. "I
never saw them again."

Her throat tightened in a strangled knot, even as questions flew through her mind. How had he placed that
memory in her head? Why had he chosen that particular
scene to show her his life? But when she saw the pain in
his eyes, she wanted to hold him and make the hurt go
away.

Vivianne placed her head on his shoulder. She'd lost
her own parents at a much younger age than he had, but
although she'd seen Trendonis fire the planetbusters she
couldn't really imagine what it felt like to lose an entire
world. And go on fighting. He was the last of his race.

She snuggled against him. "Are you worried that if you
take me with you to Pentar, I'll lose my world like you
lost yours?"

"Do you know how many times I've asked myself why
I didn't die with them?" he asked, his voice trembling
with pain.

"Your parents would be pleased to know you've
survived."

"Would they? Would they be proud of a son who lives

for revenge? War was not our way. We were a peaceful people. An old world with proud traditions."

She could feel his heartache but didn't understand him at all. She sat up so she could look into his eyes. "Are you saying you no longer want to pursue the Grail?"

He shook his head, the agony in his eyes scaring her. "It's my fate to unite the Grail and the Staff, and then I will finally be at peace. But I worry about you and how you'll go on after I am no longer here."

"You're worried about me?" Understanding hit her like a fist to the gut. He wanted to spare her the pain of loss. He believed that if Earth lost to the Tribes, she'd be better off dying with her world than the alternative.

But in truth, whether she stayed with him or not, she was still going to lose him. It would still tear at her so badly that she didn't want to think about that terrible moment when he would be gone.

"Trust me." He drew in a deep breath and released it slowly. "It would be better if you were with your own people. Let me finish this mission as I started it. Alone."

Alas! The love of a woman! It is known to be a lovely and fearful thing.

—KING RION JAQARD

30

Vivianne shook her head. "Whatever time you have left, I want us to be together."

Jordan frowned. "But—"

"I want more memories."

His tone turned gentle. "Those memories that you want will be painful. They'll tear at you. Keep you awake nights. I didn't have a choice. You do. You know what's coming."

His death.

"Don't you think I tried not to care about you?" Her fingers closed into fists, and she forced herself to take a deep breath and slowly released the tension. She could not let him go. Not yet. They both still had more living to do. Besides, she'd already fallen for him, and if he left her today or tomorrow or next month, the pain would be the same. "I've always been a survivor." She toggled the bridge. "Gray."

"Yes?"

"Set course for Pentar."

Jordan took her hand. "You're either very brave or very foolish."

"But," Gray hesitated. "Jordan—"

"Needs to make a shipwide announcement before we go anywhere," Jordan interrupted.

"I've got you on the intercom, Captain," Gray said.

Jordan's voice boomed through the speaker system. "I'm willing to drop off anyone on Earth who isn't ready to fly into enemy territory."

"Can we afford to lose those hours?" Tennison asked.

"There's no way of knowing," Jordan replied. "Earth needs us to find the Grail, but it's a dangerous mission. It could very well be a one-way trip."

"I'm staying," Tennison said.

"Me, too," Gray added.

One by one the others agreed, Knox, Darren, Sean, even Lyle.

"Then set course for Pentar, and may the Goddess bless us all." Jordan ended the communication and pulled Vivianne into his arms.

She lifted her lips to kiss him, and she let the warmth of his heat radiate into her and fill her soul. There had been enough talk of death.

When he finally broke away, she gave him a thoughtful glance. "So how did you put a memory in my mind?"

He drew her close once more. "I'm not sure. It's like I'm developing other senses. I suspect the Staff tried to prepare me by giving me those glimpses into your mind."

She eyed him with concern. "Perhaps the data chip that Arthur gave you might prove some of your theories, but why are you so certain you'll die when the Staff and the Grail unite? Maybe you'll turn back into an owl."

"That's its own kind of death, but it won't happen. Although I was separate from the Staff, I could still receive minimal energy, even through light-years. But when the Staff is gone, there will be no energy."

And no life.

Her whole body trembled, teetering between rage and grief and hope that he was wrong. "Maybe that chip has an answer that will save your life."

He took the data chip from a pocket and held it up. "For so long I've wished for exactly this knowledge, but now that I have it . . ."

"You're reluctant to know the truth?" she guessed, wishing she could ease his pain. Would seeing his world make his memories that much more painful, or would they bring him peace?

"Knowledge is always better than uncertainty," she continued, taking the chip from his hand and popping it into the computer. After that, she wasn't much help. She couldn't read the Dominus language, and while her translator could have deciphered oral verbiage, Jordan was processing the data so quickly, it blinked by on the screen at a rate she couldn't process—even if it had been English.

She placed George on Jordan's lap, noting his hand immediately falling to pet the dog behind the ears. She kissed Jordan on the cheek and left, praying to return to find a man at peace with himself.

Vivianne stopped in the galley to find Knox sitting at the counter, typing into her handheld. With a guilty look, Knox clicked off the screen.

"What's up?" Vivianne asked.

"Nothing."

"Really?" Vivianne opened the fridge. "I was thinking about a tuna sandwich."

Knox sighed. "I was making out my will. Can you send it to Earth for me? You don't think I'm jinxing us, do you?"

"I think it's smart." Vivianne turned to Knox. "But we're going to make it. We're going to find the Grail, and Earth's going to survive."

"How can you be so sure?" Knox opened a can, then chopped up some celery and an onion before adding mayo and piling it all onto toasted wheat bread.

"The *Draco*'s a sound ship. We have a great crew. And I have faith in Jordan. I have faith in us." Vivianne squeezed Knox's hand. "We can do this."

"Thanks." Knox drew in a deep breath and let it out slowly. "I needed a pep talk."

Vivianne left the galley and took her meal to the bridge to eat. Gray was at the helm. Sean was at navigation. Lyle was pacing.

"What do we know about Pentar?" she asked, hoping Devid's star charts gave more useful information than just a spatial position of the Tribal world.

"Pentar's an artificial planet with a core of asteroid-like material," Gray told her. "It's smaller than Earth, about a third more distant from its sun, and the climate's cold. The entire society lives below the surface in a hollow core."

Lyle paced faster, his eyes worried. But he remained silent.

"You said Pentar's artificial?" Vivianne asked. "Did the Tribes build it?"

"We don't know. The world is located far out on the rim. Which means it's one of the older planets in the galaxy."

"What else do we know about it?"

"Their star's dying," Gray told her, his tone serious. "Within the next ten thousand years or so, the planet won't be able to sustain life."

"Good," Lyle said. "Maybe the Tribes will die out with their planet."

"Even if Pentar's their home world, it's highly unlikely that a race that has spread across the galaxy would die out with the death of one planet." Vivianne didn't want anyone to imagine they could outwait the Tribes.

"The Tribes have usurped over a thousand worlds." Gray agreed with her.

"But you think Pentar's their home world?" Lyle asked.

She recalled what Jordan had told her and shook her head. "Jordan said that the Tribes would never bring the Grail to their home world, for fear someone hostile might come after it."

"So they know we're coming?" Lyle asked, his voice tight.

"It's possible," Vivianne said.

"So what's the plan?" Gray asked.

"We fly in, find the Grail, steal it back." Vivianne stared into space, wondering what surprises were waiting out there for them. Earth didn't have much time. Things were falling apart fast.

"How do we know that when we come out of hyperspace, their fleet won't be waiting for us?" Lyle asked.

"We don't know," Vivianne admitted.

"And how will we set foot on their world without being shot, never mind find the Grail?" he pressed.

"Jordan is working on a clever scheme," she lied. "In

the meantime, I need to modify our sensors. Perhaps we can infiltrate their computer systems. Sean, bring up our sensor specs on my screen, plus all the data we've collected on Pentar. If anyone else has any ideas how to adapt our equipment—"

"There's no time for modifications," Jordan interrupted. He strode onto the bridge, his face a study in contrasts. While light caught his cheekbones, the skin under his eyes was dark. "People, we're flying in on nothing more than an ancient rumor and a promise of a legend, but the stakes have never been higher. If we fail, Earth doesn't stand a chance. Luckily for us, Pentar's the commercial hub of the Tribal grid. The system's overcrowded and overtaxed, so if we get lucky, we fly in without raising any suspicion."

"Is that likely?" Vivianne asked.

Jordan smiled, his eyes cold. "In the last thousand years, no enemy of the Tribes has dared to fly into the heart of Tribe territory. They won't be expecting us, and that should allow us the element of surprise."

As the *Draco* jumped into hyperspace, she hoped Jordan was right. She longed to step beside Jordan and lock her fingers through his. But she denied herself his strength. She might want to spend as much time with him as she could, but she refused to give up her independence, and as a captain, she needed to stay strong for her crew as much as for herself.

It seemed to take mere seconds, as well as an eternity, to slow from hyperspace. But at sub–light speeds they could see hundreds, maybe thousands of Tribe ships.

Sean leaned over his nav screen. "The traffic pattern's insane."

Sirens blared. "Warning. We're on a collision course. Collision course."

At the command console, Gray fought with the helm. "Translators are working. Traffic control's ordering us to veer seventy degrees to point zero eight five niner."

"Do it," Jordan ordered.

Gray corrected their flight path, and the engine warnings died. Vivianne slowly let out her breath and stared at the viewscreen. Ships of every size and description swarmed in and out of Pentar's space. Some space barges looked to be a kilometer long; others, small craft with sleek lines, darted between the heavy cruisers. Military ships, transport vessels, and ferries all intermixed into the grid.

The chaos reminded her of driving in Tokyo at rush hour—only in three dimensions. But out here, just a fender bender meant instant death.

Sean put an incoming communication from traffic command over the bridge speakers. "Vessel on path zero point eight five niner, authorized entry is denied."

"Why?" Jordan asked.

"Your registration signal is nonresponsive."

Apparently every ship possessed some kind of signal to identify it to the traffic cops. Since the *Draco* didn't have a responder, they were attracting official attention.

Jordan didn't miss a beat. "Traffic control, this is ship on path zero point eight five niner. Six days ago, we lost power and shielding after a meteor shower hit us. Our transponder was knocked out, but Trendonis will vouch for us."

"Trendonis?" The traffic controller whistled.

Jordan's pretense that they were on a mission for the

enemy leader could easily backfire. Vivianne held her breath. Would the traffic controller attempt to verify their story? Or would the name of their powerful leader alone put enough fear into him to let them continue?

Jordan sounded unconcerned, almost bored. "Trendonis isn't happy when his ships are delayed, but do what you must."

"I'm clearing. Alpha, priority two. Have a good landing."

Jordan shut off the communication. "That was too easy."

Vivianne's eyes narrowed. "You think they're still suspicious?"

"We can't trust anyone. When we dock, they might arrest us or shoot us." He turned to Sean. "Break out every hand weapon onboard. Issue the crew sidearms."

"You think we can fight our way out?" Vivianne's stomach churned.

Jordan fisted his hands on his hips. "We can't let them delay us."

Fighting didn't seem the way to go. Not this deep in Tribal territory. Not when they were so outnumbered. Vivianne scratched the back of her neck. "Chances are, low-level bureaucrats will come aboard first. Instead of shooting them, why don't we try a bribe?"

Jordan nodded. "It might be better to offer to trade power. The Staff can feed into most power grids."

They now had a surplus of food. But unless absolutely necessary, she hated to give up any of the high-end products that Devid had placed about the *Draco;* nuts, coffee, beans, and synth meat. They even had brandy, bourbon, and vodka. Without knowing when they could restock, it was better to hold on to their supplies if possible.

Vivianne accepted a laser sidearm and slid it into the

waistband of her slacks, the cool, hard metal a constant reminder of the danger. When she glanced out the viewscreen again, she could see they'd be docking at a space station in orbit over the planet.

With giant arms extending out from the core, the space station was a marvel of engineering ingenuity. Ships arrived, docked, unloaded, reloaded, and departed with a smooth efficiency that reminded her of a busy hive.

A hive that wouldn't hesitate to sting them with multiple threats if they discovered dragonshapers among them.

They had no official documents. No identity papers. No transponder.

Below the space station, the terrain was mountainous and covered by glaciers and huge polar icecaps. The frozen snowball didn't look the least inviting.

Compared to Earth, Pentar was barren. Vivianne saw no oceans, no rain forests or jungles. In fact, nothing green lived on Pentar. The weather sensors told her the surface wasn't just frigid but devoid of all animal and plant life.

No wonder the Tribes had left Pentar to expand to other worlds. Anything would be an improvement. But she shouldn't fool herself. The Tribes didn't colonize— they dominated, they enslaved, they stole a world's resources and moved on like locusts, leaving decimation and death behind.

Be glad of hyperspace, because it gives you the chance to love and to laugh and to work and to play and to travel through the stars.

—ANONYMOUS GALACTIC EXPLORER

31

❦

Jordan's motto was to hope for peace but to accept the necessity of war. So he was not pleased that Vivianne wanted to greet the Tribes' authorities herself. But he knew better than to suggest she back down. Instead, he'd stay close and stay well armed—if out of sight.

While he and Sean covered the doorway with their weapons, Vivianne greeted the Tribal officials at the main hatch. "Welcome, gentlemen." She gestured to a tray filled with assorted beverages next to tempting finger foods Knox had placed in easy reach. "Would you care for refreshment?" Vivianne asked breezily.

"Hand over your ship's papers." The gray-haired taller man in a stained uniform spoke in a gruff tone, his beady eyes staring at Vivianne's lithe figure as if she stood unclothed on the slave block.

Jordan bristled. Vivianne pretended not to notice. Instead she tucked a stray lock of hair behind her ear and put on a bemused expression. "I'm afraid we lost our papers when the space debris hit us." She opened her eyes wide. "We were lucky to survive."

"You really don't expect us to believe that," the younger man sneered.

She poured the men drinks. "Actually, I was afraid no one would believe me and was hoping you gentlemen could tell me what to do. I'm really not very good when it comes to paperwork." *Ha,* Jordan thought. This from a woman who ran one of the largest megacompanies on Earth? She really could be disingenuous when she tried. "Is there some report I'm supposed to file?"

Vivianne didn't exactly flirt, but she appealed to their protective male egos. At first Jordan didn't think they had a sympathetic cell in their bodies, but Vivianne kept up the chatter.

"It was so scary," Vivianne said in a slightly breathless voice that was beginning to captivate the men. Their frowns weren't as severe, and as they snacked and drank, the tension abated. "We had to fix our engines in a strange port," she continued. "I'm fairly certain the mechanics took advantage . . . but we had to get home, so we had no choice but to over pay for repairs."

"New paperwork can be expensive . . ." The older official left the insinuation dangling.

"Oh, I'd be so happy if you could take care of it for me." Vivianne smiled, placed her hand on the man's forearm, and leaned closer. "Trendonis is always so grateful and generous to those who help smooth over any difficulties."

Damn, she was good.

"Fifteen hundred credits." The Tribesman named his price.

Vivianne didn't blink. No one would ever guess she

didn't have so much as one Tribe credit, and Jordan reminded himself not to play poker with her. "Credits can be traced, but"—she winked—"no one could object to an appropriate gift."

"What kind of gift?"

"Trendonis is a most generous man. In my experience, it's best to leave the gift up to him." Vivianne spoke and acted as if she expected the two men to agree with her. Before they could think too hard or too long, she moved on. "We also require repairs. I'd be most grateful if you could recommend someone to install a new cosmic power converter."

As they discussed prices, models, and how long those repairs would take, Jordan couldn't help but grin. Vivianne was going to get the enemy to fix the *Draco*. He only prayed that when the repairmen boarded, they didn't note anything suspicious. Still, he couldn't blame her for wanting to replace the Staff as a power source. Every time he exited the ship with the Staff, he left the *Draco* vulnerable. If they succeeded, the Staff would cease to exist. So for the *Draco* to fly home, the repairs would be vital.

He supposed he shouldn't have been so amazed. Vivianne's negotiating skills were extraordinary, and he couldn't have been more pleased when she also talked the officials into giving them temporary IDs. By the time Vivianne finished with the two men, they were acting like her best friends.

She insisted they each leave with a bottle of scotch and some of Knox's homemade cookies. But he didn't totally relax his grip on the blaster until the officials departed and the hatch closed behind them.

That's when he realized he'd broken into a sweat, worried that the men might harm her before he could stop them. But he forced a smile onto his lips, knowing instinctively that she would not appreciate his concern. Vivianne wanted to believe that he thought she could take care of herself. And he did—but that didn't mean he didn't worry.

"Good job." He strode over and had to force himself not to hug her in a tight embrace. Taking a fake ID, he slipped the bracelet over his wrist. "You ready to go?"

She kneeled, and George scampered over. "Just let me say goodbye." She petted his head. "Be a good boy." She stood and turned to Sean. "Don't feed him too many Ping-Pong balls."

"Yes, ma'am."

"Sean." Jordan lowered his voice. "No one else is to leave this ship. Schedule the repairs during Lyle's downtime."

"Understood, sir. We'll be extra careful with strangers aboard."

"One more thing," Jordan warned him. "Once the repairs are finished, keep the engines hot. We might have to leave . . . fast."

"I'll let Gray know." Sean lifted George into his arms to prevent the dog from following them. "Safe trip, and good luck."

"See you soon." Jordan stepped through the hatch and led Vivianne down the loading dock. "You ready to fly down to Pentar?"

"Of course. I'm always ready for adventure."

His chest swelled with pride. Vivianne was walking into Tribe territory with no credit, no allies, no friends.

Yet he saw no fear in her eyes, just anticipation and the knowledge she would do what must be done.

She'd never looked more beautiful. Without makeup, her hair falling loosely about her shoulders, she walked beside him, her head high, her shoulders squared, ready to face whatever came at them next.

Jordan hoped he could keep it together. He didn't want to let her down. He didn't want to let Earth down.

The first test came as they entered the transfer station. People bought tickets and lined up for the ride to Pentar.

Vivianne whispered into his ear. "We don't have credits to buy our tickets."

He squeezed her hand. "Trust me." He walked up to the ticket counter. Jordan pressed their identity cards in a slot. Then one quick mind swipe and Jordan changed the clerk's vision, so that instead of the blank piece of paper Jordan handed him, the clerk saw a hundred-credit note. It was surprisingly easy. Without hesitation, the clerk placed the paper in his cash drawer and handed them two tickets and a handful of change.

Jordan hurried her from the ticket booth. He had no idea how long the effect would last. For all he knew the clerk could look down, realize the paper was blank, and call security guards.

Vivianne's eyes grew wide, but she said nothing until they'd joined a large group in a snaking line. "How did you—"

"I don't know." How could he explain? Placing the keys into the Staff had changed him on a fundamental level. Although he wasn't reading minds, he could hear background noise; a steady hum of thoughts overflowing, hunger, the need for sex, fear. Men worried about their work. Women worried about their children. He shut down before the thoughts overwhelmed him.

"That wasn't hypnosis, was it?" she asked, peering at him.

"It's a form of mind control."

"Can you do that to more than one person at a time? How long can you sustain it? Can you make someone think I'm their best friend?"

"All good questions, but I'm afraid I don't have any answers."

"Do you have a plan to get answers?"

"I'll figure it out as I go along."

Despite security and cameras everywhere, the ride down to Pentar was uneventful. No different than riding in a crowded passenger airplane. Without enduring the cold weather, they remained indoors and landed in an artificial crater, before taking a magnetic levitation train into the city. So far no one seemed the least interested in them, but every time they swiped their identity cards, a computer was tracking them.

Jordan wanted to get off the official grid, lose themselves in the city. The first opportunity he saw, he pulled her behind a power-maintenance unit. He unsheathed the Ancient Staff and did a quick three-hundred-sixty-degree spin.

Vivianne frowned. "No matter which way you turn, it's not pulsing brighter."

"I know." He resheathed the Staff. "I was hoping it would help us find the Grail the same way it did the Keys, but it's not working."

Vivianne looked at him, her eyes worried. "So how do we find the Grail?"

Break the rules, forgive quickly, kiss slowly, love truly.
—LADY CAEL

32

"This way." Jordan took Vivianne's hand and led her down a sidewalk. At first glance, the street scene seemed similar to a dozen cities on Earth—if she discounted the artificial sky overhead. Right now the artificial sun shined brightly, and she wondered if they ever programmed in rain, snow, or gusty wind.

She strode beside Jordan, who had shortened his stride to match the average citizen's slower pace. "Where are we going?"

"To government headquarters."

She asked, "Can you make them just *tell* us where the Grail's kept?"

"No, but if they think about the Grail, I can track down the details."

He sounded so certain. Was he reading the minds of passersby? "Suppose the military has the Grail?"

"It's possible, but if they do, someone in the government will know that."

Her stomach plummeted. Walking next to him, she'd never felt more exposed. Every time she saw security, every time they had to swipe their fake IDs to progress, she expected someone to stop them.

For all they knew, the Grail might not still be on Pentar. Their intel from Honor was months old and may not have been accurate to begin with. By now, the Tribes could have transported the Grail to the other end of the galaxy.

Still, she remained hopeful. Perhaps it was because at first these people didn't seem that different from those at home. But as she really looked at this society, she saw many cruel aspects. Young girls forced to walk behind grown men. Children who didn't smile or play. Men who didn't look one another in the eye.

Everywhere, people went out of their way to give the security people wide berths. Fear permeated the air. The Tribes didn't appear happy on their own planet. Apparently their leaders subjected their own people to the same domination as they did the rest of the galaxy.

Vivianne shuddered at the bleakness of their existence. They weren't poor in things, but in spirit. There was no art, no graffiti, nothing but basic, drab design. It struck her as a world gone stale.

Vibrant Earth would not go flat and banal like this place, she vowed. As they caught a streetcar that ran on tracks and magnetic devices, then another train, she noticed that Jordan was very quiet. He hadn't spoken in the last hour. While she understood he didn't want to risk anyone overhearing their conversation, when she turned to look at him, his eyes didn't focus on her.

It was as if his mind was missing, and an icy chill slid down her back.

She swayed nearer to him in the crowded vehicle that ran along the underground street, past dilapidated apartment buildings, gray storefronts, and windowless schools. "Jordan?"

He didn't answer.

She placed a hand on his shoulder and shook him. "Jordan?"

For a full minute, he didn't move. Didn't speak. A few people glanced at her, then looked away. If there was going to be trouble, they clearly wanted no part of it.

Come on, Jordan. Damn it, you're scaring me.

"S'okay," Jordan finally responded, his speech slightly slurred.

Was he responding to her shake of his shoulder? Her voice? Or her thoughts? She didn't have time to ask. As the train slowed and motored into the station, he tugged her toward the door.

She kept her voice low. "I thought you said we were supposed to stay on this line another half hour."

"Change of plans." He sounded very sure of himself once again, and she had to hurry to keep up with him.

This railway platform was crowded with women pushing strollers, men carrying meal boxes, and several squads of security shoving past civilians who scurried to get out of their way. When they exited the station, they spilled into a somber cement square that was far from parklike. No greenery. No children flying kites or playing ball. No pets. Just people walking through, eyes downcast, heads bowed under the strain of Tribal life.

Jordan crossed the square and headed into a narrow alley that ran between apartment buildings. "We've picked up a tail."

"Security?" she asked, matching her pace to his and forcing herself not to turn around.

"Trendonis's friends."

Jordan had thrown his powerful enemy's name at traffic control to allay their suspicions. His ploy had worked. Trendonis's name inspired fear. But apparently the man also had friends, who were now after them.

Her thoughts slid to a halt. The only way Jordan could know the tails' alliances was if he were reading their minds.

While she was grateful he had a power that might aid them in staying safe long enough to find the Grail, she realized that living with a mind-reading Jordan would be more than difficult. She supposed she shouldn't be worrying about that now. The chances of either of them living beyond this mission didn't look good.

Especially as the alley dead-ended into a five-story stone wall. Jordan shoved her behind him and turned to face three dangerous-looking men running into the alley. The leader, a burly man with a black beard and blacker eyes, had pulled out a blaster and aimed at them.

Jordan stared at the man. She braced for death.

But the gunman didn't pull the trigger. He didn't change expression. He stood as still as stone.

"Boss?" One of his cohorts shook the leader.

"We'll have to shoot them ourselves," the other growled.

When Jordan stepped to one side, jerking her with him, the lead gunman remained totally motionless. However, his associates raised their weapons.

Jordan kicked the blaster from the nearest opponent's hand. Still spinning, he back fisted the last guy in the temple and he dropped his weapon. As the man dived for the blaster, she kicked the weapon out of reach.

Jordan pounced and the men rolled. Jordan ended up on

top, straddled the man's chest, grabbed him by the throat, and glared. "What do you want from us, Gridon?"

"You know my name?" Gridon's eyes widened in fear. He glanced from Jordan back to his cohort, who still stood frozen.

"I'm only going to ask once more. What do you want?"

"My boss wants to know who you are."

Jordan slammed Gridon's head against the pavement and knocked him out. While she retrieved the blaster, Jordan rifled the man's pockets and stole his ID and credits.

"The frozen guy's beginning to thaw," she muttered uneasily.

Jordan slipped an arm around the leader's throat, choked the man back into unconsciousness, then handed her his ID, too.

The entire fight had taken only seconds. Neither Jordan nor Vivianne had so much as broken a fingernail. Between Jordan's fighting and mental skills, they might just stand a chance. Still, she was shivering, shaking.

"Come on." Jordan held out his hand to her, his eyes bleak. "Security's noted a disturbance in this sector. They're on the way to investigate."

"How far away are they?" she asked, taking his hand and jogging beside him.

"I'm not sure. All these buildings look the same to me."

So he could see what Security saw? She stumbled, and he held her hand more tightly, preventing her from falling. Was he gaining new powers, or was he simply learning new facets of the powers he already had? She supposed it didn't matter.

She held on to the belief that even though he was reading other minds, he was *not* in hers.

Jordan pulled her around a corner and slowed to a walk so their movements would blend in with the crowd. When she saw a restaurant, she jerked her thumb. "Why don't we slip in there?"

"Good idea." He opened the door for her, and they took a table in the back near the rear entrance.

They both ordered the "special," the only meal the restaurant served. The food turned out to be surprisingly good. Dark bread sandwiched a concoction of marinated meat. She downed two glasses of energy water, surprised she could eat and drink when her nerves were so raw.

They didn't speak. The other diners sat so close by, they could overhear any conversation. Besides, Jordan took on that "missing" look, which indicated he was mind scanning. Perhaps he'd luck out and get a bead on the Grail's location.

As far as she was concerned, the sooner, the better. Between Trendonis's enemies searching for them, and Security now after them, too, they were attracting attention. The last thing they needed was Trendonis himself to hear rumors and come after them again.

As she paid for the food, her stomach churned. She tugged at Jordan's sleeve. "We should leave."

He refocused more quickly this time. "We need to descend four more levels."

Four levels? She already felt suffocated under just one floor of concrete. "Is there an elevator?"

"I'm not sure. It's strange, but the knowledge of how to navigate between levels is not readily available among the general populace." He ducked his head to speak into her ear. "But I picked up several hints that no one wants to live on a lower level. Where we are now is considered the height of luxury."

If the poor sections were below, it was likely to be more dangerous. On the other hand, there might be less security. Either way, they had no choice.

She didn't allow her concerns to show, but as he led her deeper into the city, her soul yearned to go back up to the surface, to the light. Traveling deeper into the bowels of this world reminded her of that cave on Arcturus.

"This way." Jordan's voice was threaded with excitement. "There's a staircase that should take us down to the central government offices."

"Do we need special IDs?" she asked.

"They have retinal scanners."

She stopped walking. "We can't fool the machines."

Jordan slipped his arm around her. "People read those machines' results."

Uh-oh. Jordan had just revealed yet another new use for his skills. He could alter the minds of those who were in charge of the machines. The little hairs on her neck stood up. "What if the techs who read the machines aren't nearby?"

"I've got it covered."

Could Jordan trace the current all the way back to techs who monitored the system? Control them from a distance?

Sheesh. She really didn't want to think about it. So instead, she focused on trying not to slow him down. He seemed certain they could pull off the theft of the Grail, and she refused to let fear freeze her.

She tried not to think about going into the bowels of the enemy world. Or being surrounded by the Tribes. Or never feeling the sun on her face again.

Choose your friends by their character and your engine fuel by its color.

—ANONYMOUS

33

Jordan's mind kept expanding. At first he read only surface thoughts of those close by. But as he stretched the limits of his new ability, he realized he could listen in on people across the street, then down the block. It took a lot of effort, but he learned how to narrow or widen the focus. Dealing with all the extraneous thoughts complicated his search for information. A lady couldn't recall where she put her keys. A man wanted to remember to call his wife to tell her he'd be home from work late, but from the images shot at Jordan, the man didn't plan on working unless it was on top of his desk with his new secretary. Jordan picked up on others' thoughts, their plans, desires, and emotions.

It was so easy to get lost in the myriad details, but eventually Jordan filtered out the extraneous thoughts and homed in on what he needed. Finally, he tuned out everything except clues about the Grail. But after listening hard, he learned nothing. So he focused on the location of the government offices. Surely someone in power would eventually lead them to the Grail.

He moved through the street as quickly as he dared. The artificial lighting down here made him feel like a bug under a magnifying glass. There were no shadows, no dark corners, no places to hide.

"Security's questioning people back at the restaurant about us," he warned her. "So once we reach a place to descend, be ready to move fast."

"Got it." At the mention of going deeper into the planet, fear radiated from her. He wasn't reading her thoughts, because he knew she didn't want him to, but from the tilt of her chin he saw she'd hold it together just as she had in the cave on Arcturus.

He spied a long silver wall with gleaming white marble floors. "We're getting closer."

Vivianne jerked her thumb and he saw the lift. Engineers inside a nearby tower employed null-grav devices to raise and lower a huge open platform. Very few people seemed to be using the platform, but a lighted billboard showed a schedule and that the lift was about to depart.

"Hurry." Jordan broke into a run. He could feel Security closing in, see in his mind that they'd just rounded a corner he and Vi had taken earlier.

He spied an elderly couple wearing straw hats and reached into his pocket and pulled out some credits. "We'd like to purchase your hats."

The man looked at him as if he thought he was crazy, but he snatched the credits from Jordan and handed over the hats.

As disguises went, the hats weren't great, but they had no time. They ran down a ramp and reached it just as a gate closed right in front of them.

Vivianne tried to push open the gate, but it was locked tight. "We're too late."

Jordan cupped his hands. "Climb over."

Vi took once glance at Security rounding the corner, placed her foot into his hands, and scrambled over the gate. He jumped, clung, and scaled the fence, then dropped down the other side, where several citizens stared in disapproval.

Security started to climb the gate, too.

Jordan hurried her away from that end of the platform as the machinery on their left rumbled. Beside him, Vi's knees buckled.

"It's okay," he murmured. "Security didn't make it. We're going down."

"That's not reassuring, Jordan," she muttered.

When the platform stopped, most people exited. Only a few got on. Then they dropped again. He expected the living conditions on each level to worsen—just like he'd been led to expect after reading the minds of the general populace. But the opposite happened.

"Each level seems more luxurious," Vi noted, her eyes taking in the pristine white buildings at their current level. Each structure possessed stained-glass windows, blooming flowers, and sweeping lawns. By the time they reached the lowest level, the homes were mansions, the public buildings magnificent works of architecture. Fountains and sculptures decorated the landscape.

Vi peeked at him from beneath the brim of her hat. "It seems as if the Tribe government is deceiving its own citizens."

"Just like governments everywhere. Why should Pentar be any different?"

He tried to pick up thoughts about the Grail, but no one nearby knew anything valuable. Except one young man seemed to know where the government headquarters were located and was heading there himself.

The man's mood was dark, angry, and fearful. Jordan wasn't sure why, but the man felt he'd been unfairly accused.

"Follow him." Jordan gestured with his chin.

"Does he know something?" she asked.

"No, but he might know someone who knows someone who does."

Vivianne sighed. Her handheld buzzed, and she raised her wrist to her mouth. "Yes, Gray?"

"Repairs are complete. We now have a working cosmic energy convertor."

"Good job. We hope to be back soon."

She ended the conversation and then skidded to a stop at the sight of a strange three-legged animal with four eyes and two tails. "What's that?"

"Don't worry. Hartogs are vegetarians, at least according to its owner." Jordan nevertheless gave the animal a wide berth. At the moment, the hartog seemed solely focused on when it could take a nap. The animal was picturing a cool, dark room, where it could crawl under the desk and out of the light of . . . the Holy Grail?

Jordan delved deeper into the creature's mind.

"What is it?" Vivianne asked.

Jordan realized he'd stopped walking in order to concentrate better. He resumed their progress, this time following the hartog's owner. "Just a sec."

He focused on the owner's mind, sifting through memories, but he found nothing about the Grail. Weary, he withdrew. "That animal has seen the Grail. But its owner seems to know nothing."

"Maybe he's not the owner. Or maybe he was with his last owner when he saw it. Or maybe—"

"You're right. That man isn't the animal's owner but this world's equivalent of a professional dog walker. But we still need to follow them."

"What about the government offices?" Vivianne asked.

"They aren't going anywhere. And I've scanned thousands of minds. This is the first clue about the Grail, and I want to pursue it."

"So we're going into the house?"

"Maybe later. First I want to check out the home's owner. According to his paid help, he'll attend the parties tonight."

"Fine, but we aren't dressed properly for this level." Vivianne sounded tense.

So far he'd refrained from reading her mind. It took quite a lot of effort to do so, but he didn't like the anxiety he heard in her tone. "What's really wrong?" he asked, knowing instinctively it wasn't the clothing.

"I told Knox we would succeed, but I never really believed we'd find the Grail."

He raised his brow. "We haven't found it yet."

"But it seems real now. And . . ."

"And?" he prodded, uncertain where she was going with the conversation. They trailed the Hartog walker into a park. Unlike the levels up higher, this area had plants, flowers, and green grass—none of them real, but plastic replicas. Still, the animal seemed to take great pleasure in sniffing every artificial blade.

Vivianne turned to him. "Will you unite the Grail and the Staff the very moment you find the Grail?"

He stopped again and tipped up her chin. "I won't leave you alone in enemy territory."

She shook her head and swallowed hard. "I'm not ready to lose you. Not yet."

"I've gotten used to having you around, too." He kept his words light. But he realized the irony that he'd lived so long alone, and now that he'd finally found a woman he cared for, he was going to lose her before they'd had any chance to make a life together.

He'd warned her. He'd told himself to keep his distance. But he'd learned that he couldn't chose his fate. Apparently it was his destiny to love Vivianne Blackstone.

Conversation is the slowest form of human communication.

—BEN FRANKLIN

34

❦

The legends about uniting the Staff and Grail were ancient, even back in Arthur's time," Jordan told her, his blue eyes kind and looking far too sad for Vivianne's taste. But then the sparkle rekindled and he grinned. "But there's something you should know."

"About the Grail?" Vivianne wiped her sweaty palms on her pants and tried to act casual.

While she hadn't thought they'd find the Grail, she'd always believed they'd find another solution. That a man who'd spent so many years seeking justice would finally have time for his own happiness. In a fair universe they would have a lifetime together—but the universe was anything but fair.

"I love you," Jordan told her and her knees went weak. "I don't know if that knowledge will make things worse after I am gone, but Vivianne Blackstone, I love you. And I'm sorry for it."

"I'm not." She grabbed his hands, her passion rising up in a fierce swell. "It's better to have loved . . . even if—"

She couldn't voice the reality. Tears brimmed in her eyes and she blinked them away, forced herself to look at the hartog as it chewed on a flower. Jordan followed her gaze. "We need to keep moving."

"Yes. Of course." She wiped the back of her hand over her eyes. She would not cry. She wouldn't. Right now Jordan was still alive. There would be more than enough time to grieve. Later.

Jordan loved her. His words meant more than she'd thought possible. He loved her, and her happiness flowed from inside out, erupting into a giggle of joy.

Jordan shot her a curious glance. "You okay?"

She slipped her hand into his and squeezed. "I love you, too."

"I'm glad." His tone was gruff, heartfelt. She wished they could go rent a room and forget the Tribes, Earth, and the Grail. She wished they could just be two people in love, with all the time they needed at their disposal.

The hartog decided it was done sniffing. Either that or its caretaker forced it forward. In either case, the pet and its steward darted across the street, through a private gate, and up a staircase toward the double doors of one of a dozen mansions lining the block.

"Let's go around back." Jordan steered her to the corner and crossed the street. The mansions were laid out in neat rows, every lot the same size, landscaped exactly alike. But only the Hartog mansion had a stone wall around the perimeter.

She was about to ask Jordan more questions when he got that "missing" look in his eyes. He was off reading minds again.

With his special ability, they were a lot more likely to

secure information. They needn't even attract attention to themselves, and that gave them a huge tactical advantage.

Would it be enough? Surely the Tribes had to keep the Grail well guarded. Surely they would have tight security, alarm systems, locked doors. They'd be walking straight into danger.

Yet all she wanted to do was skip and dance, because Jordan loved her. She felt crazy good. And scared out of her mind that she was still going to lose him.

The optimist in her told her they'd find a way to be together. The pessimist in her replied they'd be together, all right—in death.

Get a grip.

Vivianne needed to get grounded. Do something to keep her mind busy, or she was going to fall prey to her roller-coaster emotions. She needed a distraction but couldn't use her handheld to check in, since they'd agreed to keep the communication with the *Draco* down to a minimum for security purposes. Too bad there was nothing to see beyond a bunch of mansions. No one was going in or out. No one was even on the street.

In fact, the place seemed strangely deserted. But she didn't know Pentar's customs. During the day, adults probably worked and the kids attended school, and for all she knew, the grounds were kept by robots.

She glanced at Jordan. He'd been "gone" for what seemed like a very long time.

"Jordan?"

"The hartog could have seen the Grail anywhere. The animal's primitive mind doesn't allow for details that might let me identify the location."

"We followed the hartog for nothing?"

"Not for nothing. The hartog's owner is an important man. He's going to celebrate with other important leaders tonight." Jordan paused, then continued, "There's some huge social event this evening. The city's residents are attending a gala."

"We're going to attend?" Vivianne asked. "That way you can circulate among the important people."

Her comment seemed to catch him off guard. He spoke thoughtfully. "I'm not certain I can handle so many minds coming at me at once."

She arched her brow. "Here I thought you were omnipotent."

"I wish."

She didn't press the matter.

"Fine." He changed his mind. "Let's go join the party."

"I suspect we need to go clothes shopping . . . unless you just want to brainwash everyone into thinking I'm wearing a drop-dead-gorgeous gown?"

His eyes sparkled with a glow that heated her. "Let's go shop."

"I've very expensive tastes," she warned.

"All I ask is that you buy sensible shoes."

She pouted. "Define *sensible*."

"Shoes you can—" Jordan grabbed her and yanked her behind a thick hedge. "Security," he explained before she could ask.

Fear tightening up her chest, she peered between the branches as a vehicle rolled down the road. "Are they searching for us?"

"I don't know. One guy's thinking about how his wife found his porn stash last night, and the other is so angry at his boss that I can't get a bead on whatever they are supposed to be doing."

Vivianne held her breath. When the vehicle passed without slowing, she remembered to breathe again and began to step back toward the sidewalk.

Jordan placed his hand on her shoulder. "Wait. They've picked up something on their sensors."

"Us?"

"Maybe." He squeezed her shoulder. "They've taped a picture of us exiting the *Draco* to their monitor. It's grainy, probably picked up by a pedestrian camera, but it's us for sure."

"Maybe going to the gala isn't such a hot idea, after all."

"No. I think you're right. We need to attend."

"We'll need more than clothing to attend the celebration. We'll need disguises."

Jordan frowned, and she could tell he was mind-reading the Security team. "You're assuming we'll be free that long. They're turning around."

"Do something."

"Okay. They've spotted us." He sounded calm, distracted. "They're heading right here."

Apparently he couldn't stop them. "So do we run?"

"Let them come to us," Jordan directed. "I'll try to make them see two loose hartogs instead of us, but I can't focus on the task and run at the same time."

Vivianne rooted her feet to the ground. It was broad daylight, and they were just standing there. If Jordan slipped, if the men reported in, they might send squads of guards.

She crossed her fingers. *Don't see us. Don't see us. Don't see us.*

"Whatever you're doing, keep doing it," Jordan muttered.

She squeezed her crossed fingers together harder. *Don't see us. Don't see us. Don't see us.*

Security was twenty feet away. Then ten. Five. They rolled on by.

Drained, she swayed on her feet, and Jordan reached out to steady her. "Thanks."

"I didn't do anything," she insisted.

"You did . . . a lot." He held her shoulders and ran his palms up and down her upper arms.

She'd never seen him look so serious. Almost shaken. "I don't understand."

"You fed me power."

"What?"

"I couldn't have held the image by myself."

That made no sense. He didn't need her to play mind tricks. "You faked the money at the station, and I had nothing to do with it."

"That was a tiny piece of paper for just a few seconds. This time, we made imaginary three-dimensional images look real for over a minute. The construct was so tight, even their sensors didn't suspect we'd faked them out. Your extra power made the difference."

She searched his eyes to see if he was teasing, but he appeared dead serious. Temples throbbing, she rubbed her head. "I thought you drew power from the Staff."

"That's on the physical plane. What you did was on the mental plane."

"Like telepathy?"

He shook his head. "It wasn't a message. You sent me emotional mental energy."

Had her wishing been a form of mental energy? Had she really fed it to him? It seemed impossible. But then, why else was she so suddenly drained? She couldn't discount his explanation, not after she'd recently seen so many things that she'd previously thought were impossible.

Her head was spinning. "How's it possible for me to feed you energy?"

"The Staff has fed me all my life. So I guess it's possible my DNA has evolved to the point where I can pick up additional energy from you." He looped an arm over her shoulder. "I always knew you were special."

Had he? If the Staff hadn't forced lust on them . . . hadn't forced them to share memories . . . would she be able to feed him power from her emotions?

"Jordan, what are the chances that I would have a simpatico power that feeds your own capabilities?"

"It's possible my Staff altered your DNA," he said. "That while it caused us to share memories, it somehow taught you to give off the right energy frequency."

"Out of all the beings in the universe, how many can feed you mental power?"

"That I know of," he said, his eyes darkening, "only you."

Vivianne dropped the subject. For now. But her suspicions were beginning to grow. She shook her head. It was a good thing Jordan wasn't reading her mind. No doubt he wouldn't be pleased to know that she suspected he might have programmed the Staff to do his bidding. But then again, she hadn't forgotten how those blue lights had entered her body when she and Jordan had made love, either. Perhaps neither Jordan nor his Staff had anything to do with her new ability. Perhaps those lights that had changed Jordan had changed her, too.

Courage is standing up for what you believe, regardless of the odds against you, and against the pressure that tears at your resistance.

—LADY OF THE LAKE

35

The elite of Pentar seemed to be celebrating throughout this level, with the most prestigious party taking place at the palace. The domed ballroom with crystal columns and polished, illuminated marble floors was the perfect backdrop for the festivities, and the citizens had decked themselves out. Their normal dreary and drab garments had been replaced with ostentatious finery. Women wore strings of sparkling gemstones twined into their sweeping updos, and the men sported jewel-encrusted shoulder pads over their suit jackets.

Vivianne had no idea who was paying for the party, but from the golden sculpted decorations to the glitter-scented air that lent a glow to the room, they'd spared no expense. The fountains startled her. At first she'd assumed the silver-painted statues were sculpted from polished marble, but as the figures slowly pirouetted, she realized that trained actresses and elaborate costuming had fooled her eyes.

Jordan stood beside her looking elegant in a black

jacket with black-studded shoulder pads that showed off his wide torso, and a black shirt and black pants. Vivianne had chosen a gold gown that trailed along the floor to hide the ugly flat sandals Jordan had insisted she wear.

"You're gorgeous," he said with an intimate heat in his eyes that warmed her down to her toes as they made their way through the twenty-foot-high front doors.

"The gown doesn't look right without heels," she responded, concerned that someone would notice they were strangers here owing to her footwear more than any fashion faux pas.

Her role was to deflect attention from Jordan so he could focus on scanning minds. Her plan was for them to dance together, moving around the room to give him a chance to scout without having to converse. But there was no music.

Once she looked past the brightly hued gowns and sweeping architecture, the Tribe party was really quite dreary. There was no art, no laughter, no smiles, no joy here.

"So what's plan B?" she asked.

"What makes you think I have a plan B?" he countered.

"I was hoping." She realized that just because she almost always had a backup plan didn't mean that Jordan did. He seemed to operate on the fly-by-the-seat-of-his-pants theory. So far it seemed to work for him.

"The buffet line looks long and winds through the crowd," he observed.

She slid her arm through his, and together they walked toward the drinks and finger foods. Even those didn't look appetizing. The display was pedestrian, with apparently no effort made toward making the food look appetizing.

Had the government here wiped out all creativity? Or did these people simply have other values?

A couple ahead of them in the buffet line turned toward them. Vivianne pasted on a smile. "Good evening."

The woman sized up Vivianne's gown, her hair, and her makeup with a sniff of disdain. Then, with a regal nod of her peach-tinted hair, the woman pretended not to hear Vivianne's greeting. "Looks like they've let in the riffraff."

Her husband shot them an apologetic look.

Vivianne dug an elbow into Jordan's side. "I told you these weren't the right shoes and that women pay attention. But did you listen?"

"I was wrong. Sorry," Jordan murmured, but she could tell he was distracted.

At least her feet didn't hurt. Vivianne had attended hundreds of social functions, but she'd never been so on edge. The woman's catty comment didn't faze her, but being in the middle of the enemy elite was daunting. Security was everywhere.

Jordan had done his mind-altering thing to convince the doorman they had an invite. But there were dozens of monitors in the ceiling, and they might have face recognition software. Or something that detected their alien DNA. Or—

Get a grip. Pretend this is a corporate party or a political function back on Earth.

Most couples were engaging in conversations, and by remaining silent, they would stick out. The socializing was up to her. She was an expert at small talk. The planet shouldn't matter.

Vivianne spoke to the couple behind them. "Beautiful night for a party."

The elderly woman peered through her glasses and frowned. "What's so beautiful about it?"

There was no weather underground, but Vivianne forced herself to sound happy as she recovered from her slight error. "Aren't you excited to be here?"

"I suppose." But the woman sounded bored and turned to speak with the couple on her other side. There was whispering and several odd looks thrown at Vivianne.

Fitting in was harder than she'd imagined. Undaunted, Vivianne held her chin high.

From across the room, she caught a man staring at her. Something was strange about one of his eyes. The light caught his iris, and the hair on the back of her neck rose. He had an artificial eye, which shouldn't bother her, but for some reason a chill shot down her spine. She had no idea why she was reacting to his stare and angled to take a better look. He was about halfway between her height and Jordan's and dressed in dark purple. He carried himself like royalty, his bearing haughty. She caught only a glimpse, because the group of fawning women who surrounded him suddenly closed in around the man.

"Jordan, you done?"

He sighed. "There's a lot of people here."

She nudged him. "Try to hit the guy over there in royal purple."

Jordan turned. "Which guy?"

She discreetly glanced to where she'd last seen him. "He's gone."

How had he disappeared so fast? And did his vanishing act have anything to do with them?

"Something's wrong." Jordan pulled her by the hand and threaded through the crowd to a side door.

A security guard immediately stepped in front of them. Jordan did one of his mental tricks to freeze the man, and they sidestepped and headed into the street.

The artificial sun had been replaced with artificial moonlight. The air was humid and dank. Jordan merged into a shadow and kneeled. She thought he needed to tie his shoe. Instead he ripped off the bottom of her gown.

He stood, took her hand again. "Run."

She hated running when she had no idea what was going on, but she didn't dare question him, not when he'd used that serious voice he saved for emergencies. Her pulse pounded as her feet slapped the pavement. While Jordan seemed to know exactly where he was going and she saw no sign of pursuit, she still felt like a fox with the hounds nipping at her heels.

He zipped down an alley, zagged through an empty playground, and backtracked twice. They sprinted past a shopping center into a residential area, through several yards, and over a footbridge.

Her lungs burned, but finally he slowed. "We've lost them."

"Did you get what you needed?" she asked between giant gulps of air.

"Maybe." He steered her onto the sidewalk.

"Care to explain?" She tried to keep the petulance from her voice. She'd never liked being kept in the dark. Without information, she couldn't make good decisions, and if she couldn't make good decisions, she wasn't in control.

"Trendonis was in that room." He spoke as if choosing his words with care. As if he didn't have every reason to hate the man.

She knew better. Jordan controlled his deep emotions

by shutting down his anger and hatred of the man who'd destroyed his world.

"You think Trendonis was the man I saw? The man with the artificial eye . . ." Sweet stars. "The eye you pecked out when you were helping Arthur to leave Pendragon?" The years hadn't been kind to the Trendonis she'd seen destroy Dominus in Jordan's memories. Years of cruelty had aged his face, hardened him.

"That was him." Jordan kept walking through a path along a creek.

"But you didn't see him. His face looked different from the one I saw in your memories."

"Trendonis is known for using many names and disguises, but I got just a hint of his thoughts before he closed them off."

She sucked in a deep breath. "Are you saying you couldn't read him?"

"Something blocked me. Too much alcohol or drugs."

She shook her head. "I saw his eyes. Trust me, that man can think like a computer."

"Yeah, his intelligence is off the charts." Jordan crossed a bridge. "The hartog's house . . . that was Trendonis's home. And the Grail's there. I managed to pick up that much before Trendonis shut me down."

"Why do you choose your words so carefully when you speak of the Tribe leader?"

"Do I?"

"Yes."

"Perhaps it's the only way to control my hatred." He took her hand and squeezed. "My father worked for the Dominus Defense Department, and he and his coworkers specialized in maintaining a planetary shield that could stop the weapons that destroyed Dominus. I wasn't supposed to speak about his work to anyone. But in a casual comment I mentioned to a friend that my father worked on the Hill."

"The Hill?"

"A nickname for his job location. Like your CIA calls their headquarters the Farm." Jordan gathered his thoughts. "Anyway, after that comment, it wasn't difficult for the Tribes to follow my father to work, infiltrate the Hill, and turn off the planetary defense system."

"So you link that casual comment to the destruction of your world?"

"Trendonis was my best friend. I should have suspected. I should have known he wasn't who he claimed." He held her gaze a moment too long, then turned away, plainly unwilling to reveal any more of his guilt.

"How could you know?" she asked, softly, stunned he'd carried this burden for so long.

Her tenderness only seemed to make him be harder on himself. "Because I overheard him send a transmission once. And when I questioned him about it, he told me he was simply sending messages to the stars, hoping someone would hear him. And fool that I was, I believed him."

"Of course you believed him. He was your friend."

She raised her hand to her mouth, her mind swirling at the implications. No wonder Jordan's determination to stop Trendonis had burned for centuries. Trendonis had befriended him, used him, and then destroyed his world.

"How did you and Trendonis meet?" she asked, realizing that for Jordan to feel such guilt, he had to feel responsible.

"At school. I suspect he was much older than he led me to believe."

"So he took advantage of your youth."

"Youth is not an excuse for stupidity," Jordan replied.

She ached for his loss, his pain. To carry that burden on his shoulders for centuries was too much for any man to bear. A man with less inner strength might have given up, gone mad. But Jordan had fought at King Arthur's side against the Tribes, and although they'd defeated them soundly, it wasn't enough. Jordan wouldn't be satisfied until Trendonis was stopped for good.

Even if Jordan succeeded, would he ever forgive himself? Would he be able to stop punishing himself and allow himself some happiness?

She wasn't thinking straight. If Jordan succeeded in uniting the Staff and the Grail, he would die. For him, the grim reality of success was death.

Still, she wished to ease his pain. "Jordan, you made a mistake anyone could make. But even if you hadn't mentioned your father's line of work, Trendonis would have found another way to ruin Dominus. It was an accident that he used your slip up against your world."

"That's true." His voice was angry, sad, and hard. "But it's still a stain on my soul. All those billions of lives winked out in one giant flash of light. All of them dead. What the Tribes cannot dominate, they destroy." Jordan's eyes blazed.

"Now they're after Earth." She squeezed his hand, and for the first time since they'd landed on Pentar, she felt strength and a certainty of purpose flowing through her. "We're going to find the Grail and stop him."

*Don't let someone become a priority in your life when
you are just an option in their life. Relationships work
best when balanced.*

—QUEEN MARISA

36

Stop him? Jordan would have liked nothing better than to
kill the son of a bitch. But he couldn't risk losing the Grail
for the personal satisfaction of seeing Trendonis dead.

Vivianne must have sensed his banked rage. "What's
wrong?"

He turned the conversation to a new concern. "Trendonis shut me out back there, and if it wasn't drugs or
alcohol, I'd love to know how he did it."

Vivianne walked beside him. "You think it's a natural
ability, or some kind of artificial force field?"

"At first Trendonis was open to me."

"That's when you saw the Grail in his mind?" she asked.

He nodded. "Just as I skimmed the surface, Trendonis
snapped up the barrier."

"So he felt you in his head?"

"Or his mental blocks rise automatically and naturally, or . . ."

"Or he has a device that can shut you down?"

"It's possible. He spent enough time on my world. The adults would have known about his plan to destroy us unless Trendonis had had a way to hide his thoughts."

"None of these other people on Pentar have shown any indication of possessing a mental shield, have they?"

"No." Something niggled in the back of Jordan's mind. "Actually, I have encountered that kind of shield before."

"Really?"

"Back on Arcturus, Arthur was also totally unreadable. At the time, I was still unskilled and didn't know I could read almost everyone's minds."

"You assumed you could read me because of the blue lights?"

"Yes. But now I'm thinking that Arthur must have had the same kind of shield as Trendonis."

Vivianne squeezed his hand as they turned a corner. "Doesn't it seem odd to you that Arthur and Trendonis both have the same technology or same genetic trait?"

"It's as suspicious as blue hell."

"Blue hell?"

"A Dominus expression for—" Jordan pulled her into the shadows. "Sh."

Vivianne stood quietly as a squad of Security passed by, their lights sweeping the sidewalks. Jordan perused their minds as the vehicle passed. The low-level operatives were only following orders to patrol the sector, and he picked up nothing useful.

"We're almost there," he whispered. "Let's hurry."

Trendonis's mansion loomed in the moonlight, and Jordan paused to sweep the interior. "A maid's sleeping in the chamber over the garage. Two men and the hartog are in a secret room that connects to Trendonis's home office."

"Are there alarms?" Vivianne peered through the landscaped back yard to the double glass doors that overlooked a patio at the rear of the house.

"Trendonis will have a security system."

"What about the hartog?" Vivianne reminded him.

"It's dreaming about running free."

"Can you read insects and birds, too?" she asked.

"Don't know. Maybe. Why?" He braced for a sarcastic comment. He didn't have to read her mind to know his new self made her uneasy.

"We could use a lookout."

Her practicality made him grin. It wouldn't hurt to tap into the wildlife. But as he sent his mind outward, to his surprise, he encountered nothing. "Either I can only read higher life forms, or there's no wildlife."

"Come to think of it, I haven't seen any birds," she murmured as they crossed the patio toward the back doors. Then she stopped, pointed, and whispered, "See those wires? Give me a minute and I'll disconnect the alarm."

Vivianne was sophisticated and educated. She was so polished and independent, he tended to forget that she had street skills, too. That she'd been able to pick a lock since childhood.

She pulled a multitool from a hidden compartment in her handheld. "This should work."

It took her less than twenty seconds to disable the alarm.

"Good work." He reached for the door.

She pulled him back. "Not so fast."

"What?"

"That was too easy. We're talking about the Holy Grail. If Trendonis is as smart as you say, he'll have motion detectors, hidden surveillance cameras, audio and infrared warning devices, possibly temperature sensors, too. I'm betting there's a transmitter nearby, and I need to disable it before we move in."

"Hold on a sec." He scanned the guards' minds. "The guards don't know anything," he reported, "but a few months ago, one of them noted a suspicious box on the roof. When he went to investigate, he was told to stay away, that it was for Trendonis's communications with his spaceships."

"Call me impressed." Vivianne headed toward a tree with thick branches that would allow an easy climb to the roof. "You pulled out all that in just a few seconds?"

Jordan gave her a boost up to the first branch. "The guards are worried."

"Why?" Vivianne scampered up the tree.

"Trendonis put them on alert."

"That's not good." Vivianne pulled herself onto the roof.

By the time he climbed up beside her, she'd already picked the lock on the box. She shined a tiny penlight inside. Light reflected back on her face. Eyes focused, she traced several wires. "More bad news."

"What's wrong?"

"If I cut this wire, it automatically sends an alarm."

"No problem. I can follow the signal. Whoever receives it will take a nap."

She didn't hesitate. She snipped two wires and disconnected a third. Jordan let his mind flow with the signal, curious where it would lead. Trendonis was using a private security firm. Interesting choice. Apparently he didn't trust the local authorities or the military.

Jordan put the man to sleep and withdrew. "We're good to go. You ready?"

"Have you taken care of the guards inside?"

"Not yet. I want to wait until the last moment in case Trendonis calls to check in."

"Good idea." Vivianne climbed down the tree and jumped the last few feet, landing like a cat on the back deck and making almost no sound.

He swung down behind her, expecting to land in the dark. Instead, spotlights shot on, blinding him from half a dozen angles.

Experience is what causes a person to make new mistakes instead of old ones.

—ALBERT EINSTEIN

37

❦

Vivianne swore. She'd disconnected the entire alarm system, but she'd forgotten the lights. Not part of the alarm, these lights were simply there for convenience. Nevertheless, she and Jordan no longer had the element of surprise.

Stomach dancing up her throat, she lunged toward a window, knocked out a pane of glass, unlatched the lock, and climbed through. Jordan followed.

From deep inside the mansion, she heard the hartog making noises that sounded like a seal barking. Jordan sprinted past her and straight down a hallway lined with photographs. Adrenaline pumping, she raced after him.

Rounding a corner, she sped straight through an elaborate office with a huge desk, polished steel cabinets, and several bronzed sculptures. Skidding to a halt on the slick granite floor, she almost bumped into Jordan, who had halted to press his ear to the door.

A chill of fear swept over her. Why wasn't he scanning ahead with his mind?

"What's wrong?" she asked.

"I've knocked out the guards, but the hartog isn't susceptible to my power."

Vivianne glanced around the office. A clear jar with blue twigs inside caught her eye. She grabbed it, twisted open the lid, and smelled. Hartog treats?

She couldn't be certain. The sticks might be breath mints or decoration or medicine. "Open the door."

Jordan cracked it, and from inside, the hartog whined. Just before the animal pounced, she tossed a handful of the blue twigs inside. The hartog snorted, crunched, and slurped happily, and she grinned.

Jordan pulled his blaster and reopened the door. The hartog paid no attention to them—he was too busy scarfing down his treats. Beyond the munching hartog, two guards sprawled on the floor, out cold thanks to Jordan.

Vivianne followed him inside and gasped. Antiquities from every age, planet, and race decorated the high-ceilinged room. Surreal paintings, beautifully proportioned statues, sculpted objects, and delicate carvings in wood, stone, and meteorite decorated this windowless inner sanctum.

The place of honor was reserved for a white granite pedestal. Atop the pedestal perched a large cup with graceful handles.

"The Holy Grail?" she asked, her tone filled with awe.

Jordan nodded and reached for the Grail.

"Wait." She knocked his hand back. "Check the guards' minds. See if this thing's triggered to go off when the Grail's weight is removed."

Jordan stilled, checking the men, then shook his head. "No. We're safe."

At the sight of his careful handling of the sacred chalice, both sadness and happiness flooded her.

They'd found the Holy Grail.

The healing cup that might save Earth.

The instrument of Jordan's death.

He stood still, mesmerized by the smooth metal. His eyes glinted with triumph.

One of the guards groaned, reminding her that more could arrive any moment. "Jordan. We should go."

The light in Jordan's eyes hardened to a bright glint. "It's a fake."

"What?" She spun around so fast she almost tripped.

An awful sinking sensation engulfed her. Had they come all this way for nothing? "How do you know it's not real?"

"The Grail contains a rippling energy field that's visible to the naked eye."

She stared at the cup. "Maybe it's in the dormant stage."

"There's only one way to find out." From his backpack, he withdrew his canteen and poured water into the Grail, then sipped from the cup's lip. Then he handed her his knife, hilt first, and held out his arm. "Cut me."

Damn him. The idea of cutting him made her nauseous.

"I possess the Grail and I've drunk from it. If it's real, I can't die in battle."

"But if you're right, if the Grail's a fake, I'm not about to deliver a mortal wound."

"A small cut should suffice."

Her hand shook. Sweat beaded on her scalp and rolled

down her neck. She licked her lip, and then, with a sigh, she lowered the knife. "Why don't you do it?"

"Because the wound must be in battle." He raised his brows. "Self-inflicted wounds don't count."

Her stomach twisted in agitation. "I can't carve you up like a piece of meat."

"Do it." He hardened his voice. "Earth can't afford for us to make a mistake. We can't leave unless we're certain we have the genuine article."

His authoritarian tone was just brutal enough to remind her of the seriousness of their situation. Just enough to make her angry, and that anger fed her determination. She sliced a small cut across his upper arm.

He hissed in a breath but didn't move. They both watched the blood well, then trickle down to his elbow.

"How long should it take to heal?" she asked, handing him back the knife and hoping she never had to do anything like that again.

"It's not working." He tossed the fake aside. "Search the rest of these artifacts. It must be here."

Maybe not. "Maybe the vision from the hartog was from this fake. Maybe even Trendonis doesn't know it's a counterfeit." She peered at shelves that held ethereal statues of dragons, their wings spread for flight; wooden puzzles carved from moonstone; and an entire collection of leather-clad books with holographic covers.

"In the hartog's memory, the Grail glowed. It was real."

She looked behind several paintings. "There's no safe hidden back here."

"Maybe we should roll up the area rug and look under

it." Jordan peered behind an elaborate golden mirror that dominated the room.

When he'd moved the mirror, something caught her eye, a strange reflection that was probably a trick of the light. Still, she was curious. "Do that again," she demanded.

"What are you talking about?"

"Swing the mirror."

He did as she asked, and this time her puzzlement grew. "Do you see something weird in the mirror?"

He shook his head.

"Let's change places," she insisted.

"Watch closely." She tilted the mirror from side to side, the bottom of its frame scraping the wall. "See anything odd?"

Jordan went pale and his eyes gleamed. "It's not a mirror."

"It's not?"

"It's a reflection pool." Jordan faced the mirror head-on, wonder in his eyes.

"A reflection pool?" she asked.

"I've never seen one, but according to legend, reflection pools can absorb objects. So it would be a terrific hiding place." He reached toward the mirror, but his palms didn't stop on the surface like she'd expected. Instead, his hands plunged through the mirror up to his elbows.

Vivianne gasped. She didn't understand what she was seeing. Jordan was elbow deep into the mirror, and yet the mirror was flat against the wall. It was as if the mirror held another dimension of space.

"Got it." Jordan pulled his hands out of the mirror and held up the Grail.

This Grail was shaped exactly like the fake. But the

genuine burnished cup swirled with a sparkling inner energy that mesmerized her.

The Holy Grail.

Hands shaking, she poured water into the cup and again Jordan sipped. Holding her breath, she stared at his arm. The blood dried, scabbed over. Within seconds, his flesh had healed.

The hair on the back of her neck stood on end. No one knew who'd made the Grail or how it actually healed. But the legends on dozens of worlds made the object priceless.

Jordan stuffed the Grail into his backpack, then leaned over and kissed her. "We did it, Vi. We've got it."

"Yeah." She pulled back reluctantly. The knowledge that he wanted her sent a fierce rush of pleasure through her. Then the pleasure jumbled with elation and wretchedness.

Her time with Jordan was running out.

Love is a horizon that expands as we soar toward it.
　　　　　　　　　　　　　—HIGH PRIESTESS OF AVALON

38

Vivianne watched Jordan tense and jerk his head to one side as if he was listening and focusing intently. His wince told her something was wrong. But she knew better than to ask questions and interrupt his concentration while he was scanning minds. Instead, she helped him sling the backpack with the Grail over his shoulder.

When Jordan refocused, he hurried her out of the secret chamber. "When we entered and triggered the patio lights, a guard called in the disturbance."

"Trendonis is sending Security to check on the house?" Vivianne guessed, her stomach twisting into a knot.

Jordan helped her back out the window. "He must have grown suspicious. He's sending eight squads."

Sweat broke out all over Vivianne as they crossed the back yard. "How much time have we got?"

"Not long. Maybe five minutes."

Vivianne swore under her breath. "Which way?"

"I don't know. I can't scan again while we're moving this fast. Run."

Vivianne made an arbitrary right and pounded down

the sidewalk. Her footsteps seemed loud in her own ears. A curtain moved aside in the second story of one of the mansions, and someone peered out.

They were too vulnerable out in the open. "We have to get off the street."

Jordan agreed. "I know."

They reached the park and kept running. A couple walking hand in hand stopped to stare. She was certain they'd remember them and send Security. If only they could double back, but there was no place to hide in the block of mansions.

"Can we change levels?" she asked, her breath coming in gasps, not so much from exhaustion but fear. If Trendonis caught them now, they might not ever get another chance to escape with the Grail.

"Look for another lift station."

She kept her eyes peeled for the wide gates that funneled people onto the giant platforms.

A stitch in her side burned. Her legs ached, and her muscles refused to relax.

Dig deeper.

Sirens and flashing lights behind her urged her to move her feet faster. Still, she lagged behind Jordan.

"Only a little farther," he encouraged her.

They were in the middle of this sector. They might still have miles to go. She looked right. Left. Back over her shoulder. The orange lights on the chase vehicles behind them were growing more intense by the second.

"Jordan, we need to hide. Soon."

"Shoot me some mental power."

She focused on her fear. *We need to hide.* She opened

the spigot of fear and let it flow through her, felt him siphoning it up.

"One more block. Second house on the right. It's vacant."

Thank God. She was so tired she could barely move one foot in front of the other. Pumping her arms, she forced her legs to keep churning, her feet to keep moving. One more step. One more step. She kept up the chant. Each time she yearned to slow, she told herself to take just one more step.

"Here." Jordan veered down a path and headed straight to the back porch.

"Alarms?" she gasped.

"They're disconnected."

Jordan raised his fist to break a window.

"Don't."

Sucking down air, she removed her multitool from her handheld and picked the lock. Jordan shoved open the door.

They scurried inside and sank to the floor just as a Security vehicle turned down the street. Slowly, it rolled toward them, its lights outlining the house.

"You think they saw us?" she asked between pants.

"Doesn't look like it." Jordan flattened his body and peeked out the window.

It didn't *look* like it? Jordan sounded as if he didn't know for sure.

"Why can't you read their minds?" she asked.

"I don't know." He rubbed his temple. "But I'm blocked again."

Not good. "Perhaps you need to rest."

"Maybe." His tone was tight, annoyed.

They were inside a living area. Although a sagging sofa, a rickety table, and several lamps remained, the home was vacant. Off the main room she saw a kitchen. Her stomach rumbled, reminding her they hadn't eaten in hours.

She was about to hunt down some food when she glanced at Jordan. He leaned against a wall, chin slumped against his chest.

"Jordan?" She staggered over to him and discovered he was shaking. "What's wrong?"

"Don't know." Again he spoke in that tight voice he'd used earlier.

She slung an arm around his waist. "Let's get you onto the couch before you fall and hurt yourself."

"No w-w-worries. C-can't d-die. Have the G-grail."

She placed her free hand on Jordan's forehead. "You're burning up."

After helping him to the couch, she searched the kitchen for a dishcloth, placed it under cool tap water, and wrung it out in the sink. Returning to his side, she bathed his face and neck.

But mere moments after she placed the towel on his flesh, his body heat warmed the towel. Even worse, Jordan was once again glowing from the inside out. Either she was seeing things, or this time more of those bluish lights had returned, shining so brightly she had to squint. It seemed as though the lights themselves were responsible for raising his temperature, yet back in the cave, she hadn't noticed him visibly warming.

She tugged him to his feet. "Get up. We have to cool you down."

Together they moved toward the back rooms of the house. At the sight of a huge bathing tub, her pulse skipped in relief. At least sixteen feet long and eight feet wide with a seat and jets at one end, the indoor pool's clear water lapped the steps invitingly.

Jordan tripped forward and barely kicked off his shoes before staggering into the pool fully clothed. With his flesh so hot, she almost expected to hear hissing as the blue lights struck the water. Although the lights didn't even dim, blue once again shined from Jordan's eyes.

By now she'd become somewhat accustomed to the weird glow. After all, jellyfish glowed, and their phosphorescence was not only natural but compelling. Perhaps it was because her own flesh was also beginning to glow that she didn't find him so strange.

Holding up her hand to the light, she marveled at the sparkles that tingled pleasantly. "What's happening to us?"

"You don't know?" he murmured, and then his mouth came down on hers.

And instantly she knew. Jolted by the electric zing that ripped through her core, she gasped at the wondrous sensations swirling around her, through her, inside her. Heat was transformed into burning lust. Once again she was surrounded by Jordan's sparkling blue aura, but now it was also becoming part of her.

And he felt good. Damn good.

Every cell in her body was sensitized and aching for his touch. It was almost as if those blue lights were a torch that ignited a burn so hot it consumed them.

"I want you," he whispered. "I need you, Vi. I have to have you."

"Then take me." She leaned into him, her chest pressed against him, her double hearts thudding against her ribs. Sliding against his hard length, she lost herself in the blue cloud of light.

He was thinking about her lips, how he loved the way she tasted, how she welcomed him with eagerness and yet somehow still stayed soft and willing. As they kissed, her emotions fed him, and *his* thoughts were trickling into her.

He was enjoying the scent of her skin, anticipating the removal of her clothes. As his thoughts weaved with hers, as he remembered the peachy pink color of her areolas, she reacted to his thoughts, her nipples tightening, feeding him energy.

Her response to his thoughts and the resulting energy gave him pleasure, and he smoothed his hands up her rib-cage to cup her breasts, skimmed his fingertips over the straining tips. A ripening tingle of need swooped through her.

Somehow she knew he could feel what he was doing to her. Just as she could feel how much he enjoyed playing with her nipples. Overwhelmed by his thoughts and hers, she felt caught in a swirling energy–pleasure loop that was spiraling out of control.

"Jordan?" she gasped. The man knew exactly what felt good, how much pressure to exert and where . . . because she was feeding him her emotions, and he was feeling exactly what she felt, too.

"Mm."

She tore her mouth from his. "Your thoughts are rolling into mine."

"I know," he murmured, trailing his lips down her neck.

"But, but," she sputtered. "What's going on?"

He sighed and straightened, but the effort cost him. She could feel his heavy groin, the tension in his erection, the tightness and the yearning to plunge into her. Yet he held back. "The Staff's picked you for my mate."

She blinked. "What?"

"According to the data chip Arthur gave me, the Staff senses my perfect mate. And does its best to make sure we realize what we are to each other. That first time we made love, the Staff changed our electrical chemistry to bring us together." His voice was gentle, patient, and she could feel him still holding back his desire to make love.

She recalled how lust had overwhelmed her that first time in the engine room, how her passion had seemed to come out of nowhere.

"And those shared memories? The Staff used them to make us feel closer to each other?"

"Yes."

"And now?" she prodded. "The Staff is messing with our heads?"

"When the Staff picks out a mate, there is no fighting one's destiny."

She slipped her arms around his neck. "I tried not to love you."

"Me, too." He kissed the tip of her nose. "We've bonded on physical and emotional levels, as well as on a plane of energy." He threaded one hand through his hair. "But on Dominus, there are . . . deeper bonds. *Shari-ki* is more than a mental bond."

"*Shari-ki?*"

"There's no equivalent in your language. To my people, *Shari-ki* is the total unification of everything we are, everything we feel, want, and have to give, everything we shall be."

"If we unite, will I still . . . be me?"

"You'll be a combination of both of us." By now he knew her well enough to guess her deepest fear. "It's not so much losing a part of yourself. Think of it as gaining everything that I am."

Not long ago, being part of him and him being part of her would have scared her to death. But no longer. She could love him, share his mind, and still be independent. Loving didn't change the self—loving expanded the self. She recalled his thoughts, her thoughts, melding into one. "And *shari-ki* happens when we make love?"

"Yes." He tipped up her chin, his thumb caressing her cheek. "But understand that *shari-ki* is not only a connection during lovemaking."

Her mouth went dry. "What are you saying?"

"*Shari-ki* is forever. Even after I am dead and gone, there will always be part of me with you."

"Forever?" Her eyes widened. "You're saying we'll be linked beyond death?"

He nodded. "We'll be joined for eternity."

Eternity? She might not have to lose him? Her hopes rose.

"I think I'll like this *shari-ki*." She snuggled against him. "What do we have to do?"

"You're certain?"

"Yes."

"This connection once made cannot be broken."

"So we'll always be able to communicate?"

He shook his head. "*Shari-ki* doesn't work like that. It's more of a presence."

"I'm not sure I understand." Still, if she could keep part of him, it would be a huge comfort to her. The businesswoman in her wanted to know exactly what she was agreeing to, but Jordan seemed to be having difficulty putting *shari-ki* into words.

"You'll be able to tap into my memories. But you won't know everything I know—not unless you ask. It's like having a databank at your disposal, but unless you pull out the right file and read it, you won't have the answers."

If she could tap into his thoughts, his feelings, his knowledge, she would never lose him. "*Shari-ki* is a two-way deal. You'll have all my memories, too?"

"For as long as I live." He placed his lips on her forehead.

"I'd like that."

His mouth came back down on hers and his thoughts flooded her. His hunger flooded her. Her acceptance of *shari-ki* had pleased him. She could feel his pleasure, his pride, his love, and as his feelings wrapped around her, she'd never felt so cherished, so happy, so filled with joy.

If her destiny was to have only this one moment of total connection, she was determined to enjoy every second. She marveled as Jordan skimmed his hands over her flesh and enjoyed her softness under his fingertips.

"God. You feel incredible," he murmured.

As a bolt of his heat electrified her nerve endings, she gasped. His blood was pounding, his sex heavy and hard.

"How . . . do . . . you hold back?" she asked.

"It isn't easy." He spoke between gritted teeth, his voice harsh, but she could feel the smile beneath his words. But just as important, she knew he was holding back to give her time for her pleasure to build. Only now that she could feel how badly he wanted her, she felt as if the heat was consuming her, too.

The swirl of blue lights thickened. Dozens of fleeting impressions rushed through the new mental bond they were forming. She saw Jordan as a small boy in his mother's arms after he'd skinned his knee. His father swinging the boy up onto his shoulders at a fair. The taste of Dominus berries. The sound of a waterfall pounding into a river as he kissed his first girl. Enjoyment of a deep friendship with Arthur. His painful loss of the Ancient Staff, flying in the shape of an owl, satisfaction at getting back his human form.

His memories of her brought a lump to her throat. The first time they'd made love. She saw her own face through his eyes, her lips soft and pouty, the way she swept her hair off her face to reveal her cheekbones. The love for her that burned so brightly at his core.

She focused on that love. Drew on it. Pulled it around her like a warm blanket. Jordan even liked when she was stubborn. He wasn't at all threatened by her ability to run a vast company. In fact, he was proud of her.

All those thoughts flashed by in seconds. The chemistry between them stoked the fire he'd already kindled. She wasn't certain when they peeled off their clothes. But finally they were both naked.

He turned her around. "Look at us."

She opened her eyes to see their reflections in a mirror. The water was up to her waist, her back against his chest, her head resting on his powerful shoulder. He cupped her breasts and flicked his fingers over the tips, shooting heat straight to her core.

She thrashed her head, thinking she couldn't stand to wait much longer. But she would. Because he had to wait, too. He could feel her burning up, feel the tension in her, the anticipation as she fed him energy and it looped back and swelled between them. She'd always wanted him to know how good he made her feel, and now he did.

At the same time, she wanted to give him pleasure.

Turning in his arms, she leaned forward, and as her teeth closed on the cord of flesh at his neck, his excitement merged with her own, spiraling into something greater than either of them alone.

"Feeling what you feel is so cool," she murmured.

"Here I thought I was making you hot," he teased.

She lifted her mouth to his chest, laved his nipple. "Can't you feel the burn?"

He traced his hands over her back, her hips. *Lower.*

He complied with her thought and his hands cupped her butt. Craving more friction, she wrapped her legs around him, intent on pressing against him, on merging their bodies.

She couldn't wait to know what he felt like when he was inside her. But he seemed in no hurry at all, his hands caressing, stroking, his mouth once more finding her lips. But she knew better. She could feel his anticipation as her own and fed him more energy.

His hearts battered his ribs, and his groin grew even tighter. Even as he kissed her, he was restraining a groan. The knowledge of how badly he wanted her made her frantic to have him now.

Oh, sweet stars, he had yet to touch her where she wanted him most, and she was lifting herself onto his hips, trying to slide down onto his sex.

"Stop squirming," he warned.

"I can't wait." She needed him now. *Now. Now. Now.*

With a laugh, he raised her bottom until she was just the right height. His hardness filled her, her heat sheathing him, the delicious friction radiating from his flesh as well as her own. And it was magical, marvelous, magnificent.

Her head was spinning as he thrust into her.

She began to move with him, certain she was about to explode.

Wait. He withdrew.

"Nooo."

He placed his hands around her waist, lifted her to the pool's edge, parted her thighs. With a wicked grin, he ducked his head between her legs. "I have to taste you."

Gently, he parted her cleft, blew on her hot folds. His tongue tickled her clit. Oh, God. Awash in sensation, the feel of his tongue rasping back and forth drove her to the brink. Every muscle in her clenched. He was driving her wild because he knew exactly where and how and when to touch her . . . because he was right there feeling it with her.

The more pleasure he gave her, the more frantically she squirmed; the more energy she fed him, the more excited he got. Until she couldn't tell which sensation was hers and which pleasure was his.

She didn't want to explode. Not until he was inside her. Finally, when he knew she couldn't stand another moment, he gave her her wish.

This time she didn't hold back. Instead, she let loose, exploding once, then again and again. Even as she shared the pleasure, he marveled at the multiple eruptions until she swept him right along with her.

Feeling him enjoy her was a mystical experience that she would never, ever forget. She grinned. Not only did she have her own memory. Thanks to *shari-ki,* she now also had his.

History is owned by the winner.

—KING RION JAQARD

39

Vivianne and Jordan left the house a few hours later, after the heat from Security died down. Vivianne already knew the important things about Jordan. Besides being hot in bed, he was a man of honor, brave and kind. But now that she possessed Jordan's memories, there were so many things she wanted to know about him. And all she had to do was think the question and the memory was there, but now was not the time.

With Jordan busy mind scanning and distracted from their immediate surroundings, she had to keep her eyes peeled for Security as they sneaked upward level by level. When they reached the surface and had no difficulty transferring back to the space station, she had very confused feelings about their success. While on the one hand she couldn't wait to get back to the *Draco,* on the other, dread filled her. Once they launched into space, Jordan would unite the Grail and the Staff.

She was going to lose him. Although she'd known the inevitability of what was coming, she hadn't realized how it was going to tear her apart. She'd told herself she'd ac-

cepted his death, but she'd always harbored a secret hope
that his sacrifice wouldn't be necessary.

As they strode onto the space station's loading dock,
her pulse picked up. If Trendonis was going to stop them,
this would be the place. But the mechanics seemed to pay
no attention to them. Jordan signed off on the repairs,
using his skills to fool the Tribes into thinking they'd
paid, with credits they didn't have.

Vivianne hurried aboard ship, and George raced forward to greet her, then dropped a Ping-Pong ball at her
feet. She petted his head, picked up the ball, and tossed it
toward the galley. "Fetch."

George happily ran after the ball as Jordan closed the
hatch behind him. "Traffic control's given us a slot to
leave in five minutes."

She raised her eyebrow. "That's fast."

"A bribe worked wonders." Jordan kissed her cheek
and headed for the bridge.

She accepted the ball from George, then lifted the dog
into her arms and swallowed hard. Already her throat
was tightening. Her chest hurt. Just his simple kiss to her
cheek had set off her sorrow.

And while having his memories was a comfort, memories were no substitute for his arms around her, his demanding kisses, his gentle teasing, his thinking fast on
his feet. Going on without him would be the most difficult
thing she'd ever done.

He meant everything to her. She'd do almost anything
not to lose him. But if he didn't unite the Staff and the
Grail, Earth couldn't stand against the Tribes.

But suppose the damn legend was wrong?

Suppose Earth could win in the fight to come? Suppose Jordan's sacrifice was for nothing?

Vivianne spun and headed to her cabin. She needed to talk to Maggie. Perhaps things had gotten better.

"Earth's surrounded," Maggie told her in a grim, flat tone that dashed Vivianne's hopes. "The Tribes have given us twenty-four hours to surrender unconditionally, or they'll attack. They claim they have the Holy Grail and can't lose."

"That's not true. Jordan and I stole it back."

"It's too late," Maggie told her, her voice saddened. "They've blockaded Earth with an armada. Hundreds of thousands of ships are up there."

Vivianne's stomach knotted in fear and frustration. "What's Earth's response?"

"Total panic. There's almost no food. Little water. Martial law has failed. Too many deserters. There are riots in every major city. Looting. No one goes out without a gun."

Vivianne forced herself to speak past the fear choking her. "What's Earth's response to the Tribe's ultimatum?"

"News is sketchy. Europe and Africa will surrender. The North American States are ready to fire nuclear missiles into space, even though we know that when the radiation falls back on us, it may wipe out the planet."

"Earth's got to hold on, Maggie. Just a little longer. Once we launch the *Draco,* Jordan plans to unite the Ancient Staff with the Holy Grail."

"The Ancient Staff?"

"It's a legendary energy source."

"How will that help?" Maggie's skepticism came through the channel.

"According to galactic legend, once Jordan merges the two objects in space, the Tribes can't win."

"You'd better do it soon. With the state this planet's in, we may blow ourselves up before the Tribes get the chance."

"We'll do our best."

"Just hurry."

Sick to her stomach, chilled, and hating her options, Vivianne ended the transmission and gathered George against her, his warm, furry body lending comfort. The dog picked right up on her mood and tried to lick the tears running down her cheeks. She angrily wiped them away with the back of her hand.

She didn't have time for tears or sorrow or wallowing in self-pity. She didn't have time to grieve.

The captain of the *Draco* couldn't be seen crying on the bridge, and that's where she needed to go. She hurried to the command center, all the while sharing Maggie's news with Jordan over her handheld. She arrived just as the ship floated away from the loading dock.

Jordan was at the helm. Gray was at navigation, Sean at engineering. Tennison was speaking to traffic control through his headset.

Shari-ki *love, you knew this moment was coming.*

Jordan's thought popped into her head with a rush of tenderness.

"Traffic control's asking us to pull out of the lineup." Tennison frowned and tossed off the headset. "I sent back static. But that will only work for another ten seconds."

"Tell them our recent rehaul's giving us a problem," Vivianne ordered, "and we can't power down."

Tennison repeated the message twice, then cut the communication. "I don't think they bought it."

"How long until we clear the traffic?" Jordan asked Gray.

"Ten minutes. Maybe twelve."

That was too long. The Tribes would send ships after them.

Sean's head jerked up. "Captain, a warship just took off from dock eighty-seven. It's heading straight for us, and everything in its way is skedaddling."

"How long until they have a lock on the *Draco?*" Jordan asked.

"Two minutes," Gray said.

Jordan vacated the helm. "That might be enough time."

Vivianne felt herself go faint, nauseous.

"Time enough for what, sir?" Gray asked.

Not yet. Even if Vivianne hadn't been linked to Jordan through *shari-ki,* she would have felt his determination. They were in space, and he had less than two minutes to unite the Grail and the Staff.

Goodbye, shari-ki *love.*

Jordan raced toward the airlock, the Grail in a pack over his shoulder, the Staff sheathed to his side. Every fiber of Vivianne's being wanted to race after him, to beg him not to destroy the Staff that gave him life.

She willed herself to stay on the bridge. It took every speck of willpower to let him do what must be done. Earth needed her skills to keep the ship out of the Tribes' hands until Jordan . . . died.

Oh, God.

Tennison remained calm. "Traffic control's demanding we stop or be shot down."

Vivianne gathered her panic and locked it up tight. "Tell them we're trying to comply, but the valve's stuck and if we shut down, we'll career into the space station."

"One minute until the warship has us in a lock." Sean began a countdown.

Vivianne bit her lip and followed Jordan's progress on the monitor. He'd almost reached the airlock. But even after he tugged the handle, the portal would have to cycle and equalize the pressure before it would open.

"Where's Jordan's spacesuit?" Gray asked, eyes wide with horror.

Damn him. Even if the legend didn't come true, he was going to die.

"Thirty seconds."

The airlock opened. Now it had to cycle closed before the outside door would allow him to exit. He'd have to time his actions, uniting the Staff and the Grail in the critical moment just before the outer hatch opened. Because after the airlock opened to space, every cell in his body would explode due to the pressure differential.

Vivianne was going to be sick.

"Twenty seconds."

As the airlock cycled, Jordan kneeled, opened the backpack, and removed the Grail. He unsheathed and extended the Staff to its full length, then carefully positioned the bottom of the Staff over the center of the Grail.

A scream bubbled up from her chest to beg him not to do it. To forget the legend. She needed him. But so did Earth . . . She prayed the distance between them prevented her from feeding him her emotions, that his dying memory of her wouldn't be her anguish.

"Ten seconds," Gray said.

Vivianne held her breath, clenched her fists, and pressed her lips tightly together so she wouldn't make a sound. Jordan could hear the countdown through the speaker system. She had so many things she wanted to say. But there was no time.

She should look away from the monitor before she saw the man she loved disintegrate before her eyes. But she couldn't stop watching.

Eyes fierce with concentration, Jordan showed determination in every tight muscle of his body.

Sean monitored the gauges from engineering. "The hatch should be ready to open. On my mark. Now."

Jordan kicked the handle down to open the hatch. At the same time, he slammed the Ancient Staff into the center of the Holy Grail.

Nothing happened.

"The hatch." Jordan kicked the switch again. "It's jammed."

Gray spoke urgently. "Captain, the warship's locked on to us."

"Raise shields," she ordered, then spoke to Jordan, her hearts pounding. "What's wrong with the airlock?"

"The circuit's blown."

"Sean, go replace that faulty airlock circuit," she ordered.

"On my way." Sean hurried from the bridge.

That circuit had worked just fine when Vivianne and Jordan had come aboard just a few minutes ago. Had a circuit really blown?

Or had one of the Tribes' mechanics rigged the airlock circuit to blow after they left the space station? But why? The Tribes couldn't have known their plans, or the

Draco would never have been allowed to pull away from the dock. Nothing made sense, including the fact that the warship had yet to fire a weapon.

"Why haven't they shot at us?" she asked.

"I don't know," Gray answered.

"They don't want to destroy the Grail," Jordan muttered through the speakers, recycling the lock to reenter the main body of the ship.

Jordan was correct, of course. And that gave her only a measure of relief. Because not only could the firepower from the warship kill them a hundred times over, they couldn't out run the warship, either. Or even try Jordan's dangerous trick of jumping straight into hyperspace. With so many ships nearby, trying to jump now would pull other ships out of sub–light space with them and create a massive collision that would kill them all.

"Holy shit." Gray's fingers danced over his screen. "The mother of all energy beams is shooting straight for us."

Vivianne jerked her gaze from the monitor and Jordan to Gray's data screen. The burst was wide, dense, and constant. "Evasive maneuvers. Hard port forty degrees."

"It's a clutch beam," Jordan yelled. "If it catches us, we're dead meat."

Vivianne had never heard of a clutch beam, but after she accessed Jordan's memories, she knew that if the beam imprisoned the *Draco,* her ship couldn't cough up enough power to shake loose.

Vivianne prayed they could evade the beam long enough to fix the airlock. "Sean, hurry."

"I'm on it," he replied.

Gray fought with the controls. Sirens screamed. The engines protested.

"Throw the power from the shields into the engines," Jordan ordered as he sprinted onto the bridge.

Vivianne stared at the data stream in horror. The beam was just a hundred meters off the *Draco*'s bow. "We're not going to make it."

Dream as if you're immortal, live as if you'll die today.

—KING ARTHUR PENDRAGON

40

The clutch beam engulfed the *Draco,* and it felt as if they were swallowed by Jell-O, then held in place with Super Glue. Vivianne threw every ounce of power into the engines.

"We're redlining," Tennison warned.

"All right, power down," Vivianne ordered. There was no point in burning up the engines when they might need them later.

Gray frowned. "They've launched a shuttle."

"How long have we got?" Vivianne asked.

"Four, maybe five minutes."

Bleakly, she stared out the bridge viewscreens. There had been many times in her life when she felt like she'd come to a dead end. After her parents' deaths. Back in that cave on Arcturus.

Never had so many people been counting on her, and she was at a loss what to do next. They were trapped. In enemy territory. Surely it wouldn't take long for the Tribes to board the *Draco.*

Jordan took one look at the data and spun on his heel. "Vivianne, come with me."

"Gray, you have the com." Vivianne had no clue why Jordan wanted both captains to abandon the bridge at such a critical time, but she was doing no good here.

He hurried down to the engine room. "We have to make certain Trendonis doesn't get the Grail."

"How?"

"The Tribal shuttle will dock with the *Draco* in three minutes," Gray informed them over the speaker system.

Jordan slammed his hand on the intership communicator. "Sean, have you replaced the blown circuit?"

Sean's voice echoed back. "Almost done."

"What's your ETA?"

"Five minutes."

"Shuttle will be here in two," Gray said.

"Sean." Jordan began climbing into the second spacesuit. "Forget the repairs."

"Repeat that?" Sean asked.

"Don't fix the door. It'll only help the Tribes to board."

"Understood, Captain."

Jordan grabbed a spacesuit and shoved it into Vivianne's arms. "Get in."

Gray's voice filtered down from the bridge. "We've got a problem. I'm watching Sean on the monitor, and despite your direct orders, he fixed the circuit."

"Stop him," Jordan ordered.

Vivianne froze. "Oh, my God. Sean's the mole. He jammed that door so you couldn't get out. Now he's fixing it to let the Tribes inside."

Vivianne eyed Jordan. "What's the plan?"

He shot her a hard look. "I'm going to set off an explosion from engineering. The only thing between this deck and space is one bulkhead. The spacesuits will protect us from the explosion long enough . . ."

He wanted to blow a hole in the *Draco*'s hull? Even if the spacesuits protected them, no one else would survive. "That will kill . . . the crew."

"I know—" Jordan's voice was tight, hard, and angry.

"But—"

"Every one of them agreed that they'd do whatever it took to save Earth. In times of war, terrible sacrifices must be made." He grabbed her shoulders. "There's no time to argue. I need you to finish suiting up."

"We're the only two with spacesuits. That's cowardly."

"When our air runs out, we'll die, too. And if I fail, if the blast knocks me out, you're my plan B. It'll be up to you to save Earth."

"Why me? Why not—"

"Because you are the only other dragonshaper here. You are Earth's next-best chance to stop them."

Jordan wanted to destroy her ship. Horror filled her. "We can't just kill everyone . . ."

"You have a better idea?"

She didn't, and he knew it. Jordan gave her a quick hug. "I'm sorry."

His mouth crashed down on hers for a quick kiss. Her pulse quickened, and automatically she fed him fear, hope, and love.

She heard shouting, then Lyle over the com. "Sean's dead." He was panting. Clearly, Lyle had overpowered and killed the traitor. Who would have thought Lyle would take out the enemy mole all by himself?

They heard a clang. Gray spoke calmly, "The shuttle's latched directly over our airlock."

Lyle spoke in a high-pitched but fierce tone. "I've got a weapon. Whoever comes through first is dead."

"Hurry." Jordan helped her with the helmet and handed her the Grail. He clamped his own helmet on. Then he ripped the spare oxygen tank from the wall.

"Ready?"

She nodded. But no one was ready for this.

"Keep a firm grip on the Grail."

She wrapped her arms around it.

With one gloved hand, Jordan held the Staff tight. He removed his ax from his spacesuit's belt loop and swung it down hard, knocking off the valve.

Oxygen burst out of the tank's broken valve, rocketing the tank straight into the hull, where it exploded. Metal moaned, twisted, and screamed. Air rushed into space. The vacuum of space rushed in.

Jordan slammed the hilt of the Staff into the cup of the Grail. The two ancient relics burst into pure energy and erupted with a shock wave that slammed her backward. She banged her head, and for a moment her vision narrowed. When she could see once more, the Staff was glowing dark purple and the Grail swirled with a reddish-coppery glow that radiated in brilliant shimmering waves of energy.

Then the Grail and Staff vanished. Simply disappeared as if they'd never been.

"Look!" Vivianne spoke through the speaker of her spacesuit and pointed, her arm shaking. "The glow . . ." Energy released from the Staff and the Grail rippled through space, enshrouded the space station. And Pentar. *Oh, my . . .* "The wave's sweeping across the solar system."

Maybe even farther.

She stared in awe at the galactic-sized energy storm. The former blackness of space now shimmered with energy.

Everywhere she looked was now glittering with a coppery glow.

"What's happening?" she asked.

Jordan didn't answer. She turned to him and watched as he collapsed. Unmoving, eyes wide open, he floated, staring blindly ahead.

The Staff was gone, and so was he. With the hull blown wide open, her crew was dead. And soon she'd join them. Yet, along with the sorrow, fierce pride raged though her.

Tears streaming down her face, she gathered Jordan to her. "We did it, Jordan. It's done. You can finally rest in peace, *shari-ki*, my love."

When you give up, hope ends.
—KING ARTHUR PENDRAGON

41

❖❖❖

*V*ivianne, Jordan, are you all right? Gray shot a telepathic thought straight into her head.

You're alive? Vivianne asked, wondering if the stress
had made her lose her mind.

Yeah, I'm alive. Just don't ask if I'm still breathing.

What? She must still be in shock. Gray couldn't possibly have survived. Or be speaking to her telepathically.
Her mind was simply flailing from the stress. A person
could take only so much.

She'd obviously just reached her limit.

Spinning, she stared out again at space. The coppery glow
that reached as far as her eyes could see was slowly fading.

Gray's thoughts came through again, this time with
confusion and amazement. *The* Draco *has no air, but apparently none of us needs to breathe anymore.*

None of them? The implications staggered her. That
meant she no longer needed oxygen. She no longer needed
an atmosphere to survive. She could live on Mars or Venus
or thousands of other worlds that lacked air.

What about the boarding party?

Gone. The Tribes still need air and pressure. After that explosion, they . . . disintegrated.

Jordan united the Staff and the Grail. Had he altered some universal fundamental constant? She recalled back on Arcturus how Jordan had evolved, how he'd no longer needed to breathe. Arthur had whispered into her ear that her weakness would strengthen her. Was he referring to evolution? Had their weakness of requiring air, which so severely limited their galactic exploration, been turned into a strength? If their bodies no longer required oxygen, had they all evolved to a new level? The possibility of exploring oceans, as well as new planets with all kinds of atmospheres, was now open to them.

We have all changed, evolved.

Jordan suddenly blinked and sat up.

Vivianne's jaw dropped. Either she really was cracking up or she was dead. But if Jordan was here, she must be in heaven.

Vivianne floated over to him. "Jordan? Are we dead?"

"Apparently not so much." He grinned, his cocky attitude warming her.

She straightened until she could look him straight in the eye, their helmets almost touching. "But you said you needed the Staff to survive—"

"I was wrong."

She scowled. "Now I know I'm dead and have gone to heaven."

"What?"

"You're never wrong."

He chuckled. "The unification of the Grail and the Staff has changed the old rules of evolution."

"What are you saying?"

"I've changed on a critical biological level. Mitochondria in my cells are creating energy for me . . . just like you."

Gray interrupted. *The warship's out there and bearing down on us. It still has us in the clutch beam, and they're sending another boarding party.*

Hang tight. I'll handle them, Jordan answered.

Vivianne gestured to the hole in the *Draco*'s hull. "We can't fix this."

"True, but there's no reason we can't fly." Jordan placed an arm on her shoulder and began to unbuckle his helmet. Excitement burned in Jordan's eyes. "Take off your spacesuit."

"What?"

His eyes sparkled with a newborn energy. "And then let's shred our clothes."

She frowned at him. "I think being dead twice was too much for you. You should rest."

Jordan unfastened his helmet seal and stepped out of his spacesuit. *Haven't you ever wanted to dragonshape and fly through space?*

She felt nervous and edgy and just elated, too. *We're going to dragonshape and fly?*

Yes.

But how'll our wings propel us without air?

The same way the Staff powered the ship.

We're going to convert cosmic energy? she asked, shocked once again.

Yes.

As she took off her spacesuit, she began to think that anything was possible. She realized something else, too. People hadn't worn spacesuits just so they could breathe. Spacesuits shielded them from pressure, temperature, and radiation. Yet here she was floating in icy space without so much as a shiver.

Her hand should be frozen. She lifted it. Healthy enough. Normal pink. Maybe they were dead and this was their next life.

Stop.

She couldn't let herself become unhinged. "How's this possible? What's happened to us?"

"We've just climbed the next rung in the evolutionary ladder. Must be some kind of genetic skin adaptation that shields us." He strode toward the hole in the hull. And dived out.

Once he was free of the *Draco*'s confines, his clothes shredded as he dragonshaped. When he unfolded his wings and tucked up his feet, he was beautifully streamlined. But his wings' coloring caught her attention. Shiny crystals glowed along the surface, no doubt his cosmic energy collectors.

While she stood there admiring him, he soared straight toward the enemy shuttle.

Without hesitation, Vivianne immediately dragonshaped. *Oh, wow. Wow.. Awesome.* Normally when she changed shape she gave up much of her human intelligence. But with these new evolutionary enhancements, Vivianne possessed all her natural human intelligence in her dragon form.

Gray's mind touched hers, his amazement attached to his message. *Jordan? Vivianne? Are you flying outside the ship?*

It's us. Jordan flew straight for the oncoming shuttle.

And joyously, Vivianne flew after him, relishing the freedom, the awesome power, and the glory of flight.

Jordan, I'm so glad you didn't die on me.

Me, too, shari-ki *love. Now help me take out the shuttle.*

It is not sex that gives pleasure but the woman.

—Sir Lancelot

42

The Tribes' shuttle opened up her ports in preparation for firing missiles at the *Draco*.

Still caught in the mother ship's clutch beam, the *Draco* was like an injured bug in a spider's web. Vivianne and Jordan had to stop the slaughter.

With the mother ship clearly trying to haul the *Draco* into her cargo bay, Vivianne and Jordan both flew around the alien shuttle that had shaken loose during the explosion on the *Draco*. The tube the boarding party had used hung broken, but the hull looked intact.

Vivianne peered into the shuttle through the viewport and she could see the Tribe crew scurrying about, getting ready to fire at the *Draco*. If she could spread her wings to block their view, it would shake them up, maybe enough to throw off their aim enough to miss the *Draco*.

Be careful not to block a weapons port with your wings, Jordan warned.

She slammed into the bow and her weight rocked the ship. Gripping the hull with her claws, she changed plans and beat her powerful wings.

She spun the tiny shuttle, shaking the crew from their stations.

You're brilliant. Jordan flew onto the stern, and together they shook the ship.

No one could survive the shaking. The ruthless killing troubled her, but she had to remind herself that the shuttle crew had been about to fire on and board the *Draco* and the mother ship still had the *Draco* in a clutch beam.

When Jordan released his grip, she did, as well. The shuttle quickly spun away, out of control. Until it ran into the gravity well of a planet or star, it was fated to tumble through deep space.

Now what? she asked Jordan, glancing back toward the *Draco* to make certain it was still in one piece.

We destroy the mother ship.

Finding the Tribe warship's hulking mass was easy, since Pentar's silvery atmosphere outlined her dark silhouette. Apparently the warship's captain was certain of his tactical superiority. As she flew toward the huge beast of a ship, she understood why.

We can't shake her mass. Vivianne flew, keeping a sharp lookout for any advantage.

But it was Jordan who found a garbage chute. No dragon could insert so much as a claw through the narrow opening. It was too small even for a human.

Wait here. Jordan suddenly shifted from dragon form. If not for her sharp eyesight, she wouldn't have seen the owl he'd morphed into fly right up the trash chute.

She knew how much Jordan detested that form, yet he hadn't hesitated. *Can you get in?*

No. I've hit a sealed air hatch, and the metal's too thick for me to break.

Come back. We'll find another way inside. She didn't like him being that small and vulnerable.

Jordan flew back out and once again dragonshaped. *There's got to be a way inside.*

Too bad she couldn't breathe fire on it until it caved. But she required an atmosphere to create fire.

Jordan, what if we sling the Tribe's shuttle at the mother ship like a cannonball?

He caught on quickly. *If they think the shuttle's damage is limited to communications, they might open the bay doors in an attempt to recover their own people.*

Together, they veered away from the mother ship in search of the damaged shuttle.

Shari-ki *love. I see the shuttle.*

They landed on the shuttle and swung it in a giant circle, using its speed to sling it back at the warship. *If we can't slow the shuttle down,* Jordan suggested, *we could lob it at the warship like a bomb.*

She grinned, liking the idea of using the shuttle the Tribes had sent at the *Draco* against the mother ship. But even more, she liked the give and take of working with Jordan. Being with Jordan was like being with an extension of herself. Only better, because they stimulated each other, bounced ideas off each other, encouraged each other, supported each other.

The warship loomed large in the heavens as it bore down on the *Draco.* No, she had that wrong. *The clutch beam is still pulling the* Draco *toward the mother ship. Why aren't they just firing on the* Draco? *The Grail's gone, and they can't recover it.*

They don't know that.

But they had to have spotted us flying out here in dragon form.

True, but maybe they think we're a new kind of weapon, or a new kind of spaceship.

They had to have seen the glow after you united the Grail with the Staff. The entire solar system turned coppery.

Jordan's silence told her he didn't understand the Tribe tactics, either. But then as they neared the huge warship he suggested, *Their hauling in the* Draco *might be a trap.*

For us?

Trendonis has to be beyond pissed right now.

That had to be the understatement of the millennium. By uniting the Grail and the Staff, they'd destroyed Trendonis's two-thousand-year-old plan to dominate the galaxy.

Ready to let this shuttle fly home? Jordan asked.

On your mark.

Now.

She retracted her claws and prayed the Tribes wouldn't realize the shuttle was out of control until too late. That they'd think they could still recover the vessel. A shiver of apprehension grazed her scales as for a moment she feared the shuttle would swing wide of target.

But as usual, Jordan's calculations were right on. The shuttle collided with the great warship, taking out a huge chunk of metal.

Watch out.

Debris scattered, some of it coming their way. Jordan shifted to avoid part of the hull. She ducked and let a piece of pipe soar by.

When she swung around to look again, she could see

the clutch beam still steady, still drawing the *Draco* into the mother ship's underbelly. But they'd done enough damage for Jordan and Vivianne to fly into the ship through the gaping charred hole in the side.

Let's go.

They landed amid a pile of wreckage, twisted metal parts and debris so burned she couldn't identify their original use. But they still didn't have access to the interior. The warship had closed internal emergency hatches to contain the damage.

Jordan clawed at a hose spraying gas into the vacuum. *Bingo.*

What? She'd felt his elation come through but didn't understand his excitement.

This is oxygen. He ducked his head into the gas and roared out a flame. The heat did no damage to the hatch. But the oxygen caught fire and shot back up the tube of gas.

Get back.

They huddled behind a giant pile of smoking metal. Explosions rocked the warship, and the deck rippled under her feet. She waited a few seconds for the dust to clear, then peered outside. The clutch beam was gone. *The Draco's free.*

Go back to our ship, shari-ki, *my love. I have unfinished business here. I need to make sure Trendonis never destroys another planet.*

We don't even know if he's here.

He's here.

You're scanning his mind?

I can feel him blocking me. And that shield has a signature I'd now recognize anywhere.

Keep your lifestyle positive, because your lifestyle becomes your destiny.

—LADY CAEL

43

*W*e *have unfinished business here.* Vivianne's thought came to Jordan, determined and strong. They were a team, and she was the best of partners. Although he would have preferred for her to remain at a safe distance, as long as Trendonis lived, nowhere was safe.

After they humanshaped, their nanotech clothing repaired itself, and Jordan led Vivianne toward the bridge. The Tribes' crew in this area had disintegrated. But after going through two internal airlocks, they reached an area that had maintained pressure, heat, and gravity. Here, Vivianne avoided looking at the burned bodies and Jordan sensed her eagerness to leave, but he wouldn't go on without making certain Trendonis was no more.

With the warship's shuttle bay destroyed, Jordan had Trendonis trapped, yet he took nothing for granted. Until Trendonis was dead, danger could come from any direction.

Vivianne might be squeamish, but that didn't stop her from picking up two blasters from the dead. One she tucked into her pants, the other she kept in hand. Jordan kept his eyes peeled for weapons, and when he spied a space ax, he seized it as well as another blaster.

Looks like the officers have barricaded themselves on the bridge. It's likely the last remaining pressurized spot on the warship.

Unless the Tribes wore spacesuits, all Jordan and Vivianne had to do was break through a bulkhead. Pressure and the cold of space would do their fighting for them.

Jordan searched the perimeter of the bridge. *Look for a weakness.*

The Tribe warship was built with thick metal plating. Yet parts of the metal I-beams were twisted, charred, and melted. Jordan tested several joints with his space ax. *No good.*

Over Vivianne's handheld, static squawked. Then Gray's mental thought. *The warship's firing at us. I'm pulling back.*

Status? Vivianne asked.

We're hit. A loud boom and the communication ended.

Gray?

He didn't answer, and Vivianne's face paled. *We need to help them.*

Jordan found an electric box. After opening it, he picked up a fire extinguisher and rammed it into the circuits. Sparks flew everywhere.

And a hatch that had prevented them from entering the mother ship's bridge opened. Blasters drawn, Jordan and Vivianne rushed into the opening and skidded onto the bridge.

As blaster fire rushed by his ear, Jordan grabbed Vivianne's waist and rolled. *Take cover.*

They ended up half hidden behind a counter with several dead bodies. Jordan kicked the bodies out and tugged Vivianne to safety. He peeked out and counted four opponents. *Two men at weapons. One in a spacesuit at the com. And one creeping toward us.*

He blasted the man stationed at weapons. With a cry of pain, the man spun and then fell to the deck. Jordan missed the man on the attack, but Vivianne took him out.

Betting Trendonis was the one wearing the spacesuit and who was busily typing commands over the command center, Jordan edged toward him.

"Trendonis. You're done," Jordan taunted his enemy, hoping to distract him. He had a bad feeling. A real bad feeling. Why wasn't Trendonis trying to flee or fighting? Why was he holding his ground? And what was he so busy doing?

Jordan had no idea why his mind scanning wasn't working. His major advantage was gone. But he kept creeping forward. *Vi. Stay covered. Let the enemy come to you.*

And why aren't you taking your own advice?

Trendonis is up to something.

Jordan crawled behind an overturned module. He still didn't have a shot. He had to get closer. Staying low, he used elbows and knees to belly crawl. And all the while, he heard the beeping of the touch screen as Trendonis laid in orders.

Was he calling in reinforcements? Were they about to be surrounded by the Tribe fleet?

Centuries of rage surged in Jordan. Trendonis was pure evil and the son of a bitch needed to die. His time had come.

Rising to his feet in a sudden heave, Jordan fired his

blaster. Trendonis fired back. Jordan dived, and the blaster fire missed Jordan by inches. But even as he'd lunged behind another console, he'd seen his blast nick Trendonis's shoulder. Jordan aimed and fired again.

Across the bridge, Jordan heard more blaster fire. *Vivianne?*

I got him.

Stay there.

No problem. Her mental communication sounded weak, shaken.

You okay?

I'll live, and if Trendonis shows, I've a blaster waiting for him.

He's cornered and injured, which only makes him more dangerous. You'll need eyes in the back of your head. Look up, down. All directions. A snake can come from anywhere.

A blaster fired.

He's advancing on my position.

Jordan's pulse raced. His mouth went dry. Trendonis had killed everyone Jordan had ever loved. He would not hurt Vivianne.

He lunged from behind cover, rolled, and ended up behind an exposed I-beam. Shari-ki, *love. I'm coming.*

I have him in my blaster sights.

More shots fired.

Vi?

She didn't answer.

Life would indeed be dull if there were no such difficulties.

—LUCAN ROARKE

44

Vivianne?

When she still didn't answer, Jordan tensed, his flesh crawling with sudden sweat.

Vi?

She must be hurt. Or worse. Jordan sprinted across the bridge, leaping over furniture, skidding on debris, knocking electrical wires dropping from the ceiling out of his way.

Blaster fire singed his hair. Jordan kept running, scrambling, dodging. *Vivianne. Talk to me. Please, love. Say something. Anything.*

Bracing for the sight of her broken and bleeding body, he rounded the console where he'd left her. She was lying on her side, eyes closed. He couldn't tell if she was still alive. And then, from behind a column, Trendonis kicked the blaster from Jordan's hand.

Filled with fury, Jordan seized Trendonis's neck with both hands and squeezed. But with a sharp twist to one side, Trendonis broke his grip and clapped his hands over Jordan's ears.

Pain in his eardrums drove Jordan into a white rage. With an uppercut, he slammed his knuckles into Trendonis's cheekbone. The crunch of bone forced Trendonis to stagger back, but he was far from defeated. The wily fighter grabbed a loose crossbrace and raised it, ready to swing at Jordan's head.

Before Trendonis could deliver the deathblow, Jordan hurled his space ax. And with a thunk, it lodged dead center in Trendonis's chest.

The impact lifted Trendonis off his feet. His arms flailed, and he dropped the crossbrace. Knees giving out, he sank to the floor. But even as his eyes clouded with his coming death, they gleamed with triumph. "Earth . . . is . . . no more."

"Oh, God." Vivianne sat up, raised a hand to the wound on her head, and staggered to her feet. Blood matted her hair and streamed down over her face.

But she was alive.

"Thank the Goddess." Hearts welling with relief that she'd survived, Jordan gathered her into his arms, holding her, touching her to assure himself she was really there. "When you didn't answer . . ."

"He hit me on the head. I blacked out."

"Let me take a look." He gently pulled back her hair to reveal a jagged cut that oozed with congealing blood.

"I'm fine." She jerked back, eyes wide with horror. "Jordan. He said, 'Earth is no more.' What does that mean?"

Jordan took her hand and helped her to her feet. "Let's see what we can find out."

Her hand tucked in his, they headed over to the command console. With a squeeze, Vivianne released his hand and headed to the navigation center, where she tried to find the *Draco*.

Jordan pulled up the last commands Trendonis had sent out. He went icy-hot with renewed anger. Trendonis's last order personified the man himself. Pure evil.

"I've located the *Draco*." Vivianne lifted her head from the data stream, her eyes wide. "And there's a baffling communication in Trendonis's log."

Jordan put off telling her his bad news. "What did you find?"

"Trendonis sent a communication to Arcturus. To Arthur."

To Arthur? Jordan's mind raced. "And what was the message?"

"His exact words were, 'You've lost Earth, my son.'"

"*My son?*" Jordan repeated, his forehead wrinkling. Had she misheard? Was this a code?

"And he signed it 'Uther.'" Her words flowed with excitement. "Remember I told you that I'd read medieval history about this coat of arms?"

"Yes."

"Well, it was Uther's coat of arms. No wonder he and Arthur used the same family symbol. Trendonis is Uther—he's King Arthur's father."

Stunned, Jordan rocked back on his heels. Uther was Arthur's sire? Uther had stood for everything Arthur was against. Uther was a man of darkness and destruction. Arthur loved everything good and honorable. No wonder Arthur had hated the man. And he must have been ashamed, or he wouldn't have kept the secret. "Arthur has a lot of explaining to do." Jordan couldn't delay the bad news any longer. "But we have to leave. Right now. Trendonis just ordered his fleet to prepare planetbusters and lob them at Earth."

Vivianne squared her shoulders and lifted her chin. "We'll stop them. Can we send another message? Cancel his order?"

Jordan tried to hack into the weapons system, wasting precious seconds. But Trendonis had fail-safes in the system. "We don't have the code."

"Maybe Arthur . . ."

"All his life Arthur fought his father. I assure you, he may have kept secrets from me, but Arthur won't have the code. Our only shot is flying the *Draco* back to Earth. Maybe after the Tribe fleet commanders realize Trendonis is dead, they'll change their minds about destroying Earth." Jordan hefted Trendonis onto his shoulders. "We'll need his body to prove he's dead."

Pain and desperation in her eyes, she asked, "And will that be enough?"

"I don't know." He wished he had a better answer.

Love is like a fine wine, born with the bloom of ripe fruit, made with gentle care, sipped slowly to make it last.

—LADY GUINEVERE

45

Vivianne humanshaped and pulled the *Draco*'s airlock handle. *Nothing's happening.*

When Gray feared the Tribes would board, he must have locked it from the bridge.

Vivianne peered through the tiny airlock window. *I see Knox lying on the floor in the corridor. She's either unconscious . . . or dead.* She didn't like even thinking the words.

Jordan slung Trendonis under one arm, shoved around the hull, and headed toward the stern. *Let's try the engine compartment.*

She'd forgotten they'd blasted out of the engine room to leave the *Draco*. Hopes rising, Vivianne followed him.

But Gray had repaired the giant hole. He and the crew had patched the opening with metal plating, then rough-welded it.

Company's coming, Jordan warned, and she peered out to see two ships growing in size on the port-side horizon.

They had to get inside the *Draco* before those ships reached them. But how?

The crew couldn't hear their telepathy. As a last-ditch effort, she placed her mouth to her handheld. "Gray, Knox. Tennison. Lyle. Darren. Anybody in there?"

No one answered. And she feared the worst.

Without atmosphere to carry your voice, it's doubtful they can hear anything.

She scrambled around the *Draco*'s hull, looking for an opening. But they couldn't even see onto the bridge, not with the force field sealing it off.

Vivianne tried banging her hand on the hull.

Jordan shook his head. *I'll fly back to the warship and bring back a cutting tool.*

Vivianne kept banging but looked up to check the on-coming ships. *No time.*

We have no—

There's George. The dog raised up on his hind legs and scratched at the lock. *He must have heard me banging. Maybe he can pull the handle and engage the airlock.*

He's a dog.

A smart dog. And the end of the handle has a ball on it, not too different from his Ping-Pong balls. She sent a mental order, *Fetch.*

He's not telepathic. He can't hear you.

Perhaps he can. The wave that evolved us hit him, too.

But Jordan appeared to be correct. George kept scratch-ing. Vivianne spoke right against the metal door. "Fetch, George. Fetch."

Suddenly, Jordan pounded the window. George looked straight at him. Jordan motioned with his hand as if he'd just thrown a ball. George turned around to look for the ball.

The dog jumped excitedly at the door handle. *Oh, my . . . God. He grabbed the end with his mouth.* She heard a hiss. *He did it.* George did it. She was going to buy him steak dinners for a month, for a year. Hell—for life.

After the inner airlock opened, they tumbled inside. With Trendonis's body it had been a tight fit, but Vivianne was too excited to care. "You did it, George. Good boy."

Jordan closed the lock, leaving Trendonis inside the airlock. "The cold should preserve him until we get back." Squeezing past Vivianne, he kneeled next to Knox. *Her hearts have stopped. But she doesn't need air. And a pressure change or cold or radiation couldn't have done this.*

"What was in those Tribe weapons?"

"Maybe an electrical charge? Although why it didn't knock out George I'm not sure."

Maybe he'd been in midair when the strike hit. Vivianne set George down and ran down the hall for the defibrillator. She rushed back and they placed it on Knox. "Get back."

Jordan zapped Knox. Vivianne felt for a pulse. "It's beating."

Knox moaned and opened her eyes. "What happened?"

There was no time to answer. Vivianne patted her shoulder. "Stay here. We have to go help the others." Then she followed Jordan.

Ten minutes later, they'd revived the entire crew. And jumped into hyperspace. Heading for Earth.

Praying that Trendonis's orders to blow up the planet

hadn't arrived before they would, she watched the *Draco* burst from hyperspace. The Tribe fleet surrounded Earth. The hundreds of thousands of ships that Maggie had told her about still blanketed the planet.

"Open a channel to the Tribe ships," Jordan ordered.

Gray frowned in frustration. "I've used every channel we've got. No answer."

"Send this message anyway, along with a picture of Trendonis's body," Jordan ordered, then composed his message. "Your leader, Trendonis, is dead, and the Tribes no longer possess the Grail. That means in battle, you can die. But Earth doesn't want war with you. Go home. This confrontation is over."

"I've set your message to repeat in a loop, but there's still no answer." Gray moved over to help Darren monitor weapons.

Vivianne looked out the viewscreen. Dozens of ships simultaneously opened their weapon ports, and her stomach tightened. "What's going on?"

"They're preparing to fire," Jordan told her, his voice grim.

She closed her hands into fists. She couldn't let them fire and destroy her world. "We've got to stop them."

But how? They were one tiny ship against thousands.

Lyle paced on the bridge. Tears streamed down his face. "They're going to kill our world and everyone on it, and there's not a damn thing we can do."

The best defense against a planetbuster is not to be there when it goes off.

—TRENDONIS

46

There had to be something they could do. Vivianne searched Jordan's memory for information on the planetbuster that had destroyed Dominus. To break up a planet required thousands of bombs. And while all of them didn't have to land to destroy a world, most of them had to hit their target.

"What about Earth's antimissile defense system?" she asked.

Jordan shook his head. "It's not aimed to defend a threat from space."

"Suppose we fly out there and stop the missiles?" she suggested.

"This ship can't—"

"I'm not talking about the ship. I'm talking about flying out there as dragons, and manhandling those weapons like we did that shuttle. We don't need to breathe. We can stop those bombs in space before they hit the atmosphere."

"There's too many bombs. We can't do it alone." Jordan hurried after her.

Vivianne spoke on her handheld. "Gray, send the word to Earth. Let the dragonshapers spread the message telepathically. Tell them that to save Earth, they need to fly up here and stop those bombs."

"Yes, ma'am."

Even as Vivianne raced toward the airlock with Jordan close on her heels, she was praying she was right, praying that if enough dragonshapers got the word, they could divert enough bombs to save the planet.

Inside the airlock, Jordan embraced and kissed her. "*Shari-ki*, I adore the way you never give up."

"Being with you makes me braver. Smarter." She kissed him with fervor, knowing it was true. And to think she'd feared love would make her less independent. Instead, sharing her life and knowledge with Jordan had made her more confident, more of a risk taker.

The airlock opened, and she and Jordan dragonshaped, then flew straight at the newly released bombs. With a swat of her wing, she sent a bomb back the way it had come, directly into the Tribe ship. The hull collapsed and elation filled her. They could save Earth.

Help came, and it was the most beautiful sight she'd ever seen. Tens of thousands of dragons rose en masse from Earth's upper atmosphere into the heavens. Together the dragonshapers rounded up the bombs, telepathically coordinating the attack.

Dragons from every nation patrolled the skies, and whenever they found a bomb, they flung it spinning toward the Tribe ships. It didn't take long for the Tribes to retreat.

Only two bombs broke through Earth's atmosphere, one landing harmlessly in the ocean, the other doing little damage at the South Pole.

Finally, Earth was safe.

Vivianne flew beside Jordan, speculating on a wonderful future. A future where people could survive in space without suits or ships, where they could communicate with their minds. As she soared toward Earth, the possibilities seemed infinite. As did her love.

She had no doubt Jordan would achieve hero status. And he deserved Earth's thanks. But even better, they were linked forever. He was her *shari-ki*—for all time.

In your thoughts be kind, in your life be honorable, in your heart be true.

—LADY OF THE LAKE

47

Three months later

Camelot's graceful walls rose into a blue sky, and Arthur once again rode out, then escorted Vivianne and Jordan into his home. He and Lady Guinevere made them welcome at his feast-laden dining table. Lancelot was away on a spiritual retreat but hoped to return soon. George curled up under the table, where he knew Jordan and Vivianne would sneak him scraps.

"To good friends." Arthur lifted his cup and drank his wine.

Jordan, Vivianne, and Guinevere followed suit. Jordan raised his wine in another toast. "To success."

Vivianne clinked hers with Guinevere. "To love."

"And family," Guinevere agreed. "I hope you know we consider you part of ours."

"Speaking of family"—Arthur lowered his voice—"I can't thank you enough for ending Trendonis's tyranny."

"He was your father?" Jordan asked, his tone gentle.

"Yes." Arthur hung his head.

Guinevere patted his hand. "You have nothing to be ashamed of. You did not pick him to give you life. And you did everything you could to stop him. You are honorable and good."

"I'll drink to that." Jordan lifted his glass.

Arthur raised his head, then clapped Jordan on the back. "You deserve the truth." Arthur cleared his throat. "My father was born under a power-hungry star. And coveting the power of a dragonshaper, he roamed the galaxy until he stopped on Pendragon. Centuries ago, he mated with a dragonshaper. I was born of that union."

"And you were supposed to follow your father's path," Vivianne guessed.

"Exactly." Arthur's eyes burned with fire. "Uther was very disappointed when his methods of domination disgusted me. He had a sickness inside him. And over the centuries it grew worse. The more worlds he conquered, the more evil he became. That's why I gathered the knights on Earth to stop him." Arthur clasped Jordan's forearm. "Thank you for finishing what I could not."

"Thanking you for saving him from patricide," Guinevere added.

"After the worlds he destroyed, the people he murdered, you'd think I wouldn't care if he died by my own hand . . ."

But clearly Arthur's heart was torn, and Vivianne was grateful that he did not have to live with his father's death on his conscience.

Guinevere glanced at Vivianne's engagement ring and changed the subject. "I'm sorry we'll miss your wedding, but Arthur, Lancelot, and I wanted you to have this gift."

With a shy smile, Lady Guinevere handed Vivianne a lacquered box, embedded with gemstones so rare that Vivianne couldn't identify many of them. Firestones that seemed to capture starlight flickered among opals, aquamarines, and rubies. "It's gorgeous."

"Open it." Arthur poured more wine.

Hands shaking, Vivianne carefully opened the box. Inside was an obviously very ancient scroll. The parchment appeared too delicate to touch. "What is it?"

Arthur grinned. "A legend is written on one side. There's an ancient star map on the other."

Jordan watched Vivianne with warmth and curiosity. "What's the legend say?"

"No one knows. The language is ancient, and we haven't been able to translate it. But my best scientists believe the map is as old as the Holy Grail."

Vivianne carefully closed the box to protect the ancient scroll. "Thank you."

Are you ready to soar off on another adventure, dear? she asked.

Every night is an adventure with you, shari-ki *love.*

Vivianne hoped her host and hostess wouldn't see the blush rising up her neck. Jordan was a most inventive and creative lover. And the pleasure he gave her kept her a very happy woman.

Wait and see what I have planned for you tonight, she teased back and sent him a mental picture.

Jordan shifted in his chair. Even as she felt the blood tightening in his groin, she could feel his desire flaming to the surface. And coating that desire was a love as strong as the man himself. A love that would keep burning brightly. A love that was so much a part of her that she could no longer tell where her emotions began and his ended.

Vivianne smiled at her handsome husband. She had no idea if they were going back to Earth. Or off to follow the treasure map. But one thing she knew for certain. Wherever they went next, they would be together.

For always and eternity, Jordan promised.

He was reading her mind again. And wickedly, she shot him another image of what she intended to do once they were alone.

Two can play this game, he warned.

Vivianne almost choked on her wine. And then she laughed happily. Life with Jordan would be long . . . and it certainly would never be dull.

Life is a gift that is wasted if not lived to the fullest.
                              —KING ARTHUR PENDRAGON

48

❦

"Don't open your eyes," Jordan told her as he carried Vivianne, "or you'll spoil my surprise."

Vivianne snuggled against his chest. "You've been so secretive. I don't even know where in the galaxy you've taken me."

"Angleterre."

"Never heard of it."

"That's because Angleterre isn't on any star map." He kept walking, and she heard George padding beside them. Lifting her head for a clue, she smelled salt and flowers, heard the sounds of waves rolling ashore, felt the tension in his arms as he gently set her down onto her feet in soft grass.

Jordan placed his hands on her hips and angled her slightly. A warm breeze bathed her face. Sunlight heated her skin. And birds chirped in song.

"Now? Can I open my eyes now?"

"Yes."

Vivianne opened her eyes and gasped. The most perfectly proportioned house perched on a grassy hilltop

overlooking a turquoise sea. The gentle slope of the palm-
frond-shaded roof suggested a cozy invitation to proceed
up the stone path edged with wild ferns and blooming
lilies.

"What is this place?" she asked, spying a hammock
tied between two palms and instantly feeling at peace.

"Come look." He took her hand and led her up the
walkway. "Angleterre has four seasons, mild winters,
warm summers."

She gasped, recognizing the soaring ceilings, the wide
expanses of glass, and the exotic proportions. "You had
my favorite architect design this house."

They walked through the beveled front doors. The living area only had three walls. The back was open to the
stunning seascape and a pink sand beach but could be
closed for cooler weather. Jordan had even decorated the
home in her favorite blush and apricot color scheme.

"This house is lovely." She twirled around, eyes wide.
He'd bought paintings from her favorite artists, picked out
sleek contemporary furniture that she loved and mixed
it with rich mahogany pieces. The effect was inviting.
Warm. Stunning.

"There's a whirlpool on the back deck and a transporter
in the basement."

She spun around to face him. "A transporter?"

"So you can commute to Earth to work. Welcome
home, sweetheart."

"You built this house for us?"

"There's five bedrooms upstairs. I wanted to make sure
we had room to grow. I want lots of babies."

"Me, too." She took his hand, letting him see the joy she
felt spilling over her. "And I'd like to get started right now."

"Really?"

"Yes, really. Where's the closest bedroom?"

Jordan led her to two arched doors with a design etched across them. She'd seen writing like that before on the glass dome that held the Key of Soil.

"What does it say?" she asked.

"I wanted us to each have something from our pasts. The script is my native language and it says, You're the missing piece of my puzzle."

He'd remembered the necklace she'd given to her parents. Her hearts swelled with love. "Oh, Jordan."

"That means you like the house?" Jordan asked, his eyes sparkling and as blue as the sea outside their back door.

"How could I not like it?" Her hearts beat with joy. "I love the house. And I love you. Let me show you how much."

Jordan picked her up and spun her around. "Now, that's my kind of plan."

Unlock the origins of a legend . . .
DON'T MISS THE
PASSIONATE FIRST BOOK IN
SUSAN KEARNEY'S
PENDRAGON LEGACY
SERIES!

•

Please turn this page

for an excerpt from

Lucan

AVAILABLE NOW

The precious myths of our heritage are our way of understanding things greater than ourselves. They are tales of the inexplicable forces that shape our lives and of events that defy explanation. These legends are rooted in the spilling of our life blood, in the courage of brave hearts, in the resilience of humanity's tenacious spirit.

—ARTHUR PENDRAGON

PROLOGUE

In the near future

Slow down, Marisa," Lucan Roarke warned his twin.

They were deep inside the cave he'd discovered in the Welsh countryside in the shadow of Cadbury Castle, and his helmet light had settled on a gaping crack in the compacted clay of the cavern's floor. "Don't step on that—"

"What?" Marisa looked back at him just as the ground opened beneath her feet. Falling, she flailed her arms and clawed at the cave wall for a handhold, but the loose earth crumbled beneath her fingertips, and gravity dragged her down through the crevice into the darkness below.

Lucan lunged to grab her, but the unstable earth lurched

and dipped under him, throwing him off balance, and his fingers missed her by inches.

"Marisa!" The sound of splashing water drowned out his cry.

Lucan had brought his sister to Cadbury Castle for a vacation, and he'd been excited to show her this cave—his latest discovery in his quest for the Holy Grail. Although many dismissed the Grail as mythical, his years of exploration and research had convinced him the vessel actually existed.

Lucan peered through the gloom into the chasm, but his helmet light couldn't penetrate the blackness. Even worse, the earthen sides of the hole made a steep vertical descent. Reaching for the heavy-duty flashlight he carried in his back pocket, he yelled, "Marisa? Talk to me, damn it."

Nothing but silence answered him.

Closing his eyes, Lucan inhaled deeply and concentrated on linking his mind with hers, a telepathic communication the two had shared since they were little.

Marisa. Where are you?

In the water. Help me. I'm cold.

Heart racing, Lucan shined the flashlight into the darkness and spotted her head above the rushing water.

"Lucan. Here." Smart enough not to fight the powerful flow of water that tried to sweep her downstream, Marisa swam for the wall at an angle and clung to a rocky ledge.

"Hang on."

She coughed and sputtered, then shot back, "If I let go, it won't be on purpose. Hurry. It's freezing."

Lucan reached for the rope in his backpack and cursed himself for bringing his sister into the bowels of the cave.

He'd sweet-talked her into coming along, desperate to break her out of her funk. Since her latest miscarriage, she'd been fighting off depression. He'd hoped this excursion would take her mind off her loss, at least for a little while. He hadn't intended to distract her by risking her life and scaring her to death.

He uncoiled the rope, then leaned over the hole to see her lose her grip on the ledge. The current pulled her under. "Marisa!"

A split second later, a pale hand broke through the water and clutched a rock jutting from the wall. Marisa pulled her head and shoulders above the torrent, spat water, and forced her words through shivering lips. "I knew . . . I should have gone . . . to Club Med."

He looped the rope around the biggest boulder within reach. Then he tossed the line down the narrow shaft. "Grab on and I'll book the next flight to Cancún."

Marisa stretched for the rope. And missed. Water surged over her head. Again she swam to the surface, but the current had carried her too far downstream to reach the lifeline.

With no other choice, Lucan jumped into the dark shaft. He fell about twelve feet before frigid water closed over his head and ripped away his glasses. His flesh went numb, but he managed to keep a grip on his waterproof flashlight. His lungs seized and his vision blurred. Forcing his shocked limbs to move, he kicked for the surface. And heard Marisa's scream. Turning around, he swam in the direction where he'd last seen her.

Already his teeth chattered. He struggled for breath, and his waterlogged clothing and boots weighed him down. The raging current swept him under, but his concern was for Marisa. She'd been in this icy water too long. Clenching his teeth, he kicked harder until he was finally close enough to grab Marisa's shoulders. They had only minutes to find a way out before hypothermia set in.

He pulled her close. "I've got you."

When she didn't reply, fear poured through his system. Fighting to lift her head above the surface, he shined his light around the cave in search of a shoal or a shallow pool.

Marisa lifted a quaking hand. "There."

Just ahead, the river forked. One side widened, the other narrowed.

Using most of his remaining strength, he steered them toward the wider fork, praying it wouldn't take them deeper underground. His prayers were answered when they rounded a bend and the water leveled out onto a dirt embankment.

He pulled Marisa out of the river, and together they lay on the bank, panting, shivering, and exhausted. When she didn't speak, he aimed the light on her. Her eyes were closed, her face pale, her lips blue. He wrung some of the water from her clothing, then rubbed her limbs with his own freezing hands.

Her eyes fluttered open. "One word . . . about my hair, and I'll s-smack you up side the head."

"You look good in mud."

She slapped at his shoulder but didn't have the strength to land the blow.

He smoothed her hair from her eyes. "Save your strength. I don't want to have to carry you." She needed to walk to keep the hypothermia at bay.

"W-wuss." She crawled up the bank until her back rested against a dirt wall.

Lucan focused on survival. "We've got to get moving or we'll freeze."

"You wrung the water from my clothes. What about you?"

"I'm fine."

"Of course you're fine. J-just like when y-you were in Namibia and that black mamba bit you?"

"I lived."

"Barely." Marisa took his hand and tried to stand, but her knees buckled. She grabbed the wall behind her for support and it began to collapse on top of them.

Lucan lunged and threw his body over hers, shut his eyes, and prayed they wouldn't be buried alive. Clumps of cold mud cascaded over them and bounced aside.

"You okay?" Lucan asked.

"Oh, now I'm really having f-fun." Marisa spat dirt. "So glad you s-suggested"—her teeth chattered uncontrollably—"th-this little vacation."

Lucan shoved to his feet. "Think what a great adventure story you'll have to write."

"I don't want to *be* the story." She rolled her eyes and sighed. "But you love this shit. You're probably getting off on—"

Wow. Her telepathic thought interrupted her words midsentence. And her amazement came through in waves—surprising waves that peaked with astonishment.

"What?" He spun around to see exactly what had shocked her, and he froze. He focused his flashlight on the unearthed urn, hardly believing his eyes or his luck. The intricate design made dating the piece easy. "It's Tintagel ware."

"Tinta-who?"

"Tintagel ware is an ancient indigenous pottery. Fifth or sixth century. More evidence that Cadbury Castle really was King Arthur's home base."

They both jumped aside as another slice of wall and more pottery crashed down, revealing a hidden room. At the sound of breaking terra-cotta, Lucan winced. An ancient scroll poked from the shards, and he dashed to pull the paper from the muddy earth before the dampness reached it.

Old and fragile, the antiquity had survived in amazing condition. He balanced the flashlight between his shoulder and chin, unfurled his find, and squinted, wishing for his lost glasses.

Marisa peered over his arm, her reporter's curiosity evident. "What is it?"

Lucan stared, his pulse racing in excitement. The astrological map revealed the Sun, the Earth, planets. And many stars. But what had his heart battering his ribs was the line drawn from Earth to a star far across the galaxy. He was looking at an ancient map of the heavens. His mouth went dry. "This is a star map."

"Why do you sound so surprised? Even the most ancient cultures were into astrology."

"Astronomy," he corrected automatically. "I'm no astronomer, but this looks . . . far too accurate for its time. King Arthur, remember. The Age of Chivalry."

"Yeah, right."

Lost in thought, he ignored her sarcasm. "This map has details the Hubble telescope might not pick up, yet it's thousands of years old. It's unbelievable."

"So it's a fake?"

"I'll have to perform tests . . ." He squinted at the map.

His gaze moved on to the distant stars and their planets. "Hell."

"What now?"

He pointed to the map. "This moon is named Pendragon."

"Wasn't that King Arthur's last name?"

He nodded and squinted. "And written right under Pendragon is the word *Avalon*."

"Avalon? Is that significant?"

"Avalon was a legendary isle ruled by a Druid priestess called the Lady of the Lake," he answered. "She helped put Arthur on the throne. And according to the stories, Avalon was also where King Arthur left the Holy Grail."

"The Holy Grail?" Disbelief filled her voice.

"The powers of the cup are legendary. If the myths are true, the cup might cure physical ills—cancer, heart attacks, and . . ." He hesitated before breathing out the word. "Sterility."

Though neither his sister nor her husband was officially sterile, like most of Earth's population, they couldn't have children. Her recent miscarriage had been her second in as many years. If the cup truly existed and he could find it, his sister—and hundreds of thousands of others—could finally carry a child to term.

"Throughout the ages," he continued, "many men, including Arthur's own Knights of the Round Table, have searched for Avalon and the Holy Grail. Legendary stories of the Grail's healing properties exist in many cultures, yet no one has found it." He pointed to the small moon on the ancient map. "Maybe that's because Avalon wasn't on Earth."

"You've lost your mind." She sighed, but the catch in

her voice exposed her wishful thinking that after all this time despairing, she might be able to hope again.

"A search for the Holy Grail might be the most exciting thing I'll ever do."

"It might also be the last thing you ever do. Didn't you learn your lesson when you went in search of Preah Vihear antiquities?"

"The golden statue of the dancing Shiva I found in the Khmer temple was worth—"

"Ending up in a Cambodian jail?"

"Just a little misunderstanding. We got it squared away."

She cursed under her breath. "You sure you don't have a death wish? Or are you just an adrenaline junkie?"

She was fussing only because she loved him, so he ignored her rhetorical questions. Besides, he wasn't the only twin who took calculated risks. As a reporter for the *St. Petersburg Times,* Marisa had placed herself in danger often. They were some pair. She wanted to report the present to change the future. Until now, he'd believed humanity was headed for extinction, and he had studied the past because the future looked bleak. But if he could find the Grail, the past just might offer hope.

Marisa sighed. "We need to dig out of here."

He carefully rolled up the parchment and placed it in the dry sample bag he'd pulled from his backpack. Then he shined the light on the broken pottery. Kneeling, he began gathering as many shards as he could carry.

He reached for a particularly large piece, covered in an array of signs and symbols, when he spied daylight glimmering through a tiny opening on the far wall of the hidden room. A way out. "Time to go."

"Now you're in a hurry?"

"Don't you want to find out if this map's authentic?"

She sighed. "I'm more interested in warm, dry clothes."

"Do you realize what we may have found?"

"We? Just you, my brother. Avalon? The Holy Grail? A cure for cancer? The idea is more than crazy. It's nonsense. But knowing you, you'll find a way to follow that map to Avalon."

"If the star map pans out, you'll want first dibs on the story—don't deny it."

"You're a restless, adventure-seeking fool. That stupid map is going to take you straight to outer space."

He could only hope.

As they deny the world, not only in the spirit realm but in the material plane, the world will cease to exist.

—THE LADY OF THE LAKE

1

Eight years later, half a galaxy away

Cael was going to die. Not with the dignity a High Priestess was due. Not even with the respect afforded a physician.

And it was all her own fault. When she'd thought she'd seen her owl, Merlin, flapping frantically in the cooling conduit, she'd foolishly attempted a rescue. That had been mistake number one. Instead of calling maintenance for help, she'd grabbed a ladder, yanked off the outer grid, and crawled into the ductwork. Mistake number two. She'd forgotten to take a flashlight. Mistake number three. And now she was stuck in the dark conduit, half frozen, her hair held firm by the intake valve, her hand caught in the mesh screen meant to keep out rodents.

She'd shouted for help, of course, but no one had heard. With her robes and feet dangling into the hallway, she would have been hard to miss, but her coworkers never came down the hall to the High Priestess's office. Being High Priestess wasn't all it was assumed to be. Yes, she lived in a magnificent residence, free of charge, and her people revered her, even enacting a special law to allow her to be both priestess and healer, but the average Dragonian wouldn't think of stopping by for a chat, never mind asking for her medical opinion.

While she believed her empathic ability was a gift that enabled her to use her healing skills wisely, her people too often looked at it as a curse. A curse that might blast them if they looked at her the wrong way . . . so most preferred not to look at her at all.

To her regret, she'd treated only a few patients since she'd joined the Avalon Project's team of specialists, which included astronomers, archeologists, physicists, engineers, geologists, and computer technicians. Unless they had an emergency, her coworkers preferred other, less daunting healers. And if she didn't turn up for work in the lab tomorrow, she doubted anyone would search for her. They'd assume she was attending to her High Priestess duties.

So she was stuck. Alone as usual.

And Merlin wasn't even here. Mistake number four. Had she imagined that the owl had needed her help? She should have known better. The bird was crafty. He wouldn't fly into a conduit that had no exit. He wouldn't get stuck as she had. It would be just her luck if she died here of dehydration.

"Damn it." She pounded on the metal wall with her free hand and yelled. "Just turn off the cooling coils, hand me a knife, and I'll cut myself free."

No one answered. The suction from the intake valve threatened to snatch her bald. Again she wrenched her wrist, but the mesh held her fingers in a clawlike grip. Tired, cold, she closed her eyes and dozed.

"Lady?" Someone tugged on her foot.

She awakened with a jerk and almost yanked her hair out by the roots. Teeth chattering, her side numb, she figured she must have been dreaming of rescue.

Then she heard the same deep and sexy yet unrecognizable voice again. "Are you stuck?"

What did he think? That the High Priestess slept here because she liked being frozen into an ice cube? "Please, can you get me out?"

A warm hand grasped her ankle, and an interesting tingle shot up her leg as he tugged.

"Ow! My hair is caught in the intake valve, and my hand got stuck in the mesh when I tried to free myself."

She was about to ask for a pair of scissors or a knife, when she heard the duct metal creak and a thud. Then a man's chest was sliding over her legs. And his movement was tugging up her gown.

Holy Goddess.

She'd never been this close to someone before. No one dared touch the High Priestess.

Yet he'd crawled right into the duct with her and was inching his way past her hips. Both her hearts jolted as if she'd taken a direct electric charge. His heat seeped into her, and the feel of his powerful, rippling male muscles had her biting back a gasp of shock.

It was impossible not to feel the heat pulsing between them. Studying the signs of arousal in a medical book was one thing. Experiencing them was quite another.

The stranger was edging up her body, and her senses rioted. Never had anything felt this indescribably good. She wished she could see his eyes and his expression. Even her empathic gift was failing her. Her own excitement was preventing her from reading him. Was he enjoying the feel of her as much as she was him? Did he have any idea that her hearts were racing? That her skirt was above her knees?

Ever so slowly, he crawled to her waist and his head slid between her breasts, his warm breath fanning her flesh. His mouth had to be inches from her . . . oh, sweet Goddess.

"The air duct really isn't made for two," he joked.

Her pulse leaped. Her nerves were on fire. "There isn't enough air," she gasped.

"It's fine." He wriggled until his cheek pressed hers and she could feel the fine growth of a beard one day past a shave. His broad chest warmed her. Her hips nestled his, and she felt him harden against her.

She stiffened. So he wasn't unaffected, and that fact secretly pleased her. Although it shouldn't have.

Apparently not the least embarrassed by his physical reaction, he chuckled, his breath warm and tantalizing in her ear. "Don't worry. It's not like we have enough room in here to get any closer."

She squeezed her eyes tight. "You don't know who I am."

"You feel . . . beautiful." He reached above her head and ran his hand along her hair, his fingers strong and gentle. "I'm going to remove the grate so we don't have to cut your hair."

His muscles flexed, and he popped the vent from the duct. "Now let's free your hand."

He skimmed his other hand up her body, lightly teasing her waist, the side of her breast, her cheek. She sucked in her breath as a ripple of pleasure washed through her.

"I'll be happy to do more of that after I get you out of here," he murmured and ran his fingers up her arm to her trapped wrist. "Hmm. I've got a screwdriver in my back pocket. Think you can reach it?"

She licked her bottom lip and moved her free hand across his firm hip to his curved buttock. Her fingers itched to explore. After all, she had to find his pocket, didn't she?

"Try a little higher, sweetheart," he urged, his voice amused.

"If you want to live, don't call me that," she said in her best High Priestess voice. But instead of sounding authoritative, her tone was breathy and light.

She fumbled her fingers over his buttock, enjoying the hard muscle and the sensuous curve, and finally found and unsnapped the pocket. Oh . . . my. The material inside that pocket was so thin she was almost touching his bare, warm flesh. At the thought, her breasts tingled and, certain he could feel her nipples hardening against him, she flushed.

"What should I call you?" he teased.

She hesitated. If she told him her name, he might not finish freeing her. "I'll introduce myself once we're out of this mess."

"Honey, we're way beyond the need for formal introductions—not when your sexy little hand is grabbing my ass."

She snatched the screwdriver from his pocket. "Got it."

He gave instructions with an easy self-confidence that told her he was enjoying himself. "Reach up my back, over my shoulder, and place the screwdriver into my hand."

She did as he asked and found herself admiring his broad back, the muscular shoulders. She was wrapped around him, and the feel of his hard male body had her trembling. She hadn't known a man could feel so good.

His maleness was erotic, exotic. Exciting. Her blood rushed though her veins with a heat that made her feel more alive than she'd felt since she'd first taken to the skies in flight.

"You're awfully quiet." The rough texture of his words was almost as exciting as his muscles straining over her. "Am I too heavy?"

Too heavy? He was perfect.

She swallowed hard. "How much longer . . ."

"Until we're done unscrewing? Now, there's a question I haven't been asked before." She could hear the grin in his wry tone and was grateful when he changed the subject. "How'd you get stuck in here, anyway?"

Every time he turned the screwdriver, his pecs tensed against her breasts and his erection pressed hot against her thigh.

She tried to distract herself by talking. "I thought I heard a bird trapped in here."

She expected him to tell her she was silly, but he paused in his handiwork. "So you're the adventurous type?"

Was she? She had no idea. From the moment she'd been born, her destiny had been set. The Elders had trained her as High Priestess. It was her duty to perform religious ceremonies, to bless babies, to mediate high-level disputes. But she'd wanted to connect with people, so she'd insisted on becoming a healer, too. That was the reason she worked on the Avalon Project, hoping to find the Holy Grail and cure her world of all illness. Was that the same as adventurous?

He popped out the last screw, and she tugged her hand free. Her fingers landed in his thick, soft hair. "Sorry."

"Don't be. I'm not."

"You might be really sorry—once we get out of here."

"Why's that?" He began to wriggle down her body. "Are you married?"

"I'm never getting married." The High Priestess wasn't allowed to wed. Even if it wasn't forbidden, who would want a woman who had the strength to kill her own mate?

"You have seven big protective brothers who'll want to beat me up?" he teased.

"There's just me and my two sisters." She couldn't keep the wistfulness from her tone.

"No husband. No brothers. And you don't want to marry. Honey, you're ideal," he said, his tone soft and husky. Finally, he jumped down, and she found herself missing his warmth. Then his strong hands slid up her legs.

"I can get out . . . by myself." She tried to wriggle away but couldn't, of course, with the duct restricting her movements. "Is anyone else out there?"

"No one. It's past midnight."

"Thank the Goddess." His large hands almost spanned her waist. He lifted her from the conduit and set her down on her feet. Her skirts dropped to the floor, and she smoothed them while avoiding his gaze.

As the ceremonial robes swished around her legs, her customary decorum returned. "Thank you. You saved my life. But I won't tell anyone, so please don't worry . . ." She raised her head and met his eyes.

"I'm not worried." Cocking his head to the side, he'd spoken as if he found the idea absurd. He smiled as if he was seeing Cael the woman, not the High Priestess, and it charged her with intense awareness. Of him.

In the dim light she recognized him. Lucan Roarke. The new archeologist on the team had dark hair, compelling blue eyes, and a sculpted jaw. And he wore glasses. Obviously he needed a new prescription, since he didn't seem to recognize her.

"If anyone learns that you touched me, the State will execute you."

"Really?"

"The only exemptions are during my healing duties or for blessings bestowed in religious ceremonies."

She expected him to back away, tremble, even grovel as others in his position would have. Automatically, she braced for the normal blast of fear, but instead he leaned toward her, his voice seductive. "Lady Cael"—obviously he *did* recognize her—"I wouldn't mind if more than my fate was in your hands."

LUCAN HAD SCREWED UP. So much for keeping a low profile. He knew better than to flirt with any woman . . . much less Pendragon's High Priestess. So much for taking an inconspicuous walk around the complex to clear his head. What had he been thinking?

That she was soft and toned. That her hair was like silk. And her scent . . . her scent reminded him of summer rain. Lucan had seen some unusual things during his thirty-two years, but nothing as unsettling as Cael's irises, which he could have sworn had flared with tiny golden flames.

"Get back to work," he told himself.

He couldn't let the experience sidetrack him. It didn't matter that she was the most fascinating woman he'd met . . . ever. Or that every time he closed his eyes the memory of her soft curves pressing against him made him forget how much work he had to do. And how little time he had left to do it.

His career had taken him to dozens of ancient archeo-logical sites and thrown many puzzles his way. But Lucan had not spent five years flying across the galaxy, then three more learning a new language and establishing himself as a respected Dragonian linguist, to settle for anything less than the Grail. He'd endured years without the compan-ionship of his friends and family, the taste of spicy Buffalo wings and cold Corona, the smoky sounds of hot jazz and the smooth roar of his Classic Harley, deprivations he'd tolerated, all for the sake of finding the Grail.

He shifted his gaze to the large observation port that filled one side of the lab. Just beyond the wall of glass and illuminated by floodlights, Avalon punched into the night sky, an alien gray marble obelisk. Only a third of the massive structure was visible above ground, and the entire edifice was shielded by a mysterious energy that allowed no one and nothing to penetrate its secrets. Lucan was certain the Grail lay behind the shielded wall.

"The answer to breaking through that shield has to be right here in front of me." He scowled at a copy of the ancient, alien glyphs that the Avalon team had discovered on the obelisk's wall earlier the previous day.

These same glyphs were on the star map he'd found on Earth, suggesting that there had been travel between Earth and Pendragon over fifteen hundred years ago. According to Arthurian legends, King Arthur left the Grail in Avalon. But this Avalon was across the galaxy from Earth. The idea seemed outrageous, yet Lucan couldn't ignore the facts. This moon bore Arthur's last name. And the ancient Dragonians had named the imposing obelisk Avalon.

Coincidence? Lucan didn't think so.

"Think." He glared at the symbols, willing them to respond. Was he looking at an alphabet, or did the glyphs stand for individual sounds? "What are you hiding? What's your secret?"

"If only I had a coin for every time someone asked *me* those questions."

Holy hell. He'd assumed Cael had left for the evening. How long had she been in the lab? What had she seen?

Like an idiot, he'd left the star map in plain sight. Had she seen enough to recognize the parchment hadn't originated on this moon?

Forcing his mind out of a tailspin, Lucan leaned over his desk and deliberately knocked over his mug of tea. Then he whisked the damning star map into a drawer while the dark, hot liquid oozed into papers of much lesser value.

Lucan forced a smile at Cael, as if he welcomed her interruption. "*You* have secrets?"

"Doesn't everyone?" She strode across the lab, her steps graceful, her bearing regal. "Maybe I can help." Cael spoke with casual confidence, and Lucan couldn't pull his gaze from her. The light danced in her eyes in a way that mesmerized him. He saw not only intelligence, but a vibrancy, a mystery. "Or do you prefer to work alone?"

He shrugged and wiped at the mess on his desk. Lucan wasn't a loner by nature but by necessity. The less he shared with his coworkers, the less chance he had of slipping up, blowing his cover story and fake résumé, and revealing his true identity. And if these Dragonians figured out he wasn't one of them, they'd make sure he never got within a thousand yards of Avalon. They wanted the Grail as badly as he did. For Cael and Pendragon, finding the Grail would be a boon that would eliminate disease and suffering and the need for hospitals, medical research, and drugs.

"Right now I need to decipher these glyphs," he said.

She glanced at the symbols. "You think they're the key to breaking through the shield?"

The Dragonians had been trying for centuries to bring down Avalon's outer protective shield so they could search inside for the Grail. Modern technology, bulldozers, acids, and blasting had failed to win them access.

Lucan threaded his fingers through his hair. "If I could translate the glyphs, I could answer your question."

He poured more caffeine-laced tea and offered her a mug.

"No, thanks." She eyed the almost empty pot, and her hair brushed her shoulders. With the two of them alone in the lab it was impossible not to recall her hair in his hands, or her fresh-rain scent, and his pulse raced as she raised her eyes to his. "You think going without sleep will help?"

He sipped the tea, and over the brim of his cup he read concern in her eyes. And female curiosity that he couldn't afford to encourage.

He was so aware of her, it was almost as if pulling her out of that vent had ignited something between them. "I can't waste time sleeping, not when that subsurface cavity might open up and swallow Avalon tomorrow."

Last summer's drought had created a massive water shortage. The Dragonians had pumped water from the subterranean aquifer into their cities until they'd emptied the underground reservoirs, leaving a vast sinkhole beneath Avalon, one that grew larger and more likely to collapse the ground above it by the day.

"The latest estimates say we have weeks, maybe

months." She hesitated as if she didn't want to say more but then continued, "But even if the ground holds, General Brennon's newest satellite data show that the expanding sinkhole has weakened the area so much that it may be dangerous to bring down the shields."

"How dangerous?"

"The shields are reinforcing Avalon's stability. If the ancient walls collapse, the adjoining part of the city might fall into the cavity."

Lucan's eyes narrowed. "So what's he want us to do? Give up?"

"We won't." Her curious gaze settled on his desk and the copy of the runes. Her eyes, a startling mix of old soul and pure innocence, drew him in. "Are you any closer to an answer?"

He set his cup aside and chose his words carefully. If he gave Cael a reason to report anything suspicious, Sir Quentin, Avalon's chief archeologist and head of the government's Division of Lost Artifacts, would take her seriously.

"I'm no closer to translating the glyphs than when we uncovered them yesterday afternoon."

Despite years of study in ancient runes and hieroglyphics, he hadn't been able to make any sense of the connection between his map and ancient Avalon.

"You might want to give yourself more than a day to solve one of our moon's ancient puzzles." With an encouraging raise of her brow, she moved aside several of his books, and together they finished mopping up the spilled tea. When their hands accidentally touched, his flesh tingled in response. Her violet gaze jerked toward his in surprise. "You're driving yourself too hard."

That was so not his problem. The only thing too hard around here, suddenly, was his dick.

Damn it. Not now. He needed to play this cool. He bristled, then tried to hide his reaction. But a telltale flicker in her eyes told him she'd noted his irritation.

The lady was perceptive. Too perceptive? He raked back his hair to give him time to cool his jets. The last thing he needed was her ordering him to come in for a checkup. "I'm sure I look like hell. But a shower and a shave should—"

Cael placed her hand on his shoulder. "Relax." What was she up to? She seemed to be deliberately touching him now, and it occurred to him that she was scanning him with her empathic ability.

He prayed to God she couldn't read his mind, then forced himself to relax. She read feelings, not thoughts. For now, his real identity was still safe. And if she was picking up any of his lusty yearnings, she was pretending otherwise.

Cael knelt, scooped the rest of his books from the floor, and placed them back on his desk. "I won't send you to the medical bay—"

"Thanks."

"If you promise to sleep for a few hours—"

"Agreed."

"In your bed. Not at your desk." She smiled, perhaps to take the sting out of her words.

He cocked his head to one side and shot her his most charming grin. "You want to come tuck me in?"

Damn it. He'd been keeping the conversation on a professional level, and then he'd blown it again. He kept forgetting Cael was not just a colleague. No Dragonian he knew would venture such an innuendo with the High

Priestess, even in jest. But then, he doubted any other man had shared an air duct with her, either.

When she placed her hands on her hips and frowned, he thought she was offended. Then the corner of her mouth quirked to form a saucy grin. "Will that be necessary? My tucking you in?"

Necessary? *No.* Pleasurable? *Oh, yeah.* He envisioned her leaning over him, her eyes widening as he tugged her into his arms for a kiss.

Stop. He had to stop fantasizing. Stop looking at her.

He cast his eyes down to his desk. "Maybe if I hit the sack, the answer will come to me in my dreams." Fat chance. He was going to toss and turn. And think about her.

"I'm glad you're optimistic. It's terrible to think these glyphs might be our last chance . . ."

She looked worried, and not asking what was on her mind took all his willpower.

He cleared his throat and put the remaining items on his desk to rights, willing her to step away so the rainy scent of her hair didn't flood his lungs, so the light in her eyes didn't dazzle, so her lips weren't close enough to tempt him.

Too much was at stake to think about anything but his mission. He must have been more tired than he'd realized. But exhaustion was no excuse. What the hell was wrong with him? And what was wrong with *her?* He might have admired her long, long legs and flowing blond mane since he'd arrived at the lab, but she'd never shown him more than a passing glance.

When she spoke, Cael's voice was low and silvery, threaded with sorrow. "You know, finding the Grail means . . . everything . . . to me, too."

Looking away, perhaps deliberately avoiding his gaze,

she fingered her necklace beneath her tunic's collar. "My nephew . . . is sick. He's"—her voice broke—"only five."

The hint of desperation in her voice revealed a deep, black agony. One he knew all too well. "You can't heal him?"

She shook her head, her fingers rubbing the necklace. "I shouldn't have said anything. The last thing you need is more pressure. I'm sorry."

Lucan nodded in understanding. "My sister's unable to have a child. All her life she's wanted to be a mother, and her dream was ripped away. I'd hoped the Grail . . ."

Marisa's doctors had eventually declared her barren after the last miscarriage, and watching her be torn apart by grief was almost more than Lucan could handle. More and more people on Earth were being given the same diagnosis. Infertility was reaching epidemic proportions. Without a miracle, people on Earth faced extinction.

That's why the Vesta Corporation had funded his mission. That's why Lucan had crossed a galaxy to achieve his goal. Always in secret. Always alone. Always hiding his real past from everyone around him.

Cael touched Lucan's arm, infusing him with an awareness he was certain could be his undoing. "Then you understand," she whispered.

Reluctantly he pulled away from her touch. "More than you'll ever know."

The legend continues with
THE SPELLBINDING
SECOND VOLUME
IN SUSAN KEARNEY'S
PENDRAGON LEGACY
SERIES!

•

Please turn this page

for an excerpt from

Rion

AVAILABLE NOW

She who lives without taking risks dies without love.
                                          —ENGLISH PROVERB

1

London, the near future

"You call that relaxing?" A deep male voice reverberated through the exercise room, and Marisa Roarke opened her eyes. "Meditation is so overrated."

Rion Jaqard stalked with predatory zeal across the Trafalgar Hotel's workout room, flung a towel onto a chair, and whipped off his shirt before sliding onto the weight bench.

During the few times Marisa had run into Rion at her brother Lucan's apartment, she'd noticed Rion was built. But she hadn't realized he was so solid. Talk about walking testosterone. She'd bet even his sweat had muscles.

Rion always emitted a sexy aura. But tonight he seemed to have turned his charms up a notch. Almost as if his alluring appeal was a veneer. And beneath was an undercurrent of banked urgency. Intensity. She couldn't pinpoint exactly what was different about him but her tired mind was reluctant to question, preferring simply to appreciate his . . .

She had to stop looking.

Even if he was totally irresistible, she should have been immune. He may have been a first-rate flirt with other women, but he'd always treated her like a pesky kid sister. And who could blame him? A nasty divorce many years ago had left her with the expectation that most relationships were built on a mountain of lies.

Trying to ignore the size of Rion's very broad, very muscular chest, she frowned. "These days I find relaxing pretty much like trying to fly with only one wing."

Conversation over. She shut her eyes again. But the image of his ripped chest and totally toned, totally etched abs remained.

Marisa imagined those powerful arms around her. Strong, yet gentle. Warm and tight with a current of need. She imagined his eyes filled with desire . . . for her.

Stop it.

Stop imagining. She didn't imagine.

Not anymore.

She halted her wandering thoughts with hard facts.

Rion was from the planet Honor. The first chance he got to leave Earth, he'd be gone. But if all Honorians were built like him, Earth's women would be rioting for interplanetary travel visas. Of course, no such documents existed. Not since the United Nations had shut down travel from Earth to the rest of the galaxy.

For the moment Rion was trapped on Earth. She sneaked another glance. All that sculpted maleness was dazzling. Seductive. A woman could have a night to remember with a body like his. She suppressed a sigh. Too bad she wasn't that kind of woman. Since her failed marriage she'd become even more careful. Maybe too careful.

If he'd ever, even just once, shone any of his alpha sex-machine machoness in her direction, she might have succumbed to temptation and flirted. But he wasn't interested. He'd never been interested.

Stop drooling. Just look somewhere else. Anywhere else.

Marisa had thought herself past the age of ogling men who showed no sign of ogling back. She figured her reaction was due to work-related stress from her new career.

Just six months ago, Marisa had been a successful correspondent at the *St. Petersburg Times* in Florida. She'd covered everything from war in the Mideast to the story about her brother Lucan and his wife, Cael, who had brought back a cure from the planet Pendragon for Earth's fertility problems, which had been Marisa's last assignment.

While the cure had saved humanity from extinction, it had side effects, a genetic shift that required some people to periodically morph into dragons. But humans were not accustomed to their new dragonshaping abilities, which required controlling their more primitive side. So after discovering her own telepathic powers could be used to calm the dragons' highly sexed and predatory tendencies, Marisa had switched careers.

A fifteen-hour shift, exhaustion, and her not-so-successful attempt to erase the emotional aftereffects of dealing with her oversexed dragonshaping clients had clearly upset her equilibrium.

She closed her eyes. *Out. Out. Out.* Rounding up the stray emotions, she corralled them into a tiny corner of her mind, then squashed down hard.

But she still couldn't block out the man across the room. The weights clinked as Rion raised and lowered them, and Marisa peeked again through her lowered lashes. The guy was gorgeous.

He slanted a glance in her direction. The gleaming interest in his eyes startled her. "Hard day?"

"Uh-huh." She looked away. The one-on-one telepathy she'd originally signed up for wouldn't have made her this susceptible to Rion's sexuality. But after Marisa had begun to work with the dragonshapers, she'd discovered she could simultaneously communicate with an entire group of dragons. Her unique ability to help many dragons at once made her a valuable asset to the Vesta Corporation. Unfortunately, the side effects subjected her to all of the dragonshapers' angers, fears, jealousies, and passions at once.

Don't think about work.

Left with residual sexual tension, all her cells hummed with need.

Let it go.

Unclenching her teeth, she forced her lips to part, breathed deeply through her nose, and told the muscles in her aching neck to loosen. Or at least to stop throbbing so she could go up to her hotel room and sleep.

"Maybe lifting would relax you."

She arched an eyebrow. Something had to be wrong with her hearing because his voice sounded coaxing.

"If you need help, I could spot you," he continued.

"No, thanks." Surprised by his persistence, she spoke without looking at him.

Why couldn't he just leave her alone? Surely by now

even his oversized biceps had to be burning, his lungs aching for oxygen. But he didn't sound out of breath.

"Let me know if you change your mind." His tone held a hint of disappointment.

Disappointment?

No way.

Her tired mind had to be misinterpreting his signals. As much as she'd have liked to believe he was interested in her, she knew better. So she had to accept that the dragons' residual passions were affecting her judgment.

"Meditation works better in silence," she said calmly, pleased that her voice didn't give away how aware she was of the way his buttocks tightened and relaxed in a fascinating rhythm that made her mouth go dry.

"Seems to me your meditation isn't working."

He was right. She couldn't stop staring at him. A light gleam of sweat glistened on his skin, emphasizing his muscles as he set down the weights.

He straightened and raked her with a gaze that settled on the vein throbbing in her neck. "Your pulse rate must be over one thirty," he said.

Hell. Any woman within ten meters of him would have an elevated pulse. "Are you deliberately trying to annoy me, or do you come by it naturally?"

She expected him to take off, but he grabbed his towel, slung it over his shoulders, and wiped the sweat from his brow. And gave her a look brazen enough to heat every flat in London—for the entire winter.

Whoa. She might be tired. But not that tired. No way could she misread his male interest. Just what was going on here? He'd never looked at her like this before. What was he up to?

His tone oozed charm. "There are better ways to relax."

"Like?" Marisa couldn't prevent a tiny smile raising the corners of her lips.

His dark gaze flicked to her mouth, tracked it with hot male interest. He'd taken her smile for an opening. Of course, he would. She doubted anyone had ever told Mr. Irresistible no. Approaching with a long-legged saunter that made her eyes narrow with speculation, he sat on the mat behind her and placed his palms firmly on her shoulders.

She should pull away until she knew what he was up to. But she couldn't. Not when he looked so damn good.

He went still behind her, drawing out a moment of silence that thrummed with tension. Her sizzling awareness of him seemed to fill the space between them with a rush of heat.

At the first touch of his hands on her shoulders, she had to bite back a gasp of pleasure. Gently, ever so slowly, he kneaded her neck and caressed her shoulders with a sensual thoroughness that melted away the tension. Circling in on the tight spots with soothing caresses, he feathered his fingertips over her sore muscles.

Her pulse leaped. She swallowed hard.

Rion eased the heels of his palms into her tight shoulders with lingering, luscious strokes. After several mesmerizing minutes, he leaned forward and his breath fanned her ear. "You carry tension in the neck."

"I do?" She sighed and leaned into his hands, grateful for the relief.

He kneaded gently, gradually going deeper, until her muscles melted, until she felt as warm and pliable as taffy.

His fingers were so clever, but as he released one kind of tension, a sensuous anticipation began to build.

"Am I too hard for you?" he asked, almost sounding innocent.

She jerked upright and made a choking sound. He was sitting behind her, but she could see his chiseled face reflected in the mirrors and caught a reckless I-shouldn't-be-messing-with-my-best-friend's-sister-but-I'm-going-to-do-it-anyway gleam in his eyes. "My hands. Am I rubbing too hard?"

"You feel great. And you damn well know it." She lifted an eyebrow and shot back her best I-know-what-you're-up-to look.

But she really had no idea what his intentions were. He might have been a first-class flirt with other women, but with her, he'd merely been friendly.

"I'm glad you like my touch," he murmured.

At his flirting, her heart fluttered, but she tamped down her excitement and cast him a curious glance. "From what I hear, you've had lots of practice."

Rion worked on a knot next to her spine, applying tension until the tightness ebbed. "You have an Earth saying, 'Practice makes perfect.' But I'm not certain if a massage can ever be perfect. After all, there are so many variations of where to touch . . . how to touch . . . when to touch . . ."

No one could accidentally be *that* suggestive—not even a man from another planet. And while she'd love to find out exactly where and how he would touch her next, all her caution signals flared.

Leaning forward, he whispered into her ear, "Did you know you have a very sexy neck?" His gray eyes met hers in the mirror, and she could have sworn they smoldered. When he brushed a wispy tendril from her nape, heat shimmied down her spine.

Damn, he was smooth. Real smooth. Although she'd already been burned by her ex-husband, she was long over the hurt. Yet when it came to men, she remained cautious, unable to trust her own judgment.

Ignoring the desire surging through her veins, she scooted from under Rion's hands and stood. "Thanks. It's been a long day. I need to hit the sack."

"Good night, Marisa." He stood, too, and grabbed his shirt. As she left the workout room, he called out to her. "Sweet dreams."

Sweet was out of the question. Sizzling hot was more like it.

THE DISH

Where authors give you the inside scoop!

♥ ♥ ♥ ♥ ♥ ♥ ♥ ♥ ♥ ♥ ♥ ♥ ♥ ♥

From the desk of Cara Elliott

Dear Readers,

Pssst. Have you seen the morning newspaper yet? Oh, it's too delicious for words. The infamous Lord H—yes, Mad, Bad Had-ley in the flesh—has made yet another wicked splash in the gossip column. You remember last week, when his cavorting with a very luscious—and very naked—ladybird ended with a midnight swim in the Grosvenor Square fountain? Well, that was just a drop in the bucket compared to this latest *ondit*. Word has it that Hadley, the rakishly sexy hero of TO SIN WITH A SCOUNDREL (available now), has really fallen off the deep end this time. He's been spotted around Town with . . . the Wicked Widow of Pont Street.

Don't bother cleaning your spectacles—you read that right. Hadley and Lady Sheffield! The same Lady Sheffield who stirred such a scandal last year when it was whispered that she may have poisoned her husband. Yes, yes, at first blush it seems impossible. After all, they are complete opposites. The fun-loving Lord Hadley is a devil-may-care rogue, and the reclusive Lady Sheffield is a scholarly bluestocking. Why, the only thing they appear to have in common is the fact that their names show up so frequently in all the gossip columns. But appearances can be deceiving, and a friend tells me that a fundamental law of physics states that opposites attract.

Not that *I* would dare to wager on it. However, the betting books at all the London clubs are filled with speculation on why Hadley is paying court to the lovely widow. Some say that it's merely one of Hadley's madcap pranks. Others think that he's been bewitched by one of the potent potions that the lady brews up in her laboratory. But I'll let you in on a little secret: Whatever the reason, the combination of a scoundrel and a scientist has passion and intrigue coming to a boil!

How do I know? I'll let you in on another little secret—as the author of the book, I'm familiar with *all* the intimate details of their private lives.

So why did I choose to make my hero and heroine of TO SIN WITH A SCOUNDREL the subject of rumors and innuendos? In doing my research, I discovered that our current fascination with gossip and scandal is nothing new. Regency England reveled in "tittle-tattle," and had its own colorful scandal sheets and "paparazzi." Newspapers and pamphlets reported in lurid detail on the celebrity bad boys—and bad girls—of high society. And like today, sex, money, and politics were hot topics. As for pictures, there were, of course, no cameras, but the satirical artists of the Regency could be even more ruthless than modern-day photographers.

Hmmm, come to think of it, the hero and heroine of TO SURRENDER TO A ROGUE, the second book in the series (available June '10), are likely to generate quite a bit of gossip too. Lady Sheffield's fellow scholar, the lovely and enigmatic Lady Giamatti, finds that someone is intent on digging up dirt on her past life in Italy while she is excavating Roman antiquities in the town of Bath. That Black Jack Pierson is a member of the learned group stirs up trouble . . . Oh, but don't let me spoil the fun. You really ought to read all about it for yourself.

Now don't worry if your butler has tossed out the morning newspaper. If you hurry on over to www.caraelliott.com, you can sneak a tantalizing peek at all three books in my new Circle of Sin series.

Enjoy!

Cara Elliott

♥ ♥ ♥ ♥ ♥ ♥ ♥ ♥ ♥ ♥ ♥ ♥ ♥ ♥

From the desk of Susan Kearney

Dear Readers,

I came up with my idea for JORDAN, the third book in the Pendragon Legacy trilogy, while sipping a wine cooler in my hammock. I was rocking between two rustling queen palms when a time machine landed on my dock. And the hottest dude ever strode up the wooden stairs and pulled up a chair beside me. His eyes matched the blue of the sea and his muscles rippled in the Florida sunshine.

Jordan.

He'd arrived just as the sun was dipping into the Gulf of Mexico. And did you know that Jordan's history is as interesting as his looks?

Did I mention this guy may have looked in the prime of his life, but he's more than fifteen hundred years old? Did I mention that centuries ago he fought at King Arthur's side? And that not only is he a powerful dragon-shaper but he knows secrets to save us all?

Jordan raked a hand through his hair. "Rion told me that you write love stories about the future."

"I do." Somehow, I knew this was going to be one hell of a story.

"In the future, Earth will be threatened by your greatest enemy."

My fingers shook. "Did you save my world?"

"I had help from a smart, beautiful woman."

"And you fell in love?" I guessed, always a romantic at heart.

"She was my boss." His voice lowered to a sexy murmur. "And we fought a lot in the beginning. You see, Vivianne Blackstone didn't trust me."

"So you had to win her over?"

"She's one stubborn woman." His voice rang with pride, a grin softening his tone.

Oh, this story sounded exciting. Lucan had told me how Vivianne Blackstone had funded the first spaceship mission to Pendragon. Just imagining such a strong woman with Jordan sent a delicious shiver of anticipation down my spine. "But surely Vivianne must have liked you just a little bit at first?"

"She thought I was an enemy spy." Jordan's grin widened. "And she wasn't too pleased when I stole her new spaceship . . . with her on board."

Oh, my. "I'd imagine it took her awhile to forgive you."

While Jordan was quite the man . . . still . . . he'd stolen her ship and taken her with him into space. Vivianne must have been furious. And scared. Although, the writer in me told me Jordan had been good for Vivianne. "So how long did it take her to believe you were both on the same side?"

Jordan chuckled. "It must have been after the second, no, the third time we made love."

I swallowed hard. Oh . . . my. "You made love while she believed you were enemies?"

He raised an eyebrow. "We didn't really have a choice."

I gave him a hard look. "Um, look. I'm afraid I'm going to need the details. Lots of details."

If you'd like to read the details Jordan told me, the book is in stores now. Reach me at www.susankearney.com.

Susan Kearney

♥ ♥ ♥ ♥ ♥ ♥ ♥ ♥ ♥ ♥ ♥ ♥ ♥

From the desk of R. C. Ryan

Dear Reader,

Blame it on Willy Nelson. My heroes have always been cowboys.

Whether they're riding the trail in the Old West or dealing with today's problems on a modern, up-to-date ranch tricked out with all the latest high-tech gadgets, I simply can't resist loving a cowboy.

In my mind, the tall, silent hero of a Western is the equivalent of the savage, untamed Highlander. Noble, loyal, fiercely independent. Impossible for this woman to resist.

Now add to that a treasure hunt for a priceless fortune in gold nuggets, and you have a recipe for adventure, intrigue, and romance.

MONTANA LEGACY is the first book in my Fool's Gold trilogy. Three cousins, long separated, are brought together by the death of their grandfather, who has spent a lifetime searching for a lost family treasure.

Of course they can't resist taking up his search. But that's only half the story. Equally important is the love they discover on the journey. And more than love—trust. Trust in one another, and in the women who win their hearts and enrich their lives.

If you're like me and love tough, strong, fun-loving cowboys in search of a legendary treasure, come along for the adventure of a lifetime.

I enjoy hearing from my readers. Drop by my Web site and leave me a message: www.ryanlangan.com.

Happy reading!